ACCLAIM FOR ALLEN ESKENS'S

Forsaken Country

"The best stories test our view of the moral universe, which is one of the many reasons I love the work of Allen Eskens. *Forsaken Country* is a shining example of what fine crime fiction offers—a tight plot, intriguing characters, and important ethical questions. In this tale of a kidnapped boy and the men who desperately seek to save him, Eskens offers no easy answers, but delivers a taut Northwoods thriller with a raging pace guaranteed to sweep you along from first page to last. This is one of our best crime writers at the top of his game."

—William Kent Krueger, author of *This Tender Land*

"Eskens provides an irresistible hook, a clever spin on a classic suspense plot, and a series of expertly escalating confrontations...Guaranteed to keep your heart pounding till the end." —*Kirkus Reviews*

"The search for mother and child fuels the brisk plot, but *Forsaken Country* spins on Eskens's in-depth character studies. Eskens imbues *Forsaken Country* with vivid scenery, especially in the Boundary Waters...Eskens is at the top of his skills."

—Oline H. Cogdill, *South Florida Sun Sentinel*

"In *Forsaken Country*, Allen Eskens's expert storytelling is on full display. Eerie and beautifully told, it had me mesmerized from the very first page... The suspense never flags in this chilling and layered portrait of a man's desperate search for a missing child and his own redemption. Heart-pounding and heartfelt, *Forsaken Country* should be at the top of your to-be-read list."

—Heather Gudenkauf, author of
The Weight of Silence and *The Overnight Guest*

"*Forsaken Country* is Allen Eskens at his most raw and brutal as he produces some of the best cat-and-mouse games I have read... There is redemption to be had, but the price may be too high for his characters to pay. This is a novel that you will not easily forget."

—Ray Palen, *BookReporter*

"An excellent suspense novel that will keep you riveted."

—*Globe and Mail*

"In *Forsaken Country*, Allen Eskens delivers in all the ways that matter. Story, character, suspense—I loved it all. This author deserves a round of applause, and this book a massive audience."

—John Hart, author of *The Unwilling*

"*Forsaken Country* is a story of darkness, love, and redemption; a novel that will stay with you long after you mourn turning the last page. And it solidifies Allen Eskens as one of the finest literary crime writers working today."

—Alex Finlay, author of *The Night Shift*

"Eskens weaves a gut-punching and deeply satisfying story. His characters are indelible. His protagonist becomes a familiar friend with an unflinching honesty about who he is and what his past means. *Forsaken Country* is not only a propulsive mystery with a lot of soul, but also an addictive chase into the untamed wilderness of the Boundary Waters and the Quetico-Superior country."

—Diane Les Becquets, author of *The Last Woman in the Forest*

"Beautifully written and expertly crafted, *Forsaken Country* has everything we've come to love about an Allen Eskens novel—deeply developed characters, a smart plot, and plenty of suspense to keep the pages turning." —Charlie Donlea, author of *Twenty Years Later*

FICTION BY ALLEN ESKENS

The Life We Bury
The Guise of Another
The Heavens May Fall
The Deep Dark Descending
The Shadows We Hide
Nothing More Dangerous
The Stolen Hours
Forsaken Country
Saving Emma

FORSAKEN
COUNTRY

ALLEN ESKENS

MULHOLLAND BOOKS

Little, Brown and Company

New York Boston London

Copyright © 2022 by Allen Eskens
Excerpt from *Saving Emma* copyright © 2023 by Allen Eskens Ltd.

Mulholland Books / Little, Brown and Company
Hachette Book Group
1290 Avenue of the Americas, New York, NY 10104
mulhollandbooks.com

Originally published in hardcover by Mulholland Books, September 2022
First Mulholland Books trade paperback edition, September 2023

Mulholland Books is an imprint of Little, Brown and Company, a division of Hachette Book Group, Inc. The Mulholland Books name and logo are trademarks of Hachette Book Group, Inc.

ISBN 9780316703543 (hc) / 9780316703536 (pb)
Library of Congress Control Number: 2022940797

Printing 1, 2023

LSC-C

Printed in the United States of America

I dedicate this book to the memory of Calvin P. Johnson, a mentor, a sage, and a true friend. You are missed.

FORSAKEN
COUNTRY

CHAPTER 1

Max Rupert laced his fingers behind his head and settled into his pillow to await the ghosts. He knew that Mikhail Vetrov would be lurking on the other side of sleep. It had been three and a half years since he had shoved Mikhail through that hole in the ice, and very few nights had gone by where the memory of that killing didn't come to visit him.

In dreams, Max still had the short hair and clean-shaven face of a homicide detective, but that face was long gone. Max hadn't shaved or cut his hair since the day he started his exile, so now his beard reached to his chest and his hair fell in a ponytail between his shoulder blades. Living alone in the woods, Max found that unkempt look fitting.

But there were other changes that didn't sit so well with Max. His eyes seemed empty, and his cheeks had grown thin. At forty-five years old he felt too young for the tiny lines that now fanned out from his eyes and creased the edges of his mouth. And his features seemed to sag a touch, as though something inside of him, something dark and heavy, weighed him down with years that he had not yet lived.

But those parts of Max that he'd hoped might change as the years went by — his heart, his conscience — clung stubbornly to the past. He had shut himself away from the world to face his reckoning, willing to accept forgiveness or retribution in equal measure, but after three and a half years, he had found neither. His reclamation had become stagnant.

But was he really isolated?

Max's cabin was a small A-frame that had been in his family for more than a century. To the west lay a lake. To the south and north, Max could walk for miles and see no other human. But to the east, a thin trail snaked through the pines connecting his cabin to the county blacktop that ran south to Grand Rapids, Minnesota, a town of about ten thousand souls. So long as he could simply drive into Grand Rapids to resupply, his exile seemed destined to fail.

That failure had been on his mind on his last trip into town when he ran into Lyle Voight. What had it been, a week? Ten days? Time was unreliable at the cabin: minutes lingered, days lasted for weeks, and months disappeared into a fog. But Lyle had helped him put his finger on the problem: Max had been cheating. He needed to live like a true hermit, with no electricity, no running water, no trips into town. Lyle's remark had been offhand, but it touched a nerve.

Max had met Lyle five years earlier, when Lyle was sheriff of Itasca County and the first to respond to Max's 911 call the night his brother Alexander passed away at the cabin, a night Max still tried not to think about. And while they weren't close, Lyle, a quiet man in his sixties with thick hands and thin gray hair, remained the only person in Grand Rapids that Max recognized by face.

On that recent trip to town, Max had just exited the Super One Foods carrying two paper bags filled with soups, and canned vegetables, and meat, when he saw Lyle in the parking lot, sitting in the cab of his pickup truck, tapping a finger on the steering wheel to the faint sound of music. Max had never been one to talk to himself, at least not out loud, so since moving to the cabin he had rarely said more than a few words a week, usually only a mumbled thank-you in the checkout lane of the Super One—and as his beard and hair grew longer, folks seemed just fine with not talking to him. But because Lyle had parked right beside Max's SUV, Max felt obliged to at least say hello.

Lyle wore a beat-up ball cap and a frayed blue-jean jacket instead of his sheriff's uniform. When he saw Max, Lyle turned down his radio and leaned out the truck's window. "Hey, Max."

Max opened the back of his Jeep Cherokee and put his bags inside. "Working up the gumption to go in?" Max asked, trying to sound more lighthearted than he felt. The words were like gravel in his mouth.

"Waiting for my daughter and grandson. They're grabbing candy for the trick-or-treaters. I swear, we'd save a ton if we just bought a bag for the kid and called it a day."

Max cleared his throat before he spoke again. "Yeah, but where's the fun in that?"

"I suppose."

Even before he had retreated to the cabin, Max disliked chitchat, but now it seemed a painful thing. Still, despite the overwhelming urge to get in his car and go, Max couldn't bring himself to be rude to the one man in town who could call him by name. So he leaned on Lyle's rear fender and tried to come up with something to say. In the bed of the truck lay two enormous pumpkins. "You planning on doing some carving later?"

Lyle smiled. "It's kind of a family tradition. Me and the grandson do the jack-o'-lanterns, then I take him trick-or-treating. I used to wear my sheriff's uniform. That was costume enough for the kid, but now that I lost the election..." His words trailed off.

Max knew that there had been an election—he'd seen the lawn signs—but he hadn't heard that Lyle had lost. He shook his head. "Voters can be a fickle bunch."

"I guess I'll just be Grandpa this year." Lyle took off his cap and ran a hand through his thinning hair. "Truth is, I kind of feel...I don't know. I'm not sure what to do with my time anymore. I walk around all antsy, like there're just too many minutes in a day." Then he smiled to himself.

"If it were only me, I'd move out to the woods and become a hermit like you, but Meredith would have my head."

Until that moment, Max had never thought of himself as a hermit, a word that conjured up a crazy man in rags, living in a cave, eating bugs. Sure, he had let his beard and hair grow, but he still bathed, and clipped his toenails, and brushed his teeth. His cabin was sound and well insulated, with electric heat and appliances and a beautiful view of a lake.

That's when it dawned on him that his exile—his attempt at penance—was the kind of existence that some people paid good money to experience.

Something caught Lyle's attention and he turned to look at a woman and child walking toward them. The woman, in her midthirties, wore the tired face of a mother nearing the end of a long day. Her gray sweatshirt had a large chocolate stain just left of center, and her black hair fell in looping strands from the remnant of a bun atop her head. She pushed a cart of groceries with one hand and held her son's hand with the other.

"There's my crew now," Lyle said, stepping out of the truck. He walked to the back and opened the tailgate. "You ever met my daughter?"

"Not that I remember."

"Max, this is Sandy." Lyle began lifting bags of groceries from the cart, nestling them next to the pumpkins.

The woman smiled but it didn't reach her eyes. She had the lithe body of a runner, with strong cheeks and dark eyes that gave her a look of quiet confidence. Max held out his hand. "Max Rupert," he said.

Lyle said, "He's that detective I told you about, the one living north of town?"

Sandy looked like she had no idea what Lyle was talking about, but shook hands with Max anyway, her eyes narrowing slightly as though trying to find a big-city homicide detective behind the flop of hair and beard. "Nice to meet you," she said. Her hand was soft and warm, and her fingers gave a light squeeze as she wrapped them around Max's hand.

"And that little bugger there…" Lyle pointed at the boy, maybe five or six years old, who stood behind his mother. "That's my Pip Squeak."

The boy tucked his face into his mother's leg as if to hide. It was official—Max had a face that could scare children. Maybe Lyle's hermit comment wasn't that far-fetched after all. Max would have preferred to ignore the boy, but his apprehension bothered Max. He didn't want the child to have nightmares about the scary man he'd met at the grocery store. Slowly, Max squatted down to be eye to eye. "Your grandpa tells me you have quite the gift for carving pumpkins," Max improvised.

The boy remained silent.

"What are you going to be for Halloween?" Max asked.

When he didn't answer, Sandy patted the boy's head and said, "It's okay, Pip. You can tell him."

The boy looked to his grandfather too before answering in a voice so small that Max could barely hear it. "A pirate."

"A pirate," Max said, his voice cracking as he tried a whimsical lift to his words. He softly cleared his throat again. "That is a great costume."

Pip looked at Max as though he still wanted him to go away.

Max tried one more time. "Do you know what a pirate's favorite letter of the alphabet is?"

The boy gave an almost imperceptible shake of his head.

"It's the letter arrrrrrrrr." Max sold the joke by scrunching up the side of his face and pinching one eye shut. Pip's cheek twitched and then a wispy smile fought its way through his bashfulness. Max smiled back, content in his small victory.

Max stood and nodded. "It was nice meeting you both, Lyle." He held out his hand and gave the old sheriff's hand a shake.

The first thing he noticed, on his half-hour drive home, was a feeling of warmth in his chest. Lightness. His face wore the remnants of a smile. Max thought back; had he smiled since retreating to the cabin? He didn't think so. He wasn't supposed to be happy. He had gone there to be alone, to be forsaken by the world. This seemed all wrong.

The cacophony of pleasantries from that day brought his hypocrisy into sharp focus. The grocery bags in the back of the SUV held wild rice soup and ribeye steaks. Apparently Purgatory came with fresh cuts of meat. No wonder atonement remained beyond his reach. Then he thought about Lyle's words: *If it were just me, I'd become a hermit like you.*

But Max wasn't a hermit — not yet. The solution seemed both obvious and elegant.

First thing the next morning, Max drove to town and had his electricity shut off. When he arrived back at the cabin, he went to work preparing for his deprivation. He buried two coolers in the crawl space beneath the cabin to store what vegetables he had already and those he intended to grow. He dug a hole outside where he would lay his refrigerator to hold frozen meat once winter came. He fixed the old hand pump in the front yard so he could have water. His main source of food would be the fish, so he rowed out every morning and cast a line until he caught enough for the day. By the sixth day, he had grown sick of eating fish.

Max's father had left him two guns when he died, a twenty-two-caliber rifle and a twenty-gauge shotgun; they were among the few possessions Max had brought to the cabin. He hadn't used either since he'd hunted with his father as a teenager, back before his father's drinking had affixed him to the cushions of the living room furniture. Max had never actually shot anything on those outings, but he had watched his father. He believed he remembered enough of how to skin a rabbit or field dress a pheasant to make a go of it now.

On the seventh day of his hermitage, he decided to hunt down some red meat, choosing the twenty-two for that outing.

He stepped into the woods at daybreak, the air infused with the scent of wet tree bark, the world chilly and quiet beyond the crunch of pine needles under his boots. He walked south across land he had played on as a child, taking a path he and Jenni had walked the first time he'd brought her to the cabin. Some of the trees had already dropped their leaves for the fall, but most hadn't. The brilliant yellow of the poplars and aspens mixed with the rust of the oaks and the bright red of the sumac. The woods looked like a child's finger painting.

He carried the rifle into the state forest, no hunting license, the gun still registered to his father, and he considered the laws he was about to break. There was a time when rules meant everything to him. But Max was no longer that man—that much he knew. Who he had become remained lost in a fog.

After about an hour, Max leaned against a fallen tree, his gun at his side. He tried to remember what his father had taught him about hunting: Be patient, stay quiet, keep a keen eye out for movement. Max scanned the trees and was about to start walking again when he saw the rabbit, thirty yards out, moving carefully beneath the branches of a small pine.

Max raised the rifle butt to his shoulder and pressed his cheek to the stock, eyeing down the barrel to line up the front and rear sights. The rifle felt foreign in his hands after so many years carrying a pistol, and when he squeezed the trigger, the gun fired with a muffled pop.

He missed.

The rabbit turned and looked at Max. He had no idea whether the bullet went high, wide, or short, but he sighted on her and fired again. This time the rabbit collapsed, flipping onto her back, and something in Max's stomach knotted up.

He plodded forward like a man in leg irons, and as he drew near he saw that the rabbit was still alive, blood oozing from a wound in her hip. Max should have put a second bullet into her right then, but he hesitated. The rabbit twitched and looked up toward Max, and he was sure that he saw fear and confusion in her eyes, as if she were asking, "Why?"

He finally pulled the trigger a third time. He squatted on one knee next to the rabbit, and pinched his eyes closed to fight back the tears. He wanted to throw up. What the hell was wrong with him? He had tied up a man and dropped him into a frozen lake, watched as his face disappeared into the darkness of the water, and had felt nothing. But a rabbit's pain churned his gut and knotted his throat. How could a man be so utterly weak? If Jenni were still alive, she would see him for the pathetic wretch that he was, and be ashamed.

But if Jenni were still alive, he would never have had to execute Mikhail. How different his world would have been.

That night, he cooked the rabbit on a spit over the fire pit out front, the evening chill turning his breath white, and when he ate he could barely bring himself to swallow. But he did because the only thing worse than eating what he had killed would have been to let it go to waste. By the time he had finished his meal he understood that his attempt to live as a hermit had failed. He would go back to the electric company in the morning.

Across the lake, the setting sun blazed against the stratus clouds, as though the world beyond his land were on fire. Jenni would have pointed out the beauty in that glowing sky, in the dance of the trees as they swayed in the light breeze, their leaves drifting down to the lake, but all Max could see was the cold of another long winter gathering its strength.

He wished he hadn't run into Lyle. He wished that he hadn't felt the warmth of that woman's hand or seen the simple courage in that little boy's smile.

That night, under the glow of a short, fat candle, Max slid an oak log into the stove to prepare for the night. Then he climbed the steps to his bed in the loft. Outside, the thin clouds had parted and a full moon bathed the room in moonlight. He blew out his candle, climbed into bed, and stared at the ceiling to await the onset of dreams and nightmares that had become his nightly observance — unaware that the walls he had worked so hard to build around him were about to be breached.

CHAPTER 2

The man rode his bicycle west along the two-lane blacktop, the glow of the full moon lighting his way. The temperature had dropped to twenty-eight degrees, but the exercise of pedaling kept him warm beneath the black hoodie. He tried to focus on the small details of his trip: the cadence of his breath, the crunch of grit beneath his tires. It kept his mind busy, distracted from the terrible thing that he was about to do.

"Don't obsess on the big picture," his partner had said. "It's just a series of small steps, one thing following another."

One step at a time—the man liked that suggestion because it calmed his trembling nerves. Step one: Ride the bicycle from the motel room to her house, a route that took him out of Grand Rapids and across a bridge that spanned the Mississippi River. After the bridge, he took to the bike path next to the highway, twice hiding in the woods as cars passed by.

"You'll have second thoughts," his partner had said. "Don't give in to them. Focus on the plan."

After an hour, he turned onto the narrow road that led into the woods and to her house, the lane twisting its way through birch and pine. He passed three other houses on the way to hers, all of them set back far enough from the road that he could scarcely make out their shadowy silhouettes through the trees.

When he arrived at her driveway, he rolled the bike into the trees and knelt on the ground, his knees weak, his fingers trembling. A wave of misgivings churned his stomach. His little hiding spot smelled of mud and pine. Soft nettles covered the ground beneath him, and the sky above glittered with stars. The tranquil beauty of the night nearly brought him to tears. How had his life come to this?

He tried to think of the greater good—the ends that justified the means—but that kind of thinking only confused him, filling his head with questions he should have asked but hadn't. *One step at a time,* he thought. *Follow the plan.*

The house had been built in the seventies and had a picture window at the front flanked by two single-hung windows with no screens. His partner had promised that the window on the left had warped years ago, preventing the lock from setting. The man pulled a ski mask down to cover his face and slipped on a pair of thin gloves.

He had been assured that there would be no dog, and so far there wasn't. At the window, he ran a finger along the sash. A tiny voice whispered that this was the point of no return, but in truth, he had stepped beyond that point months ago. He gave the window a little push, but it didn't move.

Had his partner been wrong? Had someone fixed the bow? Reset the lock? It was too dark to see inside, to know for certain. Maybe this was his way out. How could he be at fault if the window couldn't be opened? With all the tools in his rucksack, he'd never thought to bring a flashlight. That wasn't part of the plan. If he could just see the latch, be certain that it had been fixed...No, that wouldn't fly. He would not be forgiven for his failure. He had to see it through, one way or another.

He thought about using the knife he carried to drive the window upward, but that would leave a mark, which might alter the narrative. He tried again with his fingers, applying so much pressure that spikes of pain shot down through his knuckles and into his palms. He was about to let up when the window gave way and slid an inch, issuing a squeak like the chirp of a bird.

He paused, waiting for movement or a light turning on inside the house. Nothing happened.

Using his wrists as levers, and then his forearms, he pressed the window slowly upward until he was sure he could fit his six-foot-two frame through. He reached inside to see if anything lay in his way and felt a potted plant. He moved it to the side.

He shrugged off his rucksack of supplies, leaned it against the outside wall of the house, and stepped one leg inside. He had to duck his head and twist his torso to fit himself through the opening. Once inside, he paused again to listen. He was in her world now, and it smelled of scented candles. The carpeting beneath his feet was hers, Berber, a light color that, once his eyes adjusted, helped him distinguish between furniture and the path to her bedroom. Somewhere in the darkness a clock ticked.

His heart beat hard against the walls of his chest as he lifted his rucksack through the window and carefully unzipped it, muffling the sound by pinching the slider between his thumb and index finger. He removed the knife from the sack, his palms sweating beneath his gloves. He unsheathed it and turned it so that the blade caught the moonlight.

He had accomplished step one. Now on to step two.

CHAPTER 3

Her door stood partially open, and he watched her for a minute, pretty in her slumber, a far cry from the demon that had been described. But then again, if someone had snuck into his own mother's bedroom when he was a child, would they have seen malevolence in the soft contours of her face? Her cruelty often came with a smile, so the man knew well how a demon could hide behind a disguise.

A memory of his mother came to him as he stood outside of the woman's door. It had been the year after his father's death, so he would have been eleven. A teacher caught him cheating on a math test, copying answers from the girl who sat beside him. He had been sent home with a note for his mother to sign, and when she read the note, she had lost her mind. She'd called him a thief and a thug, as though he had beat the girl up to get her answers. But what stung the most was when she told him that he was a no-good miscreant.

He'd had to look up the word *miscreant* to understand. He was only eleven and she had already made up her mind about him. How could any woman do that? Children should be protected by their mothers—and when that didn't happen, then children needed to be protected *from* their mothers. He shook the memory away. The last thing he needed was another distraction. He raised the knife and quietly slid the door open.

Once inside her bedroom, he closed the door behind him, locking it with a muted click. Moonlight streaming through slatted blinds cut the room into ribbons, and up close she didn't look anything like his mother. She had dark hair that fell softly across her face, and as he stood over her, a small line formed between her dark eyebrows as though she were having a bad dream. If she only knew.

He stepped beside the bed, held the knife where she would see it, and clapped his hand over her mouth.

The woman opened her eyes and for a couple seconds just stared at him. Was he part of her dream? Then, as he had expected, she screamed into his gloved hand, her eyes fixed on the glint of moon reflecting off his knife.

"Shut up!" The words were both a yell and a whisper. "I won't hurt you, but you have to be quiet."

She didn't obey. She was disoriented—terrified. She tried to pull away, sinking her head into her pillow as if that held some route for escape. She swung her right hand at his face and he jumped on top of her, straddling her chest and arms to stop her from moving. "I'm not going to hurt you, but you need to shut up right now."

He could feel her chest heaving beneath him, and he squeezed his hand harder against her mouth to stop her from turning her head. He pressed the flat side of the blade to her throat and saw understanding pass behind her eyes. She stopped struggling but remained stiff.

After a few seconds of silence, the man loosened his hand from her mouth, a sign of good faith. She didn't scream.

"What . . . what are you . . . gonna do?"

"Not what you think," he said in a low, gravelly whisper.

Her breath came and went in shallow spurts. She looked up at him with big, fearful eyes—a damsel in distress, and he was the cause.

The woman spoke with a quaver of fear in her voice. "My boyfriend will be home soon."

He smiled at her feeble attempt. "No. David won't be home soon."

She shuddered when she heard David's name. He could use that fear to his advantage.

"Yes, I know his name. And I know that he works the night shift at the taconite plant in Hibbing. He's there now and won't be back until just before eleven. I've done my homework, so don't insult me by underestimating me. You do exactly what I tell you to do and you'll be fine. Step out of line just once and you will force me to do something I don't want to."

"What do you want?"

"Where's your computer?"

She looked up at him in confusion then nodded toward a laptop on the floor in the corner. He got off her chest and stood next to the bed, the knife brandished between them. "Get dressed."

The woman hesitated before getting out of bed, as though her modesty mattered in that moment. Then she slid out from beneath the blankets, wearing a T-shirt that covered to her thighs, and went to her closet for a pair of jeans and a sweatshirt. He watched to see that she didn't grab anything she could use as a weapon. When she finished dressing, he put the laptop on the bed and told her to turn it on. She did as she was told, sitting on the edge of the bed as she typed.

They shared an awkward silence as they waited for the computer to warm up. He was hot under his ski mask and hoodie. His palms sweated beneath the gloves. He was glad that she couldn't hear how loudly his heart was beating. When the computer came to life, he told her to access her bank account.

"What for?"

"Because I told you to." He tried to put grit into his words, but they sounded weak to his own ear, so he tried something else: "Because I have a knife and you don't."

She typed.

Once she pulled up the account, she turned the screen to him. She had over thirty-two grand in the bank, more than he had expected. He clicked back a couple of screens and saw on the bank's website that its doors would open at eight a.m. He and the woman would have to spend some time alone as they waited. He came prepared for that.

"Call your office. Tell them you're sick and won't be in today."

"What are you going to do? I don't understand."

"I'm not going to hurt you as long as you do what I say."

"How do I know that?"

"If I came here to kill you, I would have done that already. If I came here to rape you . . ." He watched her eyes as she did the math, and she seemed to calm. Then he recited the lines he had practiced on the long bike ride over. "I am a thief. I'm here to take your money. That's all. It's what I do. In a little while, you're going to drive to your bank and withdraw thirty thousand dollars in cash and bring it to me. I'm not taking all your money—I'll leave you with enough for groceries and stuff—but I'm taking most of it."

"I'll write you a check right now," she said.

The man almost chuckled. A check? How stupid did she think he was? "And when I go to cash that check, don't you think I might have a problem? Not to mention security cameras. You think they'll cash a check for thirty grand if I walk in wearing this ski mask? I'm going to rob you, but you'll be bringing the money to me."

He looked for signs that she believed that he would not hurt her, but saw none: no settling of the shoulders, no loosening of the worry lines around her eyes. He needed her to be scared, but hated making her so. She would never know how much he wanted to be anywhere other than where he was. His mother had been right about him.

"I know that you work at the vet clinic and that you start work at eight, so you need to call your office and leave a message that you aren't feeling well. You're taking a sick day."

Her phone was plugged into a charger on her nightstand. She picked it up and turned it on. He watched closely as she touched a contact. She moved too quickly for the man to read the name of the contact identified as Poppy—not her employer.

The man grabbed the phone before the call went through, disconnecting it, and throwing the phone to the bed. He grabbed her by the hair, pushed her onto the bed and shoved her facedown into the brown satin comforter. He had gone out of his way to be polite, and this was how she repaid him?

"What did I say?" he hissed into her ear, his words emphatic and menacing. "You do what you're told and I won't hurt you. That was our agreement. You fuck with me like that again and all bets are off."

She was crying, her shrieks muffled by the bedding. He had her attention.

"I know what your office number is. I told you, I did my homework. So who were you trying to call?"

She answered, but he couldn't make out what she said, so he eased up on the fistful of her black hair and lifted her face out of the bedding.

"Who were you trying to call?"

"No one."

He shoved her face back down. "Now you're gonna lie to me? I thought you understood. This can go easy for you or it can go hard. It's all in your hands. Who's Poppy?"

He eased up again, but she said nothing. He was mad, and a little scared. She had tried to trick him, which meant that she didn't believe he would carry out his threat—and if she didn't believe he would hurt her, the plan wouldn't work. He put the knife to her throat, the spine against her skin instead of the blade, and applied pressure. "I'll kill you if you lie to me. And I'll find out who you were calling and kill that person too. Now tell me!"

"My dad." The words sputtered as she sobbed her confession. "I was calling my dad."

The man let go of her hair, stepped back, and paced the floor as she cried. He had never been aggressive like that with a woman, and it made him want to throw up. He took a couple breaths to center his thoughts, and to take on a quieter, more calming tone—a parent exploiting a teachable moment. "I can't stress enough how important it is that you obey me. In a little while I am going to have to trust you, and if I can't trust you . . . well, things are gonna go badly."

The woman turned, tears glistening on her cheeks. "I'm sorry. I'll do what you want, I promise."

He walked to the bed and sat next to her. "I need you to calm down and make that phone call. You need them to believe you. Can you do that for me?"

She nodded, and this time she dialed the correct number, leaving her message on an answering machine.

"Mark, I'm under the weather today. I don't think I can make it in. Hopefully it's just a bug. Sorry to leave you shorthanded, but it's for the best. I don't want to get everyone else sick. Talk to you later."

After she disconnected the call, she looked up at the man as if seeking his approval. He gave her a nod. "See? All you have to do is follow my instructions." Her eyes were red, her cheeks wet with tears, so the man pulled a tissue from a box on the nightstand and handed it to her. Then in his gentlest voice he said, "You need to stop crying."

She looked up at him with what he thought might be appreciation, and she nodded. Maybe she finally believed him that this was nothing more than a business transaction. He had handed her a tissue. This wasn't his fault; he was just doing his job.

Outside, the night sky was starting to give way to the encroachment of day. He had accomplished step two of the plan—get her to trust him. Now on to step three.

"Are you okay now?" he asked.

She nodded and blew her nose into the tissue.

"Can you show me a smile?"

She looked puzzled.

"I need you to look like nothing is wrong—like it's just another day."

She nodded and forced the corners of her lips up. It would have to do.

"That's good." He stood and stepped away from the bed. "Now, Sandy...it's time to go wake up Pip."

CHAPTER 4

Max was woken by the nightmare, the same one he'd been having for three years now. But this time, something had changed. He sat on the edge of his bed, trying to understand why his heart hammered so hard. He'd been on the frozen Canadian lake with Mikhail again, his hands and toes numb, the wind hitting his face like sandpaper. Night had fallen and he was turning the auger on the last of the eight holes he needed to drill to make an opening in the ice big enough to push a man through. He'd turned and turned the auger but the ice seemed to grow thicker beneath the dull blade. Mikhail lay tied up in the snow, laughing at Max.

Sometimes Max would argue with Mikhail in his dream, lay out the proof of Mikhail's crime, only to have Mikhail deny what was so obviously true. Other times he would beg Mikhail to confess. Still others, he drilled his holes in the ice in complete silence, knowing that there could be only one outcome—Mikhail's death.

This time, a small rabbit had watched as he dragged Mikhail to the hole, standing on her hind legs, her front paws folded together for warmth—or maybe in prayer. Max often woke before the moment he sank Mikhail through the hole, unwilling to relive those last few seconds, but on those nights when the dream persisted, he would push Mikhail through the hole only to see Jenni's eyes looking back up at him.

But this dream was different from all the others, because as Max watched Mikhail sink, it wasn't Jenni who looked up at him. It was a child.

Shaken, Max walked out of the bedroom as the first light of morning bled into the dark sky. He gripped the loft's rail, closing his eyes and trying to conjure the exact image that had jolted him from sleep.

Did he know that child? Had he seen those eyes before?

Max thought about Lyle's grandson. Were those Pip's eyes in the frozen lake? They had to be. Max hadn't had contact with any other child in years. Had their brief interaction meant that much?

The cabin had grown cold overnight, the fire in the woodstove never enough to keep the cabin warm. He returned to the bedroom and slipped into a flannel shirt and jeans, wool socks for his feet, before descending to load fresh wood into the stove on top of the embers of the oak log, barely breathing among the ashes.

It wasn't Pip, he decided, but there *was* something familiar about the child's eyes. Or had he made them familiar? Something cold filled Max's veins, spreading out from his heart. He walked back up to his bedroom, not quite able to shake a growing thought.

Back when he had sold his house to move here, he had made a single trip to the cities to sign the paperwork. He'd packed only a few items: clothing, his dad's guns, family keepsakes. What didn't fit into the back of his SUV remained for the new owners to deal with—those were the terms of the sale. It dropped the house's value, but he didn't care.

He kept the keepsakes in the bottom drawer of his dresser: pictures, wedding license, rings, Jenni's funeral notice. Now, Max laid the box on the bed. He hadn't opened it since he left Minneapolis. Tentatively, he flipped the lid and pulled out a stack of pictures of Jenni as a child. He culled through them to find one from when she was maybe four or five. He held the picture up and looked hard into her eyes. Here they were, the eyes from his dream—but it had not been Jenni's face he had seen.

He returned to the box, moving aside a stack of letters Jenni had written to him in college. Beneath the letters lay a bracelet, a chain with seven flat charms, golden plates each about the size of a dime. Jenni's great-grandmother had started the tradition of adding a new plate with each new baby born. And when Jenni's grandmother inherited the bracelet she continued the tradition. By now, the charms held the names of Jenni's grandmother and her two siblings, alongside Jenni's mother and uncle, and of course, of Jenni herself.

Max rubbed his finger gently across the seventh plate—the one with no name on it.

He hadn't known that Jenni was pregnant when she died. He'd learned about the child afterward—after the autopsy. The medical examiner was the one who told Max that he would have been a father. All those nights of talking and dreaming, planning a family, a future. There hadn't been a Christmas when he hadn't envisioned at least three stockings to be filled. There hadn't been a Halloween when he didn't envy the fathers ushering tiny goblins around the neighborhood. He hadn't understood the true depth of all he'd lost until the medical examiner told him.

For a long time, Max had believed that Jenni hadn't known about the pregnancy—she was only a month or so along. But the day before Max killed Mikhail, Max had found this bracelet in Jenni's car, a blank charm added. Jenni had known, and that thought had burned hot inside of Max as he drilled the holes in the ice. He had killed Mikhail not just for Jenni, but for their child.

Before last night, the child had never been more than a nameless charm, a line on a medical report. But now, could it have been his child who stared up at him from the icy water?

There were so many ghosts floating around the cabin already: his wife, his brother. To have his child now cling to him seemed too cruel. But hadn't that been why he came to the cabin in the first place—to accept his punishment? Something in the air seemed to shift as Max set the bracelet back into the box.

He had been waiting for a reckoning. Could the child in the dream be it?

CHAPTER 5

The man in the ski mask knew a great deal about Pip. He knew that the boy's real name was Reed, and that his mother refused to call him that after she divorced Pip's father—whose name was also Reed. The man knew that Pip was in first grade and stayed with a neighbor named Linda after school until his mother got off work.

"I want you to go wake up Pip and tell him that there's no school today. Tell him that his teacher is sick or something. Then take him to the rec room downstairs. Turn on the TV—find something that will keep him entertained for a couple hours. He'll eat his breakfast there."

"No. Do what you want to me, but leave my son alone."

The man rolled his eyes. "And if he wakes up? If he walks out here and sees me? What then? I'm doing this for you—for him. He must not know that I'm here; don't you understand that? Take him downstairs. Get him distracted—turn on the TV or whatever. It's imperative that he stay in the basement until you get back here with my money."

The man hesitated, but added one more point of persuasion: "I'll be taking my ski mask off while you're gone. If he peeks his head up those stairs and sees me...I'll be forced to do something I don't want to do."

Her breath went shallow. Then she said, "I'll make sure he stays downstairs."

They stepped into the hallway, and at Pip's door the man whispered,

"I'll be in the living room. I'll hear everything you say. If you fail me, you will suffer the consequences."

He was wrong, though. He couldn't hear them from the living room, and after a couple minutes of silence, he began to worry that he'd messed up. But then he heard them coming down the hall, a tired Pip asking why he wasn't going to school. Sandy sounded calm as she told him a lie about a pipe breaking and flooding the school. The two walked to the stairs and then down to the basement.

He moved to the top of the stairs to listen, the distance between them making him nervous. He wished that he had brought a gun, but his partner had said no. A gun would make noise and screw up the plan. The man moved closer to a glass sliding door that led to a deck and steps to the backyard. If she tried to escape out the basement door, he would be on her quickly, but thankfully she made no attempt.

When she came back up, she went to the kitchen to gather the supplies for Pip's breakfast: a box of cereal, a bowl, a spoon, and a jug of milk. Again the man listened at the top of the stairs as she delivered the meal.

When she came back up, the man turned one of the dining room chairs away from the table so that it faced the wall. "Here's what we're gonna do," he said, pointing for her to sit. "I'm getting hot in this mask, so I'm gonna take it off. I want you to face that wall and not look at me. Am I clear?"

She nodded.

"I can't stress this enough. Your life depends on my belief that you won't be able to identify me. Do you understand?"

"Yes."

Sandy sat perfectly still on the chair, obediently facing the wall. He walked to the living room and retrieved his rucksack, which lay inside the open window. Returning, he took a seat at the opposite end of the table and laid the sack in front of him. "Until the bank opens, we're gonna sit here and wait."

The man lifted the ski mask from his face and let the cool air wrap around him. He kept his gloves on, though. No fingerprints. No epithelial DNA. When the time came for him to leave that house, there would be no evidence that a crime had even occurred.

As he waited for the bank to open, the man set up a small command center on the dining room table. He'd brought his own hot spot so that he could connect to the internet without having to go through the woman's router. The cell phones he would use were burners, to be tossed into the river once he finished with them. If anyone searched cell tower data, they would see unidentified phones had pinged off the nearby towers, but numbers for those phones would be dead ends. It was the one part of the plan that would raise a flag, but there was no way around it. Besides, if he did his job well there would be no suspicion of a crime—no reason for the police to request cell tower data.

Other than the faint murmur of cartoon voices coming up from the basement, their time waiting for the bank to open passed in silence.

Just before eight o'clock, the man put his ski mask back on, picked up his knife, the two phones and his open laptop, and said, "Grab your purse. It's time to go."

He led her into the garage and placed his laptop on the hood of her SUV. Then he opened the door, affixed one of the phones to a cupholder attachment on the console, and aimed the phone's camera at the driver's seat.

"Get in."

"Please don't hurt my son."

"I said get in." He half shoved her into the driver's seat. "If you do as I say, you'll be back before your son even knows that you've left." The man dialed a number and the phone in the console buzzed. "Answer it," he said.

She followed his instruction, her finger trembling slightly. He showed her his phone which had a face-to-face app set up so that he could see her but she could not see him. "I'll be watching everything you do," he said.

Then he pulled an earpiece from the bag and handed it to her. "Put it in." She did, and he put an identical piece into his ear, connected to the phone via Bluetooth. He said, "I'll also hear everything you say. When you go in the bank, I want you to take the phone from the holder and carry it in your hand. Do you understand?"

"Yes."

"Point the camera up at your face, but do it casually—don't make a scene. You cannot draw attention to yourself in any way. That would be a mistake."

He took the laptop off the hood and showed her the screen, which held a map of her neighborhood, a tiny blue dot hovering over her house. "I'll be tracking you, so don't get any ideas. Do you understand?"

She seemed out of breath as she answered, "Yes."

He didn't want her to be any more freaked out than she already was, but he also needed her to obey him without question, so he gave her the warning he'd prepared. "You'll find yourself trying to come up with a way to stop me. You'll want to be a hero. When you have that thought, ask yourself this one question: How much is my son's life worth? It's simple math, really. If I were to ask you how much you would give me to save your son's life, what would you say? Is thirty thousand a fair price?"

Her breath came in stuttered puffs, a Morse code tapping out the depth of her fear.

"I'll see and hear everything. If you deviate from my plan in any way, I will kill your son and disappear. Do you understand?"

The tremble in her fingertips grew, and she gave the steering wheel a tight squeeze. "I understand," she said.

"Oh, and just in case you have any notions about passing a note to the teller, you should know that I have an accomplice. That person might be the woman filling out a deposit slip, or that bald security guard who sits at the desk just inside the door. Or . . . it could be the teller. They are waiting for you now. Don't do anything stupid. All you have to do is bring me thirty thousand dollars and I'll let you and Pip go. Do we have a deal?"

"Yes."

He stepped back from the vehicle. "It's time."

He watched her back out of the garage before going back into the house. Once inside, he put his laptop on the table and walked to the stairs. Standing at the top, he whispered into the phone, "You're doing fine, Sandy. Just stay calm and this will soon be over."

Then he muted the phone, pulled the stocking cap off his head, and walked down the steps to the basement, where Pip sat watching a cartoon.

The man gave the boy a smile. "Hello, Pip."

CHAPTER 6

Max arrived at the electric company before the office opened, having had no bath in a week. He had put off bathing because he'd have had to haul water in from the hand pump out front and heat half to a boil on his woodstove—a lot of work.

As he waited, he gave thought to the questions he might face inside. Last week, the woman behind the window, a matronly lady of sixty years or better, had seemed confused when Max asked that she shut off the power to the cabin.

"Closing down for the season?" she had asked.

"No, just doing without."

She looked at Max as if there was a punch line coming. "Doing without...electricity?"

"That's right."

"And you're still going to live there?"

"I am," Max replied.

"Without electricity?"

"Yes," he said. "I plan to live deliberately."

The woman had looked at Max like he was speaking nonsense—obviously not a fan of Thoreau. "And so...you want me to shut off your power."

Max closed his eyes, a slow blink to hide his exasperation. "Yes, please."

He had lasted only a week, and now he imagined her grinning with smug satisfaction as he asked to have his power restored. He wanted to tell her that he didn't lack the fortitude to make it without electricity. He had no problem hauling water in from the pump. He didn't mind the chill of night as the fire died down. He could make do with cooking his meals over the fire pit. What he lacked was the ability to kill a god-damned rabbit without losing his shit.

If Max could have, he would have *called* the electric company, but he'd terminated his data plan shortly after moving to the cabin, a measure he took to cut ties with the one person who had cared enough to try to call him after he disappeared, his former partner in Homicide, Niki Vang.

She had been at his side as he suffered through the memory of his dead wife, turning a blind eye as Max pieced together the puzzle that led him to her killer. She had kept his secret, telling no one about what he had been up to in the days before his sudden resignation. She had been a true friend, and Max repaid her by mailing his badge and gun to her for her to turn in to the chief. His resignation had been a deal that he made with himself just before he pushed Mikhail through the hole. Giving up his badge was a price he would pay for exacting his revenge.

Niki had tried to contact him, of course. As her unopened messages piled up, he deleted his email account, canceled his internet and then his phone contract. On his trip back to Minneapolis to sign off on the sale of his house, he could have explained things to her, but he didn't. It was cowardly, he knew that, but if he had met with Niki face-to-face, she would have tried to persuade him to come back, and he didn't want to hear her voice—he didn't have the strength. Niki had been his last link to his old self, something that needed to be severed.

Although if he was honest with himself, she had been much more than that. There had been something between them that neither had ever put into words, as if talking about it, exposing it, would have opened a crack in the earth beneath their feet. She would be happier without him — surely she was by now.

A car pulled into the lot, the driver glancing toward Max. It was the electric company employee he had spoken with before. She must have recognized Max, because she smiled to herself as though she had just won a bet. Then she got out of her car and walked into the building.

CHAPTER 7

Pip was a cute little guy. The man had seen pictures, but those pictures didn't quite capture the innocence of the boy's eyes. He wore pajamas with stars and moons on them and walked in bare feet. Pip didn't look frightened so much as curious. The man waited for Pip to say something, and when he didn't, the man said. "My name's Spud. I'm a friend of your mom's. She asked me to stay with you while she runs some errands."

"Where's Linda?" the boy asked.

"Linda is sick today, so your mom called me." He walked to Pip and squatted down. "Are you hungry?"

Pip shook his head.

"Thirsty?"

Again no.

"I need you to stay down here for a little while—is that okay?"

Pip nodded, but didn't speak, keeping his eyes on Spud as he made his way back upstairs. Once there, the man checked the dot on the computer screen to see that Sandy was driving a direct path to the bank. He unmuted his phone and whispered a few words of encouragement. "You're doing great, Sandy." Through the app he saw her nod.

He muted his earpiece and walked out to the garage, which held a well-ordered bench under a pegboard filled with tools, each outlined in black ink to show its proper place. In a cupboard, he found some telephone wire. He untangled it and gave it a tug to test its strength. He was about to close the cupboard when he saw a spool of wire, the kind a person might use to hang a picture. That would work even better. He unrolled a length and cut it with a tin snips.

He picked up two small paintbrushes with plastic handles and tied an end of the cable to each. He gave the wire a tug, and just that easy, he'd made a garrote—so simple and yet so lethal. Looking at the weapon nearly made him nauseous. He folded the garrote into the pocket of his hoodie and went back into the house.

The computer showed that Sandy was pulling into the parking lot of the bank. Even with her phone in her hand, he would be blind to most of her actions. This was the shakiest part of the plan, so he gave her a final pep talk.

"Don't forget to take the phone with you. Don't mess up now. And remember, I have eyes on you."

She didn't answer.

He had no accomplice inside, of course. He knew about the bald security guard because he made a visit to that bank as they were putting the plan together. All he could do now was hope that she believed his lie.

The earpiece picked up just enough of the teller's voice for the man to hear "Good morning."

"Hi," Sandy said. "I'd like to make a withdrawal."

The phone's camera pointed up at an odd angle, catching the top of Sandy's head and the ceiling beyond. After that, the voices became too muffled to understand. Spud began to worry as seconds ticked into minutes. How had he let himself get talked into this? What had he been thinking? He wasn't a bad guy, but here he was, doing a very bad thing. There could be no half measures now—he was all in. The plan had to work.

Then he heard, "Here you go." It was the teller. A few seconds of shuffling as she put the money into a bag and then: "Would you like someone to walk you to your car?"

"No. I'll be fine."

"Well, have a nice day."

He heard the squeak of the door, and a few seconds later Sandy put the phone back into its place in the cupholder. Spud breathed a sigh of relief and then spoke into the phone. "You did well, Sandy. David will be proud of you. I'm proud of you."

"I did what you asked," she said, her voice trembling. "You promised not to hurt us."

"I'll leave once I get my money, I promise. You kept your end of the bargain, and I'll keep mine. Just so you know, Pip was a perfect little boy while you were gone. He never came upstairs. He'll never know any of this happened."

She whispered, "Thank God." He watched her wipe tears from her eyes. He turned the phone facedown on the table. He didn't want to see her cry. The next step would be hard enough without that.

The dot on his computer screen made its way back to the house; Spud couldn't seem to catch his breath. The air around him grew inexplicably thin. He put his hands on the dining room table and heaved big gulps of air into his lungs. When he became too dizzy to stand, he sat, the world around him going blurry through the tears that filled his eyes. Somewhere in that blur, he saw the movement of a small boy.

"Pip." He wiped his eyes and blinked until the boy was no longer blurry.

"I have to go to the bathroom."

"Okay. That's fine. Can we do that downstairs?"

Pip gave no reply. So the man picked him up, carried him back down the steps, and set Pip at the door to the bathroom. Sweat gathered at Spud's temple as he paced the rec room waiting for the boy to finish.

The room was sparse, with outdated carpeting, paneled walls, and a fireplace that had been converted into a wood-burning stove. There was a couch, a television, and a bumper-pool table, furnishings that spoke of frugality, a family that worked hard to save up the thirty-two thousand dollars in the bank.

Spud went to the door that led outside to the backyard and pressed his hot forehead against the cool glass, his breath fogging up a lower pane. When he stood back, he saw the smear he'd left behind. Was there DNA in sweat? *Damn it.* He used his elbow to clean the glass.

When Pip finished, he took the boy back to the couch. "Can you sit here for a little while longer?"

The boy nodded and Spud gave him a smile. "You're a good kid."

Spud ran back upstairs in time to see the SUV turn into the driveway — no cops in tow. He felt discombobulated. He thought he'd have more time to prepare himself for what came next.

He grabbed his knife and went to meet the woman in the garage, remembering at the last second to pull his ski mask back down. She stepped out of the car with her hand outstretched, a bag of money clutched in her fingers. She looked so hopeful.

He took the money and motioned for her to go inside. "You did good," he said.

"I want to see my son. I want to see Pip."

"Pip's downstairs. He's fine—"

"I want to see him."

That wasn't part of the plan. Pip might say something about the man named Spud. If he did, everything would fall apart.

"You'll see him later." The man tried to be forceful in his command, but it sounded disingenuous, even to him. "You need to go to your bedroom."

She turned to him, her eyes wide as though she had somehow been betrayed. "You said you'd leave us if I did what you said. You promised."

"I can't have you running to the cops as soon as I leave. I'm just gonna tie you up in your bedroom. It'll take some time for you to get loose. If nothing else, your boyfriend can untie you when he gets home. Either way, I need a head start."

"And I need to see my son. Let me see him and I'll do what you want."

She was in no position to make demands, but something in the way she looked at him got to Spud. What he did next was absolutely not part of the plan, but he did it anyway.

"Outside."

"What?"

"I don't want him seeing you. He might want to come upstairs. You can look at him through the basement door."

She hesitated only a second before walking out onto the deck and down to the backyard. They walked side by side, his eyes scanning the woods behind the house. She had neighbors, but they were far enough away that he could barely see their houses through the trees.

At a basement window, the woman peered in and saw Pip sitting on the couch, the back of his head bobbing slightly to the music of a cartoon. The little boy was oblivious to their presence.

As Sandy watched her son, the man pulled the garrote from the pocket of his hoodie, a paintbrush handle in each hand. His heart pounded, and he had to swallow to keep the bile from creeping up his throat. He wanted to run away. He wanted to throw up. He didn't want to do this—but he had no choice.

He quickly looped the garrote around her neck and pulled it tight.

The woman grabbed for her throat, but the thin wire dug deeply into her skin. She clawed at his gloved hands, but made no sound. How could she?

"I'm sorry," he whispered. "I'm so sorry."

He wanted to explain. He wanted her to know that her death had a purpose, but how could he tell her? "I'm sorry," he said again.

As the fight left her body, her legs gave out and the two of them dropped to the ground. Her hands and arms went limp, and her head fell loose on her shoulders—but she was not yet dead. He knew that she would go unconscious within a few seconds, but death would take a couple minutes, at least. He kept the pressure on as tears soaked the wool of his mask.

His stomach started to heave, and he swallowed to stop what seemed inevitable now. *Just a few more seconds.* When he could no longer hold it back, he let go of the garrote, pulled his ski mask off his head, and puked into the cap. He would leave no DNA. That was the plan.

CHAPTER 8

When his stomach stopped heaving, Spud sat back on his heels and wiped his chin with his sleeve. Sandy lay next to him, dead—her lips blue, her face pale, her eyes open and dry. He looked around to be certain no one had seen him. Then a shudder rose up from somewhere deep inside and he started crying, hard tears that shook him as they fell. He was a murderer. He'd taken a life. He clutched at the grass beneath him to keep from collapsing. What had he done?

He took a breath and focused on why he was there. He was saving the boy, wasn't he? And he was keeping his word. Spud had made a deal with the devil—and the devil had already honored his part. And anyway, the debt would have been paid, one way or another. Spud promised himself that he had done the right thing.

As strength returned to his knees, he put the garrote back into his pocket, lifted Sandy's dead body onto his shoulders, and carried her to the garage, where he placed her body in the back of her SUV. It was just past nine o'clock. David would be home before eleven and Spud had a thousand tasks to do.

First, he found a plastic shopping bag in the garage and put his puke-filled ski mask in it. He would keep that in the front seat of the SUV so that he could get rid of it somewhere along the drive. He put his ruck-sack with the phones, computer, and knife on the passenger seat and the thirty grand into the glove box. He placed Sandy's cell phone on the console, still turned on. David would call once he arrived home, and that call would be used to locate the path of her phone—the false trail that Spud would leave.

He went down to the basement where Pip still sat on the couch. The boy looked at him with curiosity as Spud gathered suitcases from a storage room. He gave the boy a smile as he passed by on his way back upstairs. He carried the suitcases to Sandy's bedroom and began filling them with clothing from her closet and drawers. Like the Grinch in the Dr. Seuss story, Spud took everything that looked like it might belong to the woman, and when the suitcases were full, he used garbage bags. He took the pill bottles from the medicine cabinet with her name on them. He took her jewelry box, her laptop, her hair products and makeup—everything.

When he had finished in Sandy's bedroom, he did the same in Pip's, loading toys and clothing into a bag. He loaded school records, pictures and mementos, everything that a woman would take if she were running away to start a new life with her son. That would be the story the police would uncover.

He set aside some clothing for Pip to wear now, along with a coat and hat. He also set aside a portable game console to keep the boy entertained as they drove. Within an hour, he had the cargo area of the SUV filled with garbage bags and suitcases, Sandy's body buried beneath it all.

The final thing the man packed was Pip's pillow, the one that the boy hugged every night when he went to bed, the one he'd had since he was a toddler, the pillow he'd named Bobby. Pip would never leave home without his pillow. Spud had done his homework. With his task complete, he took Pip's clothes downstairs, where the boy had fallen asleep on the couch, curled up with his hands tucked between his knees. He looked cold, and the man regretted not giving Pip a blanket earlier. He knelt down in front of the boy and gently shook his shoulders.

"Hey, buddy, wake up."

Pip opened a tired eye, looking confused. He sat up slowly, and the man handed Pip the clothes. "Can you put these on?"

Pip nodded. He seemed a very polite and quiet child. "Where's Mommy?"

"We need to run a little errand. Your mom said you should do what I say. You can do that, can't you, buddy?"

After putting Pip's coat on him and taking him to the SUV, he buckled him into the booster seat and handed him the game to play with.

With Pip in the car, Spud did a final walk-through of the house, making sure that everything was in the proper place. He closed the window he'd used to enter and put the plant back beneath it. Then he strapped his bicycle to the top of the SUV. He'd left no footprints, no fingerprints, no hair, no DNA. There was nothing that pointed to any story other than a woman taking her child on the run.

Satisfied with his effort, the man got behind the wheel and backed the SUV out of the garage. He headed south, knowing his route would skirt Grand Rapids and lead to the Twin Cities. Just past a small town called Hill City, he turned off the main highway onto a dirt trail to toss his puke-filled stocking cap into the woods.

A few minutes later, he turned Sandy's phone off and exited the highway again onto a gravel road, a detour he didn't want showing up on the phone's tracking system. The road led into Hill River State Forest, an area about as secluded as you could find along that stretch of highway. The road, barely more than a one-lane trail, took him west for a mile or so before cutting past the tip of a marsh. That's where he'd had hidden a bag with weights in it—where he would leave Sandy's body.

He backed the SUV up to the water's edge, stepped out, and listened carefully, hearing only the chirp of a bird in a nearby basswood tree. In the woods, buried under dead leaves, he found the nylon duffel, filled with eighty pounds of barbell weights. He dragged it back to the car.

Before pulling her body out, he gave a peek in at Pip, reassuring himself that the stack of suitcases and garbage bags was blocking the child's view. Then Spud dragged Sandy out from beneath her belongings and dropped her on top of the opened duffel. It took some work to get her folded into the bag, but he had purchased the biggest one he could find. Once she and the weights were inside, he zipped it shut and lugged the package out into the marsh.

The marsh was cold, but the work kept him warm as he dragged her out into water that went up to his chest. He dropped her there, stepped around the sunken duffel, and trudged back to shore. Inside the SUV, Pip seemed to be taking this little adventure in stride. Spud gave the boy a reassuring smile as he took the rucksack from the front passenger seat. Using one of the burner phones, he typed a message to his partner. On the road. No problems. He sent the message, returned the phone to the sack, filled the sack with stones from the side of the trail, and heaved it out into the marsh too.

Back on the main highway, Spud turned Sandy's phone on again to await David's calls. How long would the worried boyfriend wait before he phoned the sheriff?

The phone buzzed eight times in the remaining couple of hours it took to reach Minneapolis, the last call coming just as Spud pulled into the gas station to fill up. The stop had been carefully planned. The gas station had no surveillance cameras and there were no banks or ATMs between it and his exit from the interstate. Spud pulled the hood of his sweatshirt up over his head as he put gas in the car.

As the tank filled, he pried Sandy's phone open, removed the battery, and tossed both into the trash. The gas station would be the end of Sandy's trail. He paid with one of Sandy's credit cards and headed back to the highway, now driving north, the direction from which he'd just come.

The rendezvous point had also been carefully chosen, a secluded farm at the edge of the Mississippi River. It was an hour's drive from where Spud had filled up with gas—a little more than that after a stop to buy him and Pip a couple hamburgers. He ate as he drove, watching as the strip malls and truck plazas gave way to farm fields and woods.

Spud searched for the landmark that would tell him when he was nearing the designated field, a grove of pine trees with a single cottonwood sticking up in the middle. It was dark now, though, and he couldn't be sure that he'd be able to see the cottonwood tree when he came to it. To make things worse, the field he was looking for had been full of cornstalks before. The crops had now been harvested, so the landscape was mile after mile of dirt.

He began to doubt himself and was about to turn around when he came upon the cottonwood tree silhouetted in the moonlight. With a sigh of relief, he killed his headlights, turned onto the field, and bounced along the tractor path that led to a bluff at the far end. As he neared, he saw a shard of moonlight reflecting off the windshield of a waiting car.

He parked the SUV so that its nose faced the bluff, turned off the engine, and let out a deep breath. The plan had worked.

Someone stepped out of the waiting car, a man with a military haircut and cold eyes. He approached the SUV, walking around to the back passenger side. Spud turned in his seat to watch as the man opened the door and bent down to be face-to-face with Pip in his car seat.

"Hi, Pip," the man said in a gentle tone. He paused as if to take in Pip's confused reaction. When Pip didn't respond, the man smiled and said, "Do you remember me?"

Pip looked hard into the man's eyes. Then he said, "Daddy?"

CHAPTER 9

In the three years since he had last held his son, Reed Harris had grown accustomed to waiting, in the same way a man who loses his right hand gets accustomed to eating with his left. He waited as the custody battle played out, even when his hearing landed while he was still in jail for assault. They made him wear his orange jumpsuit to court. Of course the judge came down hard on him.

He waited as the two years of probation ticked down, his discharge date being the start of his new plan. Did Sandy think that there would be no price to pay for her treachery? Had she been that shortsighted? For two years, Reed followed the rules, put on a show so the world would believe that he had capitulated.

As the SUV bounced its way across the dusty field, Reed couldn't help but puff with pride. He had won. It didn't matter that some bitch of a judge had deprived him of his son—not even allowing visitation. It didn't matter that Sandy had brought another man into his son's life. He had the boy, and she was dead. He had slammed his checkmate down on the board with authority.

When the vehicle came to a stop, Reed went to the back where Pip sat in his car seat. Pip—the name stabbed Reed in his heart. She had gone out of her way to erase Reed from the boy's life, going so far as to take away the boy's true name—Reed Harris, Jr.—and calling him Pip like he was some Dickensian orphan. Reed would soon change all that.

When the time was right, he would whisk the boy away and they would start a new life with new names. Until then, he thought it best not to confuse his son any more than he had to. He would grit his teeth and call the boy Pip.

Reed opened the door and leaned into the car. "Hi, Pip. Do you remember me?" He smiled and waited for his son to recognize him. But when that recognition came, there was no excitement. What Reed saw on the boy's face was puzzlement.

He lifted his son from the booster seat and held him for the first time since the night of the fight. The child had grown so much. Reed had seen Pip a few times in town, hand in hand with his mother, the restraining order forcing Reed to turn and walk in the opposite direction. But he had created a fake Facebook account under the name of a woman that Sandy vaguely knew. He then tricked Sandy into friending him so that he could watch his son grow up through the pictures online.

Pip didn't hold on to Reed or fold into his arms as Reed carried him to his Tahoe. Reed understood. They were strangers. It would take time to work through all of the destructive lies that Sandy had told the boy. He put Pip into the warm vehicle and buckled him into a new car seat. Then he returned to Spud, waiting next to Sandy's SUV.

"Roll the windows down a couple inches," Reed said. "We want it to sink fast but we don't want her stuff to float out."

The vehicle faced the bluff. Below it, the river turned in an oxbow, where the water would be deep enough to hide the car as long as it didn't float around the bend before it sank.

"Here." Spud held out the pillow with the dinosaur pillowcase.

"Everything goes into the river," Reed said.

"You said he needs it to sleep."

Reed rolled his eyes, a gesture lost in the darkness, and took the pillow. "Put the car in neutral."

Reed took the pillow back to the Tahoe and threw it in the backseat next to Pip. Then he climbed into the driver's seat and maneuvered the

Tahoe behind Sandy's SUV, the headlights of both vehicles off. There was a slight thump as his bumper nudged hers. Reed dropped into his lowest gear and slowly pushed the SUV forward, over the edge of the bluff, the sound of small trees breaking against the metal of the car lifting out of the valley.

Reed joined Spud at the precipice, the moon lighting the path that the SUV had taken into the river. It left no debris trail and sank quickly. Again, Reed felt like puffing his chest. His plan was working like a dream.

The next part was, again, a waiting game. Deposit Spud and Pip in the cabin they had secured in the woods north of Grand Rapids, a hiding spot rented with cash and a fake name. They had the cabin for six months. Reed figured that that would be enough time for the dust to settle. He would go back to his life tending bar in Grand Rapids, play the distraught father. How could she have run off the way she did? All the while, Spud and Pip would be waiting in the woods.

Yes, Reed was good at waiting, but he had no faith in his partner. Three years ago, Spud had simply been in the right place at the right time. He had been easily manipulated by Reed's sad story. Reed had listened to Spud go on and on about his messed-up childhood before sculpting the version of Sandy and Pip that Reed knew would feed his partner's maternal resentment. And with the right story, Spud had become a malleable and useful recruit.

But Spud was also impulsive; that would be a problem. One would think that murder and kidnapping would be the most difficult part of the plan, but Reed knew otherwise. The following days, and weeks, and months would be the challenge.

As they both climbed back into the Tahoe, Reed looked at Spud. How long would his partner last before he forced Reed to execute the final step of the plan — the step that Reed kept to himself?

CHAPTER 10

Five days passed before Max dreamed of the child again. He'd been holding Jenni's hand as they walked through a park when he felt tiny fingers press against his other palm. Max tried to see the child's face, but it was like staring into the sun. He wanted more than anything to know him or her, but he awoke with a deep emptiness in his chest, an emptiness that he carried out to the fire pit along with his morning coffee.

The day had rolled in with a light fog on the lake, the grass wet with dew. The air was crisp with the coming winter, fall colors dancing off the water as the sun rose up behind him. Max had been watching an eagle in one of the trees at the water's edge, the brilliant white plumage on its head and tail marking the bird as at least five years old. It seemed to be enjoying the last throes of autumn as it stared down at the lake in search of a meal. Max tried again to conjure the face of that child, but distractions cut through: Jenni, Mikhail, the rabbit. He gave up, took a sip of coffee, and tried to refocus on the eagle.

As a homicide detective, Max had grown used to his brain zipping from thought to thought, connecting dots faster than the flap of a hummingbird's wings. Like a child sent to the corner to think about what he had done, Max had expected the stillness of the woods to guide him to Nirvana or Perdition or wherever the hell he was supposed to go now, but instead of bringing clarity, the absence of stimuli had made him restless. He wanted to be like the eagle, her world reduced to the simple task of catching her next meal. Max was fairly certain that she had never felt sick at the death of a rabbit or awoken from a dream shaken by the eyes of a child staring up from a watery depth.

It was the eagle who heard the pickup truck first, turning her head toward the county highway beyond the trees. She took flight before Max heard the hum of the truck's engine as it weaved its way down the trail toward his cabin, the crunch of its tires muffled by pine needles, wet leaves, and grass.

The truck rolled to a stop next to the cabin, Lyle Voight behind the wheel. At first the intrusion struck Max as damned offensive. No one had come down that trail in years. Who did Lyle think he was? They'd chatted on occasion—that was it—and here he was rolling in like he owned the place.

But the detective in Max took a closer look at the older man. Lyle stayed in the truck for a good minute or two, his hands gripping the steering wheel, his head tipped forward. True, Max didn't know Lyle all that well, but he'd guess the old sheriff wouldn't drop by uninvited unless he had a good reason. Max felt ashamed for his initial reaction.

In time, Lyle stepped out, making his way toward the sliding glass door of the cabin. Max held up his cup of coffee and called out, "Hey, Lyle." Lyle didn't wave, but nodded grimly, turning to walk Max's way.

Lyle was fit for a man in his sixties, if not particularly big, and Max had little doubt that Lyle could outlast him in a log-splitting contest. But Lyle's slow gait, the way his head dipped down on his shoulders, told Max that Lyle was carrying somber news.

Lyle stopped short of Max to look out at the lake, and then up into the trees, before saying, "This sure is a slice of heaven you got here." Even in that compliment, Max could hear sadness.

"You okay?"

Lyle seemed confused and said, "You haven't heard."

"Heard what?"

Lyle looked at the bench as though asking for permission to sit. Max gave a nod, and Lyle sat, resting his elbows on his knees and folding his hands together, his fingers trembling slightly. "You met my daughter, Sandy, remember?"

"Yeah, outside the store. Had your grandson with her ... Pip, right?"

"They're missing."

Max leaned forward, matching Lyle's posture. "Missing?"

"Three days ago, her boyfriend came home from work and she was gone — Pip too."

"I'm sorry."

"It ain't like that, Max. Something's wrong. She wouldn't do that — not in a million years. You don't just up and leave when you got no cause for it."

Indulging an old habit, Max began to shuffle through the possible explanations: ran away, kidnapped, taking a break from the boyfriend. "What about her stuff, clothing and the like?"

Lyle paused before answering. "Her clothes were gone," he said finally. "Her clothes and Pip's clothes were gone."

"What about other things ... medications, makeup?"

"Gone. I know what you're thinking, Max, but it ain't so. She didn't run off. I know my daughter."

"What about the boyfriend?"

"His name is David Haas. They've been together about a year now. A stand-up guy by all accounts."

"And she lives with him?"

"More like he lives with her. Sandy's ex-husband, this piece of shit named Reed Harris, destroyed her credit rating, so after the divorce, she couldn't get a loan to buy a tent. My wife and I gave her our place to live and we moved into an apartment. Then after I lost the election ... well, I didn't see any reason to stick around where I wasn't wanted. We're up in Ely now."

Max found he had a hundred questions, but asking those questions might pull him into Lyle's situation, which was probably the reason for

Lyle's visit in the first place. Max decided to pull back. "I assume you reported this to the new sheriff?"

"The man has no business wearing my badge. He says she ran off and that's all there is to it. But that's not what happened. I know it in my gut. That's why . . ."

"That's why you came here," Max said. He took a slow drink of his coffee, and considered the gentlest way to turn Lyle down.

"I know how it sounds, but I also know my daughter. That's the thing. I know with all my heart that something bad happened. Tell you the truth, Max, I'm scared. It's been three days and we ain't heard a word. It's not like her. Even if she did run off, she'd have called." For the first time since he took his seat, Lyle looked at Max, his features already thinner than Max remembered. "Max, I need your help."

"I'm not a cop, Lyle. You need someone with a badge."

"But you *were* a cop, and a damned good one."

"How would you know?"

"When you first moved up here, I made a call. Couldn't figure out why a young fella like you—a detective and all—would quit the force and move to the woods. Your chief couldn't figure it out either. Said you were the best he had."

This wasn't how it was supposed to go. The world was supposed to leave Max alone—no favors, no friendships. Lyle had no right to ask this of him. Max sipped his coffee again and stared at the ashes in the fire pit. He finally said, "I'm just not the guy you need."

"What I need is someone to tell me the truth. I need someone with the eye of a cop. It doesn't matter that you don't have a badge. I don't care about any of that."

Max thought about Mikhail and that day on the lake. He thought about the deal he'd made as he slid Mikhail through the hole. He wasn't part of that world—not anymore. That part of Max died on that lake and he couldn't let anyone or anything pull him back there. "I'm sorry, Lyle. I can't."

Lyle seemed to deflate, his head sinking into his chest, his hands on his knees, fingers drained of blood. Max hated to see Lyle that broken, so he looked back to the woods, where the eagle had taken to the air. Lyle pushed himself up to his feet and walked slowly back toward his pickup.

"They'll turn up soon enough," Max offered, a clumsy gesture of hope.

Lyle stopped at the front of his truck and slowly turned to Max. The look of recrimination in his eyes was just about enough to blacken out the sun. "I don't know what you have going on that's more important, but right now you're turning your back on my daughter—on my grandson. You've met them. I don't understand how you can..." Lyle took a breath as if fighting off a well of emotion, then he said, "He's just a child, for God's sake."

Max dropped his gaze as Lyle's words hung in the air. Eventually Max heard the engine of the pickup start, and the crunch of dead pine needles as it pulled away.

Long after the truck had receded, Max could still hear Lyle's parting words: *He's just a child, for God's sake.*

CHAPTER 11

By the fourth day at the cabin, Spud was wondering just how well he knew his partner. Had Reed always been this way, or had something changed? The day began as had the last three, with Spud waking up on the floor of the room where Pip slept. That hadn't been the plan.

The cabin—little more than a rickety old hunting shack—had two bedrooms, one for Spud and one for the boy. Reed still slept at his place in town just in case the sheriff dropped by. The shack had a tin roof, slate siding the color of rotted teeth, and a wooden porch that dipped to one side, the wood soft and wet even on dry days. The interior walls were pine boards painted the color of creamed corn, and it had linoleum floors. There were rust stains in the sinks and gaps around the windows, and doors barely sealed with tacky foam insulation. The shack was squalid, sure, but it was tucked in the woods and would keep them hidden until the heat died down. When the time was right, Reed would take Pip far away, and Spud would return to St. Paul a wealthy man.

He'd thought his task of babysitting Pip would be easy. Feed the boy, keep him mildly entertained, put him to bed—but on that first night the boy had cried out in his sleep, a chilling wail like a wounded dog. Why had they not expected this? They had snatched a child from his home—from his mother—and whisked him into the dark, cold night. Of course there would be fallout.

Pip had stayed awake for the entire drive to the shack, his eyes fixed on his father behind the wheel. Reed didn't talk. He had given Pip no explanation as to what was happening, no words to patch up three years of absence. Spud had tried to get the father and son engaged by asking Pip if he had missed his father, but the boy remained mute. Spud even offered to drive so that Reed could sit in back with Pip, but Reed snapped at Spud, telling him that no one drove Reed's vehicle other than Reed.

Spud tried to remember the stories that Reed had told him about how things had been before Sandy tore the family apart. There had been stories, hadn't there? Tales of a loving father and son? Fishing trips? Playing in the snow? He was sure that there had—or maybe those had been Spud's stories, memories of him and his father before his father died when Spud was only ten years old? He shook the thought away. They were doing the right thing—they were saving the boy.

On that first night at the shack, when Pip woke up screaming, Spud had run into the room to find him sitting up in bed, his eyes closed, his arms wrapped around his pillow. When Spud put his hand on the boy's back, Pip's eyes flashed open, and he kicked and flailed, backing himself into the corner at the head of the bed.

"Pip, it's me, Spud." He stepped back and flicked on the light. That didn't ease the boy's fear, so Spud smiled as warmly as he could manage. "It's me...your buddy."

Pip looked around as if searching for a monster, keeping a bear hug on his pillow. Spud took a step closer, approaching the boy as he might an animal. Spud had never before been responsible for a child, or spent any length of time with one, but he remembered his father's gentleness. At the side of the bed, Spud took a knee and held out his hand. It was then that he saw the tear on Pip's cheek. "What's the matter?"

The boy looked around the room again. He didn't answer.

Thinking that Pip might be looking for Reed, Spud said, "Your dad's at work, but he'll be here soon." Spud had said those words to comfort Pip, but instead they caused him to grip the pillow tighter.

In a soothing tone, Spud whispered, "Hey...buddy...it's okay.

Ain't no one or nothing gonna hurt you—not while I'm here. Don't be scared." He patted the mattress. "Go ahead. Lie down. I'll stay right here."

"You'll stay here?" Pip finally asked in a small voice.

"Right beside you." Spud leaned against the wall, his knees up and his forearms resting on them. He waited as Pip considered his words. Then the boy scooted out of the corner and slid back under the covers.

Spud figured he should tell Pip a bedtime story as they lay in the darkness of the room. He had started the tale of Rumpelstiltskin but remembered that it led to the kidnapping of a child, so he switched to the story of the king with no clothing. By the end, Pip was asleep. Spud went to his own room, retrieved a blanket and pillow, and returned, curling up on the floor so that he would be there if the boy woke up. He would keep his word.

That first day at the shack began with Pip asking where his mother was. Spud dodged the question by asking Pip about his father, a subject that made Pip strangely quiet. They had no toys or games at the shack, so Spud made up a game where Pip would hide a spoon and Spud had to find it—because the shack was too small to play actual hide-and-seek.

Reed finally stopped by before going to his evening shift, pulling into the yard around two in the afternoon. When Pip heard his father walking up the steps, he ran into the kitchen to stand beside Spud.

"I bear gifts," Reed called out as he entered the shack, a bag of groceries in each hand. He placed the bags on the kitchen table and unpacked a jug of milk and a box of cereal without so much as a glance at his son.

"Did you bring a coloring book for Pip?" Spud asked.

Reed dropped his smile and shot Spud a look, his eyes narrow and cold. Spud had a good four inches on Reed, and although Reed was thick for his size, Spud probably had thirty pounds on him as well. But the look on Reed's face made the big man feel small. Reed turned his back on Spud, putting the milk into the rusted refrigerator without answering the question. Of course he hadn't brought a coloring book.

Reed returned to the table to lift a package of Oreos out of the bag. It was only then that he sought out the boy. "You like cookies, don't you?"

Pip remained quiet, standing behind Spud's leg.

Reed opened the package, took out a cookie, and popped it into his mouth. Then he held the package down for Pip. "Go on. I won't bite you."

Pip took a single cookie and walked to his bedroom, shutting the door behind him.

Reed watched the boy walk away and said, "It's gonna take some time to work the poison out. I knew she messed with his head, but... Christ."

"He needs games," Spud said. "Something to bring him out of his shell."

Reed cocked his head slightly. "You're an expert on raising kids? Here I thought you said you were a college dropout."

"I didn't say I was a—"

"Or maybe you've raised a few kids of your own?"

"He needs to feel like this is a good place."

"He's not with that bitch." Reed's lip twitched up in a snarl, and he pounded his pointer finger into the tabletop. "So this is a good place."

"He had a nightmare."

That seemed to get Reed's attention. "About what?"

"I didn't ask."

"You should have asked."

"He was scared. I told him a story and stayed with him."

"Stayed with him?"

"In his room."

"You stayed in his room? In his bed?"

"No, I slept on the floor."

"That's not what we discussed." Reed's eyes bored into Spud, causing Spud to take a step back.

"He was scared, Reed." Spud's words sounded like an apology. "I want him to be able to sleep."

Reed smiled at Spud, as if taking pleasure in watching the man's retreat. Then his eyes softened. "I appreciate that, but . . . you're under-mining what I'm trying to do. I have to break the spell his mother cast on him. You see that, don't you? I have to teach Pip to be strong. He needs to face his fears. If we go rushing in to save him . . . well, it'll be like his mother's still here, hovering."

Spud nodded as Reed spoke, but none of it made sense to him. Reed was talking about a six-year-old boy like he was an experiment. Reed's visit lasted under an hour, and before he left, he made Spud promise to let Pip cry through his nightmares. Spud gave his word, but went to sleep on the floor next to Pip that night anyway.

The morning of the fourth day found Spud, once again, waking up next to Pip's bed. He woke to the sound of a truck engine — Reed's Tahoe. Spud slipped out of Pip's room into the kitchen just as Reed mounted the porch. Again he carried food in grocery bags. Spud opened the door to let him in.

"It happened," Reed announced with a sweep of pride. "Just like I said it would."

"What happened?"

"Sheriff Bolger came out to interview me yesterday. I told you there'd be an investigation. Damn, it's playing out just like I thought."

"Does he suspect . . ."

"Not a thing. I could tell by the questions he asked. He bought our story about the runaway wife hook, line, and sinker. Asked me if I'd heard any rumors about problems between Sandy and David Haas. Wanted to know if Sandy ever talked about moving out of state while we were married. I told him that Sandy always had a thing for beaches. Talked about California and Florida."

"But if he's investigating . . . doesn't that mean that he suspects some-thing's wrong?"

"No. It's David Haas and probably Sandy's old man. No doubt, they're pushing it, so Bolger has to at least go through the motions. He even searched my house."

"He had a search warrant?"

"Hell no. A search warrant needs probable cause. Ain't no way he'd get a prosecutor or judge to sign off. I invited him to search. I wanted him to see that I have nothing to hide. I want him to believe that I'm desperate to find my son, and the sooner he searches my house, the sooner he crosses me off the list. She's a missing person—at best—and that's all."

"So now what?" Spud asked.

"I can start spending more time here ... with you and Pip. I'll put on a good show about my son being taken away by his mother, make sure that people see that I'm upset about it. And then it's just a waiting game. In time, I'll move out of Minnesota because there's nothing to keep me here. You see? Then you're free to go back to your life. It's working just like I told you it would."

"So when you say you'll be spending more time here ..."

"Starting tonight—after my shift. I have a cot in the truck. We'll move your bed into Pip's room for me, and you can have the cot."

"I get the cot?"

Reed's smile fell away. "Which one of us has to work every day?"

He stared at Spud until Spud nodded, although to himself Spud thought, *You could have just as easily brought a bed.*

They unloaded the Tahoe of groceries, clothes for Reed, and a box of magazines: sports magazines, hunting magazines, but nothing for a child. Spud wanted to throw the magazines at Reed. Had he forgotten that he had a son there at the shack? Where were the children's books? The games? Did Reed think his six-year-old son cared who the Vikings traded or what power of rifle worked best for hunting deer?

But then Spud thought about his own father. Yeah, they read books and played games together, but those weren't the moments he cherished. The memories that held their color over the many years were the times they just sat together and talked, moments of respite away from his mother, when they were Spike and Spud, the nicknames they used when they were alone.

Spud hoped that Reed had plans to take his son for a walk in the woods, or cook a meal with him. But Spud's hopes were short-lived.

Reed spent five hours at the shack that day, four of them sitting in the living room reading magazines. Pip stayed in his room for most of that time. When he came out for lunch, he sat beside Spud, a move that caused Reed's nostrils to flare. And when Pip accidentally spilled a glass of milk, Reed stood, went to the sink, picked up a washrag, and tossed it to the table.

"Clean it up," he said to Pip.

Pip wiped up the milk and Spud took the rag back to the sink, Reed glaring at him the whole way.

After Pip went back to his room, Reed motioned for Spud to join him on the porch. "I know you think you're helping things, but when I tell my son to do something, I do it for a reason." Reed smiled at Spud, but the smile seemed forced. "He's been spoiled by his mother ever since he was born, taught that life is all candy and marshmallows. I have to break him of that softness. I need to make Pip strong, and having him do for himself sometimes is part of the process. So I need you to back off a bit. You understand, right?"

Spud didn't understand. Pip was so small and scared. He had been plucked from his world and dropped into a shack in the middle of nowhere. A little kindness seemed warranted. So that night, as he had done every night since they arrived at the shack, Spud sat beside Pip's bed and told him a story—the cobbler and the elves. And just as he had done every night, Spud stayed in Pip's room, sleeping beside his bed, breaking the rule that Reed had laid down. But unlike the other nights, Spud didn't stay there the whole night. He crept out of Pip's room in the early morning hours, sneaking to his room and the cot before Reed returned to the shack.

Spud was still awake when Reed came home from his job at the bar, the man lumbering through the house like no one else lived there, slamming doors and kicking a chair in the kitchen. He heard Reed fling off his shoes and toss his clothes to the floor before plopping into the bed in Pip's room.

Spud imagined Pip lying quietly in bed, pretending to be asleep so that his father would take no notice of him. Pip would know that Spud was gone, and in that moment, Spud knew he had let Pip down — a thought that kept him awake much of that night.

CHAPTER 12

Max did not sleep well that night, not with Lyle Voight hounding his thoughts. No matter how hard Max tried to clear his head, Lyle kept at him, pushing and pushing. Max argued back, but their clash always ended with Lyle saying, "He's just a child, for God's sake."

Waking to that echo, Max again took his coffee out to the lake, this time sitting on a stump at the water's edge, the autumn chill crisp in his lungs. A duck squawked somewhere down the shore, and the water lapped gently against the rocks. It was a beautiful morning, but Max couldn't deny his anger. Lyle shouldn't have come to him. He shouldn't have heaved the weight of a missing woman and child onto Max's shoulders. Sandy was probably sitting in the sun in California, or Florida, the boy playing in the surf. She wouldn't be the first woman to feel penned in by a small town.

And what did Lyle offer as evidence? Nothing—other than his belief that he knew his daughter. Could anyone know another that well? Max thought of Jenni. Had he known her that well? He nodded to himself. Yeah, he had. If she had turned up missing, no one in the world would have convinced him that she had run off.

Max thought about the boy, his bashful smile, the touch of sadness in his eyes; he was the kind of child that you want to protect, so it made sense that Lyle would show up at Max's cabin. But what could Max do?

That thought dangled as Max showered, brushed his hair into a neat ponytail, and put on his only white shirt. As much as he wanted to sit this one out, he needed to at least talk with Sheriff Bolger. If nothing else, Max might be able to get Bolger's take, find a nugget of hope to take back to Lyle.

Max had never been to the Itasca County sheriff's office, and just stepping through the door brought on a sense of loss. There was a time when a sheriff's office — any sheriff's office — had the effect of calming Max's heart rate. He was at home among badges and uniforms. Radio chatter was the background music of his life. But now he saw the divide, a wall beyond which lay his old world, guarded by a receptionist sitting behind bulletproof glass.

"Can I help you?"

Max cleared his throat and then thought that it made him sound nervous — which maybe he was. He hadn't prepared himself for the conversation ahead, and after three and a half years in the woods, a tendril of self-doubt inched up his spine. "Is Sheriff Bolger in?"

"Do you have an appointment?"

"I don't," Max said, stroking his beard, a habit that started about the time it grew long enough to touch his chest. "If he has a moment, I'd like to talk to him about the disappearance of Sandy... um..." Lyle had never mentioned whether she went by his last name or that of her ex-husband. "I'd like to talk to him about Lyle Voight's daughter."

The receptionist narrowed her gaze. "Your name?"

"Max Rupert."

She pointed toward an empty meeting room adjacent to the reception area. "Have a seat in there and I'll have a deputy come talk to you."

"If you don't mind, ma'am, I'd like to talk to Sheriff Bolger."

That seemed to aggravate the receptionist, and she gave an audible huff.

"If that takes an appointment," Max said, "I'll make one, but I'd like to talk to the sheriff."

Maybe it was the hassle of setting up an appointment, or maybe he had impressed her by wearing his best white shirt, but the receptionist rolled her eyes, picked up the phone, and punched a button.

"Sheriff, do you have time to meet with a walk-in?"

She paused.

"Says his name is Max Rupert. Something about Sandy Voight." She looked at Max as she listened to Bolger's instructions. Then she nodded, hung up the phone, and said, "Go have a seat—he'll be with you in a minute."

Max walked into a small room about the size of a jail cell, four off-white walls surrounding a table with four chairs, a room designed for this exact purpose: meeting with people without bringing them into the guts of the operation.

Max didn't expect Sheriff Bolger to drop everything, but after nearly an hour—or what seemed like an hour because he no longer wore a watch—Max's mood had turned foul. As a cop, he had often let murder suspects stew in the tiny interrogation room back in Minneapolis. It unnerved them. Silence could loosen a rusty tongue, but it pissed Max off.

When Bolger finally showed up, he offered no apology. He struck Max as the aging high school star, a sizable gut diminishing his broad shoulders and solid arms. He shut the door and said, "What can I do for you, Mr. . . ."

"Rupert. Max Rupert."

Bolger gave no indication he'd heard of Max or cared. He took a seat at the small table and looked blankly at Max.

"I was hoping I could talk to you about the disappearance of Sandy Voight."

"Disappearance?"

"It's my understanding she turned up missing about four days back. Or do I have that wrong?"

"Let me guess," Bolger said with a grin. "You're a psychic and you know where she is?"

"I'm a friend of the family. I'm just trying to help."

"There's nothing to help with here. There was no disappearance. Sandy Voight took her boy and ran off. That's it. The case is closed."

"How can you be so certain?"

"I'm not gonna talk about a case with some rando off the street. It's confidential."

"So it's an *active* investigation."

Something stirred in Max, a sense of potency that had gone dormant. Like watering a starving plant, turning the questions on Bolger had invigorated Max. It felt good.

"There's nothing active about it," Bolger said.

"If it's not an active investigation—if it's closed—then it's not confidential."

"Now you're gonna tell me my business?"

Max felt like a runner hitting his stride. "Someone probably should."

The narrowing around Bolger's eyes was unmistakable—umbrage— but before he could feed off that anger, Max continued:

"If it's not an active investigation, then it's not confidential. Minnesota Statute Thirteen Eighty-Two."

Bolger shifted in his chair, turning from irritated to curious. "What did you say your name was?"

"Max Rupert."

Bolger stood, said, "Excuse me," and left the room.

Max pushed his chair away from the table, leaned back, and crossed one leg over the other to wait. He knew that Bolger would be looking up whatever he could find on Max Rupert. He also knew that when Bolger returned to the room, there would be a shift. It would no longer be a sheriff deigning to listen to the whims of a hermit; it would be one trained investigator talking to another.

Ten minutes later, Bolger came back carrying a couple sheets of paper. Max could see that one had his picture, an article that ran when he was awarded a citation for saving a young woman's life. As Bolger took his seat, he looked back and forth between the picture and Max.

"It's me," Max said.

"You're a detective? Why didn't you say so?"

Max started to clarify that he was a former detective, but thought better of it. "What makes you sure that Sandy Voight wasn't kidnapped?"

Bolger shifted back to his angry face. "Did Lyle send you here?"

"It's natural that he'd want answers."

"I gave him answers. The problem is he won't accept the truth."

"Maybe I can help with that," Max said, shifting tack. Interrogation 101—make them believe you are on their side. "If he hears it coming from me, he might take it better. My understanding is that you and Lyle have a rough history."

Bolger tapped a finger on the table as he considered Max's pitch. Max hadn't yet sealed the deal, so he added, "The man's hurting. What have you got to lose, Sheriff?"

Bolger tipped his chair back, opened the door, and hollered out, "Joanna, get my laptop and bring it here along with the Sandy Voight file."

He closed the door and leaned in to put his elbows and forearms on the table, his hands clasped together. "David Haas and Sandy Voight lived together down off Sixty-Three in the woods there. David works the two-to-ten shift at the taconite plant in Hibbing. Comes home from work to find that Sandy moved out. Took her clothes, the kid's clothes, everything. You don't have to be Sherlock Holmes to know you don't clean out your closet if you're getting kidnapped."

The receptionist entered with a laptop and a file, laying both on the table in front of Bolger.

"And here's the kicker." Bolger talked as he loaded a CD from the file into the tray of the computer. "She drove to the bank that morning and cleaned out their savings. Thirty grand. We have footage. Shows her walking in calm as can be. Goes up to the teller..." He cued up the video and turned the computer to Max. It showed a split screen. On the left, a light-colored SUV pulled into the bank's parking lot. On the right, Max recognized Sandy as she entered the lobby.

"She's a woman on a mission," Bolger said. "A woman about to leave Grand Rapids in the rearview."

Max went back and forth between the interior view of the bank and the empty car in the parking lot. "Did you talk to the teller?"

"Yeah, and she didn't notice anything unusual."

"What about Sandy's friends? Have they seen a change in her recently?"

"Not sure she has any, at least not close friends. We talked to her coworkers at the veterinary clinic. They didn't know all that much about her personal life. They said she was an introvert. She has a neighbor who watches her kid after school—a woman named Linda. All she could give us was that Sandy seemed protective of her boy, Pip. Didn't let her boyfriend do any of the picking up or dropping off."

"When did the babysitter last talk to Sandy?"

"The day before, when Sandy came to pick up the boy. She didn't recall any conversation beyond hi and goodbye. Like I said, Sandy was a quiet type."

Max watched as Sandy took the money and left the bank, her stride a little faster than what he thought normal, but nothing obvious. She got in her SUV and left the parking lot.

"She has an ex-husband," Max said.

"Reed Harris. Did Lyle tell you that he used to be a deputy here?"

"We didn't get that far."

"There's a lot of bad blood between Lyle and Reed."

"What about between Reed and Sandy?"

Bolger shifted and shrugged. "The divorce was...Let's call it acrimonious."

"How acrimonious?"

"There was an assault. Reed lost custody because of it. He also lost his job and spent some time in jail."

"Sheriff Bolger, that's a far sight more than acrimonious."

"But Reed Harris was at the White Oak Casino. Went there after tending bar at the Dizzy Duck. We have footage of him there all night. Didn't leave until eleven in the morning. David Haas was home from work by then, so we know Reed had nothing to do with it."

"You talked to Mr. Harris?"

"Yes. Even searched his house."

"You..." Max hadn't expected that. "You had probable cause to search his house?"

"Consent search. Did it myself."

"Just you?"

Bolger crossed his arms and leaned back in his chair. "Yeah. Just me. And I didn't find a thing to suggest that his wife or boy had been there—ever."

"What was his demeanor?"

Bolger shook his head as his umbrage reared once again. "He was upset, but cooperative. He acted like a man who had nothing to do with his wife skipping town."

"Ex-wife."

"Whatever."

"I assume you took a look at Sandy's phone records?"

"I did. Haas called her a bunch of times, but that's it. We tracked her through the cell towers down to Minneapolis. She stopped at a convenience store on the north end of the city to gas up. Used her credit card there. After that, she must have gotten tired of Haas calling, because she turned off her phone. That's where her trail ends."

"Did you get surveillance footage from the store?"

"They didn't have any."

"Did you look for footage from any of the surrounding businesses?"

"What for? We know what happened."

"Do you?"

"Yes, we do." Bolger's voice turned stiff. "I know Lyle doesn't want to believe it, but his daughter ran off. She got tired of Haas and Grand Rapids, so she left. I don't need video of it to know what's what. If my ol' lady comes home carrying bags of groceries and a receipt from the grocery store, I don't need a goddamned video to know she went shopping."

"This is a missing-person case," Max said, keeping his tone even. "We're not talking about a trip to the grocery store. You have two people gone and—"

"Jesus, you're just like Lyle."

Max couldn't help but let his voice tick up a notch. "Did you check Haas's time card? Did you talk to his fellow employees? What about calls made by other phones near her home? Did you check the cell towers for other traffic?"

"I sat down with you out of common courtesy, Detective. I'm not going to entertain Lyle Voight's fantasy no matter who he sends in here to spin it. His daughter ran off. That's the end of it. Now, I've wasted more time than I care to on this crap. If you want to be a sidekick to Don Quixote out there, be my guest. We're done here."

Bolger stood, gathered up his laptop and file, and walked out without another word.

Max remained seated for another minute before walking across the hall to the receptionist. She was an older woman, and Max thought it likely she was a holdover from Lyle's time. If that were the case, she might have a soft spot for the request Max was about to make.

"Hi...Joanna, right?"

She looked up but didn't answer.

Max did his best to come across as meek. "I don't know if you overheard the yelling..." He gave her an impish smile. "But Lyle has asked me to...well, kind of look into this mess regarding his daughter."

Joanna looked after Bolger, probably making sure he wasn't watching her.

"Problem is," Max continued, "Lyle told me he moved up to Ely—so that Sandy could live at his place here—but he didn't give me his address. Any chance you might...help me out?"

Again, Joanna looked in the direction of where Bolger had gone. Then she wrote an address on a piece of paper and handed it to Max.

"You didn't get this from me," she said.

CHAPTER 13

L yle had moved to a faded brown mobile home in a park on the northern edge of Ely, a rusted air conditioner sticking out of one of the windows, wooden pallets leaning against the foundation to keep out the bears. The front stoop and stairs were metal grate and in need of a new coat of paint. Max didn't know why he expected something different; a sheriff's salary—and now an ex-sheriff's pension—never made sense to Max, given the risks of the job. But men like Lyle Voight didn't do it for the money.

The stairs squeaked enough that a knock on the door was unnecessary, but Max knocked anyway. A curtain in a nearby window moved to the side and then a lock unclicked.

"Max?" Lyle looked stumped.

"I was in the neighborhood."

Lyle smiled at that. He opened the door and waved Max in.

The inside of the mobile home was outdated but pleasant: paneled walls, yellow kitchen cabinets, faux wooden floors, all of it kept tidy. The living room had a cloth couch and two leather chairs facing a flatscreen television mounted on the wall. Lyle patted the back of one for Max, and the two men sat.

Lyle scratched the stubble on his neck as he gave Max an appraising look. "I'm kind of surprised to see you."

"I'm kind of surprised to be here," Max said. "Truth is, I felt bad about how we left things yesterday. It wasn't right of me to shut you down like that."

"You don't owe me anything."

Max wanted to agree with Lyle, but the thought got all balled up in his chest. He owed a debt to someone, didn't he? Wasn't that why he still had nightmares? "I'm not sure why I'm here, or what I can do, but...a couple questions have been gnawing at me, and I was hoping you could help me out."

"Sure."

A woman came into the room from the hallway. She had dark hair, and dark eyes, and high cheekbones like Sandy's, suggesting she might have some Ojibwe blood in her veins. She wore blue jeans, a sweater, and a look that could have been either curiosity or dread.

"You haven't met my wife, Meredith, have you?" Lyle said. He gestured toward Max. "This is Max Rupert, the guy I told you about."

Max half stood and nodded toward Meredith. "Ma'am."

"Nice to meet you, Mr. Rupert."

As she neared, Max could see that she had been crying, or maybe her eyes were red and puffy from the lack of sleep. Either way, she moved past him as though his presence mattered little in her world. She went to the kitchen and Max returned to his conversation with Lyle.

"What can you tell me about David Haas?"

"Haas? He's a good guy. Why? You don't think Haas had something to do with it?"

"I'm not saying one way or the other. It's just...something's been bothering me about the situation. I stopped by the sheriff's office this morning and had a chat with Bolger."

Lyle looked like he'd just bitten into a rotten apple. "Did he talk to you?"

"A little. He buys that Haas has an alibi, but admits he's got no time card or witness statements. It leaves open a window of opportunity."

"What else did he say?"

"He said the case is closed. He's convinced that Sandy ran off — and that's all there is to it."

"The person we need to look at is that son of a bitch Reed Harris. If anyone —"

"Reed has an alibi."

"The casino. I know. Did I tell you that Reed used to be my deputy?"

"Bolger mentioned it."

"That's how he met Sandy. I'll regret that to my dying day. I tried to talk her out of marrying him, but you can't make someone see what they don't want to see." Lyle went on like a steel spring uncoiling. "The man got violent when he drank. You can't hide something like that from a cop. I saw the bruises — heard the excuses. I wanted to fire him, but Sandy talked me out of it."

A sniffle came from the kitchen. Max looked over his shoulder to see Meredith leaning over the sink, her hair covering her face as she scrubbed a dish.

Lyle continued in a quieter voice. "It's been hard on her."

"I can only imagine," Max whispered.

"We thought Sandy would be safe once she divorced Reed."

"How did that come about?"

Lyle straightened up. "Reed came home one night — drunk — and he and Sandy got into an argument. Somehow, Pip got in the middle of it, and Reed hit Pip hard enough to send him flying. My daughter's always been a timid thing, but when that happened, she lit into Reed like a scalded cat. He hit her and broke her eye socket. She called me but he was gone by the time I got there. Honestly, Max, if he'd have been there when I saw Sandy — her face swollen like that — I'd have shot the bastard. I swear I would have."

Lyle looked at Max as though expecting judgment, but Max had none to give.

"He went on the run, lived up in the Boundary Waters for that summer. Finally caught him when winter set in; he started breaking into cabins for food. He did a year in county for the assault and the burglaries. Lost his Post Board license and Sandy got full custody. He didn't even get visitation rights."

"How long ago was that?"

"Three years or so."

"Does he have any close friends—someone who might be willing to throw in with him to do something to Sandy?"

"Not that I know of, except...well, Tate Bolger."

"Sheriff Bolger?"

"He and Reed go way back. There was something that happened when they were younger." Lyle rubbed his forehead as if trying to loosen up a memory. "They were seniors in high school. A waitress died... They found her body floating in the Tioga Mine Pit. She was married, but there were rumors that she and Tate stepped out now and again. Reed was Tate's alibi. Said they were hunting."

"And you hired them both as deputies?"

Lyle's head sank. "It can be hard to get deputies up here—at least ones who want to stay in the North Country. So many of 'em just want a couple years under their belts before they head south to the Twin Cities. I hired Tate first. He wasn't bad as deputies go—showed up on time, took overnights without complaining. I gave him the benefit of the doubt. Maybe that was a mistake."

"And Reed?"

"Bolger talked me into hiring Reed. I was against it from the get-go. Reed was a hothead, and that was the last thing I wanted on my team— but Bolger vouched for him. Looking back, I wonder if Bolger wasn't repaying some debt."

"You think that Bolger might still be repaying that debt?"

"I don't know. So my question is, what do you think?"

"I think Occam's razor fits here: The simplest answer is usually the correct one."

"So, you think she ran away?" Lyle said.

"But..." Max paused as he pieced together his thought. "When I was at the sheriff's office today, there was this one small detail that... well, it stuck in my craw."

"What was that?"

"Did you get a look at that video from the bank?"

Lyle nodded. "Bolger showed me. He made a point of how calm Sandy was."

"What about the car in the parking lot?"

"Well...I saw her get out of it, but..." Lyle studied Max's face, as if looking for clues as to where this was leading. "What did you see?"

"It's not what I saw; it's what I didn't see. The car was empty."

Lyle didn't make the connection at first, but then his eyes widened. "Pip."

"Exactly. Where was Pip?"

"Sandy would never leave him home alone."

"That doesn't seem likely. And his regular babysitter said she didn't see him that day."

"So where was he?" Lyle pondered.

"All I'm saying is that something's out of place here. Pip might have been home alone or maybe Sandy left him with someone else. It's also possible that...Now, don't get upset, but it's possible that Sandy had another boyfriend waiting with Pip at the house."

Lyle opened his mouth as if to object, but closed it again. "I suppose I should be hoping that Bolger's right about all this, because if he's not..."

Max didn't say it out loud, but he finished the thought in his head. If Sandy hadn't run off, then foul play was involved.

In the kitchen a plate crashed to the floor, splintering into shards. Max turned to see Meredith bent over the sink, her knuckles white as she gripped the edge of the countertop. Her knees seemed to weaken and she slid partway to the floor before catching herself. She looked at

Max and then at Lyle with a venomous glare, her breath coming and going in jagged twitches. Then she walked out the front door without saying a word.

Lyle closed his eyes and shook his head slowly. "We probably shouldn't have had this conversation here."

"Bolger's theory has the strongest legs." Max tried to sound convincing, but his words betrayed his true feelings. "Let's focus our energy on finding Sandy."

"Where do we start?"

"I know you don't want to hear this, but we should start by figuring out if there was another man in her life. You could put together a list of Sandy's friends—anyone she might have shared that kind of a secret with. We won't make any assumptions one way or the other. Agreed?"

Lyle gave a nod.

"Also, a trip up to the taconite plant would be a good idea. Ask around about David Haas, see if anyone saw him that morning. I want to lock his alibi down."

"I can do that."

"At some point we'll need to have a chat with Mr. Haas. See what he has to say about his relationship with Sandy."

"And what will you be doing?"

"They tracked Sandy's cell phone to a convenience store on the north end of Minneapolis. I'm gonna drive down there . . . shake a tree or two to see if anything falls out."

"This feels good," Lyle said, looking energized for the first time. "At least I'm doing something instead of sitting on my thumbs. The last few days have been pretty damned dark."

They parted with a handshake, Max promising to touch base once he got back from Minneapolis. Leaving the mobile home, he was about to get into his Jeep Cherokee when a woman's voice called out to him.

"Mr. Rupert?"

It was Meredith, standing behind a small shed at the edge of the lot. She held the collar of her sweater up tight around her throat, as if trying to keep warm as she'd waited for him.

"Mrs. Voight."

"Do you have children?"

Immediately, Max thought of the bracelet and his dream. Even though he hadn't known about Jenni's pregnancy, he wanted to believe that he had been a father. But he had no desire to explain that here, so he answered, "No."

"My daughter's name is Sandy, and my grandson's name is Pip. They're flesh and blood and they're alive."

"I never said—"

"Did Lyle tell you that Sandy had cancer when she was a child? Wilms tumor. She spent seven hours in surgery the day before her first birthday. If you want to know what kind of bargains a person is willing to make with God, just go through that. And Pip is scared of spiders and bridges. He holds his breath every time we drive over one. He calls me Nana, and Lyle is his Poppy. They're not just names on a piece of paper; they're my family. They're what keep me alive."

She took a step closer, and in the sunlight, Max could see the wrinkles around her eyes and the light streaks of gray in her hair, the desperation in the taut lines around her jaw. "Do you think my daughter's alive?"

"I hope so."

"Don't patronize me, Mr. Rupert. Do you think she's alive?"

"I honestly don't know. But if she is, I'll do my damnedest to find her."

"I know she is. She's out there, Mr. Rupert. Maybe she's hurt or maybe she just needs time to come to her senses, but she's out there."

Max let his eyes drop. "You're probably right, ma'am."

Meredith reached out and touched Max's arm as if she could make Max understand. "Promise me something."

"If I can."

"Bring my family back to me. I won't survive without them. Promise you'll find my family and bring them home."

A nod was the best Max could offer. Then he said, "I'll do everything I can."

CHAPTER 14

Pip was a quiet child, not only in his refusal to speak, but in his movement around the shack. On that first morning after Reed moved into Pip's room, Pip had awakened and crept into the living room without making a sound. Spud had been in the kitchen sweeping up the pine needles that Reed had tracked in the night before. Catching movement out of the corner of his eye, Spud turned to find Pip sitting on the couch, watching him.

Spud smiled and summoned Pip to the kitchen with a twitch of a finger. "Pancakes?"

Pip smiled back and nodded.

They had eaten pancakes every morning since arriving at the shack. Spud remembered making them with his father, and it was the one meal he could whip up with confidence.

The door to the room where Reed slept was closed, and somehow both Spud and Pip knew to stay quiet. A sleeping Reed — like a bear in his den — was best left alone. Spud mixed the batter in a plastic bowl, whispering as he asked Pip, "Did you sleep all right?"

Pip looked away and didn't respond. How could he have, with all the noise Reed made when he came home from the bar? Spud handed the bowl and wooden spoon to Pip to let him stir, something that the boy seemed to enjoy.

They ate the pancakes with syrup and a glass of milk, and Spud asked

Pip to tell him about something he liked. Spud learned that Pip liked dinosaurs and some cartoon about a monkey with a tool belt. They kept their conversation low so as not to wake the sleeping bear, but when breakfast was done and Pip scooted his chair back, one of the legs caught on a tear in the linoleum. The chair flipped backwards, falling to the floor with a bang.

Reed shouted through the closed door. "Goddammit! I'm trying to sleep."

The color drained from Pip's face.

"My fault," Spud called back. "Knocked a chair over."

The door opened and Reed leaned against the jamb in a pair of blue boxers, his face creased, his eyes hard and cold. "I need sleep. I don't have the luxury of going to bed whenever I want."

"It was an accident," Spud said.

Reed looked at Spud, then at Pip and the chair lying on the floor and said, "Be more careful." He went back inside the bedroom and closed the door.

Spud put a hand on Pip's shoulder and gave him a pat. "It's okay," he whispered. "He's just tired."

Why was Reed being such an asshole? Where was the man who loved his son so much that he'd do anything to save him from an abusive mother? Uneasiness crept up Spud's back and into his chest. How had he gotten so knotted up in this? He had pledged himself to a plan that would give Reed his son back, and in exchange set Spud up with wealth for life. Had he so been blinded by that promise that he hadn't seen the truth about his partner? And now he had to spend weeks, maybe months, in this shack before he would be free of his pledge.

But if Spud was being honest, he would admit that it wasn't his pledge that kept him there. It was the boy. Pip needed Spud in a way that made Spud's heart ache.

Spud went to Reed's bedroom and opened the closet door slowly, the hinges squeaking to announce his presence.

"What are you doing?" Reed grumbled from his bed.

"I'm getting clothes for Pip. I'm gonna take him outside so we don't bother you."

"You bother me by coming in here...so that you won't bother me? You see the flaw in your thinking, right?"

"Maybe you should sleep in the other room and I'll set up in here. That way me and Pip can get up in the morning without waking you."

It was an idea that came to Spud without much forethought, and after he said the words, he expected Reed to get mad, but Reed never even opened his eyes. Instead, he pulled the covers up around his shoulders. "Yeah, we should do that."

Spud was so stunned by Reed's swift capitulation that he almost forgot to grab Pip's clothing. He would be able to stay with Pip all night. He could honor his promise.

Spud dressed Pip in his warmest clothes, with a coat, hat, and gloves, and then the two of them slipped quietly out the front door.

The shack faced an open space just big enough for a vehicle to turn around; beyond that was a marsh. A fallen cottonwood lay at the edge and Spud used it as a bench. They sat and watched a muskrat swim across the water.

Spud thought about telling Pip another fairy tale but decided to make up a story instead. He told Pip about a Sioux woman who left her son at the base of a large pine tree. She loved her son, but soldiers were searching for her tribe, and so she hid her boy to protect him.

After many days, when the mother didn't return, the boy went searching for her. He walked from when the sun came up until it was about to go down and came upon a pack of wolves. The leader of that pack, a large wolf named Red, wanted to eat the boy, but another, a wolf named Sparky, saw that the boy was a good child. He took the boy in as his brother, teaching him to run and to hunt, and the boy lived forever in the woods with Sparky.

When he had finished, he saw that Pip was crying. "What's wrong, buddy?"

"Where's my mommy?"

Spud swallowed hard. It had been a mistake to tell Pip that story. He put his arm around Pip and told the lie that Reed had prepared.

"Your mom...she wanted to marry David." God damn that Reed. It should have been him out there breaking that little boy's heart. "Your mom and David...they want to start a new life."

Pip started to breathe heavily. Spud held him tighter.

"I'm sorry, little buddy, but they wanted to start a new family. They... want your dad to take you from now on."

Pip had been crying in silence, but now burst into a wail. Spud picked him up and held him. "It's gonna be okay. Shhh." He stroked Pip's hair. "I'll be here with you. I promise. I'll take care of you."

Spud thought back to when he was Pip's age. Had his father swooped in to take him away from his mother, he would have cried for joy. A memory came to him... coloring in a book, his father at his side. Spud had come home from kindergarten, crying because another child made fun of his poor coloring skills, jutting lines that slashed across the pictures. He had interrupted his mother, who was on the phone, to show her.

"Jesus, that looks like it was done by a monkey." His mother laughed. She returned to her phone call, telling the person on the other end about the atrocious piece of art. Spud went to his room to sit with the abomination, tears filling his eyes. Why couldn't he do what the other kids could do?

When Spike came home and found Spud curled up on his bed, he went to work teaching his son how to color. They sat on the floor with a coloring book and Spike drew tiny circles inside the lines. "Just take your time," his father had said. "When you touch the line move the circle to another spot and fill that in. Use your fingers instead of your hand to move the color." Spud did what his father told him, and it worked.

Pip seemed to be tiring, the sound of his cry folding in half, then in half again until it was barely more than a whimper. Reed had said that Pip's mother was cold and neglectful. She beat the boy. Pip needed to be rescued. He and Reed were the good guys.

But what if Reed had lied?

He shook away that thought. Reed's stories were true, they had to be. Spud had not killed a good person. He had freed Pip from a cruel life. He had to believe that—otherwise, he was the evil one. He was the monster.

Spud hugged Pip tighter and tucked his doubt away, making a mental note. He would press Reed to buy crayons and a coloring book. He could teach Pip to color the way Spike had taught him.

CHAPTER 15

Since moving his few possessions into the cabin three plus years ago, Max hadn't once traveled beyond Grand Rapids. But from Ely he was now on his way to Minneapolis, driving roads he'd never wanted to see again. How had he let his plans get so interrupted?

Something about going back to the city felt like he was crossing a threshold, stepping through time into a past life. There had been a time that nothing seemed more important than his dream to be a homicide detective. He had dated, and played sports, and did the kind of things that young men did, but his eyes never left the prize. He would become a detective and serve in Minneapolis.

Then he met Jenni.

In college, Max worked for Campus Security, mostly escorting women home from the library after a late night of studying. One young lady had a particular knack for requesting an escort only when Max was on duty. She was pretty and flirty, going so far as to invite him up into her dorm room, a breach that would have gotten Max fired. Max always politely declined.

It was on the fourth or fifth trip that Max met the woman's roommate, Jenni. The encounter had been brief, a shared glance and a nod of the head, but that had been enough. He couldn't get Jenni out of his mind—her smile, the way her eyes caught the light.

The world changed on a Thursday night when Max was working

security at an event and he saw Jenni again. She was with a group of girls waiting to enter, and when she saw him, Jenni waved.

"You're Officer Romeo," she said.

"Officer Romeo?"

"That's what my roommate calls you."

That made Max smile. "It's Max . . . Rupert." He extended a hand, but instead of shaking it Jenni held it — and that was it. Max knew in that moment that he wanted to hold Jenni's hand for as long as she would let him. How many hours had he spent reliving their time together? Now here he was, on a four-lane interstate, heading to Minneapolis, despite his promise to her that he would have nothing more to do with that world.

After three years of driving the curvy back roads of the Northwoods, Max thought the other cars seemed to be going unusually fast. He locked in his cruise control, a maneuver that took him a couple rusty tries, and stewed anew on his predicament.

Why *was* he making this trip? Because Lyle refused to believe that his daughter could do what countless other women had done — run away? Why was that so hard to believe? People disappoint you and abandon you. No one thinks it can happen to them, but it does. *Just ask Niki Vang,* Max thought darkly.

As he neared Minneapolis, Max began to regret making the trip. He hadn't expected the memories to be so strong. He would keep the visit short. He would find proof that Sandy had run off and help Lyle come to terms with that truth. Once he had done that, Max would crawl back to his little corner of the woods.

Max arrived at the convenience store where Sandy's trail had ended, looking for surveillance along the drive. Security cameras had become ubiquitous in the past couple decades, and hiding from them usually took effort. But on the short drive from the off-ramp, he passed no banks or ATMs. There were no stoplight cameras along the route, and with the exception of one bar, he saw no businesses that might have an exterior surveillance camera. There were other paths she could have taken, but this was the most direct one.

He filled up at the pump. If someone didn't want to be seen or remembered, they need only pay with a credit card. Before going in to pay, he walked around the outside of the building just to make certain that it held no cameras. It did not.

Inside, a thin man with jaundiced skin manned the cash register behind a glass partition. Max walked the aisles in search of a camera and found none. He handed the guy behind the register cash for his gas along with a picture of Sandy and one of her 2002 Honda Passport.

"Have you ever seen this woman?"

"If I had, I sure as hell wouldn't tell you."

"She's missing. I'm trying to find her."

"I'm sure you are." The man handed Max his change. "Get the fuck out of here."

"She might be in trouble."

"Listen, asshole, my sister was stalked by a nut job like you. If you don't leave right now, I'm calling the cops."

Max looked at his reflection in the partition, his beard and hair grown wild. When he didn't move right away, the man repeated his demand. "I said git!"

Max walked out of the store and to his car, looking around a little more carefully at the nearby buildings. Not a camera to be seen.

He drove back in the direction of the highway, pulling over every third block to get out and look around. This had to be the one street in the entire city with no cameras anywhere. His last stop was outside of a bar he'd passed on the way in. Bars were a special case. They often had cameras, but didn't want that fact advertised. While camera footage might capture a vandal or someone trying to break in after hours, it might just as easily show someone getting served underage or a bouncer crossing a line.

Max parked beside the bar—the Rook—and was about to go in

when he saw it. The building had red awnings that loomed over the sidewalk, and in one corner, a galvanized pipe arched out with a flood light on the end. Attached to the pipe, tucked inside the awning, was a small camera aimed at the front door. If it was set to capture a wide-angle view, it would pick up the intersection, too.

Max walked in and asked for the manager. The bartender yelled, "Janelle, someone to see you!"

A minute later a woman came out, forty-something, with the voice and skin of a lifelong smoker.

"I'm trying to find a missing person," Max said. "She was in this neighborhood on November sixth." Max pointed at the window and the camera beyond. "I was hoping I might take a look at the footage from your camera."

The woman both coughed and laughed. "Like hell."

"I know this is an unusual request —"

"I ain't showing you dick — not unless you have a badge. You don't have a badge hiding under that mop, do ya?"

"This woman may be in trouble."

"Buy a beer or get the fuck out." She turned away, dismissing him.

He knew someone with a badge — many, really, but one in particular he'd once trusted with his life. He shook the thought away. It would be cruel to ask her for a favor after the way he had treated her. Could he be a bigger asshole?

He should go home, tell Lyle that he'd found nothing. That was the truth, wasn't it? For all Max knew, the surveillance camera didn't even work, and if it did, what were the chances it had caught anything useful?

He got in his car, sat behind the wheel, and stared at the brick wall of the bar. He thought of meeting Sandy and Pip, that morning at the grocery store. Lyle was right. They had been preparing for Halloween, not an escape. Pip was going to be a pirate. He had smiled at Max. Now he was out there somewhere — missing.

Max knew that he had not done all that he could. Maybe he could call up one of the other detectives he'd worked with? Surely he had been liked well enough that he could ask such a small favor now? But if Niki ever found out, he might as well just walk up to her in the Homicide unit and slap her across the face. She was the last person he should ask a favor of, but he could think of no alternative.

If she still worked the day shift, she would be off duty already. He could drop by her house, assuming she still lived at that address, but an ambush like that seemed all wrong. He decided to bed down at a cheap motel—consider what he was about to do. Had he exhausted every alternative? He needed to be sure before he ripped the bandage off that wound.

CHAPTER 16

Reed Harris hated bartending. He hated smiling and pretending and sucking up to assholes for tips. But right now, he had to walk a fine line. He needed the world to see that he was a man grieving for the loss of his son, but at the same time, a man who hadn't been allowed to see his boy for going on three years. He packaged his faux grief as disappointment: disappointment that he'd lost the possibility of a future with his son, disappointment that Sandy had been so selfish, and disappointment that he had stuck around Grand Rapids in the forlorn hope of once again seeing his boy. With that last one, he had started laying the groundwork for his own eventual departure.

Reed turned out to be a pretty convincing actor. People went out of their way to comfort him in those first few days, patting him on the back or putting an extra buck in his tip jar. He wallowed in false sadness as he let folks know that he wasn't all that surprised that Sandy hit the road—that she'd often complained about living in Grand Rapids. He kept it subtle, letting people read what they wanted to into his words.

Of course, none of it compared to that performance he gave when Tate Bolger had shown up at his house to interview him.

"When's the last time you saw Sandy?" Bolger had asked at his door.

"Are you talking, like, seeing her around town?"

"Anything."

Reed pretended to think. "I saw her...had to be about a month ago. I was walking out of Target and she was walking in with that guy she's been living with."

"Did you talk to her?"

"No, why?"

"Do you remember the date?"

Reed paused for effect. "It was a Sunday. I remember because the Vikings were playing the Packers that day. I went to Target to pick up some chips for the game, around ten in the morning. Target might still have it on tape if you want to check."

"And you haven't seen her since?"

"No, why? Is something wrong?"

The look on Bolger's face when he broke the news told Reed all he needed to know. Bolger had shrugged his shoulders and used the word *gone* as opposed to missing. Bolger had bought Reed's narrative. And why wouldn't he?

Still, Reed's reaction to the news was crucial. He had to look confused—stunned. He had practiced his reaction in the mirror. Reed paused as though processing what Bolger had said, then replied, "What?"

Bolger repeated his news, again using the word *gone*.

"What do you mean, 'gone'?"

Bolger didn't have to give Reed details. In fact, if Bolger thought that there might be foul play, he surely wouldn't have laid the evidence out the way he had. Bolger told Reed about the empty bank account and the clothes.

That's when Reed interrupted him. "What about...my son?"

When Bolger told Reed that Pip was also gone, Reed sought out a chair to sit on.

The interview lasted a half hour and included a cursory search of the house. Reed, for his part, asked a lot of questions, most of which Tate answered even though he probably shouldn't have. They had been friends since high school. They had been deputies together. They had history, and at the end of the interview, Bolger put his hand on Reed's shoulder and said, "Wherever Sandy ran off to, keep in mind that she's a good mother. She'll take care of Pip."

"You're gonna keep looking, though, aren't you?" Reed said. "You gotta find Pip."

It was the exact opposite of what Reed wanted Tate to do, but he had to play the part.

"She'll turn up. Her folks live up in Ely. I expect she'll be in touch with Lyle inside of a month. When that happens, I'll let you know."

"I appreciate that, Tate."

That should have been the end of it, but Reed knew that Lyle would be sticking his nose in. Reed had to always think ahead—a burden his partner needn't care about.

Now, as he poured a pint for one of his regulars, it grated on Reed's nerves that Spud held no appreciation for the heavy lifting that Reed had to do. Spud didn't have to calculate the moves of Bolger or Lyle. Spud didn't have to pour drinks till two in the fucking morning. Spud didn't have to put on performances to deflect suspicion. He could make all the damned noise he wanted to, waking Reed up at the butt-crack of dawn. He could sit at the cabin and play with Pip all day. What did it matter to him? Didn't he realize that Reed needed his sleep? Their lives depended on Reed being sharp.

And the whispers—the fucking whispers—they would sneak around, whispering and giggling. Reed was sure that he had heard his name mentioned in hushed tones on more than one occasion. They shut up when he walked in the room, but as soon as he turned his back again, he heard the *stss, stss, stss*. And if they weren't whispering, they were off in the woods. Pip had seemed cold, distant, when they came back that morning. He'd barely looked at Reed. What was Spud telling the boy? What kind of lies was he putting in Pip's head? It's like Sandy all over again.

But now was not the time to deal with Spud. Spud was an idiot, but he was a useful idiot and Reed needed him—for now. While Reed kept up appearances in town, Spud needed to keep the boy hidden. In a few weeks the heat would be off and Reed could leave Grand Rapids without raising any eyebrows. That's when he would deal with Spud.

CHAPTER 17

Max knew a lot about Niki Vang, having been her partner in Homicide for three years. Her parents had escaped from Vietnam before Niki was born, crossing over the mountains into Thailand and landing in a refugee camp. That's where Niki was born. She came to America as an infant and grew up with one foot in each culture.

Max knew that Niki loved music but couldn't sing. He knew that she preferred burgers and fries to Asian food, a secret that she kept from her proud Hmong mother. And he knew where she parked when she came to work. So that morning, Max sat on a short wall alongside the path he knew she would take to City Hall, hoping that his old partner might be in a forgiving mood.

When she arrived, he noticed she had trimmed her hair, wearing it just off her shoulders, her bangs grown out and swept to the side of her face. She was attractive, but Max knew that nothing pissed Niki off more than being judged by her appearance. The new cut gave her an air of maturity, but she still looked younger than her thirty-eight years.

Coffee in hand, she walked like a woman on a mission, which was by design. At the office she was all work and no play. But when the two of them were alone, she unleashed a wit that could get them both rolling with laughter. Other detectives, those who didn't know her as well, thought her arrogant. She once confided in Max that she didn't smile because men dismissed women who smiled, and she never wanted to be dismissed.

As she approached, Max found himself wishing that he'd taken the time to buy some clean clothes. He hadn't planned to be in Minneapolis overnight. His shirt and frayed blue jeans had passed the smell test that morning, but now he had doubts. The rubber band he had used to tie his hair back had broken, so his hair fell loose and scraggly on his shoulders. He wore a thick canvas coat, stained with dirt and chain saw oil from cutting firewood. Had he held an empty cup to the people passing by, he probably would have made a couple bucks.

He also found himself wishing he had come up with something better to say. He had tossed and turned on the motel's lumpy mattress, trying to figure out a way to say hello. In the end he decided that he would offer no excuse for his past behavior, no defense. He would take what he had coming, even if it meant a cup of coffee to the face.

As he stood, a wave of cowardice almost caused him to turn away. But when she was close enough, he said, "Hello, Niki."

She stopped abruptly and looked at him, a question behind her eyes. She moved her coffee cup to her left hand, her right undoing the button of her coat to free up the Glock attached to her right hip. She narrowed her gaze to study his face, as if she couldn't place it.

To help her solve the puzzle, he spoke again. "Long time no see." It was a stupid thing to say, but it was the only thing that came to him in that moment.

With that, her eyes turned sharp and hard. "Max?" Her fingers tightened around the cardboard coffee cup and Max readied himself. She half yelled through gritted teeth: "What the hell? Max? You... son of a bitch."

Max had nothing to say to that.

"You drop off the face of the earth. You completely disappear, no warning. And now..." Her lip lifted in a snarl. "You've got balls showing up here."

"I deserve that—"

She stepped close enough to hit him. He braced himself. "You send me your gun and badge...It's been three years...and now this? I was your partner...and I thought I was your friend."

"I'm sorry." Max wanted her to hit him now. Get it out there.

"Why did you..." She took a step back and held up her hand as if to stop him from answering. "You know what, I don't want to know."

"I am...sorry."

"Stop saying that." She was angry. "Why are you here? Why today? Why?"

Max wished he hadn't come. But he was there, and to leave without explaining his visit would have been even more selfish. And he couldn't shake Pip's shy smile. "I'm looking for someone. I need...a favor."

It was the exact wrong thing to say. Niki waved a finger, cutting the air between them. "No. You don't get to...No." Then she turned and walked into City Hall without another word, her heels clapping hard on the concrete.

Max leaned against the wall to let a wave of nausea pass. In some ways, it had gone better than he'd expected. She hadn't done him any physical harm. But on the other side of the ledger, the shame he felt hit harder than any punch.

The last time they had seen each other, he had been narrowing in on Mikhail and she'd had his back. He had convinced himself it was because they were partners. But deep inside, he knew it had been more than that. She had put herself on the line for him, risked her career, her reputation. Max knew deeper feelings lurked in the shadows, beyond work, beyond even friendship. And the way Niki had just laid into him—she must have felt something more as well.

He should have stayed in Grand Rapids. He should have never agreed to help Lyle. He had no business opening such a deep wound and no business turning his back on his penance.

He heard Niki before he saw her, her heels clicking as she marched back toward him. He stood again, ready to receive another dose of her outrage. She stopped short, looking him up and down as if to take in just how far he had fallen.

"You look like shit," she said, the anger still in her eyes.

"I know."

"What happened to you?"

It wasn't curiosity he heard in her voice, but rather clemency. Was she asking him about Mikhail? What did she expect him to do, blurt out that he had killed a man in cold blood? A man she had helped him track down? A smarter man might have found a better answer to give, but Max fumbled into a joke.

"I lost my razor," he said.

Whatever compassion he had seen on Niki's face disappeared. "One favor, and that's it."

"You don't—"

"Tell me now before I change my mind. And it better be worth it."

Max couldn't look at her eyes as he spoke, so he focused on her chin. "A friend... his daughter went missing. He's beside himself with worry. I'm looking into it. There's a bar up on North Lyndale called the Rook. I need to take a peek at their surveillance footage, but they won't release it to anyone without a badge."

"That's why you came here—to use my badge?"

Max glanced up and noticed for the first time that Niki's eyes looked red, as if she'd been crying. In all the years he'd worked with her, she had never cried.

"It was a bad idea," he said. "I'm sorry."

"Stop saying you're sorry. It's pathetic."

How had he convinced himself that she might understand? "I know that I have no right to ask..."

"I know the bar," Niki said, in a matter-of-fact tone. "I'll meet you there at five."

With that, she was gone.

CHAPTER 18

Max sat on the wall outside of City Hall for several more minutes, watching people in suits and dry-cleaned coats pass on their way to work. He recognized some of the faces, but none looked his way—not that they would have recognized him if they had.

He hadn't eaten breakfast yet, so he returned to his car and drove to a little diner he and Niki used to frequent called Ida's, one of those old-fashioned joints with a lunch counter and a single row of booths along the outside wall. They used to go there to comb through homicide cases over coffee and a plate of steak and eggs.

Ida's was packed that morning, as it usually was for breakfast, and Max took a seat on a stool at the lunch counter. The waitress was a middle-aged woman named Marilyn, who used to flirt with Max back in the day, good-natured teasing to keep a customer coming back and tipping well. He had somehow expected her to recognize him, maybe give him a smile, but all he got was a menu and a flat statement about the specials.

He ordered, and Marilyn took the menu back without even looking at him.

As he waited, it occurred to him that this was the first time that he had eaten at a restaurant in years—he wasn't going to count his convenience–store hot dog from the night before. He had gotten used to people in Grand Rapids looking at him sideways as he walked the aisles of the grocery store, but sitting in Ida's seemed to amplify the stares. Every booth in the place was filled, as were each of the stools—with the exception of those to Max's immediate left and right.

After his coffee arrived, Max noticed a woman at the entrance. Marilyn stood next to her and from the corner of his eye, Max saw Marilyn point to the empty seats beside him. The woman shook her head and waited by the door until a man at the far end vacated his seat.

Max's first reaction was anger. He wanted to tell that woman that he had once been a police detective, a husband, a respected man—but that urge died away quickly. She had chosen wisely. He was a murderer, after all.

By the time Max finished his steak and eggs, he had made a decision. If Niki was going to help him get a look at that surveillance video, the least he could do was show up looking a little bit professional. Max paid for his meal and left Ida's in search of a barber.

He drove to three barber shops before finding someone who would agree to tackle the challenge. The first place had a sign that read *Walk-ins Welcome*, but they told Max that they were too short-staffed. The second place was a lone barber who looked at his watch and said that he didn't have enough time. The third shop had two barbers, an older man and a kid who looked too young. The kid had an empty chair and invited Max to have a seat.

There were pictures of models on the wall, and Max pointed to one who had a haircut similar to what Max had before he drove into the woods. "I want you to make me look like that."

The kid started to laugh, but stopped once he realized that Max was serious. A license pinned to the wall identified him as Neil Tandon, a barber with less than a year of experience. In the mirror, Max saw Neil glance at the older man, who had a big grin plastered on his face.

"I'll pay you double," Max said.

Neil looked at the picture again and nodded. "I can do it."

Neil started with the beard, cutting most of it off with scissors before getting out the electric clippers. Neil tipped Max's head left, then right as he clipped away. His fingers against the side of Max's head felt oddly intrusive after all the years alone. Max kept his eyes closed as Neil worked. Soon the clipper blade moved across his skin. "If it's okay with you," Neil said, "I'm gonna leave a bit of stubble. Otherwise your pale chin and cheeks will stand out. They haven't seen the sun in a while."

Max didn't really like that idea, having been a stickler for a clean-shaven face for most of his life, but said, "If you think it's best."

As the beard fell away, Max could feel the chill of air against his face, a sensation he hadn't felt in years. When Neil finished with the electric clippers, he used a razor to shave the edges. When he was done with that, Neil stepped back and said, "Damn, I'm good."

Max kept his eyes shut.

Neil then went to work on Max's hair, again cutting off big clumps before wetting it down so he could trim it. He spent forty-five minutes clipping, combing, and working out knots before he again stepped back and said, "I should have taken a 'before' picture."

"You're done?"

"You tell me."

Max opened his eyes and could hardly believe what he saw. He ran a hand through his hair—short and neat. Leaving the stubble was a good call, as it not only covered up the paleness of his skin but added a rogu-ish twist to the new look. Here was a man who could walk into any establishment and not be thought a stalker. Max almost laughed at his image in the mirror. "You did well, Neil."

The older man came over to inspect his protégé's work. "I'll be damned."

Max paid what he had promised, shook Neil's hand, and left to find a men's clothing store. Maybe it was the new haircut, but Max was aching to get into a pair of business pants and a new white shirt.

In the hours he spent waiting for Niki in the parking lot of the Rook, Max began to have second thoughts about his haircut and new clothes.

He felt unfaithful to his exile, as though he was slipping into a skin that he had shed three years back. It didn't feel right to look like the old Max when he had worked so hard to leave the old Max behind.

He was still knee-deep in that internal debate when Niki pulled into the parking lot. Max stepped out of his car. When she got out she still looked angry, glancing at Max and not recognizing him at first. Then she looked again and something shifted behind her eyes. For a split second, Max thought he saw the hidden softness that he remembered in her. But then it left again.

"I hope you didn't go through all that trouble for me," she said.

"Thought I'd try and look...well, not like a crazy man."

"It'll take more than a haircut to do that."

Max saw the slight twitch of a smile. "You have any suggestions?"

"A long list. I'll email it to you—Oh wait, that's right. You don't have an email address anymore."

And just like that, Max was back in the doghouse. "I'm—" He stopped himself before saying *sorry*, and by the look in Niki's eyes, that was a good thing.

"Who's this friend you're helping out?" she asked.

"Lyle Voight. Former sheriff from up north. His daughter vanished. Took her kid and all their clothes and left."

Max talked as they walked into the Rook. "Honestly, there's nothing unusual about the case. It's just that her father swears she would never run off like that. She cleaned out her bank account before going. The one thing is...her six-year-old son wasn't with her at the bank."

"Maybe she didn't run away alone."

"That's my working theory, and if I can prove it, I can give Lyle something to help him sleep at night."

Niki looked around the bar. "Who's the manager?"

Max spotted her putting popcorn seeds into the popper at the end of the bar; he pointed.

"She got a name?" Niki asked as they crossed the room.

"Danielle, I think—no, Janet...maybe."

"Mind like a steel trap," Niki muttered. She unclipped her badge from her belt and held it up. "Excuse me, ma'am. Are you the manager here?"

The woman closed the lid to the popcorn popper and turned her attention to Niki. "I am."

"My name is Detective Niki Vang and this is my...trainee, Max Rupert."

"Janelle Donohue," the woman said, sweeping a lock of dyed red hair behind her ear.

"Janelle?" Niki looked at Max.

Max shrugged.

Niki returned her attention back to Janelle. "I was wondering if that camera out front works."

"Sure does."

"Would it be possible to take a look at footage from November sixth?"

"I knew you'd be coming by," Janelle said. "I knew something was up."

"Something was up?" Niki repeated.

Janelle leaned in as if she had a great secret to tell them. "Some homeless dude came by yesterday asking about that same thing."

"Homeless guy?" Niki slid a glance at Max, and he could see the joy she suppressed behind her pursed lips. "Can you describe him?"

"Long, straggly hair. A beard down to here." Janelle tapped her finger on her sternum. "Real meth-head-looking character."

"I think I know who you're talking about," Niki said. "Has a face that could scare children?"

"That's him," Janelle said. "I figured he was up to no good. Told him to get the hell out."

"You did the right thing. If he is who I think he is, the man's an unstable nut job. A real piece of crap."

"Is he the suspect? What kind of case is it?"

"I can't really talk about it, but can we take a look at the video?"

"Sure. Follow me."

As Janelle led them to her office, Max leaned into Niki and whispered, "Piece of crap?"

Niki whispered back. "I was being nice."

Janelle took a seat at her computer and spent some time pulling up the footage. Max narrowed the time frame down to the half hour before Sandy's credit card placed her at the gas station. After she cued up the footage, Janelle left the room. Max put the picture of Sandy next to the computer screen on the left and the Honda Passport on the right.

The Passport was white, which, if Max remembered correctly, was the most popular color for passenger vehicles on the road in the United States. They had a license plate number, but they saw right away that the resolution and the angle of the camera wouldn't allow them to see a plate. The one thing they had going for them was that one of the Passport's roof racks was broken off.

Max and Niki scanned the footage for a while before Niki said, "You promise this woman we're looking for isn't your girlfriend or something? I'd hate to be aiding and abetting a stalker."

"Why do people keep thinking I'm a stalker?"

"It's your shifty eyes—a common trait among meth heads."

"And I shaved for this."

"You weren't exactly rocking that caveman look, Max."

"I was going for lumberjack."

"Swing and a miss."

The camera picked up vehicles in the lane closest to the bar. If Max was correct in his assumptions, Sandy would have traveled that lane to get to the gas station. A light-colored SUV passed in front of the camera and Max stopped the footage and backed it up. The angle of the camera caught the roof with two intact racks. It was close, but it was definitely not Sandy's car.

He tapped the play button again and they watched, the color of the passing cars becoming more unreliable as the bodies reflected the light from a setting sun.

After a minute, Niki said, "The thing I have never been able to figure out is how you thought it would be a good idea to mail your badge and gun to me — make it my problem to do your dirty work. I can't for the life of me understand how that seemed okay."

What could Max say? How could he explain it without admitting that he had killed a man? He was searching for an out when the surveillance footage offered one. A white vehicle entered the screen. "Is that it?" he said.

Niki froze the frame and zoomed in on a white SUV with a broken luggage rack. A match.

"Can you see her face?" Max leaned in eagerly.

Niki moved the frames forward and back, bringing the SUV closer and then farther away from the camera. The angle was wrong. Niki again moved the footage frame by frame, stopping it when she had the clearest view. "That looks like an arm with a hand on the wheel."

Max leaned in. "Yes, but the arm of a woman or a man?"

"I can't tell." Niki zoomed in, but that only made the image blurry beyond recognition. Then she zoomed back out and studied the frame for several seconds before saying, "It's definitely not a woman."

"How can you tell?"

"Look for what's not there, Max."

Max leaned even closer to the screen. "I don't..."

"What kind of car do you drive now?"

"Jeep Cherokee."

"About the same size as a Passport, wouldn't you say?"

"Pretty close."

Niki stood. "Come with me."

They walked out of Janelle's office, stopping at the bar so Niki could ask Janelle to copy the surveillance footage for them. Then Niki took Max outside.

"Pull your Cherokee around and park it where the Passport was at in that last shot."

Max drove his car out of the lot and parked it in the street where the Passport had been. Niki pulled her unmarked squad car behind the Cherokee and turned on her strobes, so that they could block the lane. She told Max to stand beneath the camera, and then she climbed into the Cherokee.

"Can you see me?" she asked.

Just like in the surveillance video, all he could see was an arm and a hand. "No."

"How tall is your missing woman?"

Max pulled out a piece of paper where he had written down Sandy's information. "She's five-feet-six."

"I'm five-five," Niki said. "Now watch." She moved the driver's seat forward and slowly came into view. "Can you see me now?"

"Son of a bitch."

They pulled their cars back into the lot and went inside, taking seats at the bar to wait for the footage. Niki was the first to speak. "If she had the seat adjusted for her height, we would have been able to see her in the video—maybe not a clear shot, but more than just an arm. The person behind the wheel is taller than five-six."

"It's not Sandy."

"So what does that mean?"

"I'm not sure. It's possible she's in the backseat. The tint on the window is too dark to tell. But my gut...I don't know. I don't have the instincts I used to. What do you think?"

"I'm probably not a good one to answer that question," Niki said.

"Why is that?"

"People like us...we see the worst side of humanity. Every day it's another homicide, or sexual assault, or...Well, you remember. After a while, you start to see every situation as a worst-case scenario. You get jaded. I suppose it's enough to make a person want to disappear from the world."

Max thought that Niki was taking another jab at him, but she stared straight ahead with neither anger nor insult in her eyes.

"I can't thank you enough...for helping me out," Max said.

Niki shrugged. "I hope you find her. I know that if I ever went missing, you'd be the one I'd want looking for me."

Max didn't deserve a friend like her, but before he could think of something to say, Janelle walked out of the office with the thumb drive. She handed it to Niki, who gave it to Max.

As they left the bar, Niki asked, "Are you staying in town tonight?"

"I should get this to her father."

"Yeah," she said with a hint of sadness in her voice. "I suppose you should. I hope it helps."

They stopped at Niki's squad car, Max unable to pull away just yet. "You did good...picking up on the camera angle and seat position and all."

"Just doing my job."

"You went above and beyond." Saying goodbye came harder to him than he thought it would. "You're really something."

Niki flashed a smile. "And by 'something,' you mean brilliant? Astonishing? The best damned detective you've ever met? And remember, all of the above is a viable answer."

He wanted to say all of the above. He wanted to tell her that he had missed her, and would miss her. He wanted to say a lot of things, but what he said was, "I owe you."

She got into her squad and closed the door, but as Max walked away, Niki rolled down her window. "Max, I know I said just the one favor... but..." She hesitated as if reconsidering her words. Then she said, "If you need me, I'll be here for you."

Niki's kindness touched a tender place inside Max, and he smiled and nodded a thank-you that he could not put into words.

CHAPTER 19

S pud knew that Reed saw him as a dolt. In those early days when they
were devising their plan, Reed found a reason to dismiss every idea
that Spud offered. Reed had been polite about it, of course, but none of
Spud's suggestions measured up. That was okay with Spud, because he
had made some secret plans of his own.

For example, the plan had been for Spud to rent the shack using his
name and credit card, a six-month lease. Reed had delegated the cost
to Spud because if the plan worked, Spud had money coming—lots of
it. But Spud had sneakily maxed out his credit card, so when the time
came, Reed had to pitch in most of the money to cover the rental.

In truth, Spud had the money—sort of. He had borrowed against
his credit card to purchase three thousand dollars' worth of cryptocurrency, one twentieth of a single coin. It would be his emergency fund
in case Reed's scheme fell apart. If Spud had to go on the run, he could
pull the money out from anywhere on earth except China.

But that wasn't the biggest secret.

Reed knew that Spud had money coming, believing it would arrive in
the next three to four months. What Reed didn't know was that the money
was almost in Spud's hands already. The day before he rode his bike to Sandy's house, he had received an email from the lawyers. They reported that
the logjam they had been working on was about to get cleared up. What
that meant, Spud wasn't sure, except that his ship was about to come in.

Another secret was that Spud had been sneaking away from the shack to check his emails every day. His cell phone had lousy reception — zero bars at the shack. The burner phones had connectivity there, but no data package. Reed's phone worked just fine at the shack, but Spud couldn't use Reed's phone to look at his email account. Reed would blow a gasket if he knew what Spud was doing. *It wasn't part of the plan.* So Spud took to sneaking away once a day.

It had been easy at first. Pip went down for a nap every day after lunch. He was such a well-behaved boy. Spud would stay in Pip's room until Pip fell asleep and then slip out of the house.

He and Reed had parked Spud's car at the shack the day before the kidnapping. From there, Reed had driven Spud and his bicycle into town to the motel where Spud waited until it came time. Spud's car hadn't been driven since — or so Reed thought. But after Spud put Pip down for his naps, he would drive toward Grand Rapids until his phone picked up a signal. There he would pull onto a trail that had a small turn-around and check his emails for word from the lawyers. When he returned to the shack he was careful to park his car in the exact same spot and at the exact same angle as it had been before. Reed never noticed.

But now that Reed was staying at the cabin, Pip took his nap while Reed read magazines in the living room.

So Spud waited for Reed to leave for work that night before sitting Pip down. "You know what a secret is, don't you, Pip?"

The boy nodded.

"So if we do something, can you keep it a secret from everyone — even your father?"

Pip didn't respond. It was as if Spud's words didn't quite make sense.

"If we do something like go for a drive, could you keep that a secret?"

Pip nodded.

"Even from your dad?"

Again the boy nodded.

Spud smiled. "I thought so. We're buddies, right?"

Now Pip smiled as well. "Yeah, we're buddies."

Spud held out his fist and at first Pip just looked at it. Then he raised his own hand up for a bump.

They kept Pip's car seat at the shack, as it would be hard for either Spud or Reed to explain why they had one in their vehicle. Spud strapped Pip in and headed to the small turn-around about ten miles south where his phone finally got reception. Once there, he parked and opened up his email app. No message yet from the lawyers.

Disappointed, he put the phone away and edged back up to the highway. An SUV approached from the left and Spud waited for it to pass, but as it drew closer, he saw the light bar on top.

Damn it! A cop!

He glanced at Pip sitting in the back. Were the police looking for him? The front seats were probably tall enough that Pip would be hidden, but the gap between was a problem. Spud casually laid his arm across the back of the passenger seat, his elbow bent, his sleeve taking up as much space as it could. Down the tree line, he saw what looked to be the edge of a sign nailed to an oak tree. A No Trespassing sign? His pulse quickened. Was he on private land?

The car passed. It was a sheriff's vehicle. The deputy looked at Spud as she passed, her speed slowing a touch. Spud turned on his blinker to go left, waited a second, and then made the turn.

He looked into his rearview to see the squad car brake lights flash. Spud now saw the No Trespassing sign nailed to the tree.

Son of a bitch.

He locked in his cruise control exactly at the speed limit. He gripped the wheel with both hands to keep even between the lines. The squad car pulled to the shoulder and made a U-turn.

Crap! Crap! Crap!

Had she seen Pip? Was there another problem? His tags were up-to-date. His lights all worked. Was she really going to pull him over for stopping on that trail? For all she knew, he had just been turning around.

The highway ran for three miles before his turn to go north. He began debating whether he would make that turn. He couldn't lead the deputy to the shack. That was their hideaway. But if she pulled him over—and found Pip—he would have no need for a hideaway. The game would be over. He'd go to prison.

Fuck! Fuck! Fuck!

His mind flooded with panic, but he kept the car steady and calm. Amid all the noise in his head he could hear Reed yell, *You should have stuck to the plan.*

Two miles to his turn.

The deputy had nearly caught up to him. Her lights weren't on yet. Maybe she was just curious or bored. Or maybe Reed had been wrong about them closing the investigation. Spud looked around for a weapon. She would have a gun, but he would have the element of surprise. There was a screwdriver beneath his seat. He had put it there the previous winter because his trunk would freeze shut. He could stab her in the neck. Drag her body into the woods and ditch her car.

He looked at Pip in the backseat, humming to himself as he watched the trees go by. *Damn it.* He couldn't kill anyone in front of Pip.

One mile to go.

If Spud hit the gas, could he outrun her? His car was probably no faster than hers, and she knew the roads. Besides, she could call for backup. He was screwed. He glanced at the mirror without tipping his head up—he didn't want her to know that he was looking. She was right behind him.

He rounded a curve and saw his turn. *Take it or not?*

He hit his signal and tapped the brakes. Behind him, she slowed, but didn't indicate a turn. He slowed more, easing onto the northbound road. She also slowed, almost to a stop. Then he saw her vehicle turn—but it didn't head north. Instead, she made another U-turn and headed back toward Grand Rapids.

Spud realized that he had been holding his breath. He felt dizzy with relief. In the back, Pip played with the drawstrings of his coat's hood.

By the time he pulled onto the trail that led to the shack, Spud's heart rate had settled back to normal. He parked carefully. He trusted that Pip would keep their secret and Reed would never know about their trip. And as Spud was starting to understand, the less Reed knew the better.

CHAPTER 20

Back at his cabin, Max had stayed up late, watching the surveillance footage over and over, hoping to catch something they'd missed. In the end, he went to bed with nothing more than what Niki had found earlier, that the seat of the Passport had been seemingly set too far back for a woman of Sandy's size.

When he arrived at Lyle's trailer in the morning, it was Meredith who answered the door. Her eyes were even more sunken, as if she hadn't been sleeping well, and she looked at Max like she had never met him before. "Can I help you?" she asked.

"Meredith, it's me... Max Rupert."

She studied him for a moment, the clean face, the new haircut, before cracking an empty smile. "You've changed." She stepped away from the door and let him in.

Lyle was in the dining room, sitting at the table. He didn't get up.

"Holy crap! You look like a new man—or more accurately, you look like your old self again."

Max almost winced at that, his exile feeling more and more like an afterthought.

"Any luck?" Lyle asked, his hope written on his face.

"There's movement," Max said. "Whether it helps us... I don't know."

Lyle looked past Max, to his wife. "Mere, could you make a run to the store? We're running low on milk."

Meredith shook her head. "I'm staying." She sat down beside Lyle before he could object.

Max set his laptop on the table and leaned in between Lyle and Meredith, cueing up the surveillance footage. As soon as she saw the Passport, Meredith said, "That's Sandy's car!"

"Where'd you get this?" Lyle asked, visibly shaken.

"A camera near where her credit card was last used."

Meredith said, "Is that her... in the car?"

"That's the thing," Max said. "Watch." He advanced the footage frame by frame until the vehicle was out of sight; then he backed it up and played it again. "You never get a clear look at the driver, but..."

Meredith leaned toward the computer screen, and Max could only imagine how desperately she wanted to see her daughter in those shadows.

"A friend of mine noticed something. If a woman of Sandy's height had been sitting in the driver's seat... the seat would have been adjusted forward. You should have been able to see her."

Meredith looked at Max, then at Lyle. "What does that mean?"

Lyle's head sank. "It means that it's not Sandy. Someone else is driving her car."

"But... she could be in the back, right? She could be back there with Pip." Meredith took over the computer, moving back through the frames. "I mean, that—right there..." Meredith pointed at the rear window. "That's someone's head, isn't it?"

Max had looked at that frame the night before. He had run the footage back and forth and watched the shadow move across the face of the tinted window, a reflection that came from outside of the vehicle. But to Meredith, he said, "It could be. It's just too dark to say for sure."

"Meredith..." Lyle took hold of his wife's hand. "Who's driving the car? If Sandy's in back... who's behind the wheel?"

"I... I don't know, but... if she's in the back with Pip, at least we know they're okay, right?" There was a desperate hope in the way she spoke.

Lyle nodded and whispered, "Absolutely." Whether he was saying that for Meredith's benefit or because he truly believed it, Max couldn't tell.

"Maybe Bolger was right," Meredith said. "Maybe there was someone else. We don't know. How do we . . . There's got to be a way to find out?"

Lyle said, "We have a pretty good idea how they got to Minneapolis. Maybe he stopped for food at a McDonald's or at a convenience store; they all have videos nowadays. We could canvas every inch of their route."

Max frowned. "People don't just give surveillance footage to random guys like us. I had to call in a big favor to get this. We're civilians, Lyle. Besides, do you have any idea how many potential stops there are along that highway? We'd need manpower for something like that. We need to call in the cavalry."

"What cavalry would that be?"

"Like it or not, we have to take this to Bolger, give him a chance to step up."

"Bolger's gonna see what he wants to see." Lyle pointed at the computer screen. "There's no way he's gonna get off his ass for this. He'll say this proves his theory, and that's it."

"I don't disagree, but without his help, we're kind of at a dead end."

"We'll talk to David Haas," Lyle said. "If there was another man, David would have to have seen something."

Max thought about it. It might not do any good, but then again, it would be better to muster all of their evidence before meeting with Bolger again. This might be their best hope, maybe their only hope, to get Bolger off his ass.

CHAPTER 21

Reed woke up in a foul mood. Spud had kept Pip out in the woods too long—at least that was the reason Reed gave. Yet had Spud brought Pip back any earlier, Reed would have been mad that they woke him up. There was no pleasing him. Was that the reason Pip kept his distance from his father?

Their walk that morning had been a good one. They saw a deer and a fox, getting close enough to both animals for eye contact, which made Pip squeal with delight. Spud held Pip's hand when the woods were thin enough to allow it, Pip's tiny fingers wrapping tightly around two of Spud's. He told Pip another story, this one a take on Hercules slaying the Hydra, a little boy battling a multiheaded boa constrictor in the jungles of Brazil.

But when they got back to the shack, Reed was sitting at the table, bags under his eyes. He had a bowl and spoon in front of him and a box of cereal off to the side. He didn't smile when they came in, or offer any greeting. Pip stepped behind Spud's left leg.

"Have a nice walk?" Reed asked, his tone anything but pleasant.

"We were exploring," Spud said.

"You had your breakfast?" Reed asked.

Spud had made himself a meal of bacon and eggs before Pip woke up. Pip liked to make his own meal by pouring a bowl of cereal while Spud cleaned up the dishes. The frying pan and plate Spud had used that morning were in the drainer. Spud glanced at them, wondering where Reed was going. "I had bacon and eggs." He pointed at the dishes. "Pip had cereal."

"I know Pip had cereal," Reed said. "And do you know how I know that Pip had cereal?"

Reed looked at Pip, as if waiting for his son to answer. Then he said, "You left the milk out." Reed pointed at the jug on the counter beside the fridge. Spud hadn't noticed it there before he took Pip for their walk.

"That's my bad," Spud said, crossing the room and picking up the milk.

"Don't make excuses for him," Reed said, still looking at Pip. "He left it out and now it's warm."

Spud put the milk into the refrigerator. "It was an accident, Reed."

"I said don't make excuses." Reed stood so fast and hard that he knocked his chair backwards. "You left the milk out, Pip. Now I can't eat my cereal because the milk's warm. This is our only jug of milk—and it's ruined."

Pip backed up toward a corner. Spud started to walk to him but Reed held out an arm. "That's your mother's doing. She taught you to be irresponsible . . . lazy. Well, that stops now."

Reed stomped over to Pip and grabbed him by the back of his coat. "You're gonna stand outside for a while and think about what you did."

"He's probably cold, Reed. We just—"

Reed shot a finger in Spud's direction, his face red with anger. "You stay the hell out of my business." He half carried, half shoved Pip out the door. "I'm sick and tired of people telling me how to raise my kid. He's gonna be a man if I have to kick him there myself."

Reed stopped in the middle of the yard, planted Pip there, and said, "You stand here until I tell you that you can move. Maybe next time you'll be a little more careful."

From the front door of the shack, Spud could see a tear glistening on

Pip's cheek, but Reed didn't care a lick. The Reed who talked Spud into this plan had been a gentle man, worried about his son's safety. He had cried when he told Spud about the ache he had in his heart. Had that all been an act?

Reed marched back to the cabin, but Spud stepped in his way, blocking him at the door. "It was my fault, Reed. This isn't necessary."

Reed looked mad enough to beat him. "I will not have my boy growing up weak," he said. "You think you can take me because you're big? You think size has anything to do with it? Well, go ahead, take your shot."

Spud couldn't move. He couldn't speak. Reed wanted to fight him—over a jug of milk?

"I thought so," Reed said. "Pip's gonna grow up tough...not a wuss like you."

With that, he shoved Spud out of the way and went inside.

CHAPTER 22

Lyle had to knock several times before David Haas came to the door, wearing a T-shirt and jeans — no shoes or socks. His hair was tossed about like he'd just gotten out of bed, which apparently he had.

"Sorry to get you up," Lyle said. "I was hoping you might have a chat with us."

David stepped back to let them in. "Always got time for you, Lyle. Has she called?"

"No. Sorry. I'm afraid I came here with questions, not answers." Lyle gestured to Max. "This is Max Rupert. He used to be a detective in Minneapolis." Max shook hands with the tired younger man. "He's kinda helping me out with this." They walked to the kitchen table and sat down. "How you been doing?"

"I'm not really sure," he said. "My brain is like a wet paper towel. I keep waiting for the phone to ring or to hear them coming through the door. I can't figure it out. I'm going out of my mind."

"I know how you feel, David," Lyle said. "Went to make bacon and eggs this morning and forgot the eggs. Sat down to eat and just sat there staring at a plate of bacon."

"You have questions for me?"

It was Max who spoke: "I know you talked to Sheriff Bolger about all this, but I was hoping you might tell us what you saw when you came home that morning."

"Sure. I got here, had to be around eleven, like usual. The first thing I noticed was that she'd left the garage door open. She never does that. But her car's gone, so I figure she's at work and maybe the door wasn't working right. I come in and I hear the TV on downstairs. Why the TV was on, I don't know, but it was set to one of Pip's cartoon channels. Then I went to the bedroom, and that's when I knew something was wrong. All of her clothes were gone—everything—even stuff she don't never wear."

"Stuff like what?" Lyle asked.

"You know. Sweaters she got that she never liked. Pants too small for her. That kind of thing. She took everything. Same with Pip's room. Everything was gone. I tried calling her, thinking she was mad at me, but she didn't answer."

"Was she mad at you?" Max asked. "Did you guys have a fight?"

"No. We were fine."

Max said, "Were there ever times when Sandy might slip out of the room to take a call or come home from work later than you might expect?"

"You could set a watch by her schedule. Every day the same thing—and that's the way she liked it."

"Unexplained credit card purchases?"

"She kept track of the money, but we talked about everything. We were hoping to buy a house in a year or two. But it's not like I was holding her back. If she wanted to buy something, well, it was okay with me. Like the new couch. That was her idea."

Lyle sat up with attention. "New couch?"

"She'd been wanting a new couch for some time, and I kept telling her to get one. We had the money. Finally, she took me down to Rivertown and we bought one of those wraparound...what do you call 'em...sectionals. I called it an early Christmas present—you know, to ease her worries."

Both Lyle and Max looked toward the living room, at a worn brown couch.

"It ain't got here yet," David said. "They're shipping it up from a warehouse in the Cities."

"When did you buy it?" Lyle asked.

"That would have been... the Saturday before she went missing."

Max and Lyle shared a look.

"Is that important?"

It was Max who spoke next. "We're just gathering information right now." Max leaned in to the table, resting on his elbows, and made eye contact with David, hoping that his next question didn't come across as an insult. "You're aware that Sheriff Bolger believes that Sandy ran off with another man. I don't mean for this to sound... disrespectful, David, but is it possible Sandy was seeing someone else?"

"No!" David's answer came fast and hard. "I know that's what Bolger thinks, but no. There's no way. I mean, Sandy and I weren't... you know, grabbing at each other all day. We'd both been through bad relationships before. But we love each other. We're like... You ever cross a lake in a well-balanced canoe—both people paddling in sync? That's what Sandy and me are like."

Lyle said, "What if I told you that we had a picture of her Honda Passport in Minneapolis and there was a man at the wheel?"

"Then he stole it. You have a picture?"

"Surveillance video," Max said.

"No." David stood up and began pacing around the room. "I don't believe you. There was no other man. This is bullshit."

"David..." Max patted the chair next to him and David sat down. "I don't mean to put this indelicately, but of all the possibilities, having her alive and well with another man is one of the better ones."

"What possibilities?" David asked.

Max paused and looked around. The house was pleasant and well kept, and David Haas struck Max as being a caring man who genuinely loved Sandy. If there was no other man in Sandy's life, then what would she be running from? A terrible feeling washed over Max as he paid heed to what his instincts were telling him. He wanted to believe that he would bring Sandy home alive, but in his heart, he didn't.

Max held his tongue until that thought passed. Then he said, "If there is no other man, then what? Was she robbed? Carjacked? There are other possibilities out there, but..."

The cogs in David's head seemed to fall into line and he gripped the edge of the table. "Oh, Jesus."

Max regretted where he had led the conversation, and again wished that he had never left his cabin. Sandy wasn't his daughter; she wasn't his girlfriend. Pip wasn't his child. But there he was amid a pall of despair so thick that he could feel it pressing his shoulders, the weight of this woman and child another burden for him to carry.

He should have kept his mouth shut. He should have left Niki alone. Then, at least, they could all have held on to their hope.

CHAPTER 23

Bolger kept Lyle and Max waiting for half an hour. When he walked into the meeting room, he carried himself like a man ready to wrestle a steer, his stride impatient and purposeful. He plopped down in a chair and looked at Lyle and then at Max and said, "Okay, let's hear it."

They had decided that Max would do most of the talking, keep the personal animosity on the sidelines as much as possible. Max had his laptop ready, the footage from the Rook cued up. "We just wanted to run something by you," Max said. "To start with, is it still your theory that Sandy Voight left her home voluntarily back last Tuesday?"

"That's what the evidence supports," Bolger said.

"Are you still of the opinion that Sandy ran off with another man?"

"That's my deduction."

Lyle stepped in. "If there's no evidence one way or the other, it's not a deduction—it's speculation."

Max reached over and patted the older man's arm. Then he returned his attention to Bolger. "You're drawing that . . . conclusion because of the clothing being moved out."

"That's right."

"Because a person getting kidnapped wouldn't pack their clothes."

"Not in my experience," Bolger said with more than a touch of condescension.

"It's logical," Max agreed.

Bolger must have felt that he was being led into a trap, because he answered cautiously. "Yes...logical."

"Would it be logical for a woman — as frugal as they come — to buy an expensive couch if she was planning to skip town?"

"What couch would that be?"

Max slid the paperwork to Bolger. "Cost them near four grand."

Bolger leaned back and smiled. "Running away can be an act of impulsivity. You don't think Sandy Voight has the capacity to be impulsive?"

Max said, "Sheriff, she took all the clothes from her closet. She took clothes she didn't like — clothes that didn't fit her anymore. Is that logical?"

"She was in a hurry. She had to get out of there before Haas came home."

"She had all night to pack. Haas worked the night shift."

"Now who's speculating?" Bolger said.

Max looked at Lyle, whose nostrils flared with the strain of keeping quiet. Max turned the laptop so that the screen faced Bolger. "This is a video from a surveillance camera outside of a bar on Lyndale Avenue. Sandy would have passed this spot on her way to the convenience store where her credit card was last used. This is her Honda Passport."

"How do you know?" Bolger asked. "Can you read the plate?"

"No, but it's missing part of its luggage rack...and both Lyle and David Haas agree it's her car."

Bolger, not wanting to concede an inch, said, "For the sake of argument, let's say that's her car. So what? We already knew she gassed up down there."

"Sandy's not driving the car. Look." Max pointed at the driver's window. "The seat is set too far back for that to be a woman of Sandy's height. There's a man in the driver's seat, and no one on the passenger side."

"*If* that's her car."

That was apparently more than Lyle could take. "It's her goddamned car, Tate. It is because I'm telling you it is. You want to turn a blind eye...Jesus Christ! You're the goddamned sheriff. When are you gonna start acting like it?"

"Shut up, Lyle." Bolger pointed a thick finger at Lyle's face as he spoke. "You come in here with this...this cock-and-bull...Buying a couch don't mean a damned thing. You have an SUV near the convenience store—great—but you can't even prove it's her car. And if it is her car, she could be in the backseat. You close your eyes to the obvious and expect me to buy into your delusion. Well, that's not gonna happen. Your daughter went to the bank and emptied her account. Then she packed her shit, took her kid, and left. If you come up with any actual evidence to contradict that, I'll be happy to take a look. Until then..."

"Aren't you the one who's supposed to be looking for the evidence?" Max said. He tried to keep his tone even, but there was no way to disguise the insult.

"Are you telling me how to do my job now?"

"Well, let's see. Did you subpoena the cell tower data near Sandy's house yet? There might have been calls made that morning. If you think Sandy was seeing another man, his phone number should come up. Did you look for fingerprints at the scene? What about video? If Sandy's vehicle drove through Grand Rapids, some other camera might have caught it too. Did you check businesses along the route?"

"What about Reed Harris's phone?" Lyle said. "Did you check it to see who he'd been calling?"

"Maybe someone *should* tell you how to do your job," Max said, "because you've made a mess of it so far."

Bolger stood up. "We're done here."

Lyle stood as well. "You're protecting that son of a bitch, aren't you?"

Bolger leaned over the table. "You'd better watch your step, Lyle."

The older man didn't flinch. "What does he have on you? Is it that girl—the one that drowned in the Tioga Pit?"

"Lyle, you can go straight to hell." With that, Bolger left, slamming the door behind him.

Max and Lyle looked at each other. Max shrugged. "That went well."

"No worse than I expected," Lyle said. He looked around the tiny room, a room that was part of an office that used to be his. He grimaced with anger and said, "Screw him. I'll go it alone."

"No, you won't." Max closed the laptop and stood beside Lyle.

"You ain't stopping me, Max."

"No—I'm not stopping you; I'm going with you."

CHAPTER 24

M ax hadn't had a beer in over three years. It was one of those things he'd felt he no longer deserved. Lyle, on the other hand, didn't suffer that deficiency, and purchased a twelve-pack on his way out to Max's cabin. They had driven separately to pay their visit to Bolger and had decided, after that fiasco, it was time to put together a plan.

A strong November wind ushered in the kind of cold that seeped through the walls and made a man's joints work slower, so Max began setting a fire in the cabin's woodstove.

Lyle popped the top on his beer and sat on the couch. "Did you see the way his hackles stood on end?"

Max, who knelt in front of the fire, didn't have to look at Lyle to know that the old sheriff was smiling. The showdown with Bolger had invigorated him.

"I think I hit a nerve," Lyle continued. "You saw it, right? How he got all twisted when I mentioned Tioga Pit? I swear there's something there."

Max joined Lyle, taking a seat in a chair across the coffee table from him, where a cold beer sat opened and waiting. One more marker on Max's slide back to a world he didn't deserve. Still, he took a drink, thick and smooth. He hadn't realized how much he'd missed it.

"So what's our next move?" Lyle said.

"We look at this from a new angle. If Reed had a hand in this, he'd have to have had an accomplice because Reed was at the casino. I doubt that Bolger looked for evidence of that when he searched Reed's house."

"Evidence like what?"

"They would have to communicate somehow and Reed's probably smart enough not to use his personal cell. Maybe we can find proof of a burner phone—a receipt or bill, something like that. If I could get a look inside his house..."

Lyle sat back on the couch and appraised Max. "You understand what that means, right? You'd be committing a burglary. They'll lock you up if they catch you."

"I understand."

"You got no dog in this fight."

Max thought about his dream, the child he couldn't save. It seemed an easy calculation. He could die alone and forsaken in the woods, waiting for a reckoning that might never come, or he could go down fighting for something good. And although it went against everything he once stood for, Max felt at peace with this particular felony.

"Dog or no dog," Max said, "I'm going."

"Okay, tell me your plan."

The plan was simple: Max would break in while Lyle sat outside of the Dizzy Duck to keep an eye on Reed. But the plan had one big, obvious flaw, and Lyle called it out right away. "So how are you gonna get inside Reed's house without breaking a window?"

"I thought I'd try picking the lock."

"You ever pick a lock?"

Max had entered hundreds of homes searching for suspects or executing warrants. He had seen a lock pick used, but admitted he had never actually picked a lock himself. "From what I hear, it's not all that hard."

"It's not. Most people would piss their pants if they knew how easy it was. But it does take finesse. My uncle was a locksmith; I can do it with my eyes closed. Which might come in handy since it'll be dark."

"So, you can teach me."

"I can, but I won't because you're not going in. If someone's gonna commit a felony here, it's gonna be me. You go to the bar and watch."

"It doesn't matter if I'm at the bar. I'm aiding and abetting the crime, so I may as well—"

"I'm not gonna argue with you on this, Max." Lyle gave him a look as heavy as stone. "I'm going in and that's nonnegotiable."

Max tried to come up with an argument, but he had nothing. "You'll need a lock-pick set."

"You got a hacksaw blade and something to grind it with?"

"In my shed."

"Then I'm good. It'll take about an hour."

"Okay then . . . I'll go buy a couple burner phones. That way I can signal you if there's a problem."

"Now you're talking," Lyle said. "We'll do this right. Might as well put all that cop training to good use at last."

Max found his hacksaw and a drill with a grinder bit out back, and Lyle set to grinding a lock-pick set right there at Max's kitchen table.

Max had kept a single debit card that he used for food and gas and the like, just one more tether that he worried made his exile a sham. But he would use cash to keep the burner phones anonymous. He went up to the loft and dug out a tin can he kept in his drawer. He was about to turn away when he saw the box of keepsakes, and he thought of Jenni.

Max wasn't one to believe in angels or spirits, but in his darkest moments, he sometimes wondered what she thought of his downfall. And here he was, preparing to commit another crime. Would she understand? Would she see that this time he was doing it to save a child—to try to make things right?

He opened the box, lifted out the bracelet, and looked at the empty golden charm. In a world full of tradeoffs, this one seemed easy. There was a little boy lost, and no one else looking for him. If it was their child out there, she would want him to go to the ends of the earth—to hell and back—if that's what it took to bring him home. Max was sure of it.

He slid the bracelet into his pocket along with a roll of twenties from the tin can, and tucked the box and can carefully back away.

CHAPTER 25

Spud had learned a valuable lesson when that sheriff's deputy followed him the previous day. He needed to wait until dark to make his daily trip. In the daylight, people could see into his car, but at night he was just another pair of headlights.

That evening, after Reed had gone to work, Spud played a game of Go Fish with Pip, using a deck of cards he'd found in a kitchen drawer. By the third hand, Pip started talking, cautiously at first, as though he had momentarily forgotten to be shy. Spud smiled and asked questions. Pretty soon, Pip was telling Spud about a girl he liked at school, and his favorite flavor of ice cream, and a dog that had licked his face when he was visiting a friend. He was still guarded as Spud drew him from subject to subject, but there was a definite and encouraging thaw in his demeanor.

When it was sufficiently dark outside, he again strapped Pip into the back of his car and eased down the trail. He drove to where he normally parked to check his emails, but he did not stop—another lesson he had learned. As dangerous as it was to check his phone while driving, he wasn't about to have some deputy catch him trespassing again. He would stay on the road and be extra careful.

When he reached the point where he knew he had reception, he touched the email icon on his phone and returned his eyes to the road. The highway curved slightly, and he waited until he was out of the curve to look at his screen. There was a message. He lifted his phone closer to his face and saw it was from his lawyer. In his excitement, he jerked the car over the center line and back. This was it. It had to be.

He opened the email and again focused on the road as another pair of headlights came at him. The two cars passed and then Spud looked at his phone.

I am happy to inform you. . .

The road curved around a bend. After the bend he read,

The documents are ready to be signed.

There was more to the email, but now that he had it loaded onto his phone, he could read the rest of it at the shack. He pulled onto a gravel road, turned around, and headed back, his heart beating with joy. His jackpot was sitting in the lawyer's office, more money than he ever thought he would see in his lifetime. All he had to do was fulfill his end of Reed's bargain and he could return to St. Paul a rich man.

Then again, although he had given Reed his word, Reed had deceived him. Sandy wasn't an abusive parent; Spud knew that now. Reed was the cruel one, the one whose mere presence could turn his son mute. If Spud had known that, he never would have gone along with Reed's plan, no matter how much money was in it for him.

Reed was a liar. So why honor a promise to a liar?

Still, Reed had lived up to his end of the bargain, which was the only reason Spud had this money waiting for him. Spud had agreed to the plan, shook on it. But how was it fair that Spud had to stay in that crappy shack when he had so much waiting for him in St. Paul? What if he just walked out, left Reed to fend for himself and went back to St. Paul for good?

Reed could hurt him. He might even go so far as to kill Spud if he went back on his word. Spud hadn't believed that to be a possibility when this all began, but the way Reed had been acting lately...Spud had to admit, he was scared.

Spud looked at Pip in the backseat, quietly staring out the window. What a perfectly wonderful little boy. Pip was never supposed to be part of the equation beyond a few weeks of babysitting, but something had changed. Of all the terrible things that Spud had done, none tore at him as much as the thought of what he was about to do—leave Pip with his father. How could he do that? The thought of what Reed would do to toughen his son up turned everything in Spud's stomach sour.

"How you doing back there?"

"Fine." Pip kept his head turned toward the window.

"Can I ask you something? You like me, right?"

"Uh-huh."

"We're buddies."

Pip looked at Spud, his lips arcing up in a little smile. It was a beautiful smile.

"We're more than buddies," Spud said, "don't you think? I mean..." It might have been the elation of everything that email represented, but the swell of emotion in his chest had Spud saying things he shouldn't. "If it was just you and me...if we were—you know—a team, that'd be okay with you, wouldn't it?"

He saw Pip nod.

Spud tucked the thought away. He shouldn't put ideas into Pip's head until he'd had time to work them through. If Pip slipped up and said something about the car rides or the two of them...Spud was treading on very dangerous ground.

He drove back to the shack but didn't bother to park in the same spot or at the same angle. He'd decided he would not be there when Reed came home from work.

CHAPTER 26

Technically, Max owned a cell phone already; it lay in the bottom of a drawer, its battery dead, its screen dusty. He had canceled his provider back when he moved to the cabin, and now the phone was little more than a paperweight.

Still, he brought his old phone with him to the store, thinking he could fire it up with a new account, one that wouldn't have a pile of unanswered messages from Niki waiting. But the woman at the store convinced him to upgrade, selling him the smartest phone she had. It needed an email address, so he created a new one. He promised himself that all this was temporary, a necessity that he'd shut back off as soon as they found Sandy and Pip.

Next, he drove to Walmart, where he bought two cheap burner phones. Just to be safe, he wore a ball cap and kept his head down for the cameras. He paid cash and loaded sixty minutes of time onto each phone.

When he got back to the cabin, Lyle was just finishing up his lock-pick set. He had filed a hacksaw blade down to make two different versions of a rake, the part of the set that he would slide into the lock to move the tumblers out of the way. He had pulled the metal insert off of one of his wiper blades and fashioned a tension bar, a simple twist of metal that looked like a paper-thin Allen wrench. He would use that to turn the lock once the tumblers were pushed back. "It's a thing of beauty," Lyle said holding up his creation.

"Kind of scary that it's so easy." Max handed one of the burner phones to Lyle. "Keep communication to a minimum," Max said. "Nothing that can be used as evidence."

"Got it."

Max also gave Lyle a dark stocking cap and a black sweatshirt to help him blend in with the night. Max didn't own any latex gloves but had a pair of leather ones that would work. As Lyle dressed, Max looked around as if there might be something lying on the floor or countertop that they were forgetting. It was their last chance to back out.

"I think we're ready," Lyle said.

Max nodded, and they walked to his Cherokee.

Other than Lyle giving Max directions to Reed's house, neither spoke on the drive. It was a rental, small and surrounded by overgrown shrubbery. It had brown siding, broken in a couple places, and the paint peeled off the shutters in leafy strips.

Max drove past the house, looking for a place to drop Lyle. About fifty yards away, he saw a stand of trees. He pointed as he passed them. "Stay in the woods until I text you that it's clear."

Lyle nodded. "Let's do this."

Max turned the SUV around on the empty street and rolled to a stop by the trees. Lyle opened his door and slid out quickly, the interior light staying on for only a second or two. As he drove away, Max looked in the mirror for Lyle, but the man had already disappeared.

The Dizzy Duck was on the southern edge of the city. Part sports bar, part family restaurant, it overlooked a small lake. Max had eaten there with his brother a time or two back when Alexander was alive, so he had a basic memory of the layout. Again he wore a baseball cap and kept his chin down, taking a seat at a table near the bar but not so close that he might stand out to Reed.

About half of the tables in the restaurant were occupied, and only three people sat at the bar, a slow start for the night. A waitress in a black T-shirt brought Max a glass of water and a menu and told him that the special was deep-fried walleye.

Reed hadn't changed much from Lyle's picture. He was maybe five-eight, thin with dark hair that he kept short. He had the thick arms and the barrel chest of someone who lifted weights on a regular basis. Once Max confirmed that Reed was behind the bar, he sent a text to Lyle: Good to go.

Max's first impressions of Reed Harris fell far short of the monster that Lyle had described. The man seemed affable as he chatted with the three men at the bar. Max had found nothing of value when he searched Reed's name on his new phone, so everything that Max knew about Reed came from Lyle Voight, a man who admittedly hated his former son-in-law. As a cop, Max rarely acted on the word of a single witness, yet here he was, all in with nothing more than Lyle's opinion as his bedrock.

The waitress came by, and Max ordered a burger and fries. When he turned his attention back to the bar, Reed had stepped away from the patrons and was tapping at the screen of his phone. Would he be stupid enough to text his accomplice? But then, Reed could be texting anyone — or not even texting at all. Max's part of the operation was simply to watch Reed and give Lyle the heads-up if Reed left for home. But if he could get a peek at that phone, it might offer a second trail to follow.

The men's room was past the bar. Max stood and walked over casually, his eyes cast hard to the side in the hopes of seeing Reed's screen. As he passed, he couldn't see anything, but Reed didn't seem to take notice of him, so he turned around and bellied up to the bar at a spot where he could see over Reed's shoulder. Reed noticed Max and turned. In that moment, Max saw it was a card game open on Reed's phone.

"What can I get ya?" Reed asked.

Max dropped his chin. "Grain Belt."

Reed slid his phone into the back pocket of his jeans, reached into a cooler, and pulled a bottle of beer out, popping the top and handing it to Max.

Max paid for the beer and walked back to his seat, wondering why he had made that trip to the bar. If Reed had been texting his accomplice, Max wouldn't have been able to read it from that far away anyway. He would have had to steal the phone, and even then, the best Max could have hoped for was a number he could ping. But of course, he wasn't a cop anymore, so he couldn't ping a damned thing; he would need Bolger for that, and that's where it would all come to another screeching halt.

The waitress came with Max's hamburger, thick and juicy with a stack of extras—onion, tomato, lettuce, pickles—on the side. He ate slowly, not wanting to finish before Lyle had time to search Reed's house. By the time he had downed his last french fry, Lyle still hadn't texted him, so Max ordered another beer.

The place had filled as Max ate, and Reed now hustled to keep up with the orders. Nothing in his demeanor hinted at a man burdened by murder or kidnapping. Max knew better than to judge a man by his appearance, but to be that evil and yet that calm suggested a level of sociopathy reserved for serial killers and politicians. If Lyle was right about Reed, the man had orchestrated Sandy's death, kidnapped Pip, and still poured drinks with a steady hand.

But then Max thought about Mikhail. How was Max any different? Where were the ripples in Max's surface to tell the world what he had done?

Max checked his burner phone again—still no message. Suddenly, he saw Reed frown, put down the drink he had been pouring, and pull his cell phone from his jacket pocket. Reed walked to the end of the bar, turned his back to his customers, and leaned into the call. With his beer in his hand, Max stood and walked a few steps closer to get a better look. Reed held the phone tightly to his ear and gave a short glance over his shoulder. He looked angry.

Something seemed out of place. It wasn't just the swift change in Reed's demeanor, but something else, something he couldn't put a finger on.

Max downed his beer so he could go to the bar for another, getting closer to Reed. His third of the day, the alcohol tingled pleasantly up against his better judgment, and he shook his head to stay focused.

Reed straightened up and put the phone into the breast pocket of his denim jacket, buttoning the pocket shut—and that's when Max knew.

CHAPTER 27

The phone that buzzed in Reed's jacket pocket was for emergencies only. He had even listed for Spud what might constitute an emergency: an injury to Pip, someone showing up at the shack. The last time that phone had buzzed Spud had just killed Sandy and had texted Reed to say that they were on the road. No problems.

Worried, Reed moved to a part of the bar where there were no customers. "What's wrong?"

"Everything's fine," Spud said.

Reed almost hung up, but said, "If everything's fine, then why the hell are you calling me?"

"I just wanted to tell you that I'm on my way to St. Paul. The papers are ready to sign."

"What?" Reed kept his voice as quiet as he could. "Are you out of your fucking mind? You can't leave now. You have to stay with Pip. That's the plan, and we don't fuck with the plan, remember?"

"I gotta sign this stuff sooner or later. It's ready now, so I'm going—"

"We'll talk about this when I get home—not now."

"I'm not there. I'm on the road."

"You left Pip alone?"

"He's asleep; he'll stay asleep until you get home. He won't even know I'm gone until morning."

"You're gonna fuck things up."

"I've worked it all out. You got tomorrow off, and I'll be back before you have to work again. The timing's perfect."

"Turn your ass around—"

"I got to go. I'll be back in a couple days."

"Goddammit!"

The connection went dead.

He called Spud back, but there was no answer.

Reed wanted to reach through the phone and grab Spud by the throat. How dare he? Who did he think he was? Reed's pulse thumped hard inside of his ears. He wanted to smash beer mugs and liquor bottles until his rage subsided, but instead, he eased the phone back into his jacket pocket and took a couple deep breaths.

He'd known that this might happen, but he truthfully hadn't believed that Spud had the spine. What if Spud stayed in St. Paul longer than a few days? Reed would have to call in sick. And how would that look? This wasn't the plan, goddammit.

Reed took another breath and let it out slowly. He needed to get it together—keep up the act. He forced a smile onto his face and turned around to find a guy waving an empty Grain Belt bottle at him. He wanted to hit the man for no good reason.

Instead, he gave the man a new beer. *Don't let them see that anything's wrong.*

CHAPTER 28

Max paid for his beer and returned to his table, elated by what he'd seen. Reed had been playing cards earlier on a cell that he kept in the back pocket of his jeans. The call he'd just taken had been on a phone he pulled from the breast pocket of his jacket. Reed had a burner! And the simplest answer for why he had a burner—the one that fit Max's puzzle perfectly—was that Reed was talking to his accomplice.

Max needed to look at that phone, but how? He could wait to see if Reed took his jacket off at some point, but no, Reed would keep the jacket on to keep the phone close to him. If he was going to get a look at that phone, Max would need to force Reed to take it off, which seemed impossible. And if he stole the phone, Reed would know that someone was onto him.

Max's own burner buzzed. He looked at the text, a single word: Done. Max sent a reply, also a single word: Wait. All Max needed was a few seconds with Reed's phone.

He looked around the restaurant. The waitstaff were all women, including the manager. There were probably male cooks in the back, but as far as Max could determine, Reed was the only male employee around.

He stood and nonchalantly walked to the men's room: two urinals and a single stall with a toilet. Max entered the stall and went to work. He was no plumber, but basic toilet technology hadn't changed in over four hundred years. Sure, there have been tweaks and upgrades, but most guys believe that fixing a toilet is within their genetic ken. Max was willing to bet that Reed Harris would rise to the challenge.

He lifted the lid off the tank and took a quick inventory. Pushing the handle lifted a flapper, the seal that held the water in the tank back from the bowl. Once enough water passed into the bowl to complete the flush, the flapper dropped and the tank filled again. What stopped the tank from overflowing was the float. The water lifted the float until a valve shut off the water.

Max unclipped the thin bar that connected the float to the valve, dropping it into the tank. Now the water would continue to flow.

But the tank had a fail-safe. The water would stop rising once it topped an overflow tube. Max looked around for something to shove into the overflow tube, and found only toilet paper, which might dissolve once the water hit it.

Then an answer came to him. He planted his right foot on the toilet seat, untied his boot, and removed the boot and his sock, then slipped his bare foot back into the boot. He twisted the sock and shoved it down the overflow tube. Then he stepped back and inspected his work, mentally going through the mechanics of what would happen. Satisfied, he put the lid back on the tank and gave it a flush.

By the time he finished washing his hands, he could hear water lapping onto the floor.

CHAPTER 29

It wasn't just that Spud had disobeyed him, it was his tone, pushy—resolute—as if they were equals. He hadn't asked Reed about going to St. Paul; he'd told him. Spud never talked that way to him. It was always *maybe we should*, or *how about if we* . . . And where had Spud found the balls to hang up on him like that?

Two more people took seats at the bar, one of them holding up a twenty to get Reed's attention—a mojito and a scotch.

Reed went to work on the mojito. What if Spud didn't come back? *Christ. That would ruin everything.* The world had to see that Reed was going about his life. Like it or not, he needed Spud. The plan wouldn't work if someone didn't stay with Pip.

The plan had always been to take Pip up into Canada once suspicion died down. But Reed also had a backup plan—his break-glass-in-case-of-emergency plan—that would immediately send him and Pip into the woods and into Canada, where he knew a shady pilot with a float plane. But that plan was supposed to be a last resort. If Reed took off for Canada now, everyone—including Bolger—would suspect he'd had a hand in Sandy's disappearance. The case would be reopened. He and Pip would be fugitives.

Reed served up the drinks as a group of three men slid up to the only open barstools. "Three shots—whiskey," one called out.

He had to trust that Spud would return. They were tied to one another; surely Spud didn't believe he could walk away without any consequences. Reed had to believe that Spud knew better.

He served up the whiskeys and took an order for a vodka tonic. As he opened a new bottle of tonic, he looked up to see Grain Belt man standing in front of him again. The man kept his face tilted down in an odd fashion, the bill of a cap obscuring his eyes. He pointed the neck of his beer bottle at the men's room. "Dude, you have a problem in your john."

Reed ignored him and poured the tonic into a glass.

"There's water all over the place. I think the toilet's overflowing."

Jesus Christ. Reed pinched his eyes shut. *What the hell else could possibly go wrong tonight?*

CHAPTER 30

Max waited a beat as Reed dropped his head, muttered something under his breath, and then headed for the john.

Two other men passed Max, also heading into the restroom; at last Max followed them in. By the time Max got there, Reed was in the stall, bent down, turning off the water line.

"Holy hell," one of the men said. The other just laughed and tiptoed across the wet floor to a urinal.

Max had hoped to see the jacket, but it was nowhere. Surely Reed would have to reach into the water to fix the problem. He couldn't do that without getting his sleeves wet. But what if he didn't fix it? What if he simply put up an Out of Order sign on the stall?

Max heard the scrape of porcelain as Reed removed the tank's lid. "Goddammit," Reed muttered.

The two men chatted about some plumbing mishap one had experienced after a hard freeze. They moved from the urinals to the sinks, and Max went to the urinal closest to the stall to listen. He couldn't tell what Reed was doing, and thought that his scheme might have failed. But then Reed tossed his jacket over the partition so that half of it fell on Max's side, the breast pocket with the burner phone only inches from his face.

The two men washed their hands. They could see Max in the mirror if they looked, but they weren't paying attention. Still, it was too risky.

They might have been regulars or friends of Reed's, so he waited. On the other side of the partition, Max could hear water being rippled and assumed that Reed was reaching for the float bar at the bottom of the tank.

The two men shuffled out, and Max went to work. He unbuttoned the breast pocket of the jacket and the phone slid into his hand. He was in luck; the phone hadn't timed out. Max pressed the icon for phone calls and a single number showed. Max memorized the ten digits, repeating them in a loop as he slid the phone back into the pocket.

Then Reed yelled, "What the fuck!"

Max was trying to rebutton the flap when the jacket suddenly moved. The button slipped from Max's fingers, but the phone didn't fall out.

Reed spoke again, this time an angry hiss. "A fucking sock?"

Max gave the button a second try, punching it through the hole just as the jacket disappeared over the top.

Reed slammed the stall door open. Max turned to the urinal, his face aimed at the wall like a man taking a leak. In his head, he repeated the phone number over and over. Reed washed his hands, pounding the soap dispenser, yanking out paper towels, and cursing under his breath.

Max let the seconds tick by, the phone number finding a cadence in his head. He couldn't let anything trip him up. He had to hold on to those numbers. The door creaked open and closed again. Max breathed a sigh of relief.

CHAPTER 31

M ax stopped at the stand of trees near Reed's house. Lyle stepped
out and climbed into Max's Cherokee. "Anything?" Max asked.

"This." Lyle held up a small piece of paper, crumpled as if it had been
wadded up at some point. "I went through his mail, his trash, his drawers.
Found no evidence of an accomplice. No phone bills, no notes. But then I
went through his hamper and in the pocket of a pair of jeans, I found this."

It was too dark for Max to see, so he asked, "What is it?"

"A grocery receipt. Two days ago Reed bought a jar of peanut butter,
chips, bread, mac-and-cheese, cereal, and a bunch of other food that
might appeal to a young boy."

"You don't have to be a six-year-old to like mac-and-cheese."

"True, but there was no mac-and-cheese in the cupboard. None of
those items were in Reed's kitchen."

"He's stocking food someplace else."

"The kind of thing a man might do if he's hiding someone nearby."

Max smiled and reached into his shirt pocket for the piece of paper
he'd scribbled on at the bar. He handed the paper to Lyle.

"What's this?"

"Unless I miss my guess, that's the phone number for the accomplice."

"What?"

"Reed's carrying a burner phone. That number called him tonight
and said something to piss him off."

Lyle looked at Max with astonishment. "How the hell did you manage that?"

"It's a long story that involves criminal damage to a toilet—I'd rather not go into it—but if we can ping the number we can get a location. Problem is, we'd need someone in law enforcement to do that—and for that we would need probable cause."

Lyle laced his hands together, steepling his index fingers and touching them to his lips. "The second phone proves nothing," he said. "And the food could be an early Thanksgiving donation. Everything can be explained in a way that says there's no crime."

"I agree," Max said. "And I get the impression that Bolger isn't going to budge without something more substantial."

"Oh, hell no. We take this to Bolger and he'll go ask Reed—and there goes our lead."

Max pulled into the empty lot of a strip mall and put the Cherokee in park. "I do have another idea," he said. "We could track Reed's vehicle. See where it goes. If he's spending time at their hideaway, we might be able to find it."

"Track him? How?"

Max pulled out his cell phone. "Attach this to his vehicle. I can track my phone online to see where it goes. Do you know what he drives?"

"He used to drive an F-150, but that was before I fired him. I'm not sure if he still does."

"Would you be able to pick it out of the trucks in the lot at the Dizzy Duck?"

"Absolutely."

Max returned to the bar and drove slowly through the parking lot while Lyle scanned the rows. No luck. They drove through a second time with the same result. Max pulled onto a small side street and parked to rethink the plan.

"He must have bought a new vehicle," Lyle said.

"Do you know anyone who might know what he drives?"

"Assholes like Reed don't have a lot of friends." Lyle turned in his seat to face Max. "Let's just follow him. Wait here until he gets off work and follow him."

"What if he makes us?"

"This is my family we're talking about. We could put an end to this thing tonight."

"Or he sees us and we give up our only advantage."

"If you had a kid, you'd understand how it takes everything I got not to set a blowtorch to that son of a bitch."

Max thought of the easing of tension he had felt in his chest as he watched Mikhail Vetrov sink beneath the ice. He knew Lyle's pain. "All I'm saying is that we wait one more night—find out which vehicle is his and come back tomorrow."

"That's an eternity. We're so close."

"There are too many ways to get spotted."

"I'll make a deal with you," Lyle said. "We follow him tonight, keep a good distance back. If you think it's too risky, we can abort and come back here tomorrow with a tracking device."

Max gave it some thought. He was driving, so he would be able to back off if he felt that something was wrong. "Okay," Max said. "We'll give it a try, but it's my call. If I see the slightest sign that he's checking for a tail, we come back here tomorrow and track him with my cell phone."

"Deal."

CHAPTER 32

There were only three vehicles left in the parking lot when Reed Harris walked out of the Dizzy Duck. He climbed into the biggest of the three, a black SUV that looked to be a Tahoe. Max and Lyle slid down in their seats as Reed pulled out of the lot and passed by them. Max waited until Reed was some distance away before starting his Cherokee, the headlights coming on automatically.

Reed drove north into Grand Rapids, keeping to the main highway through town, which made it easy for Max to follow without being conspicuous. He slowly closed the gap to half a mile once they entered the city limits. There were very few cars out at that time of the morning and with the stoplights flashing yellow, Max didn't have to get too close. He expected Reed to pass through Grand Rapids and head north to the woods, but Reed turned onto the road where he lived, a river road that followed the Mississippi as it left town.

"He's going home?" Max asked.

"He's being careful. He's not a fool." There was a hardness to Lyle's voice.

The road was long and straight as it approached Reed's house, but it had spurs that angled off about every quarter mile or so. Max pulled onto a spur close enough to see the front of Reed's house and driveway. He killed the engine and got out, walking back to the main road to get a better look. Lyle followed in time to see Reed park and go inside his house.

"I guess we gotta come back tomorrow," Max said. "He must not go out every day." Max was about to head back to the Cherokee when Reed walked back out of the house, a bright flashlight in his hand. Max stepped back to find cover and Lyle joined him.

Reed lay down on his back beside the Tahoe and shined the light up into the undercarriage.

"What's he doing?" Lyle asked.

Max shook his head. "He's looking for a tracker."

"Son of a bitch," Lyle said. "I guess our date for tomorrow is off."

"He's expecting us — or Bolger."

Reed popped the hood and shined the light at the engine.

"Think he'll head out of town when he's done?" Lyle asked.

"That'd be my guess. He wants to make sure his car's clean before he goes."

Reed closed the hood, walked to the end of his short driveway, and shined his light up and down the street. Max and Lyle ducked low and held still as the light passed. Then Reed got into his truck and backed onto the road.

Lyle headed for the Cherokee, but Max pulled him back into the trees. "Don't open the door," Max said. "The interior light, he'll see it." They stayed in the trees until Reed went by them, then they climbed into the Cherokee. "It's gonna be risky once he heads out of town," Max said. "We'll be the only cars on the road."

"We gotta follow him," Lyle said, almost pleading with Max. "This is our chance."

Far ahead of them, Reed turned north and Max sped up to keep sight of Reed's taillights. As the highway cut into the woods, Max dropped back so far that Reed's taillights disappeared beyond the curves and hills.

"Damn it! You're gonna lose him," Lyle said. "Get a little closer."

"We can't let him spot us. We have to—" Max crested a hill. Ahead of him the highway rolled straight for several miles with no taillights.

"Shit!" Max sped up in case a rise in the road or a slight curve might be blocking his view, but the highway ahead remained as black as night. "Shit!"

"Go back," Lyle said. "He must have turned off."

Max did a three-point turnaround and headed back slowly, watching for roads and trails that Reed might have taken. There were a few dirt paths that cut into the pines, but the best bet was a blacktop that headed north. Max took it, pushing the needle of his speedometer past eighty on the straightaways and braking hard into the turns. If Reed was still ahead of them, Max might be able to catch up. But after ten minutes of driving like a madman, no taillights appeared.

"Think he made us?" Max asked.

"I don't know."

Max pulled onto a side trail and parked. The night was heavy and dark, the moon hazy behind thin clouds. Max glanced at Lyle and saw the same slump of disappointment in his friend's shoulders that Max felt in his own.

"We have the phone number," Max said.

"But no way to ping it without coming clean with Bolger. And if I know Tate Bolger, it'll be you and I who go to jail, not Reed."

Max thought back to Niki's parting words: *If you need me, I'll be here for you.* Could he really ask her to cross the line again? To put her career in jeopardy for him? He had no right...but there was a child's life at stake.

Max swallowed his misgivings and said, "I may have an idea."

CHAPTER 33

Reed had to keep his head. His anger at Spud's betrayal had been screwing with him all night. He'd been confusing drink orders, forgetting to keep track of tabs. He had spent years putting his plan together, and Spud had thrown it out the window. The fool couldn't wait a few more weeks to get his money. He had no mind for strategy—no patience—and now Reed couldn't stop picturing his hands around Spud's throat.

But as he finally made his way toward the shack, the hum of the tires seemed to have a calming effect on Reed, and his anger dropped from a boil to a simmer. Reed needed Spud to come back from St. Paul. He would have to play nice. All would be forgiven, because the idiot was still useful. They could still salvage the plan if Spud returned.

If Spud didn't return, Reed would simply leave Grand Rapids earlier than he had planned to, making a swing down to St. Paul to tie up a loose end.

With his heart rate once again calm, Reed turned on the radio, his presets all tuned to country music stations. He sang along with a song about a woman who had done her man wrong. He could relate.

Sandy had been far worse than any country song could capture. Sure, it had been good in the beginning. Her introverted personality matched up well with his alpha-male tendencies. She could cook, and clean, and hold down a job. And while the sex wasn't mind-blowing, she acquiesced to some things she would have been embarrassed to admit.

But all that changed when Pip came along.

Sandy hadn't wanted to name him Reed Jr. She said it was because she didn't want the boy to grow up being called Little Reed, but Reed knew better. It was Sandy's first step toward pushing Reed away. Even after he won that argument and she wrote Reed Jr. on the birth certificate, she insisted on calling him Pip.

Soon after they'd brought Pip home, Sandy became demanding, as though having the kid around gave her some kind of authority. She refused to do household chores, telling Reed that if he wanted them done he could do them himself. She even went so far as to cut her hours at work so that she could spend more time with the boy. She didn't talk to Reed about it—she just did it. So Reed canceled her cell phone contract to make up for Sandy's reduction in income. Sandy blew a gasket.

She seemed to lose the ability to see or hear Reed. His shirts went unwashed even as Pip seemed to always have clean clothing. Meals that had once been steak and potatoes were now macaroni and cheese or chicken strips. And when it came to sex, although they slept in the same bed, they may as well have been in different rooms.

The final straw came when Pip was three. Reed had been at the bar when he met a woman named Carla. She was going through a divorce—her second—and couldn't seem to get enough of Reed. She squeezed his biceps, and licked her lips as she told him that he was the kind of guy most women were dying to meet. Reed could have taken Carla to a motel if he had wanted to. Instead, he went home to a woman who could barely look at him.

Why the hell didn't Sandy see him the way other women did? Why didn't she want to squeeze his arms or look into his eyes with admiration? He was tired of being treated like trash in his own home. He was tired of being second behind a three-year-old child.

The song ended and Reed looked into his rearview mirror as a pair of headlights pulled him from his memory. He turned off the radio to concentrate. Was it a squad car? No, they wouldn't be so far back. They would do like he used to do and drive up close to get a plate number. They would stay close enough to unnerve him, create a reason for a stop.

So it could be coincidence, but then again it might not be. He sped up slightly to increase the distance between them and it appeared that the headlights kept pace.

Reed knew those roads well. There were dozens of little trails cutting off the highway heading back to cabins or deer stands. He was approaching a curve that would hide him long enough to pull onto one. Then he could see if the car was following him.

The headlights disappeared as he rounded the curve and he cut sharply to the left, pulling onto a dirt trail and driving fifty feet into the woods before shutting off his engine and lights.

The vehicle passed by, although from that distance he could tell very little about it. It appeared to be an SUV, but what make or model he had no idea. He could discern no particular color, although he thought he saw a flash of red, maybe maroon. He searched his memory and could think of no one he knew that owned a red or maroon SUV.

After the car had passed, he exited his Tahoe and walked to the highway in time to see the taillights disappear in the distance. He gave thought to what had happened and could think of only two explanations. The first was that the car had been behind him by random chance, just another vehicle traveling the same route. The second was that someone was following him.

Had Bolger put him under surveillance? He wanted to kick himself for not continuing to spend his nights in Grand Rapids. It was a mistake to move into the shack. He needed Spud to get his ass back up there.

Reed was about to return to his Tahoe when he saw a halo in the distance. He slipped back into the woods and waited. What were the chances?

As the lights approached, Reed could see that the vehicle was traveling slowly. He squatted down behind a cluster of trees and watched it pass — an SUV, four doors, maroon.

Reed looked hard at the interior of the cab, hoping to make out a face. He could just see the passenger, lit by thin light from the dashboard — a man, older, with a familiar angle to his profile.

Was that . . . Lyle Voight?

CHAPTER 34

The next morning, on his drive to Minneapolis, Max ran through the discussion he was about to have with Niki, twice finding himself on the verge of turning around.

Under the Fourth Amendment, the ping of a cell phone location was considered a search, which meant that he needed probable cause that a crime had been committed, and probable cause that the phone number in his pocket would lead to evidence of that crime. Max imagined standing before a judge and laying out the facts. He had a missing woman and child, and an asshole ex-husband. But that woman was seen emptying out her bank account the day she vanished. She'd taken her clothing, called in sick to work, and used her credit card at a gas station in Minneapolis. Where was the crime?

The ex-husband had a foolproof alibi, but he carried a second phone, inspected the underside of his car, and drove north into the woods instead of staying at his house. He'd bought groceries that weren't found when his house was illegally searched.

Sandy had a relationship that wasn't one to run away from. They'd just purchased an expensive couch. Max had a video of a vehicle that might be Sandy's with a man driving it, but no proof of whether Sandy was in that vehicle.

And Max had a father who was certain his daughter wouldn't run away.

What he had was a mix of facts and opinions that, if presented to a judge, would have gotten him kicked out of her chambers.

But there was an exception to the rule. If an officer had articulable grounds to believe that a person's life was in danger, they could bypass the judge and request the ping directly—the missing dementia-patient scenario. The request came with a paper trail, however, and that paper trail would lead straight to Niki.

How could he ask Niki to risk her job for what he felt in his gut? Yet every time Max contemplated turning around, he thought about Pip. How could he live with himself if he didn't do everything possible to save the boy?

Max waited for Niki in the parking lot of Ida's Diner. He had hoped that choosing Ida's might stir nostalgia in his old partner, soften her up for his unthinkable request.

When Niki arrived, her first words were "Ida's, huh? I haven't been here since you mailed me your badge and fell off the face of the earth."

Picking Ida's may have been a mistake. "You're not gonna let that go, are you?"

"You're right. I should be more like you and get over my past."

Damn, she could cut to the quick.

They sat at a booth, and when Marilyn came to get their orders, she looked at them for a moment before saying, "Well, I haven't seen you two in a coon's age."

Max considered mentioning his earlier visit, but thought better of it and said, "I've been out of town."

"That's one way to say it," Niki muttered.

"Well, welcome back," Marilyn said. "It's the same menu, but if you need a minute..."

Niki ordered for them both. "Steak and eggs all around. Mine over easy and well done, his scrambled and medium rare." Niki smiled at Max, showing off. She knew him in a way no other human could. And she wasn't about to let him forget it.

"And two coffees," Max added. "Black, no cream or sugar." He knew her as well. He would have ordered dark roast for her if they carried it, but Ida's Diner wasn't that kind of place.

When Marilyn left, Niki asked, "So how's the investigation going?" Max was relieved to see a genuine spark of interest in her eyes.

"We have some floating pieces, but I was hoping you might help me put them together. Start with the disappearance of Sandy Voight. She and her son, Pip, haven't been heard from for a week now. Emptied out her bank account and cleaned out her closet, so on the one hand, there's no hard evidence to support foul play."

"But you think that there was foul play?"

"I do."

"Do you have a suspect in mind?"

"Her ex-husband, Reed Harris, a former sheriff's deputy. The divorce was ugly. It came to a head one night when Reed beat the boy and the mother. He did jail time for it. Lost his badge. Lost custody."

"How long ago?"

"Three years. Reed's off probation now and working at a bar up in Grand Rapids."

"Where was the ex when the boy and his mom went missing?"

"At a casino with a thousand cameras capturing his every move."

Max could almost see the wheels turning in Niki's head. "So to do this he would have had to have an accomplice."

"I think the person driving that Passport—the guy whose arm you saw—is that accomplice."

"And that brings you to me because . . . ?"

Max pulled the slip of paper from his pocket. "I have a phone number that I think belongs to the accomplice."

"Where did you get it?"

"It's from Reed Harris's burner phone—or a phone that I believe is a burner. Beyond that, it's probably best that you don't know."

"All these years and you still don't trust me." She looked at her mug as she lightly swirled the coffee inside it.

"I trust you with my life." Max leaned toward her as he spoke, hoping that she could hear the sincerity in his voice.

Niki raised her gaze. "But not your secrets."

Her words sent ripples of regret through Max. It was so easy to forget he'd been a different man when he was with Niki, so easy to slip back into his old skin.

Max dropped his head and almost pulled the slip of paper back, but Niki placed her hand firmly on top of his. "What do you need?"

"I need to track down the phone attached to that number." He released the paper.

Niki tapped a finger absentmindedly on the table as she looked at it. "And your probable cause is...?"

"Too weak to take to a judge. But I believe I have exigent circumstances."

"You believe?"

"I've been working this through in my head and I keep coming to one single conclusion. If I'm right...Reed Harris orchestrated the murder of his ex-wife so that he could kidnap his son."

"But you have no evidence to prove that."

"No, but it's the most reasonable conclusion. He had the only motive to harm his ex-wife. She put him in jail for assault and took his son away. He goes out of his way to set up an alibi, going to a casino after a long shift at the bar. If he can convince the world that she ran away, then he's in the clear. He ditches her car and her clothing and hides his son away until the smoke clears. It's the only scenario that makes any sense. All he needs is an accomplice to commit the act and stay with the boy. And to communicate with his accomplice, he would need a burner phone, which he has."

"You *think* it's a burner phone. And where's your proof that she didn't just run off with another man?"

"She hasn't called her folks. She didn't tell any friends. She and her boyfriend were getting along just fine. They were saving up to buy a house together—and she just bought a new couch, four grand, days before she disappeared. And you saw Sandy's SUV. You saw that Sandy wasn't the one driving. That driver used her credit card to buy gas, and there's been no use of it since. She dropped off the face of the earth. Something's wrong. Reed might have kidnapped her as part of some twisted fantasy, but I don't think that's the case. I think she's dead. Either way, that phone number is the key."

Marilyn brought their food, set the plates on the table, and refilled their coffee cups. Max was glad to have something to look at other than the doubt in Niki's eyes. He cut into his steak and took the first bite, the meat tasteless in his mouth.

They ate in silence for a while before Niki said, "This is no small favor, Max."

"I know."

"If you're wrong about this, it'll come back to bite me pretty hard."

"I know. You don't have to do it—and if you don't, I'll understand."

"Your argument is chock-full of what you believe to be true; your supporting facts are tenuous at best. You want me to put my ass—my career—on the line for an instinct?"

Max said, "I shouldn't have asked."

They returned to eating in silence, and Max wished he hadn't come. But after a few bites, Niki said, "When I came to Homicide, I thought I had it all figured out. I could look at a crime scene like I was looking at a piece of cloth. I could tell you the material, the color—hell, I could even give you a thread count. That's all I thought I needed to be a good detective."

She averted her gaze as if working up to a confession, her fork carving small lines in her eggs. "But then you came along and taught me a whole new way to look at things. Where I saw thread counts, you saw folds and stretches. You could look at that cloth and see in a twist of the fabric whether it had been used to strangle someone or smother them. You had this . . . incredible intuition. It was like you could see right through walls, and lies . . . and people. God, how I admired you for that."

And Max had thought that he couldn't feel any smaller.

"It was a thing of beauty to watch you follow your instincts. And I went along... diving in even when I thought the water might be too shallow. Time after time you pulled something from nothing. All because your gut told you so."

Niki paused as if to think something through one last time. Then she said, "I guess what I'm saying is that if you tell me that this woman is dead and her son has been kidnapped—if that's what you truly believe happened—I'll trust you."

Even though everything in his gut told him that Sandy was dead, Max hesitated. Had he lost his edge living in the woods? He needed to get this right. He closed his eyes and said, "She's dead and the boy's been kidnapped—and I need your help to save him."

Niki gave Max a sad smile. "Okay. I'll do the ping, tonight, after hours. I don't want anybody around to ask questions."

CHAPTER 35

A t eleven that night, Max sat in his car outside of City Hall and waited for the last of the detectives to leave. Niki's text came at 11:15: Come on in.

She met him at the door and they walked the marbled hallway that led to Homicide together, their steps echoing in the emptiness. Max had walked that hallway so many times in his life that it had become just another passageway, but now it seemed longer, and larger, and more impressive than he remembered. Niki walked with purpose, seemingly unaffected by the dubious nature of their visit.

She stopped at room 108 and unlocked the door to the anteroom, then punched a code onto a keypad, releasing the lock on the second door into the unit. Max had watched over her shoulder, curious if the code was still the same. It wasn't.

The homicide unit had two-person cubicles in which teams of detectives sat back to back. Niki walked to the one they used to share and took her seat at her same old desk. Max put his hand on his old chair but didn't sit. He was an intruder, an imposter. Worse, an actual murderer creeping around the sanctuary of those who hunted men like him. A wave of self-loathing hit him so hard that it nearly buckled his knees. This was why he belonged in the woods.

Now he was spreading his infection to Niki, corrupting her, asking her to skirt the law, a weakness that was becoming a habit with him.

He had been such a Boy Scout, living by a code that included keeping his relationship with Niki professional. She was his partner and nothing more.

Yet how many times had he sat in that chair and let his mind get lost in the scent of her perfume? Returning to their cubicle, he couldn't pretend it hadn't happened. Coffee in the mornings, lunches at Ida's, a beer after work, and always those eyes that looked up at him with such respect. And the jokes, her wit, her smile—he couldn't deny that he looked forward to each day that he worked with her. But those were behind them. He'd ended them.

Max picked up a framed photo of a man with a wife and two children, sitting on the corner of his old desk. "Is this your new partner?"

Niki turned in her chair. "That's Matty."

He was younger than Max, with dark hair and features, and he smiled like a man who was downright giddy to have his wife and kids around him.

"Handsome guy," Max said.

"I'm sure his wife thinks so."

"Is he smart?"

"He's no Niki Vang, but who is?"

"You'll get no disagreement from me."

Niki smiled and received her compliment. "He's dogged," she said. "And he loves research. Ask him to find someone's employment history or family tree, and he's as happy as a puppy with a bone."

"How about in the field?"

"He's getting there. He's no Max Rupert...but who is?" She smiled again. "Where's that phone number?"

Max handed her the piece of paper, and Niki unfolded it.

"Just in case they ask, the boy's name is...?"

"Reed Harris Jr.," Max said. "But he goes by Pip."

"How old?"

"Six."

"Is there a missing-person report?"

"His grandfather Lyle Voight reported him missing in Itasca County. The sheriff up there isn't acting on it, but there's a report."

"Okay. I'll do the ping. It'll take a few minutes to hear back."

As Niki made her call, Max stepped away from the cubicle to update Lyle, who was staying at Max's cabin. "Lyle, we're starting the ping."

Lyle sounded like he had been sleeping, his consonants blurring together as he spoke. "Yeah. Good. Um . . . will they give me an address, or just coordinates, or . . . ?"

"We'll get GPS coordinates here. I'll plug them in and get the address for you. It'll likely be out in the woods, isolated, so I want you to sit tight until I get back. We can drive out together. I don't want them seeing your headlights and getting spooked."

"I don't want to wait. There's no reason to wait."

Lyle still sounded fuzzy, and Max wondered if he might have been drinking. Max had empathy for his friend, knowing the headwinds that Lyle faced. Lyle had to know that Sandy was likely dead, even though neither he nor Max had ever said those words out loud to each other. Still, Lyle's impatience could throw their work and Niki's sacrifice into jeopardy. It had been reckless to follow Reed the night before. Max should have put his foot down but didn't. For a moment, Max questioned whether he should give the coordinates to Lyle at all. The last thing he needed was for Lyle to go off half cocked, hell-bent on appeasing his grief.

"We need to take our time, Lyle. We need to do this right."

"I'll just drive by and get the lay of the land."

"We go together," Max said.

There was silence on the other end of the line. Finally Lyle said, "Whatever you say."

"It'll take a little while to get the information from the provider, so sit tight and I'll call you back." He returned to the cubicle where Niki sat waiting.

"Everything good on your end?" Niki asked.

"Yeah. Lyle's a bit...impatient. This whole thing's got him twisted up inside. He'll be okay."

Max hovered at the opening to the cubicle, unsure what to do. Niki must have sensed his discomfort. "You can sit in Matty's chair. He won't mind."

Max nodded his thanks. The chair felt like an old friend.

"You miss it?" Niki asked.

"The chair?"

"Being a detective. Solving crimes. The hunt."

If he had been truthful, he would have told Niki that he missed it more than he could bear. It was as if he'd lost a limb and hadn't realized that it was missing until Lyle showed up at his cabin. But this wasn't his world anymore. It wasn't his chair or his cubicle, and it never could be again. He didn't deserve it. So, Max lied. "There's peace in the woods, a slowness that makes me feel like I'm living with purpose. I don't know how to explain it, but...that's my home now."

Niki looked away. He had hurt her again.

The phone rang and Niki answered it. Max looked over her shoulder as she wrote two strings of numbers, longitudes and latitudes. Before hanging up, she typed the numbers into the search box of the map on her computer. She pressed enter and a dot appeared, but it was not in northern Minnesota. Instead, the dot appeared in St. Paul.

"That's not right," Max whispered.

Niki spoke to the person on the other end of the phone. "Could you read those numbers to me again?" She touched a pen to each number on her tablet, making no corrections. "And you're sure you typed the correct phone number?" There was a pause and then, "Okay, thank you."

"That's the correct address," Niki said. "Is it possible that it wasn't a burner phone, or that he was simply calling a friend here in the Twin Cities?"

Max felt profoundly embarrassed. How had his instincts grown so dull? The whole trip had been a wild-goose chase—and to have it all play out in front of Niki. He needed to be put out to pasture—or better yet, shot. He had put Niki's career at risk for nothing.

"I'm sorry, Niki. I thought..." He shook his head in disgust. "I should let Lyle know."

He couldn't bring himself to tell Lyle that he had screwed up, so he sent a text: Stand down. Wrong number. I'll explain when I get back.

While he was texting Lyle, Niki had been typing on her computer. Max looked over her shoulder again. She was accessing a database that collected the names and addresses of crime suspects, witnesses, and victims.

"The house belongs to a woman named Olivia Molinar...sixty-two years old and—" Niki stopped and leaned in to the screen as if something had caught her attention. "Holy shit."

"What?"

"Olivia Molinar was murdered in this home seven months ago."

CHAPTER 36

Max hadn't planned to spend the night in Minneapolis. He had expected the ping to locate the second burner phone somewhere in the Northwoods. They had to be keeping Pip nearby if Reed was hauling groceries out to him. If Max's intuition had been on the mark, right now he would be driving north, with an address and a plan, certain that Pip would be back with his grandfather by morning.

But tracing that phone to St. Paul, to a house where a woman had been murdered, had shattered Max's mental picture. If anything, this was bigger than he'd thought. The two crimes had to be linked somehow. Max didn't believe in coincidences. But that meant at least one more day in the Cities for him, and for Pip, one more night as a missing child.

Before leaving the Homicide unit, Niki dug into Olivia Molinar's case. The murder had been in St. Paul—Ramsey County jurisdiction—so what they had at their fingertips was little more than what had been reported in the press.

Molinar lived on a street lined with older Victorian and craftsman homes, the kind of well-tended neighborhood that would have neighbors telling TV reporters "You never think something like this could happen here." In the early-morning hours of April fifth, a neighbor noticed Mrs. Molinar's front door hanging open. Responding officers found Olivia dead. The cause of her death had not been released to the public, but the internal database listed her as the victim of a homicide. No arrests had been reported.

Max had gone to City Hall expecting a quick answer only to find another trail of bread crumbs. Exasperation ballooned in his chest. "I need to get a look at the Molinar file," he said.

"Sure, tomorrow morning just stop by St. Paul PD and show 'em your badge and—Oh, wait, that's right, you don't have a badge."

"You're enjoying this, aren't you?"

"Hey, you made your bed. I'm just the stalker peeking in the window to watch you toss and turn."

"Will you go to St. Paul with me?"

Niki raised an eyebrow like a mother waiting for the magic word.

"Please?"

"Was that so hard?"

"I promise, this will be my last favor."

"Promises, promises. Where are you staying?"

"I'll get a motel."

"Or . . . you should stay with me. We can brainstorm before bed."

Max had picked Niki up at home numerous times, but he'd always stayed outside, on the front stoop. It was one of his rules. She was attractive, and female, and his partner. If he wasn't careful, rumors would grow like weeds, and he was determined to protect her from those rumors, kill them before they took root.

When Max hesitated, Niki gave him an innocent pout and said, "I promise I'll behave."

"I wouldn't want you to go to any trouble," he said carefully.

Niki looked at him with deadpan eyes. "*Now* you're worried about my troubles?"

"Touché. I'd be happy to stay at your place." He felt a tingle at the thought of lying down in a bed so close to her, as though some forbidden fruit lay just beyond his reach.

Niki's house was small, but cozy. Constructed early to mid-century, it stood two stories tall, filled with intricate woodwork and built-in shelves. The living room had a stately fireplace, although its wood floors were covered with a tarp. She was in the process of painting the walls, going from off-white to a royal blue.

Max pointed at a wall half painted. "You missed a spot," he said.

"Yeah. I got interrupted by a blockhead with a problem."

"I like the blue. Dark fits you."

"You should see the basement. Painted it black and bolted shackles to the wall. Got a torture rack on backorder with Amazon. I'm hoping it gets here by Christmas."

"A girl's gotta have a hobby."

"Do you think that makes it officially a dungeon?"

"Does it have egress windows?"

"No."

"Then I think you're good."

She showed him into the kitchen and dining room, bright white with royal blue tile for the backsplash. On a shelf against the wall Max saw pictures of Niki's mother and father. In one, her parents were young and her mother held a baby that Max figured had to be Niki. In another the couple stood beside a kindly looking man with a pastor's collar. Niki had told Max about how her family, refugees from Vietnam, had been sponsored by a church in St. Paul. Max thought that the man in the picture might be that pastor.

In the corner, he saw a picture of him and Niki. They were in a room — an apartment, maybe — and he stood beside Niki, his hand on his chin, as though rubbing it. She was bent with her hands on her knees. They both looked at something on the ground just out of the frame. Max had never seen that picture before, and he looked closer to try to remember when it might have been taken. Niki must have noticed.

"That was our first case together," Niki said. "The crime scene photographer took that. I had mentioned to him that it was my first day in Homicide, so he gave it to me as a memento."

"I would have thought..." Max stopped.

"What?"

"I would have thought you'd have cropped me out of it."

Niki walked to the stove and put a kettle on for tea. Without turning to face Max, she asked, "Would you have thrown it away if the roles were reversed?"

Max tried to imagine that. What if Niki had disappeared?

When he didn't answer right away, he saw Niki's shoulders settle, like a child who had just been let down. "No. I would not have thrown it away," he said, finally. He knew that those were the words she wanted to hear, and as he said them, they felt honest.

"Want some tea? A little chamomile to slow the gears down?"

"Sure."

Max sat at the table while Niki gathered cups and tea and honey. The room had gone silent, so Max filled the void. "Whoever we meet with in the morning will want to know why we're looking into the Molinar murder," he said. "We probably shouldn't tell them about the ping. I don't want you getting tangled up in my..."

"Shenanigans?"

"Sure, let's go with shenanigans. I'll just say that a confidential source gave us a tip and leave it at that."

Niki joined Max at the table, sitting across from him. "I can work with that," she said.

"What should we say about...who I am?"

"Seriously, Max? Everyone in the St. Paul Homicide division is going to know who you are, if not by face, then by reputation. Believe it or not, you were something of a legend."

"I could stay in the car."

"We'll tell them that you're consulting with me," Niki said. "We're trying to solve a crime. No one's going to care that you don't have a badge as long as you're with me."

"Watching out for me...just like the old days."

"No, this isn't like the old days, Max." She traced a finger along the tabletop. "In the old days, you wouldn't be sitting in my kitchen waiting for tea to boil."

Max felt his cheeks warm up.

"Don't think I didn't notice how you always kept the distance between us," she said.

"We were partners. I...didn't want people to think..." Max could see no way to say it without coming across like a patronizing fool.

"They were going to think that regardless. But you made the decision for both of us. You with your rules and your walls. Getting to know you was like...walking through a maze."

"I thought I was doing the right thing. We were such good partners. I didn't want to mess things up."

"And how did that work out?"

"Why didn't you say something?" Max asked, not sure if he was ready for where this conversation seemed to be headed.

"Would you have listened?"

"Probably not."

"Besides, those walls weren't there just to protect my reputation, were they?"

Max didn't see where Niki was going at first, but then it came to him. "Jenni."

Niki nodded. "It was like there were three of us in that squad car. But I was fine with it. She was the love of your life. You were grieving. Truth is, I admired the way you held on to her. I mean, who wouldn't want to be loved like that?"

Niki stood and went to the stove, where the teakettle was puffing out small breaths of steam, building up to its boil. She kept her back to Max as she spoke. "You had a road to walk, and I was willing to wait. But then you disappeared." She gave a light sigh as though surrendering something precious. "When you left...it hurt."

"I'm sorry. I..."

"I used to drive past your house—after you left. I kept thinking that I'd see a light on. I kept hoping that you'd come back. Then one day I saw the For Sale sign. I cried. I just couldn't believe it."

The kettle began to chirp.

Had he known how she really felt? He thought back and remembered the laughter and the glances, the unspoken subtleties behind the playful banter. Yeah, he had known, but he had shut it down, refused to see what was right in front of his face. All those rules—and for what? And now it was too late. He had murdered a man. There could be no coming back from that.

"I know you don't understand," Max said, "but...it's better if you keep your distance. I'm not the man I used to be."

"Still building your walls...still hiding from the world." She spoke softly, almost to herself.

"I belong in the woods," he insisted. "I'm no good here."

The teakettle began to whistle hard and loud. Niki turned the burner off and poured the water into the cups, the tea bags floating to the top. She put the kettle down and held still for a moment before turning, a cup in each hand.

"I think I'm gonna drink mine in my room," she said. "We have a long day tomorrow." She put Max's cup on the table. "Your room is the last door on the right. And if you wake up before me, you're in charge of making coffee." She smiled, but there was nothing behind it.

Max smiled back: it felt like charity.

She started out of the kitchen, but at the hallway door paused to look at Max. "You can go to the woods if you want to...hide from the world, from me...But, Max...you have to understand by now, right? You'll never be able to hide from yourself."

With that, Niki walked away.

CHAPTER 37

Spud wasn't answering his phone. In the thirty hours since he took off, Reed had left only three messages, calm entreaties to get together, the kind of innocuous statement that would mean nothing to an investigator. But behind the banal words, Reed seethed. "You stupid...goddamned...dumbass...son of a bitch!"

The outbursts did little to clear the maelstrom of thoughts that swirled around in his head all day. Two men in a maroon SUV had followed Reed. What if he hadn't been paying attention? What if he hadn't pulled onto that trail to hide? What if Bolger had men watching his house? Or maybe they were using surveillance cameras. His enemies were closing in. It was time to get the backup plan ready, just in case.

Reed had a thousand things to do before the sun came up. And because he knew that he might not make it back to the shack before Pip woke, he had locked Pip in his bedroom, propping a broom handle across the door frame and tying the doorknob to the stick. Pip would probably cry once he discovered that he'd been locked in, but even that couldn't hold a candle to what Reed had endured as a child—sitting for hours in the chill of a dark root cellar for not eating all the food on his plate. Pip never had a belt taken to his skin for misbehaving or felt the blow of a steel-toe boot in his back. It was high time that Pip learned that the world was a hard place.

Reed drove slowly down the river road to his house, searching the trees for any sign of a spy. He parked in the driveway and went around the side of the house to watch the road for a few minutes. No movement.

Once inside, he moved with efficiency, gathering the gear he and Pip would need to survive in the woods. Reed had been strategic in how he had stored it, keeping his stuff inside, scattered throughout various closets, but storing Pip's gear under a concrete slab in the backyard. Had Bolger found a child's camping equipment when he searched the house, it would have been hard to explain.

Reed had purchased expensive sleeping bags for him and the boy— rated for twenty below zero—but far less expensive gear for Spud. If Spud managed to still be around for this part of the plan, he would have to make do. It pained Reed to think of dragging Spud along, but the man was strong; if he carried the boy they could move faster.

Reed brought Pip's sleeping bag and clothing from the concrete slab into the house and laid the items on the table next to his own gear. He had made a mental inventory of what they would need, and as he worked through his checklist, something caught his eye.

A week earlier, Reed had laid a stack of bills and receipts in the middle of his dining room table, the kind of papers that might attract the attention of an officer conducting a search. Buried in the stack was a photo of him and Tate, a picture he had taken on the morning authorities found Tracy Progaski's body in the Tioga Mine Pit. He had left the picture there for Tate to find.

Tracy Progaski had been a married woman, five years older, and she'd had an eye for the eighteen-year-old Tate. She and Tate would get together every now and again to have sex in the cab of Tate's Dodge pickup. Tracy tended bar and her husband worked the night shift at a paper mill, so it hadn't been hard for them to sneak away.

Reed was Tate's best friend, and what good was having sex with a married woman if you couldn't brag about it to your best friend? Somewhere in those conversations, it had occurred to Reed that he might get a little of that action as well. He didn't have Tate's looks, or his charm, but he wasn't some half-formed troll, either. So Reed went to the bar where Tracy worked, ordered a Coke, and did his best to flirt, complimenting her smile, her looks, moving slowly as he tested the water. In time, he became emboldened and told her that her ass had the perfect amount of jiggle. At that, she stepped back and grinned, and something dark washed across her face.

"Hey, Stanley." She directed her words to a good ol' boy at the end of the bar. "This kid here just told me that my ass has the perfect amount of jiggle." She turned her back to the man, stuck her butt out, and bounced it. "What do you think?"

The guy named Stanley laughed, exposing two missing front teeth. "I think you'd better stop jiggling, or your boy's liable to mess himself."

There were a dozen people at the bar, and they all got a good laugh out of that one—all of them except for Reed, of course. He wanted to climb over the bar and beat Tracy with a beer mug and then shove the broken shards into Stanley's neck. Instead, he stood and walked out of the bar. That was the night he decided that Tracy Progaski would find her way into the Tioga Pit.

The plan had been an easy one. Reed knew that Tate would go back to the well at some point, so all Reed needed to do was wait until that trip coincided with a night that Tate's parents would be out of town.

Tate and Tracy had a routine. He'd pick Tracy up in the parking lot of the bar after she closed, and the two would drive out to the woods. When they finished, he would drop her off back at the bar.

Reed's plan began at 11:45, when he filled his truck with gas at a particular gas station, one that was on the way to the land where he and Tate liked to hunt deer. That would be the start of their alibi. After that, he backtracked to the bar and put a small board with a nail in it under Tracy's back tire—passenger side, where she wouldn't see it. Then he drove out of sight to wait for her to finish her shift and for Tate to show up and whisk her away in his truck.

Reed stayed hidden, waiting, and when they returned after having sex, Tate dropped Tracy off at her car—no lingering kiss goodbye, just a wave and a smile and Tate was gone. When she backed out of her parking spot, the nail punctured the tire, creating a slow leak. Tracy lived out in the country, on roads that had few if any travelers at three in the morning. She would be in the middle of nowhere when the tire finally gave up the last of its air.

Reed followed her out of town, a roll of duct tape, a few zip ties, a pistol, and his deer rifle in the truck beside him. He came upon Tracy and her flat tire, offered to help her before she had a chance to call someone on her cell phone. It had been almost too easy.

Two hours later—with Tracy's body now floating in the Tioga Pit—Reed banged on his friend's door, waking Tate from a deep sleep.

"We're going hunting, goddammit," Reed said.

"Jesus, Reed. What time is it?"

"Get your camo and let's go. If we hurry, we can be out there before sunup."

"Are you serious?"

"Don't tell me she wore you out?"

Tate grinned at the inside joke. "I don't know what you're talking about."

"Then get your ass in gear. I'll be in the truck."

Reed took a picture of Tate once they got into the woods. The picture would have a date and time signature, metadata to prove that they had been hunting. He would use the gas receipt to show that they had gone out to the woods long before Tracy Progaski got off work. On top of all that, shooting the four-point buck had been sheer luck.

When they got back to town, news had already spread about Tracy's body being found in the Tioga Mining Pit, and rumor had it that whoever put her there had done terrible things to her. Tate became a ball of mush as grief and panic fought for the upper hand. The dumbass wanted to go to the cops and confess to the affair.

"You were the last person to see her alive," Reed had told him, "except for the killer. They'll never believe you didn't do it." After a great deal of hand-wringing, they worked out the details of their alibi, one that Reed had planned out weeks before. This had been his true genius. When the sheriff came to question Tate — following up on the rumored affair — Tate said that he was hunting deer with Reed.

Tate walked away believing that Reed had lied to save his ass, when in truth, Tate had been the one to lie, giving Reed the alibi that he needed. That twist still made Reed smile.

That's why Reed had placed that picture on the table — the one with them posing with the deer. He wanted Tate to remember his debt.

But the picture had been moved. Someone had been in his house.

Reed looked around as if he might see some clue to explain the moved picture — and he did. If Tate Bolger had entered his house under the lawful authority of a search warrant, he was required to leave a copy of the warrant behind along with an inventory of items taken. No such documents had been left. That meant that it hadn't been Bolger in his house.

Lyle Voight? That crazy old man? Reed walked around and saw other things that had been moved: the mouse for his computer, a folder where he kept his tax documents. One of the drawers of his desk was ajar, and while he couldn't swear to it, he was pretty sure he had closed all of his drawers before he left.

It had to be Lyle.

The son of a bitch was hunting him.

CHAPTER 38

Niki's guest room had a bed, and that was about all that separated it from a storage room. She had moved some of the furniture from the living room in to prepare for repainting, and there were boxes and books spread all around. But Max didn't mind the clutter. The bed was comfortable and warm—yet he struggled to fall asleep.

Light from the streetlamps escaped past the edge of a curtain, crossing the ceiling above him, thin and long like the blade of a sword. But that wasn't what kept him awake. It was Niki's words. They hung in the air above him as he lay staring at the ceiling and echoed in his head when he closed his eyes.

Was he hiding? From whom? That wasn't why he'd gone to the cabin—was it? As he tried to understand what she meant, he was reminded of the old Wolf Man movies with Lon Chaney, Jr., the way Chaney hid from the moon to keep the monster inside him from coming out. The Wolf Man wanted to believe that he was protecting the world from who he could become, but in truth, he was trying to avoid his darkest nature.

That couldn't be him, could it? The man who stood on that frozen lake was an aberration. Max wasn't the Wolf Man. He was a man who'd temporarily lost his way, a runner who stumbled. His absolution would come in time, he was sure of it.

He tried to silence his thoughts by remembering the man he had been before Mikhail, the man he had been with Niki. He thought about the happiness he felt working with her, the thrust and parry of their conversations as they waded through those serious cases. It was the kind of job that could take a toll on a person's psyche, but Niki had somehow made it the best part of his day—of his life. There had been a connection between them that went beyond partnership. He had always known that, but like a disciplined penitent, he'd denied himself that happiness.

But as he lay there, trying to find sleep, he couldn't help but mourn the loss of what might have been.

In the morning, Max found it strange, waking up to the sound of Niki showering. He made the bed and went to the kitchen to start the coffee, nervous about how things would feel after what had been shared the night before. But when Niki padded to the kitchen in bare feet and her bathrobe, she greeted Max as though the night before hadn't happened.

"You didn't forget that I like it strong?" she said.

"Just slightly thinner than mud. I remember."

Max concentrated on pouring the water into the coffeemaker, but she stood close enough that he could smell the faint aroma of coconut-scented shampoo. She reached up into a cupboard, retrieved a Tupperware bowl, and peeled the lid back to reveal several sticks of biscotti.

"Ah, my favorite," Max said with genuine surprise.

"You got me hooked on them."

"No one can say that I wasn't a positive influence."

The repartee came so naturally when they were together. It made him sad to know that he would soon be leaving her once again.

"Yeah, when I grow old I want to be just like you." She walked away before the sting of that one could ease.

The St. Paul Police Department was housed in a building that had all the architectural charm of a brick box. Max had been there many times, coordinating cases that crossed jurisdictional boundaries. Niki had called ahead to set up today's meeting, and while he knew some of the detectives, the woman that he and Niki were to meet with didn't ring a bell. When Detective Macey Greene greeted them, Niki introduced Max as a consultant.

"Max Rupert?" Detective Greene gave him a closer look. "You used to work Homicide in Minneapolis, didn't you?"

Max smiled. "Niki and I were partners."

"I attended a lecture you gave on interviewing techniques back when I was a baby detective. I heard . . . well . . . there was a rumor going around that you . . . took a hiatus."

"I retired."

"Are you doing private-eye shit now?"

"Something like that."

Macey led them to an interview room where a file lay on the table. "I don't blame you. The hours. The pay. I hear it's better in the private world."

"And yet," Niki said, "here he is. Some things just can't get done without us."

Macey laughed. "You tell it, sister."

Macey opened the file. "I can't say we have all that much on this one. Mrs. Molinar was sixty-two years old. Lived alone. Widowed. Her late husband left her pretty well off. She had investments worth a couple million bucks. Owned thirty-two units of apartments, had a healthy stock portfolio. She could have been living in a McMansion in White Bear Lake if she wanted, but she lived very modestly."

"Robbery?" Niki asked.

"That's how it looks. A neighbor found her door wide open on the morning of April fifth. Patrol officers did a welfare check and found Mrs. Molinar dead near the front entryway. She'd been strangled with a nylon stocking."

"Any DNA on the stocking?" Niki asked.

"Just the victim's. No suspicious fingerprints, but we found shoe prints in the mud outside the garage and on the floor of the garage. Men's size-nine Adidas. We have the garage as the point of entry. It abuts an alley in the back. Beyond that is a park—nothing more than a patch of grass with some playground equipment. We think he might have waited in the park until he saw her leave. A glass pane in the side door of the garage was busted out."

Max said, "Planned attack or random?"

Greene bit at her lower lip as she considered her answer. "We've been going back and forth on that one. Molinar had a safe in her closet—bolted to the floor. The killer found the safe, but hadn't brought tools to pry it up, which suggests that he wasn't planning on busting a safe loose when he entered. He used an axe and crowbar from Molinar's garage to chip the floor away until he could pull the safe free. It looks like he had a dickens of a time. He also took her jewelry box and some electronics. We think she came home and caught the burglar in the act."

"Where was Mrs. Molinar when he broke in?" Niki asked.

"She played canasta with friends every Thursday night. She was there from five until eight. We think she surprised the burglar when she got home around eight-fifteen. Time of death fits that scenario."

"He was there that long?" Max asked.

"Getting that safe pried out of the floor took some time. It's possible he just happened by, but I tend to believe he saw her leave. He made himself a sandwich in the middle of it all, too. We found mustard and bread and turkey out in the kitchen."

"Suspects?" Niki asked.

"None that fit the bill. She hired a contractor to fix some electrical issues. That was about a month before the murder. He would have been in her bedroom, so he could have seen the jewelry box, and then found the safe after he broke in later."

"Alibi?"

"No, but . . . I don't know. He's semi-retired. Been working all his life. No priors. Everyone says he's as honest as the day's long. My gut tells me he's not the guy. He's on the list, but only because we needed names to put there."

"Anyone else?"

"She had a son, Peter." Macey dug through her reports to find a file with the name Peter Molinar on the tab. "Thirty-four. Never married. He works for a landscaping company in New Hope."

"He would have known about the safe," Niki said. "And the canasta game on Thursday."

"That occurred to us too, but why bust it from the floor if you can just open it?"

"To throw off suspicion," Max said.

"He had an airtight alibi. He was up north, playing slots at a casino." Max and Niki shared a look.

"What?" Detective Greene asked.

It was Max who spoke. "I'm here, unofficially, because of a missing woman. On the morning she disappeared, her ex-husband was conveniently on camera at a casino too."

"And you think your guy's tied to the Molinar case?"

Niki looked at Max to answer.

"I have a confidential source. It's thin, but we have reason to believe that a phone number tied to my case out of Itasca County is connected with the house where Mrs. Molinar died."

"A source?" Greene said. "What's the nature of that source?"

"I'm afraid I can't reveal that right now."

"So all you have is a source that you can't talk about?"

"That and the fact that both men have identical alibis."

"Can you connect the two men?" Greene asked.

"As far as I know, they're strangers."

Niki's eyes lit up. "Jesus Christ."

"What?" Max asked.

"*Strangers on a Train?*"

Max looked at Niki and tried to figure out where the train part came in.

Niki said, "The old movie — *Strangers on a Train*."

Greene nodded, her eyes narrowing as though she had picked up on Niki's reference.

Max shrugged his confusion.

Niki said, "They did a remake of it with Danny DeVito and...um..."

"Billy Crystal," Greene said.

Max tried to remember the movie. "What's it about?"

"Two guys meet on a train." Niki said. "They have no connection to each other, but they get to talking and in time learn that each has someone they want murdered. So they make a pact. They will each kill the other guy's target on a date and time that would give the other a perfect alibi."

Max pondered out loud. "Reed Harris killed Mrs. Molinar when Peter was at a casino playing slots, and Peter Molinar killed Sandy Voight while Reed is on camera playing blackjack."

"It's a reasonable theory," Niki said, "but we'd need to prove a connection."

"Can I see Peter's jacket?" Max asked.

Detective Greene handed Max a folder with Peter's interview statement and background information. Max flipped through, perusing for any clue that Peter might know Reed Harris. Three pages in, Max came upon a booking photo taken of Peter Molinar three years earlier. He had been arrested on charges of theft and possession of stolen property. The man looked at the camera with an expression of disgust, as though getting arrested was far beneath his station.

Then Max saw the location of Molinar's arrest—Itasca County. He'd spent time in jail in Grand Rapids.

Max looked at Niki and smiled.

CHAPTER 39

D etective Macey Greene led the procession to the house where Olivia Molinar had been murdered. The house didn't scream wealth, but the delicate woodwork that framed the porch and gables suggested that the owner had worked hard to keep the turn-of-the-century home in pristine condition.

Before driving to the house, Macey and Niki had put together a plan. They would shake Peter Molinar in the hopes that he might make a call to Reed Harris. While they didn't have probable cause for a search warrant, they thought they might have enough to get a subpoena for cell phone tower data. If Peter made that call from the house, it would expose the number of Reed's burner phone.

But Max knew subpoenas took time and getting the records from the providers took even more time. Reed might be gone by then and Pip might never be found. So Max came up with his own plan, one that he kept secret from Niki and Macey Greene.

On the drive to the Molinar house, Max placed a call to Lyle. "I need you to check on a Peter Molinar. He was arrested in Itasca County three years ago."

"Sure," Lyle said. "But you want to tell me what the hell's going on? I feel like a goddamned mushroom up here."

"Molinar might be the accomplice. We need to see if the two men have a connection."

"Who's 'we'?"

"Niki Vang, my old partner, is helping me out."

"You trust her?"

It seemed an odd question, and the tone came across as though Lyle had some reason not to.

"She's helping us," Max said in a way that put the matter to rest.

"Don't pay me no mind," Lyle said. "I didn't sleep well. Your couch is not very comfortable."

"You stayed at my place?"

"Thought you might come back here last night. Wanted to figure out our next move."

"Our next move is to find a nexus between Peter Molinar and Reed Harris."

"Sure. I got you. I'm still friends with Joanna, the secretary at the sheriff's office. I'll give her a call and see what I can come up with."

Max hung up just as he parked behind Niki's squad car out in front of the house he recognized from Olivia Molinar's file.

Max and Niki stood behind Detective Greene as she rang the door-bell. The weather had taken a turn for the worse, the wind picking up from the north, light rain falling at an angle. Max flipped the collar of his jacket up and turned his back to the wind.

Greene rang again and knocked on the glass, peering inside. "I don't see any movement." She rang and knocked a third time. "Maybe he's at his apartment in Falcon Heights."

Max's phone buzzed. He took it out to see that Lyle was calling him and slipped it back into his pocket.

"The ping came to this location," Niki said. She walked to a window next to the door and peeked in.

"Ping?" Detective Greene looked at Niki and then at Max. "What ping?"

The ping had been a Fourth Amendment violation. The fact that it brought them to a house where a woman had been murdered hadn't changed that. Max stepped in to steer the conversation away from Niki's slip.

"My confidential source..." Max cleared his throat to stall for a second. "He's in a position to ping a phone number. The important thing is we have a lead—that *Strangers on a Train* thing."

Greene said, "Why do I get the feeling you're holding out on me?"

Now it was Niki's turn to redirect. "You said Peter worked for a landscaper. He could be at work."

Macey was slow to pull her attention from Max, but eventually did, scrolling through her phone for the information about the landscaping company. Niki and Max shared a furtive glance, and Max could see a look of relief on Niki's face.

Macey placed the call. "Hello? This is Detective Macey Greene with the St. Paul Police Department. I'm trying to reach one of your employees, a Peter Molinar." There was a pause, and then Macey looked at Niki with a raised eyebrow. "Oh, really? Well, I appreciate your help."

Macey ended the call. "When did you say that woman went missing?"

"November sixth," Max said.

"Peter Molinar hasn't been to work since the fourth."

"I think we should check his apartment in Falcon Heights," Niki said. "It's only fifteen minutes away."

"How about this," Max said. "You two go to Falcon Heights and I'll stay here and watch this place. If he shows up, I'll call you."

Greene gave Max a suspicious look. "You'll call as soon as you see him? And you'll stay in your car and wait for us?"

"This is your show. I'm just a consultant."

After they got back into their respective cars, Max waited for Macey and Niki to drive out of sight and then returned the call to Lyle.

Lyle answered the phone, no hello, no greeting, instead blurting, "They were cell mates. After Reed got convicted for hitting Sandy, he did time in County. Molinar was there for possession of stolen property.

He sold some jewelry at a pawnshop and cashed a couple stolen checks. Reed and your guy Molinar shared a cell."

"Were the stolen checks his mother's?"

"Bingo. I didn't remember the case, but Joanna did. The mom wrote up an affidavit for the jewels and drove up here to testify that he didn't have her permission to write checks on her account. I guess the guy had a bit of a gambling problem. Molinar was sitting pre-trial. They were together for three months."

"We have our connection."

"What next?"

"The detective from St. Paul is going by the book. She wants to shake Molinar enough that he'll call Reed, then subpoena the phone records from the cell towers."

"That'll take weeks."

"I know."

"That's bullshit. We can't wait that long. Reed will get spooked and run. We got him in our sights."

"I have an idea."

"What?"

"I'd love to tell you, but it would make you an accessory to something really illegal."

"I don't give a rat's ass. I'm going nuts up here."

"I'll call you in a bit and fill you in if all goes well." Max hung up before Lyle had a chance to argue any further.

Max thought back to what Niki had said about his instincts, about how she had come to trust his intuition. Well, his gut was now telling him that the path to finding the boy led through Olivia Molinar's house.

The park was empty on that cold November morning. From his car, Max studied the garage. He imagined Reed Harris—on the night that he broke into Mrs. Molinar's house to kill her—parking very near to where he now sat.

It was starting to make sense. Olivia had turned her son in. She'd refused to post his bail, and she'd even testified against him. She'd had enough wealth to get him out of his jam, but Peter was a gambler, and that was the thing about gamblers — they never fully got out of their jams. She was probably trying to teach him a lesson — hard love. It was a pretty good bet that Peter Molinar hadn't learned his lesson.

Max stepped out of his Cherokee and walked casually through the park, giving a side glance to the garage of the Molinar house. Beside the overhead door was a regular door with a small rectangular window. The window had a piece of cardboard over it where glass had once been. Reed Harris's entry point. Max looked around and saw no one, although a hundred eyes could have been watching him from the windows of the nearby houses. He would have to take a chance.

He walked to the driveway of the Molinar property as though he had every right to be there. At the door, he pushed the cardboard out of the way and reached through the hole, turning the knob with a click.

Once inside he closed the door and took a moment to acknowledge that he was committing a second-degree burglary. The thought came and went carrying little weight. Not for Max. Not anymore.

CHAPTER 40

The garage was dark, the busted-out window providing the only light. The door that connected the garage to the house had no windows, and the jamb next to the dead bolt had been busted where Reed had pried it open with a crowbar. Max tested the doorknob and found it locked, but a doorknob lock could be opened with a simple credit card.

Max paused for a second. If his instincts were correct, Peter Molinar had killed Sandy Voight and kidnapped Pip in return for Reed Harris having killed Olivia Molinar. If that were true—and Max now believed it to be true with every fiber of his being—then someone had to be watching Pip so that Reed could go to work and put on a show for Bolger. It seemed logical that Peter would be that person.

What didn't match up was that Peter was in St. Paul, not the Northwoods. Max could be completely wrong about all of this, his current behavior nothing more than common burglary, or maybe Peter had brought the boy with him to St. Paul. It was possible that Pip was in this very house. That prospect had Max's heart beating loud in his chest.

It was also possible that Peter was inside the house, hiding from Macey Greene and not answering his door. Max listened for any unusual sounds but heard nothing. He pulled out his wallet and lifted his driver's license out of its holder—pliable yet strong enough to do the job. What would Niki think? It was just one more reason for Max to put that barrier up between them again. He was obviously unrepentant.

He jimmied the door, working the card into the crack between the door and the jamb, sliding it in just above the latch. Once he had snaked the card in far enough, he angled it downward, pushing and pulling the door a fraction of an inch at a time until the door clicked free.

It creaked as he eased it open. He paused again to listen and heard nothing. He closed the door behind him.

It was a beautiful home: exposed wood beams held up by tapered posts, all wrapped in cherry wood. There were built-in cupboards in the front parlor with stained-glass windows and a fireplace, the arcing brick lintel stained with soot from years of use. The house held an old-fashioned charm that explained why Olivia Molinar chose to stay there even when she had the means to move anywhere in the city.

Max went to the kitchen and found three unwashed plates in the sink along with three glasses each with a trace of milk in the bottom. He crossed to the refrigerator. It was empty except for a half-drunk milk jug, a package of ham, a bag of cheese slices, and some mustard. He opened the milk jug and sniffed it. Fresh. Someone had stocked up enough to live there a few days. Peter Molinar didn't plan on staying long.

He peeked out through the kitchen window, which looked out over the alley and park. No car. No Peter. Then he crept up the steps to the second floor.

All of the upstairs doors were closed, and he paused to listen at each before opening it. Behind the first three doors were empty bedrooms, only one of which held an actual bed. The others were being used for storage. He checked the closets. If Peter had brought Pip to St. Paul, it wasn't beyond the realm of possibility that the boy might be locked in one. But he found no Pip.

He went into the upstairs bathroom and found a damp towel in the hamper and a man's bathroom kit on the ledge of the sink—the final proof that Peter was staying there, not in Falcon Heights.

The last room he checked was the largest, decorated with flowered wallpaper and lacy curtains. A sleigh bed took up most of the room, and the covers lay rumpled on top. This must have been Olivia's room.

He opened the closet. An athletic bag lay on the floor next to a plastic bag with a Target logo. He looked in the athletic bag first; it held men's clothing: shirts, pants, socks, underwear. Enough for a few days at most.

When he opened the shopping bag, his heart jumped. It was a toy car about the size of a football—the kind of toy a six-year-old boy would love. Below the car was a stack of coloring books. A receipt in the bag showed that Peter had made the purchase the day before. Wherever Pip was being held, Peter had a plan to rejoin him soon. That gave Max an idea.

He called Lyle. "Grab my laptop from the broom closet in the kitchen. It's on the shelf up above."

"You got something?"

"I think so."

There was some muffled noise as Lyle searched for the laptop. "Here it is."

As he waited for Lyle to fire up the computer, Max peeked out of the bedroom window, which overlooked the backyard, the alley, and the garage. Two boys now played catch with a football in the park beyond the alley. Other than that, the world was quiet.

"Okay," Lyle said. "It's turning on. What's going on?"

"I'm going to try to plant my phone on this Molinar guy, use it as a tracker."

"Now we're cooking with gas. What can I do?"

"Go to Google and type in *find my phone*."

Max went to the settings of his phone to make sure that the location-services setting was enabled. He gave Lyle the email account information tied to his phone. "Did it bring up a map?"

"Just a second . . . yeah. I see a blue dot on Holly Avenue in St. Paul."

"That's me. I need you to watch that dot."

A noise—a gnarling hum—shook Max from his thoughts. Furnace? Pipes? No, the garage door!

"I gotta go!" Max ran to the window and looked out to see a car paused in the alley waiting to enter the garage. *Dammit!*

He went back to the closet, grabbed the box with the toy car, and sliced open the tape that sealed the box shut, using his thumbnail as a blade. He slid his phone inside the compartment where the remote control and battery pack were stored. It would be discovered as soon as the boy opened the gift, but by then Max and Lyle would be closing in.

Downstairs, a key rattled in the door to the garage. He put the car back into the shopping bag and was about to shut the closet door when he realized his mistake. He pulled the box back out of the bag, slid his phone out, and muted it. All he needed was for Niki or Lyle to call him and have the phone buzz. He slid the box back into the shopping bag and returned it to the closet.

He could hear Peter's heavy footsteps crossing to the kitchen downstairs. Max stayed in the bedroom, but closed the door to the hallway, leaving the upstairs just as he had found it. Then he crept to the bedroom window and eased it open, popping the screen out as quietly as he could, then hiding it between the mattress and box spring of the bed.

The creak of the stairs told Max that Peter was getting closer.

Max slipped onto the windowsill and slid down until he held himself up with a forearm on the sill, his legs dangling about three feet above the roof of the garage. Whatever atrophy he had experienced at the cabin over the past few years hadn't affected his arms, which he had built up through wood chopping. He strained to hold on to the sill as he closed the window, the act almost nudging him from his perch; then he lowered his body down until his toe touched the roof.

He let go. Two quick steps and he was at the edge of the garage, where he slid off and dropped to the ground, walking casually back out into the alley.

The two boys in the park, maybe ten or eleven years old, had paused their game to watch Max. He gave them a salute—two fingers to the forehead. If they were Cub Scouts, they would recognize that salute. He smiled at them and walked to his car as though climbing out of that window was no big deal—nothing to tell their mothers about.

Then Max pulled out his burner phone and sent a text to Niki: Max here. New phone—don't ask. Our boy just showed up.

CHAPTER 41

Spud felt as though he had grown an inch taller as he drove to his mother's house that morning. Having spent the past two hours signing documents at the lawyer's office, he was now a millionaire. He owned several units of apartments as well as the house in St. Paul, a total of over two million dollars in equity. The big surprise, however, came when he paid a visit to the bank to take control of her cash accounts. She had almost five hundred thousand dollars just sitting there, earning pennies in interest. His father would have been furious at such a foolish use of his hard-earned wealth.

Spud's father had worked himself ragged to provide for them and yet still found time to spend with Spud. Those hours had been more precious than anything. He and his father—Spike and Spud—playing and dreaming and planning for a future that would never come.

When he was ten years old, just a few months before his father died, they had been playing catch in the park when Spike pointed at the house and asked Spud if he liked it. When Spud answered yes, his father said, "It's going to be yours someday. Everything I have will be yours." Spud never forgot that promise—that pact—but it hadn't occurred to him that his mother's stubborn existence would get in the way of his father's wishes.

She never called him Spud. To her, he was Peter, the boy who could never measure up—her biggest disappointment. In the years since his father's death, what had once been a chill between Spud and his mother had become a frozen wasteland, and when the time came for her to be forgiving, she had denied him, driving all the way to Grand Rapids to condemn him in front of a judge. All he'd needed was one lucky streak to get out of trouble, just one night of good cards. But it didn't happen, so he had forged her name on a check and cashed it, knowing that he could win back enough to make good in a matter of days. It was supposed to be his money anyway—Spike had said so.

But his luck didn't hold, and by the end of the weekend, he had hocked some of his mother's jewelry. As bad as it got, it never dawned on Spud that his own mother would have him arrested. She could have refused to press charges, or she could have bailed him out, but she did neither.

And in the midst of that gloom, Spud had reached out to the only person who would listen, his cell mate, a guy named Reed Harris, a guy who said he had an ex-wife just like Spud's mother, a woman who treated their son like dirt. That's when Reed came up with the plan.

As Spud pulled into the garage at his mother's house—his house—he thought about the calls from Reed that he had ignored. Reed would be mad. He hadn't bothered listening to the messages because he already knew what Reed would say. Spud had been waiting for seven months for the estate to be cleared. Reed was just being selfish, making Spud stay in the woods.

He would be able to smooth things with Reed now that he had money. They had been living off of Sandy's cash. The cabin, the food, toys for Pip, it all came from that money, but now that he had his mother's, he could make living in the woods much more comfortable. Reed should be happy about that.

Spud carried a thick folder up to the bedroom where his mother used to sleep—his bedroom now. The folder bulged with documents, proof that he owned the house, and the apartments, and the money. He lay down and imagined that he was rolling on a bed of hundred-dollar bills.

He was rich. He stared at the ceiling and started dreaming about all the things he would do. A new car? Sure. A boat? Absolutely. And travel— of course there would be travel.

Then his thoughts came to Pip. What a life he could give that boy. He would be generous like Spike had been with him. Pip would never want for a thing. But in a few months, Spud and Reed would part ways and he would never see Pip again. The boy would be whisked up into Canada or somewhere else far away. Reed rarely talked about his escape plan, other than to say that it involved Canada. From there, Spud had no idea where they would go; Reed had kept that part a secret.

Spud would be happy to be rid of Reed, but Pip was another mat- ter. The time that Spud had spent with Pip brought into sharp focus how wrong Spud had been. Reed had convinced him that Sandy was an abusive parent, but that wasn't true. Reed was selfish and brutal, and although Reed hadn't yet hit Pip, it wasn't far off. If Pip needed to be res- cued from anyone it was from Reed. Spud had snatched Pip away from a loving parent and given him to a cruel one; that thought tightened a knot in his chest. He tried not to think about it, but he couldn't escape the crushing weight of his failure. He had murdered a woman for all the wrong reasons and had delivered an innocent boy to the hands of a monster. Now that he had money, there had to be a way to rectify his mistake. He had to save Pip.

He could kill Reed. Why not? He was already a murderer; at least kill- ing Reed would balance out the mistake he'd made. Killing Reed wasn't the problem, though. The problem would be creating a new life for him and Pip, a new life as father and son. Reed had a plan to acquire new iden- tifications but hadn't shared it with Spud. He would need Reed to explain how to do that. Once they had new names, he could be a better father to Pip than Reed ever could. Peter and Pip—he liked the sound of that.

A knock at the door startled Spud out of his daydream. He sat up and blinked away the stupor. The knock came again, along with the chime of the doorbell.

Spud walked down the steps to the front door and opened it to find Macey Greene, the detective in charge of his mother's murder investigation. She was flanked by a man and woman he didn't recognize. All three smiled pleasantly, which was unnerving.

Then Macey said, "Hello, Peter. You got a minute?"

CHAPTER 42

Spud invited the three people into his house before it dawned on him that he had a choice. Macey had interviewed him on three different occasions last spring, all taking place at the police station. It wasn't until after he let the three in that it occurred to Spud that they didn't seem the least bit surprised to find him at his mother's house.

Macey introduced the people with her as Niki and Max. Spud didn't catch their last names, but did catch that Niki was a detective from Minneapolis and Max was from Grand Rapids. Hearing the name Grand Rapids nearly caused Spud's heart to stop.

He offered them seats in the front parlor, but Macey declined.

"You have the day off?" Macey asked instead.

"The day off?"

"From work."

"Oh . . . yeah," Spud said. "It's been kind of slow lately."

"Really?" Macey turned her back to Spud and pretended to examine a porcelain figurine of a little Dutch boy on one of the shelves. "That's curious, because I just talked to your boss, and he said that he's busier than ever."

"You talked . . ."

"Yeah, and he was more than a bit disappointed that you haven't been there for a while. He said you stopped showing up some time ago."

"Oh . . . well, I . . . didn't want to say anything, but yeah, I quit. It was getting too cold to do that stuff."

Macey turned to face Spud. "Why did you lie to me, Peter?"

"I just . . . I don't know. I guess I didn't want you to think I'm a quitter."

"Is it better that I think you're a liar?"

Spud looked at the floor, unable to maintain eye contact with Macey.

Again, Macey turned her attention away from Spud as she slowly walked around the parlor. "So, where have you been keeping yourself," Macey asked, "now that you aren't working?"

"You know . . . just hanging around . . . taking care of my mother's affairs. That kind of thing."

"Hanging around here — in the Twin Cities?"

"Um . . . yeah. For the most part."

"For the most part?"

"Pretty much."

"Other than when you are *pretty much* here, where might one find you?"

"Nowhere, I guess. Just around."

"So you haven't been spending any time . . . say . . . up in the Grand Rapids area?"

Spud shot a short glance at Max, who remained stone-faced.

"Grand Rapids?"

"Yeah." Macey again stopped moving, and looked at Spud. "You've been there before, right?"

"Yeah, I've been there."

"So, when was the last time you were there?"

"Why?" Spud again looked at Max, hoping to glean some hint of what they knew. He kept his eyes on Max for all of a second before turning his gaze back to the floor. "What's Grand Rapids got to do with anything?" When no one answered his question, Spud continued. "There's a casino up that way. I go there sometimes."

"And when was the last time you were in Grand Rapids?"

"I don't remember."

"Were you up there on November sixth, maybe?"

"November sixth?" Spud felt the color drain from his cheeks. "What's this about?" He couldn't quite seem to catch his breath. He looked again at Max, but it was like looking into the sun.

"We just have some questions that we think you might be able to help us with," Macey said. "You want to help us, don't you?"

"Yeah, but I don't know anything about that."

"About what, Peter?"

"About...Grand Rapids or anything. I can't remember where I was on the sixth. I don't keep track..."

"Peter, you seem flustered. Is something wrong?"

"I'm tired, that's all. I lost my mother. And you come here and ask me all kinds of questions that I—"

"Peter, what if I told you that someone said they can put you in the area around Grand Rapids on the sixth of November. Is that possible?"

"Who said that?"

"Were you up that way last week?"

"You know, I don't...I think I want to be alone. I've had a hard day and...maybe you all should leave."

Macey stared at Spud and let the room fill with silence. Spud swallowed hard and looked at his feet.

"Okay, Peter. We'll go, but we're not done here. We'll be back."

CHAPTER 43

Max, Niki, and Detective Greene left the house and walked across the street, stopping at Niki's squad car. "We struck a nerve," Macey said. "I thought he was gonna swallow his tongue for a second there."

"He knows damned well where he was on the sixth," Niki said. "Strangers on a fucking train."

Macey looked over her shoulder at the house. "Think he's watching us?"

"I'm sure he is," Niki said. "We should stay here and chat for a bit. Let him sweat."

"I'm betting he's making the call already." Macey looked at Max. "I can expedite the data—might get it in a few days."

In a few days, Max thought, *Reed will be long gone. Peter now knows that we are onto him, and in a few minutes, Reed will know it too.*

Macey said, "I'm gonna get started on that subpoena."

"I think we'll hang here for a bit," Niki said. "Keep him worried."

After Macey walked to her car, Niki turned to Max. "So, what's the plan? Stay at my place until we get that tower data?"

"I think I should head north—be ready."

"I have some vacation time I could burn. Maybe I should head north with you."

Max didn't have the words to tell Niki just how terrible an idea that was. He would be following an illegal tracker, one that he put into Peter Molinar's belongings during the course of a felony burglary. He and Lyle needed to make first contact with Reed—and hopefully Pip—without law enforcement, just in case they were wrong about everything. Only if they were right might their many sins and crimes be overlooked. Max couldn't risk getting Niki tied up in that mess.

"What about your cases here?" he asked.

"Matty can hold down the fort for a few days."

"I don't know, Niki."

She looked at him as if he had just slapped her. "Are you kidding me?"

"It's best if—"

"Bullshit, Max. I do you a favor and now you're gonna ditch me again?" Niki seethed as she spoke. "I have a right to see this through."

"Niki, there are things I have to do that you can't be a part of."

"Why not?"

"Because . . . You just have to trust me, I—"

"Trust you? Why should I trust you when you obviously don't trust me?"

"I do trust you, but—"

"No! If you trusted me you'd tell me what the hell's going on. If you trusted me, you'd be honest about what happened three years ago and why you disappeared. Don't you dare say you trust me, because it's a lie and you know it. I'm tired of this, Max. I'm tired of being shut out by the one man . . ." Niki clenched her teeth as though fighting to keep words from slipping out.

"I know you're sick of me saying it," Max said. "But I am sorry. There are things I can't tell you, and where I'm going . . . you can't follow."

"Why? Are you afraid I might get hurt? I don't need you to protect me like I'm some child. Jesus, you can be an infuriating jackass!"

"Someday . . . I hope you'll understand."

"Someday, I might not care anymore." Niki's words came out hard, but her eyes had turned soft.

Max dropped his gaze. "Maybe that's for the best."

They stood in silence before Niki said, "I feel like a punching bag, Max, and I'm tired of it. Go north—run away again. For all I care you can go to hell." She paused as if she had more to say, but then she shook her head and walked away.

CHAPTER 44

*O*h God. *Oh God.* Spud peeked out through a gap in the drapes. The three detectives stood in front of his house. *Oh God, they know.* He could barely breathe. The room spun and he had to put his hand against the wall to keep from losing his balance.

Macey looked over her shoulder at the house—at the window where he stood. He stepped back and nearly stumbled over a chair. They knew about Grand Rapids and November sixth. They had to know he'd killed Sandy; why else would they ask him about that city, on that date? He had to call Reed.

He stopped. Which phone should he use? Did it matter? Were they monitoring his calls? Did they know about the burner phones? The world seemed to be collapsing around him.

He peeked through the window again and saw that Macey had gone but the two strangers remained, standing in front of a maroon SUV. Why were they still there? Was he under surveillance?

Spud ran up the stairs to his bedroom and dug the burner phone out of a drawer beside the bed. He played the first message.

Something's come up. Any chance you might get back here right away? It's important.

Something's come up? Did Reed know about the detectives? He played the second message.

I need your input on some stuff. Call me.

Reed seemed so calm, but the words told a different story. Reed had made it clear that they weren't to leave messages unless it was an emergency. And not to say anything in the messages that could be used against them. He played the third:

It looks like there's some really bad weather on the way. Give me a call.

Bad weather? Something was terribly wrong. Had things fallen apart that badly? They must have. He dialed Reed's burner phone.

"Where the hell are you?" Reed yelled as an answer to the call.

"St. Paul."

"I need you to get back here, right now."

"Some detectives came here."

There was a long pause from Reed, then, "What detectives?"

Spud walked down the hallway to a bedroom that faced the street. "Three of them. One was from Grand Rapids."

"What did they want?"

"They asked me about November sixth and I—"

"Shut up!" The phone went silent and for a moment, Spud thought that Reed had hung up on him. When Reed finally spoke, he seemed much calmer, returning to a voice that Spud remembered from those days when Reed explained his plans, an almost fatherly tone. "Remember the protocol we talked about? If you think someone might be watching you?"

"Yeah."

"Do that now and don't forget to flush the sims."

"I won't."

The protocol. First, check your surroundings. Look for any sign of someone parked close enough to watch you through binoculars. Spud scurried down the steps and onto the front porch. He scanned the street in each direction; the cops had gone. Then he ran to the kitchen and looked out back. Again it looked empty.

Next, he checked for tracking devices on the car. A good tracking device needed to be wired to the battery. But not all devices were that sophisticated. He had tracked Sandy with a phone. He looked under the hood, examining the battery and fuse box. Neither had extra wires attached. He searched the undercarriage of the car and the bumpers and found them clean.

He then removed the sim cards from both his personal phone and the burner, flushing them down the toilet. He pulled the batteries and tossed them in a wastebasket, cutting the tether that connected him to Reed.

Spud went upstairs and packed the few belongings he had brought. He picked up the file with the paperwork that he had signed that morning. Should he bring it? What good would it do him up north? If the plan really had fallen apart, he might never see St. Paul again, and as that thought formed, his panic turned to anger—then to rage.

Reed had fucked up. For all his big talk, Reed had to have been the one who made the mistake. How did the detectives know to find him at his mother's house? He had been careful. He had been the one stuck in the woods at that godforsaken shack for a week. It was Reed's fault—it had to be—and now Spud might never get to spend his inheritance.

Spud stopped packing and went to the bedroom that his mother had used as her office. It was little more than a storage room with a desk in the corner, but on the desk was her computer. He fired it up.

Spud had five hundred thousand dollars sitting in a bank account in St. Paul. But he had his crypto account that floated in the ether. He could get to his crypto money from almost any computer in the world. How much crypto could he buy with five hundred grand? Reed had waited for two days to hear from Spud. He could wait a little longer.

As he converted his mother's cash into digital code, he thought about Pip. He was in danger with Reed, Spud just knew it. Reed had had his son for a little over a week and already was abusing him. With this money, Spud really could take Pip. They could settle anywhere in the world. Everything was coming into focus.

He shut the computer down and went to his bedroom to finish packing his duffel, placing the toy car he had bought for Pip on top of his clothing. He smiled as he imagined handing the car to Pip— the joy on the boy's face! Then he zipped the duffel shut and walked downstairs.

In the garage, Spud tossed his bag into the backseat of his car. But before he left, he searched the garage for the lock-blade knife that his father'd had, the one he'd used when they went fishing together. Spud remembered it being in his father's tackle box, and he was pretty sure the tackle box had been stored in the rafters of the garage, out of reach of his mother.

Spud lifted himself up into the exposed rafters where a couple sheets of plywood had been laid down as a makeshift floor to hold boxes. Dust lay thick on the relics of Spud's past: board games he had forgotten about, suitcases left to rot by a woman who found no adventure in the world outside. Christmas ornaments he remembered from those years before his father died, when they did more than the bare minimum to celebrate.

Spud found the tackle box and opened it, and what he saw nearly brought him to tears. It was a half-eaten bag of Beer Nuts. He remembered eating those with his father on their last fishing trip. They had passed the bag between them and would have eaten them all, but Spud had caught a fish, a northern pike.

Spud picked up the bag and pressed it to his face as though it held the very soul of his father. He would buy Beer Nuts for Pip. He would take him fishing and do those things that Reed would not do—that Spud's mother did not do. He would love the boy.

Spud put the bag of nuts into his shirt pocket and turned his attention back to the tackle box. There, in the bottom, lay the knife, a bit tarnished but functional. He opened it a few times to work the rust out of the hinge and then slipped it into his pants pocket. *Sometimes plans change*, he thought to himself.

CHAPTER 45

M ax drove three blocks away from Peter's house, turned, and parked beyond Peter's view, walking back to the alley to take up a position behind a tree. From there he could see the garage door. He waited nearly an hour before Peter's silver car backed out.

Max called Lyle. "He's on the move. Do you have him?"

"I have the blue dot, but it hasn't moved."

"Give it a minute."

Tracking a phone online had its drawbacks. Unlike the professional tracking equipment that police forces used, the Find My Phone app could be spotty. It had to refresh the position of the phone every minute or two, moving the blue dot in fits and starts. But none of that would matter if Peter hadn't taken the toy with him. It killed Max to watch Peter disappear around the block. His impulse to follow nearly overwhelmed him, but he stayed put.

"Is the dot moving?" Max asked.

"Not yet. I don't think—Wait! I have him heading west on Holly Avenue."

Max smiled. Peter took the toy. He got back into his car and drove toward home.

Lyle called every ten minutes at first, giving Max updates. Peter had headed north on Interstate 35. That would take him as far as Moose Lake, where he would need to cut through the backroads to get to

Grand Rapids—in total a three-hour trek from St. Paul. The blue dot stopped on the outskirts of the Cities, and Max saw Peter as he passed by a convenience store where Peter was filling his tank with gas. Max would be in front of him now, but Max decided that that was a good thing. He would get to his cabin in time to see where the dot came to rest.

As he drove north, Max's mind drifted back to something that Niki had said. *If you trusted me, you'd be honest about what happened three years ago and why you disappeared.* Did she suspect that he had killed Mikhail? All those years ago, she had known that he was looking for the man who killed Jenni, but did she think that he might have killed that man?

She had invited him into her home. They'd joked the way they had in the old days. She had helped him track down Peter Molinar. She would not have done those things if she saw him as a murderer, would she? Still, she knew he wasn't being honest. How could she not suspect the truth?

The thought of her seeing him as vicious sent a flush of cold racing through his veins. The more time he spent with Niki, the more she would see through his thin and tattered façade. But as long as he never confirmed her suspicions, there was hope she'd remember him as the man that he had once been—the good man.

"The good man." Max muttered the words, and they tasted bitter in his mouth. "What bullshit."

Did he really have no choice but to kill Mikhail? He had been convinced of that at the time. Mikhail would have walked free, his confession inadmissible in court. There would have been no retribution for what he had done. But if Max were a good man, shouldn't he at least feel remorse? Where was the crippling guilt? Shouldn't he be rending his clothing and lashing his skin with knotted ropes by now? Lord knew he'd tried to get there over the past three years.

He had thought about that night on the frozen lake thousands of times, trying to remember what he had felt as he watched Mikhail sink. Max had been half frozen, his fingers and toes throbbing and swollen. Every inch of his body had seemed to be in pain, but inside, he had felt nothing as he watched Mikhail die; he'd been sure of it.

But now he knew that that wasn't true.

It had come to him as he held the toy car in Peter's closet. In a court of law, that car meant nothing. Peter could have bought it for anyone. He could have gotten it for himself. It certainly didn't amount to evidence of a kidnapping and murder. But for Max it meant everything. He was now certain that Reed and Peter had killed Sandy. He was sure they had Pip hidden away somewhere. He knew the truth and he would do whatever he had to do to save that child—and that's when he felt it. It only lasted a second or two, but he recognized it right away, his mind becoming still, his pulse calming. It was as though every cell in his body understood that in that moment, Max had evolved into his truest state. Laws, rules, justice, vengeance, black, white, and gray—none of it mattered. He had found the toy car, and now he would find Pip.

Three years ago, when Max watched Mikhail drown, he had felt that same sense of peace. He had been the judge, jury, and executioner, and that had been right. As he stood in Peter Molinar's house, staring at that toy car, he knew that if it came to it, he could do it all again.

He had been all wrong about his exile. He had banished himself to his cabin expecting to struggle under the yoke of his conscience, but his nightmares hadn't been born of guilt. Somewhere in the deep recesses of his soul, he understood that it wasn't the killing that still bothered him; it was knowing that he wasn't sorry. How can a man atone for a sin that he refuses to confess?

He had exiled himself to the cabin hoping for a crucible, something to resurrect the *good* man he had once been, but that man no longer existed—if it ever had. Max Rupert was now a man of right and wrong, not rules and laws. If the law helped him, so be it, but if not... well, then damn the law.

Max dialed Lyle's number. "Is he still on the way?"

"He should be in the area within an hour."

"Go to my bedroom upstairs," Max said. "In the back of the closet, I have a twenty-gauge shotgun and a twenty-two rifle. The shells are on the shelf above. Load 'em and be ready when I get there."

CHAPTER 46

The first thing that Reed did when he brought the camping gear back to the shack was show Pip his new sleeping bag. It wasn't some cheap slumber-party crap but a nice one rated for below zero. The boy looked at it but didn't move from his bed.

"Get down here and lay in it," Reed said. "Test it out. I want to see if it fits." Reed knew it would fit—it was a sleeping bag, for God's sake.

Pip still didn't move.

Why wasn't Pip excited? Reed yanked the sales tag off and waved it in Pip's face. "I spent a hundred and fifty bucks on this. The least you can do is try it out."

Pip slid off his bed and sat beside the sleeping bag, gently touching it with one finger.

"Get in."

The boy slipped into the bag, lay on his side, and put his thumb in his mouth.

"Stop sucking your thumb," Reed said. "You're not a baby anymore. It's time for you to grow up." Pip pulled his thumb from his mouth but showed no hint of appreciation for the gift. "You like it?"

Pip nodded but remained expressionless.

Reed stood and left the room, glancing back to see Pip climb back onto his bed and curl up around his pillow, leaving the sleeping bag wadded up on the floor. Such disrespect. Reed had a lot of work to do on that boy. A trip into the Northwoods in November might be a good place to start. But he didn't want to take that trip unless he absolutely had to. A cold rain was falling outside, which soured Reed all the more on the idea of trekking through the woods. If the plan to stay at the shack could still work, they would stick it out.

As he waited for Spud, he stewed. Someone—not a cop—had searched his house, and that person had likely followed him on the night that Spud took off. But why had detectives paid a visit to Spud's house? And what did they know about the sixth of November? How had Spud messed things up so badly?

He stepped out of the shack and stood under the shelter of the porch awning. The rain had ebbed to a trickle, and in the west, the sun peeked through the clouds as it dropped toward the horizon. They had maybe an hour of light left. If they were to make a run for it, they might have to wait until morning.

A glint of silver flashed through the trees. Spud was back. At last. He rolled his car up to the cabin and got out, not looking at Reed, reaching into the backseat to pull out his duffel bag.

"You weren't followed?" Reed asked, doing his best to keep the anger out of his voice.

"No."

Spud walked past Reed and into the cabin, and it was all Reed could do not to grab his partner and shove him to the ground. "Are you sure?"

"I pulled off the highway every half hour—just like you told me to do. No one followed me, and look..." He pointed out of the kitchen window. "No planes. No helicopters. Nothing."

Reed followed Spud into the cabin. "Tell me about the detectives."

Spud put his bag on the table next to the backpacks. "What's this?"

"Plan B—if it comes to that. Tell me about the detectives."

"There were three of them—" Spud stopped talking when he saw Pip standing at the bedroom door.

"Spud?" Pip said, a cautious smile on his face.

"Hey, little man, I got something for you." Spud opened his duffel and pulled out a box with the car in it. When he showed it to Pip, the boy's eyes lit up.

"For me?"

Pip ran to Spud, and Spud handed him the car. "Just for you."

"Oh man, it's...it's...Thanks, Spud."

"Jesus," Reed muttered. "Go to your room and play. Spud and I have to talk."

Instead of moving, Pip looked at Spud as if Spud might override Reed's order.

"I'm your father," Reed hollered. "Do as I say."

"Don't yell at him," Spud said. "He's just a kid."

The gall. Reed clenched his jaw as he pushed down a surge of rage so powerful, he could have ripped Spud's throat out with his fingers. Pip took his car and obeyed. When the door closed, Reed turned his attention back to Spud.

"What did the detectives want?"

"They asked me where I was on November sixth. How did they know about that? What happened, Reed?"

"How would I know? You're the one who broke from the plan. You shouldn't have gone to St. Paul."

"This isn't on me. I was here all week, quiet as a mouse. There's no way they could have got to us through me. You're the one who fucked this up."

Reed had had just about enough of Spud's attitude, barking like he had teeth all of a sudden. Reed glanced at his backpack. His Glock nine-millimeter lay a mere two feet away in the outer pouch. He could put an end to this partnership fast. But that would be rash, not strategic. It would feel good, but he would regret it as he tried to haul a six-year-old boy through blow-down country. He could put up with Spud for one more day, then decide whether or not to put a bullet in his head.

"Let's quit pointing fingers," he said. "We need to plan our next move. Tell me about the detectives."

"One was Macey Greene, the detective working Mom's case. Then there was an Asian woman...Niki something. The third was a guy they said was from up here."

"Grand Rapids?"

"Yeah."

"What's his name?"

"Max. I don't remember a last name."

Reed ran through the officers he knew from Itasca County and shook his head. "There ain't no Max up here. Are you sure he said Max?"

"I'm sure."

"Was he driving an Itasca County squad car?"

Spud paused to think before saying, "No. I think he was driving a maroon SUV."

Reed walked away from the table, a jumble of thoughts swirling. A maroon SUV—the car that had followed him two nights ago. But there was no Max on the force in Grand Rapids. And how was this Max guy connected to Macey Greene? How much did they know about November sixth? How the hell did they link that to Spud? None of it made sense.

"We gotta go," Reed said. "I don't know how, but somebody knows something. We can't take the chance."

"Go where?"

Reed pointed at the packs on the table. "In the morning, we'll hike up into Canada. Once we're across the border, we can use the cash we have left to either hide out or hightail it to a new beginning."

"Are you serious? What about my inheritance?"

"Won't do you no good in prison. When things cool down, we can see about getting you back to St. Paul. But right now, we have to play it safe."

The door to Pip's bedroom squeaked open and his little face peeked around the corner. It was Spud who spoke to him. "What do you need?"

The boy looked at Reed, hesitant, but then in a soft voice said, "Can you turn my phone on?"

"What phone?" Reed asked.

Pip stepped out from behind the door and held out a cell phone. "The one Spud gave me."

CHAPTER 47

When Max walked into the cabin, Lyle was sitting at the table looking at the laptop screen. He had the shotgun in his hand and the twenty-two leaning against the wall, a half-empty bottle of whiskey beside his elbow. He hadn't shaved in a while, and tufts of hair jutted out uncombed from the side of his head. He looked up at Max with eyes rimmed in dark shadows. "He veered north of town," Lyle said.

Max eyed the bottle and wondered how long Lyle had had it, and how long it had taken to go from full to half full.

Lyle said, "I'm not sure, but I think he stopped. The dot hasn't moved for a couple minutes."

Max leaned in to look at the screen and could smell the alcohol on Lyle's breath. The blue dot was about ten miles away as the crow flies, but twenty-five miles by road. "It's possible the phone lost its signal. That's out in the middle of some pretty heavy woods." He loaded the Google satellite view and zoomed in. The area was thick with trees, but he saw a small rectangle of what looked like a roof. He zoomed in as far as he could. "It's a cabin."

Lyle pulled a map up on his cell phone and homed in on the cabin's location. Then he grabbed the shotgun and headed for the door. Max hesitated, unsure about his partner's state of mind. He had kind of blocked Lyle's truck in, but with a little effort, Lyle would be able to get around him. It would be better if Max drove, both for the safety of the trip and to have some control over Lyle, just in case. He picked up the twenty-two and followed.

Max tossed the twenty-two into the backseat, but Lyle held on to his gun and climbed in, riding shotgun in every sense of the word. "Go down to Sixty and head east," Lyle said.

"When we get there, if we see any sign of Pip, we call Bolger."

"What good would that do? You've seen how he's been protecting Reed. Besides, all our evidence was gathered illegally. We're the ones Bolger's gonna come after."

"True, going to Bolger now would probably land us in hot water. But if Pip is there, it proves everything we've said. Bolger won't be able to sweep it away. Besides, we may need the manpower."

"I'm not letting Bolger turn this into a hostage standoff," Lyle said. "I wouldn't put it past Reed to do a murder suicide. That's my grandson in there. He's all that matters."

Lyle had a point. A show of force would be clumsy and loud. It could backfire quickly. Max thought about the burner phone in his pocket. If things started falling apart, he could be the one to call Bolger.

Lyle directed them through backroads that twisted around lakes, and woods, and marshland as Max pushed the Cherokee to its limits, the speedometer hitting ninety before he'd break hard for the curves.

"Around that next bend we turn left," Lyle said.

Max made the turn and weaved between some marshes.

"We're close," Lyle said. "Up ahead on the right."

Max slowed down to look for a trail, nearly passing it before he saw it— nothing more than flattened grass the width of car tires disappearing into the trees. The cabin was far enough in the woods that it wasn't visible from the road. Max parked at the end of the trail, blocking the way, but before he could turn off the engine, Lyle was out the door, the shotgun in his hand.

"Wait!" Max called out, but Lyle was charging for the trees. Max grabbed the twenty-two and ran after him.

Lyle moved fast, more like a man in his thirties than a man in his sixties. He crouched under branches and glided over fallen trees with the ease of someone at home in the woods. The ground was soft and wet from the rain, the pine trees still holding droplets, which fell down the back of Max's neck as he bumped the lower branches. Fifty feet into the woods, the contours of the cabin became visible, a small structure with a rusted tin roof and algae-stained siding. As he drew closer he saw Peter's silver car, but no black Tahoe.

Max caught up with Lyle, who had squatted down behind a fallen jack pine. "That's Peter's car," Max whispered.

They were close enough to the cabin that anything more than a whisper would give them away. There were two windows facing them, a small one that might suggest a bathroom or kitchen, and a bigger one. With the sun nearly touching the horizon behind them, the reflection turned the glass a bright gold.

Lyle pulled the pump back just far enough to confirm a shell in the breach. "They got Pip in there," Lyle said. "I just know it."

"Then let's call Bolger."

"Not yet. I want to take a peek."

"If they found my phone, we could be walking into an ambush," Max said.

"Then you stay here and cover me."

Before Max could disagree, Lyle slipped over the tree trunk. Staying low, he moved toward the cabin.

"Damn it," Max whispered to himself.

Max held his aim on the larger of the two windows and scanned the area for movement.

Lyle crept up to the bigger window, slid his back up the wall until he was standing. Then he gave a peek inside. He looked again, this time keeping his face against the window and putting a hand up to block the sun's interference. He moved to the smaller window and did the same thing, then waved Max in.

Max stayed low, but Lyle had shed his vigilance, standing squarely in front of the window, the muzzle of the shotgun sagging toward the ground. When Max got there, Lyle shook his head and whispered, "It looks empty."

Max peeked in through the smaller window and saw a kitchen and beyond that a living area. "You want the front door or the back?"

"Front," Lyle whispered.

Pine needles cushioned Max's steps as he ducked beneath the windows, skirting around the dilapidated old cabin. He scanned the woods as he moved, keeping an eye out for the possibility that Reed and Peter lay in wait.

The back storm door had been painted green and had a small stoop. Max gave a quick peek inside. Nothing. The back door led into the living room. Beyond that lay the kitchen and the front door, where Lyle looked in.

Max opened the door slowly, the creaking of the hinge announcing his presence. He aimed the twenty-two at the interior doors, bedrooms most likely, in case Peter or Reed popped out. He listened but heard no sound. He slipped inside at the same time that Lyle slid through the front door.

Max went to one of the bedroom doors, Lyle to the other. They threw the doors open and stepped back. The cabin remained eerily quiet. Each man entered a bedroom, rifles at the ready.

The room Max was in held two twin beds. On one of the beds lay a pillow with a dinosaur pillowcase. Next to that lay an open coloring book and a box of crayons. He went to the closet. Where were the mounds of clothing that Sandy was supposed to have taken when she disappeared? Of course the clothes weren't there, because Sandy hadn't run away. The empty room, Peter's car in front, confirmed what Max already knew—an inescapable conclusion that Lyle had to have known as well. Sandy had been killed and Pip kidnapped.

"Clear," Max said.

"Clear," came Lyle's reply.

Lyle entered the room behind him. "Oh, Christ." He rushed to the bed and picked up the pillow. "Oh, sweet Jesus." He pulled the pillow to his face and smelled it. "It's Pip's."

"You sure?"

"It was his security blanket."

Lyle dropped to one knee, grabbing the edge of the bed to keep from falling over. His chest heaved as he clutched the pillow. Max put a hand on Lyle's shoulder.

"I wanted Bolger to be right," Lyle whispered as he held the pillow tightly to his chest. "If he was right, my daughter was still alive. But she's not here. Her stuff's not here. She would never leave Pip." Lyle drew in a shaky breath to hold back his cry. "She's not alive...she can't be. And that son of a bitch has my grandson."

On the floor just under the edge of the bed, Max found the toy car and the box. He picked it up. "They found my phone," Max said. "They knew we were coming."

"Goddammit!" Lyle stood up and squeezed the pillow in his fists.

"We came up from the south," Max said. "We'd have seen them if they were heading south. Maybe they have another cabin farther north?"

Max walked to the kitchen to look for anything that might tell them where to go. On the table lay a pair of wool socks and a packet of water purification tablets. On the floor, next to the refrigerator he found his phone, smashed, the battery pulled out. Nearby he saw a piece of cardboard, a sales tag for a child's sleeping bag.

Lyle came out of the bedroom and Max held up the tag. "They're heading for the woods."

"The Boundary Waters," Lyle said. "That's where Reed went last time, after he beat my daughter. He's the kind of guy who will seek familiar ground."

"The Boundary Waters is a lot of ground."

Lyle held up a finger to stop the conversation. He closed his eyes as though trying to remember something. "When he was in jail back then, he told my jailer the trail he took. It was ... the Sioux Hustler Trail—that's it. He took that as far as he could and cut through the woods up into Canada. Or tried to, at least."

Max bent down and picked up a nine-millimeter bullet that had fallen under the table. "They're armed. We need to get Bolger in."

Lyle looked at Max as though he wanted to punch him.

"Bolger has resources. He can call in the state police. We can maybe cut Reed off before he gets to the trailhead."

"Okay," Lyle said, "but that's not gonna stop me from going after that bastard myself. If Bolger wants to finally do his job ... well, I ain't gonna stop him." Lyle walked out the front door, talking to Max over his shoulder. "I'll call him—you drive."

"Drive where?"

"My place in Ely. You don't go into the Boundary Waters half cocked. I'll need my gear."

"What about me?" Max said.

"What about you?"

"I'm not letting you go in there alone."

Lyle stopped walking and turned to face Max. "Listen, I appreciate all you've done, but this ain't your fight. Reed's a desperate man with a gun. Chasing him is a fool's errand, but I got no choice. You do."

"The hell I do," Max said. He thought about the unborn child he had failed to save. He thought about the three years he had wasted waiting for a reckoning. And he thought about Pip, and Lyle, and the promise Max had made to Meredith.

"This is my fight more than you know," Max said. "I'm going after them whether you take me with you or not." Then he walked past Lyle and headed for the Cherokee.

CHAPTER 48

The first part of the drive went by in silence, Spud afraid to speak for fear of reigniting Reed's anger. When Reed had seen the phone in Pip's hand, he'd grabbed it and thrown it to the floor, smashing its screen. Then he beat it against the table until it opened and he could remove the battery. He held what was left in front of Spud's face.

"You know what this is?"

Spud couldn't speak.

"This is the end of the plan. This is you messing up so fucking bad . . ."

"I don't know how—"

"Shut up! Not a word. I need to think."

Reed was enraged, pacing like a trapped animal, and Spud believed in that moment that Reed might actually try to kill him. Spud still had the knife in his pocket, but if Reed came at him, there'd be no time to pull it out. Spud slid one foot back to give himself a defensive position.

But Reed didn't attack. "We gotta move," Reed said. "I mean right now. Pip, go get your boots and coat."

Spud waited for Reed to give him an order.

"What are you waiting for," Reed said, throwing one of the backpacks at Spud. "I said we're moving."

Spud carried the backpack to his car, but Reed corrected him. "We're taking the Tahoe."

"What about—"

"Leave it. They already know you drove here. Maybe they'll think you walked into the woods and got lost."

Spud threw his pack into the Tahoe and went back inside, to Pip's room. Pip sat on his bed, his chin tucked in as if he was crying, but there were no tears. "Hey, little buddy, you okay?"

"I'm scared."

Spud knelt down in front of the boy. "There's nothing to be scared about. We're just going camping. People go camping all the time."

"Will you be there?" He whispered the question as if he didn't want Reed to hear.

Spud held one of Pip's hands. "Of course I'll be there. I'll always be there for you, Pip. I promise." Spud walked to the closet and picked out the warmest non-cotton clothing he could find. "Put this on, okay? It'll keep you warm."

Pip slid off the bed and obeyed.

Reed called to them from the front door. "Let's go!"

As they drove north, Spud regretted not insisting on taking both vehicles to the trailhead. He hadn't been thinking. If he could have gotten Pip in his car, away from Reed, he could have driven off with Pip. He needed to start thinking ahead. He needed to be smarter.

Maybe he should just kill Reed in the woods—somewhere away from Pip, so that the boy would have no nightmares. He would have Pip and the money and...no plan. Reed was the one who knew how to cross into Canada, and where to go once they got there. He knew how to get new identifications. Spud needed Reed—but Reed didn't need him. Reed had no reason not to kill Spud once they got into the woods. Why hadn't he thought of that before? Spud had no leverage—except the money.

Their bankroll—Reed's tip money, along with what they stole from Sandy—had dwindled to a mere twenty-eight grand, hardly enough to start a new life. Five hundred thousand dollars might just buy Reed's forgiveness.

"I know you're mad," Spud said. "I don't blame you. I don't know how they got that phone into my stuff."

Reed didn't answer.

"But you should know that I can make it right."

"Make it right? We're running for our lives. The whole plan is fucked beyond recognition. How are you gonna make it right?"

"Remember me saying that my mom never spent any of her money?"

Reed gave him a look but said nothing.

"It was more than I'd imagined—a lot more."

"Great," Reed said. "Bully for you. What good's it gonna do you sitting in a bank in St. Paul? Don't you think they're already watching your account? You try and transfer money out and they'll be on you in a heartbeat. Hell, they probably froze the account already."

"The money's not in the bank."

Reed gave Spud a look of curiosity. "You have it with you?"

"In a manner of speaking—yes. I turned it into cryptocurrency. It's in the ether, but I can get to it whenever I want. All I need is internet access."

"How much are we talking?"

Spud almost blurted out the actual number, but stopped himself. If he was buying his life with this money, Reed would want a big chunk, maybe half. Spud trimmed half off the top and said, "Two hundred and fifty thousand bucks."

Reed grinned from ear to ear. "Are you shittin' me?"

"Two hundred and fifty grand," Spud said. "I shit you not."

"And you can get at that from Canada?"

"I can get at that from almost anywhere in the world."

Reed whistled. "That's gonna come in real handy."

"The way I see it, after we get to Canada and get some new IDs, that money can take us anywhere we want to go."

"It's not that easy, but . . . yeah, I can make it work."

"And you can have half—you and Pip. You get me a new ID and I'll set up an account for you and transfer half."

Reed's smile fell away and his face grew tight. Spud recognized that look. It was the face Reed wore when he worked through details. It was the face of a man scheming, and Spud was pretty sure he knew the calculation twisting in Reed's head: Kill Spud now or wait to take his money first?

CHAPTER 49

Max figured that Reed had at least a thirty-minute head start by the time he and Lyle left the hideout. They could chase him and hope to catch up to him before he entered the Boundary Waters, but if Reed was driving as fast as Max, there was no chance of that. Going to Ely made sense.

The road twisted like a carnival ride and Max ignored speed limits as he cut and swerved his way toward Ely. Stopping to get gear would put them another half hour back, but Max and Lyle didn't have to hunt for Reed alone anymore. They had the proof they needed. Pip's pillow and Peter's car were at the cabin, and Max had no doubt that the place would be full of Reed's DNA and fingerprints. As much as he distrusted Tate Bolger, the time had come.

"Call Bolger," Max said. "With any luck, they can intercept him before he gets to the trailhead."

Lyle nodded as he considered that idea. "You're right." He pulled out his phone and tapped a number into it. "Joanna; it's Lyle. I need to talk to Tate."

There was a long pause before Lyle said, "Tate, we found where they've been hiding Pip."

Pause.

"Sandy's boy—my grandson. Reed and this fella named Peter Molinar had him up in a cabin off Fifty-Six."

Pause.

"We found Pip's pillow and his toys there."

"Tell him about Peter Molinar's car," Max said.

"And there's a car there belonging to that Peter Molinar guy. It proves that he's Reed's accomplice."

Pause.

"Never mind how. We think they're heading to the Boundary Waters, the three of them. They're in a black Tahoe, heading for Sioux Hustler Trail—at least I think so."

Pause.

"You can cut 'em off before they get there."

Pause.

"Damn it, Tate. Go check it out yourself. The cabin is just past mile marker forty-eight—east side of the road. You'll find a pillow in a dinosaur pillowcase. That's Pip's. And there's not a stitch of Sandy's clothing there."

Pause.

"It proves Sandy didn't run off."

Pause.

"Okay, but be quick about it. They're on the run."

Pause.

"You'll keep me posted?"

Pause.

"Okay."

He tapped the phone and shook his head. "Dumb son of a bitch. He wants to search that cabin first. The man can't put two and two together without looking at his fingers. When this is all done, I-told-you-so ain't gonna cut it."

"I'll need gear," Max said.

"You done any cold-weather camping?"

"Not to speak of."

"It's no picnic."

"Don't worry about me. Can you get me some gear?"

Lyle thought for a moment, pulled out his phone, and dialed a number. "Henry? It's Lyle Voight. What time do you close?"

Pause.

"Any chance I can get you to stick around a bit longer? I need to outfit a buddy of mine — tonight. We can be there in an hour."

Pause.

"Thanks. Get him a sixty-liter pack and a sleeping bag." Lyle looked at Max. "What size boot you wear?"

"Eleven," Max said.

"He'll need a good pair of boots, size eleven, and throw in two pairs of hiking pants, long johns, and a couple good wool shirts. We might be in the woods for a while, so pack maybe . . . ten MREs. Put it on my tab."

Pause.

"Hunting?" Lyle contemplated a thought before the corner of his mouth inched up in a smile. "Yeah, Henry, we're going hunting."

CHAPTER 50

At the trailhead, Spud stepped out of the Tahoe into a night that was dark and damp and cold—very cold—and it occurred to him that this would be the last time Pip would feel comfort until they got to Canada. Even then, Spud couldn't be sure how long it might be before they found a structure with walls and heat.

Reed had been vague about what would happen beyond the Boundary Waters. He had mentioned something about crossing into Canada at a place called Loon Falls, but after that, the plan got hazy. Spud was sure that Reed was keeping him in the dark on purpose. And why not? If Spud knew the details of the plan, why would he need Reed? Spud had the cryptocurrency. He would have Pip. He could figure the rest out as he went.

"You'll need this," Reed said, tossing a headlamp across the truck to him, the lamp bouncing off Spud's chest and falling to the ground. Using the Tahoe's dome light, Spud figured out how to strap the light to his head and turn it on.

"When we head into the woods, I'll be taking point," Reed said, "so you're in charge of Pip."

Spud walked to the rear of the Tahoe and got his backpack out, setting it on the ground near the trail. Then he went to the backseat and lifted Pip out. Reed stood at the tail of the Tahoe doing something with his own backpack. Spud heard the sound of a zipper open and close; then Reed unloaded his pack from the truck and set it next to Spud's.

"Stay here," Reed said. "I'm gonna ditch the truck."

He climbed into the Tahoe and drove out of the parking area toward the main road, crossing a small bridge that had carried them over a creek. About a hundred yards beyond the creek, he hit the gas and plunged the truck deep into a stand of trees, ramming it into the woods as far as it would go.

As he waited for Reed to come back, Spud looked inside of his backpack to find a sleeping bag, a pad, three bottles of water, a mess kit, a small cookstove, and a canister of propane. Spud would also be carrying Pip's sleeping bag and clothing. Spud took note that his pack carried no food, no money, and no weapon, not even a hatchet or a Swiss army knife.

Reed had also packed no spare clothing for Spud. Spike had once told him that there was no such thing as bad weather in Minnesota, only bad clothing. Pip was decked out in a down coat over a fleece shirt over a wool undershirt. The boy's pants were the kind you might wear in a duck blind, and his boots and gloves were high end. Reed was similarly dressed.

Spud, on the other hand, wore the dress coat and leather gloves that he had worn to visit his lawyer that morning—warm enough for walking around town but definitely not designed for November in the Northwoods. His shirt and jeans were cotton and denim, and his shoes were a cross between a sneaker and a boot. The cold seeped in through a thousand gaps.

His father would have been disappointed in how ill prepared he was for the coming journey, but then again, much of what Spud had done recently would have disappointed his father. Saving Pip from Reed might make up for some of Spud's failings, but not all of them.

"What are we doing here?" Pip asked.

"We're going for a hike," Spud said.

"But . . . it's dark."

"Haven't you ever been on a night hike before? It's fun."

There would be nothing fun about what they were about to do, but Spud wanted to buoy Pip's spirit. That was what a good father would do, wasn't it?

"I'm scared," Pip whispered.

"Don't be scared, little man. I'm here. I won't let anything bad happen. Besides, look up there." Spud pointed up into the cloudless sky, littered with stars more brilliant than Spud had ever seen. "See those? There's billions of them up there, and each one is a light pointing down at us, kind of watching over us in a way. Nothing bad can happen as long as we have those stars. I promise."

Spud thought of what dangers lay in the dark forest ahead. Black bears and wolves—but they weren't really a concern, as they preferred to stay away from humans. Spud had heard that moose could be aggressive, especially in rutting season, but they should be past that now. Then Spud thought about Reed. That's the only thing that Pip should be scared of. Spud had no doubt that Reed would sacrifice him and the boy to save his own skin.

Spud brushed his fingers across the knife in his pocket. He would keep Pip safe.

Reed came back after ditching the Tahoe and walked past Pip and Spud without saying a word, stopping at his pack. He unzipped a pouch and pulled a pistol from the small of his back.

Reed had a gun! That's what he had been fiddling with before he ditched the Tahoe. Reed had taken the gun with him so that Spud wouldn't have a chance to get at it while Reed was away.

The knife in Spud's pocket suddenly seemed a joke.

Reed tucked the gun into the pouch, zipped it shut, hoisted the pack onto his back, and said, "Let's go."

CHAPTER 51

When they got to the outfitter's Lyle jumped behind the wheel of the Cherokee and headed to his trailer to get his gear, leaving Max alone on the street. The lights at the outfitter's shop were on, even though the sign read *Closed*. Max knocked on the door and a short, rugged-looking man came and opened it for Max.

"You Lyle's friend?" the man asked.

"Max." He held out his hand and the two men shook.

"I'm Henry." He peered out as if looking for Lyle.

"Lyle went to his place to grab his gear."

"Of course."

Henry led Max to a counter, where a blue backpack lay surrounded by a stack of supplies. "I got you a good sleeping bag and pad. Do you prefer a tent, a bivvy, or a hammock?"

"A bivvy?"

"A one-person tent... about the size of a coffin."

"That's a comforting thought. Which is warmest?"

"The bivvy. It's small so it'll hold in the warmth a little better."

"Sold."

"I'm afraid I don't have any size-eleven boots, but while I was waiting for you, I called my brother-in-law." Henry picked up a pair of dirty boots from the floor and plopped them onto the counter. "Waterproofed and broken in. You'll like 'em."

"Your brother-in-law won't mind?"

"He owes me a favor...and I owe Lyle one, so..."

Henry walked Max back to a room with a selection of wool socks, fleece shirts, and down coats. Max remembered a mantra he had heard once about hiking in the Boundary Waters: Cotton kills.

"Find what fits you," Henry said. "Grab one set to wear and one to carry. I'll get that bivvy."

Max moved quickly, trying on clothing made of merino wool and polyester. In ten minutes he had two complete sets of clothing along with gloves, a wool cap, and a down coat that balanced warmth and weight. He wore one set of the new clothing and brought the spare set to Henry, who helped him roll it all into tight little packages and stuff it into the backpack.

"You said you owed Lyle," Max said. "If you don't mind my asking... for what?"

Henry paused but didn't look up, as though contemplating whether or not to answer Max's question. Then he said, "I've known Lyle most of my life. We grew up here in Ely—used to skip school to go hunting up in the Boundary Waters. A few years back, my granddaughter got beat up at a party. Our sheriff here in St. Louis County didn't seem to take it seriously, so I asked Lyle if there was anything he could do. A couple weeks later, he dragged these two boys in—confessions in hand."

"How'd he manage that?"

Henry buckled the backpack shut and again hesitated before answering. "He never told me. All he said was that he did what needed doing. I didn't care. He got results."

"The end justified the means."

"If you want to put it that way." He pulled the tie-downs tight, cinching the pack shut. "Lyle's like that—always has been. If he sets his mind to a thing, he stays on it until it's done." Henry lifted the backpack off the counter and bounced it gently in the air to feel its weight. "I'd say about thirty-five pounds. Not bad. Is this your first hike into the Boundary Waters?"

"Can you tell?"

"Lyle knows his way around up there. He'll take care of you." He handed the pack to Max. "There's paracord in the pouch in back, and a Leatherman. Those come in handy. You need a headlamp?"

"I suppose," Max said.

Henry went to a display case and picked up a small light about the size of a nine-volt battery on an elastic strap. "Had some newbies get lost up there this fall. Sent out planes and choppers with infrared cameras, but still didn't find them for almost a week. One of 'em died. It's a lot of country—beautiful—but if a person gets in trouble... Well, it can be about as godforsaken a place as they come."

"A million acres, right?"

"A million point three—and that's just on our side of the border. I don't normally second-guess Lyle, but... heading out in the middle of the night like this, I can't help but wonder if you boys thought this through."

"It was kind of a last-minute decision."

"You know..." Henry walked to a nearby display case. "If it was me, I'd take one of these babies." He picked up what looked like a small walkie-talkie. "It's an emergency GPS communicator. Push this button here and it sends out a distress signal. If those newbies had taken one... well..."

"How much?"

"We rent 'em, but under the circumstances, no charge."

Max slipped the GPS into the pocket of his hiking pants.

"I think you're set." Henry nodded toward the backpack. "Try it on."

Max lifted the pack above his head and let it slide down his back, his arms fitting through the shoulder straps as it dropped. It was heavier than he had expected, but manageable. He buckled all the buckles he could see, and Henry gave the waist strap a tug to tighten it. "Keep this tight," he said. "Let your hips and legs do the work, not your shoulders."

"I appreciate you doing this," Max said. "How much do I owe you?"

"Not a thing."

Henry's generosity embarrassed Max. He was the last person on earth deserving of such kindness. He shook the hand of the old outfitter. "Thanks."

Headlights cut through the night as the Cherokee pulled up in front of the store.

"Be careful out there and...keep an eye out for that old man." Henry nodded at the headlights outside. "He forgets that he's not a kid anymore."

"I'll do my best, Henry."

CHAPTER 52

The trek into the Boundary Waters had started with Spud carrying Pip atop his backpack, holding on to the boy's ankles to keep him from falling. The cold wind that had bothered him at the trailhead had fallen still once they entered the forest, and the hike had warmed his joints and muscles. He kind of felt like one of those dads in a TV commercial. Of course, those fathers weren't on the run. Still, the fantasy made his burden a little lighter.

In front of him, Reed walked like a man who knew where he was going and was in a hurry to get there, a pace that Spud could barely keep, especially with the heavier of the two backpacks and a six-year-old boy. Half an hour into the trek, Spud could no longer see the light from Reed's headlamp. He focused on the path at his feet. There were no off-shoots or intersections, so he knew he would eventually catch up.

But the trail ended when Spud came to his first beaver pond, the path disappearing into a muddy pool of water. He looked around but couldn't see a detour—and where the hell was Reed?

Spud lifted Pip from his shoulders. "I think we should rest a bit, is that okay with you?"

"Sure."

Spud could feel the pinch of cold at the tips of his toes, and his fingers had grown stiff inside of his leather gloves. He asked Pip, "How are you doing?"

"My face is cold."

Spud took off his gloves, rubbed his palms together to warm them up, and held them against Pip's cheeks.

"Where's Dad?"

What Spud wanted to say was that Reed had abandoned them, that he was a selfish jerk who should go straight to hell. But what he said was "He went ahead to scout the trail."

No sooner had Spud said those words than he saw the light from Reed's headlamp in the distance, walking toward them.

When Reed got to them, he said, "You got to cut through here."

It wasn't much of a path, but now that Reed had pointed it out, Spud could see the detour through a thicket of trees. He followed Reed to a bulwark of sticks and mud twenty yards long—a beaver dam. The trail tracked along the top of the dam, a berm less than a foot wide, with an icy pond on one side and a four-foot drop into a marsh on the other.

Reed scooted across with no problem, disappearing into the trees on the other side, leaving Spud alone to figure out how to get Pip across.

"We need to walk across this dam," he told Pip. "It'll be okay, just hold my hands and take one step at a time."

"I can't." Pip sounded like he was on the verge of crying.

"I won't let you fall. I promise. Look, I'll keep my light shining right in front of you and I'll be walking right behind you. You can do it, Pip. You're a big boy and you can do it."

Pip's breath, vapors in the cold night air, curled through the beam of Spud's headlamp. The boy tightened his grip on Spud's fingers and took a step onto the dam, his foot sinking slightly in the soft clay and mud. Then he took another step—and another. Spud held Pip's hands and kept the light steady on the path. The world around them fell away so that there was no pond, no marsh, and no stars. There was only the dam. Soon they reached the other side, and Pip's iron-tight grip eased.

"I knew you could do it!"

"That was scary. I thought I was gonna fall."

"I would never let that happen, Pip."

Spud could see Reed's light in the woods beyond them; he was returning to the beaver dam. "The trail picks up over here," Reed said.

Spud's world shrank to the circle of light cast off by his headlamp, his eyes focused on the few feet of trail in front of him. When the trees grew too dense for Spud to carry Pip on his shoulders, Pip walked in front, staying close so that he could see the path in Spud's headlamp. But when he could, Spud carried the child. He lifted Pip over fallen trees and mud pits; still, they couldn't seem to keep up with Reed.

As he carried Pip to the crest of yet another hill Spud stopped, his fingers and toes grown numb from the cold and his back on fire from the weight he carried. He put Pip down, and braced himself against a birch tree to keep from falling. "Hold up, Reed."

Reed, who was about thirty feet ahead of them, paused long enough to say, "We gotta keep moving," and he started walking again.

"Goddammit, Reed. I said hold up. I gotta rest."

Spud could see Reed's lamp turn on the trail and move toward him, bouncing at an angry clip. When Reed was within a few feet of Spud, he stopped, the beam from his light blinding Spud. "Are you giving the orders now?" Reed said. "Is that what I'm hearing?"

"I need a break."

"Stop carrying Pip. He's old enough to walk on his own."

"He's six years old. He can't walk as fast as you."

"We have to keep moving."

"Christ, Reed. No one's after us."

Reed stepped into Spud's face. "We're out here because of you. They found our cabin because of you. Don't tell me that no one's after us, because you don't know a fucking thing."

Spud could feel Pip's grip tighten on his thigh as the boy stepped behind him.

"It's okay, Spud," Pip said, "I can walk."

"That's my boy," Reed said. "You're no wimp. It's just a little hike in the woods, right?"

Pip stepped in front of Spud, ready to follow. Reed turned and began walking, again at a brisk pace.

Spud reached down to pat Pip on the shoulder, to let him know that things were going to be all right, and Pip grabbed his fingers. He held on to Spud as they walked through the darkness.

CHAPTER 53

There were no vehicles parked at the trailhead. No Reed. No Pip. Had Lyle been wrong? There were dozens of entry points for the Boundary Waters, many with trails that led toward Canada. And who's to say they were heading into the woods to begin with? They had a tag from a kid's sleeping bag—that was all.

Max and Lyle stepped from the Cherokee, and Max grabbed his military-grade flashlight from the glove box, shining the light through the nearby woods. They appeared empty. He turned the beam to the ground at his feet, the muddy gravel of the parking area. At first he saw nothing, but after taking a few steps he saw tire tracks.

"Lyle." Max pointed at the tracks. "It rained today, so these are fresh."

Lyle had strapped a headlamp to his forehead and looked at the tracks, then around the parking area. "But where's the Tahoe?"

The tire tracks circled as if the vehicle had turned around. "We crossed a creek . . ." Max said. "Maybe they ditched it."

Max backtracked toward the highway, but Lyle didn't follow right away. He went to the cargo area of the Cherokee and opened the hatch. Max turned, curious, and saw Lyle haul out a deer rifle with a scope, one that he must have picked up when he had gone home to get his gear.

"Jesus, Lyle," Max said.

The rifle held a five-shot magazine, and Lyle chambered a round. "I

237

can drop a deer from a thousand yards. It's not gonna be a fair fight if I have anything to say about it."

They walked to the bridge and Max shined his light across the marsh. Finding nothing, they continued backtracking toward the highway. The marsh gave way to woods, and the woods grew thicker as they walked. Ahead, Max spotted tire tracks cutting into the trees, and his beam caught a glint of something as if a reflection off glass.

"Lyle . . . there. See it?"

"Yeah," Lyle said. "I see it."

They walked in a crouch, Max shining the light and Lyle pointing the rifle. Sure enough, it was Reed's Tahoe. It should be empty, but now Max regretted leaving his shotgun in the Cherokee.

Lyle took the driver's side and Max circled to the other. The front of the truck tipped up, hung on a stump. Max stepped through the trees, his light aimed at the passenger door. He popped the door and shined the light inside the cab. At the same time, Lyle opened the driver's door. The Tahoe was empty.

"They're here," Lyle said. "Dumb son of a bitch came back. I knew he would."

Max looked through the cab, hoping to find proof that they had the boy, a car seat maybe. At first he saw nothing, but then, there they were . . . a child's shoe prints on the back of the front passenger seat. "And they have Pip with them," Max said, pointing.

Lyle came around to look, and when he saw the shoe prints he traced them with his finger. In a voice strangled with emotion Lyle said, "He's got my grandson out there."

"If they drove straight here, they have at least an hour's head start."

"Then let's get a move on." Lyle started to run back to the Cherokee. But Max called out, "Wait!"

Lyle stopped.

"We need to let Bolger know."

"Goddammit, that's a waste of time."

"We know Reed's here. We know he's got Pip. Bolger can send out a plane."

Lyle shook his head as if disgusted. "Fine." He pulled out his phone and started moving it around looking for a signal. "Go get loaded up. I'll call Bolger."

Max walked back to the Cherokee and shoved the flashlight into his already bulging pack and then checked the shotgun, pumping out the four shells—one shy of a full load—and reloading them. He strapped the headlamp to his head, but then thought better of it. If Reed was lying out there in the darkness with a gun, he didn't want to give the man such a clean target. He tied the headlamp to the end of the shot gun barrel. That way, if Reed took a shot at the light, Max would have a chance.

Still, the lamp seemed awfully bright. Henry had packed a spare pair of long underwear for Max, a black nylon-type fabric. He found the Leatherman and used the knife blade to cut material from one of the legs, wrapping it around the light, dimming it down a bit. He cut another piece of cloth to give to Lyle.

As he hefted his pack, Lyle came jogging up the trail.

"You call Bolger?" Max asked.

"I got ahold of Joanna at home. I gave her the details." Lyle lifted his pack onto his back and buckled in. "She said she'd find Bolger and tell him. Now let's go."

"I'll catch up. I got to do something." Max opened the backseat door as Lyle marched up the trail.

Max had changed into the hiking pants at Henry's shop, throwing his street clothes into the backseat of the Cherokee. Now he reached into the pocket of his pants and pulled out Jenni's bracelet. He couldn't quite explain why, but if he were to die in those woods, he wanted that bracelet near him.

CHAPTER 54

Spud had lost track of time. Had they been marching for three hours? Four? Five? His internal clock had stopped ticking, frozen like his toes and his fingers. The pain in his back blazed through every muscle and turned his shoulder blades into rusted steel wedges. Pip's weight, along with the backpack, was too much, but Spud was determined not to show it. He would swallow the pain anew with every step. He would not fail.

Pip, for his part, had been a perfect traveler, keeping his body still on Spud's shoulders, leaning forward, his head low, his chin on Spud's crown. Every once in a while a pine sprig or the crooked tip of a birch branch would scratch at the boy and he would let out a whimper. When Spud asked if he was all right, Pip answered that he was fine. That wasn't true and Spud knew it.

Reed had told him that they would cross a river at a place called the Devil's Cascade before they set up camp for the night. The promise of that river—that camp—had Spud straining to hear the rush of water in the night breeze. Up yet another hill and down the other side, across another slough, painful step after painful step—the Bataan Death March, Jesus's walk to Calvary—all of it muddled together in Spud's dazed brain.

Then he heard it, the sound of falling water in the distance, growing louder with every step. The sweet noise of a cascade lifted out of the darkness, swirling around them. Soon, the trail opened up into a campsite, flat and open atop a large hill, the stone surface of the crest disappearing as it fell into a chasm, the unmistakable roar of the Devil's Cascade rising up from below.

Reed had taken off his pack by the time Spud and Pip joined him. Spud unloaded the boy and his backpack, and though he wanted nothing more than to crumple to the ground in exhaustion, he willed himself to stay on his feet. He walked to where Reed stood at the edge of the precipice, the land dropping a good two hundred feet. It didn't fall straight down like a cliff, but it wasn't far off. In the thin light of the gibbous moon, Spud could see the froth of white water as it crashed over rocks.

"Devil's Cascade," Reed said. "We'll cross down there." Reed pointed downstream from the cascade, where a line of boulders appeared to form a chain across the water. "Then we'll camp."

"Can't we just camp here?" Spud asked, trying not to sound as desperate as he felt.

"We need to cross that ridge." Reed pointed to the crest of a hill where the trees spiked in silhouettes against the starry sky.

"You can't expect Pip to cross that river at night. It would be dangerous enough in the daytime. Let's just hole up here until morning."

"Christ, you're an idiot. This is a public campsite. Anyone could stumble by."

"At this hour? Who's out hiking now?"

"The same people who put that phone in your bag. I'm sure they found the cabin. They could be on the trail as we speak. We need to get across that river and beyond the hill. End of discussion!"

Reed shook his head as if disgusted. He walked to his backpack, unzipped the pouch, and pulled the handgun out.

"What are you doing?" Spud's chest went hollow, and he instinctively reached for the knife in his pocket, his gloved fingers too thick and too frozen to grab it.

Reed reached into his pack again and pulled out a pair of binoculars.

"I'm gonna backtrack to the last ridge," Reed said. "Look for any lights or signs that someone's following us."

Spud slid his fingers out of his pocket. Had Reed seen him reach for his knife? He didn't act like he had. Reed walked down the trail, backtracking, disappearing into the darkness.

Pip sat on the ground and leaned against Spud's backpack, his little arms wrapped around his knees. Spud walked over, lay down on the ground beside him, and stretched out his knotted back, the sharp pain stopping his breath. He did his best to hide his misery, and when he was able to breathe again, he said, "How you holding up, little man?"

"I'm hungry."

"When's the last time you ate?"

Pip didn't answer.

Spud sidled over to Reed's pack and dug his hand through one of the outside pouches until he felt the slick wrapper of an energy bar. He slipped it out and scooted back to Pip.

"Here," Spud said, opening the wrapper an inch. "Eat this."

"Daddy will be mad."

"We won't tell him, okay?" Spud handed the bar to Pip, but Pip seemed reluctant. "If it'll make you feel better, I'll go stand by the trail. If your dad comes back I'll tell you."

Pip nodded his agreement. So Spud walked back and listened. Behind him the crackle of the wrapper told him that Pip was eating.

An icy breeze crawled up the rocky slope and felt its way along the ground to where Spud stood. It wrapped around his exposed neck and ears. It seeped into his joints and muscles. He walked back to Pip and put his hand on the boy's shoulder. Pip was shivering.

"You cold?" he asked.

"A little."

Spud sat on the backpack and lifted Pip onto his lap, wrapped his large arms around him, and rocked back and forth. They were quiet for a while, but then Pip whispered, "Spud?"

"Yeah?"

"I'm scared."

"You don't have to be scared. The animals are more afraid of you than you are of them. They'll stay far away from us."

"No...I'm not afraid of the animals."

Pip was afraid of his own father. To that, Spud could find no comforting words to offer. He would not lie to Pip and put him off his guard. He needed to be wary. Finally, he said, "I won't let anything bad happen to you."

With that, Pip seemed to relax, the boy's head nestling against Spud's neck.

Spud hadn't heard Reed return—no footfalls on the path, no raspy breath in the cold night. Nothing until Reed said, "Well, ain't this cozy?"

Spud felt Pip jump in his arms; Spud may have jumped a bit too, before pulling himself together and asking, "Did you see anything?"

Reed walked past them and stepped up to the precipice. "I didn't see any lights, but that don't mean they ain't back there."

Reed stood atop a two-hundred-foot drop, his back to Spud. Was he daring Spud to act? Would the fall be enough to kill Reed? Twenty-five feet separated them. One simple shove and it would be done.

Spud set Pip down on the backpack and stood. He took a step toward Reed but stopped. The gun—Reed had it in his hand when he left. Was this a test?

Spud made a point of grunting as he lifted his pack off the ground and worked it onto his shoulders. Reed turned and looked at him, the gun resting in the crux of his crossed arms, his finger lying against the trigger.

CHAPTER 55

Reed boiled inside, to see his son sitting on Spud's lap. Spud was coddling the boy the way Pip's mother had. What was Spud telling him? No doubt filling Pip's head with lies, painting Reed as a bad guy. Hard times made strong men and easy times made weaklings. Why couldn't people understand that?

And what was that move Spud had made when Reed dug the gun out of his backpack? Spud had put his hand into his pocket. Did he have something in there? A knife perhaps? He hadn't believed Spud capable of independent thinking, but there was that trip to St. Paul. And the toy car. And Spud had converted his inheritance into cryptocurrency. Clearly, Spud had been making plans of his own. Had they reached the point where mutiny was on the table?

Climbing down the ravine wall would be treacherous. It wasn't a cliff, but it was steep enough that if one of them slipped, the tumble wouldn't stop until he hit the river. Pip would need to be brave. He would need to be strong. The climb down the wall would be a good place for Reed to show his son what it meant to be tough — to be a man.

Reed turned to Spud. "Give Pip your light," he said.

"What am I going to use?"

"I brought two headlamps. How many did you bring?"

"All I'm saying —"

"Are you suggesting that Pip should go down in the dark?"

"I was just... Don't you have anything else?"

Reed had a tiny penlight that folded into the handle of his Leatherman tool, but that tool also had a knife blade. "We only have the two," he said.

Spud took off the lamp, adjusted the elastic straps down for Pip, and knelt to secure the light to Pip's head, fiddling with the fit like some mother hen.

"Christ, would you hurry up?" Reed said.

Once Spud seemed satisfied, Reed took Pip's wrist and led him to the edge. "We're climbing down this hill." He unclipped a roll of paracord from his pack, unwound fifteen feet of it, and tied an end to Pip's belt, clipping the other end to his own waist buckle. "Stay behind me. Lean into the hill. You'll be fine."

"I'm scared," Pip said quietly.

"It only looks scary because it's dark, but you got a light. Let's go."

Reed started his descent, the hillside dipping sharply downward. The lamp on Pip's head swiveled back and forth as he looked between his father and Spud, lighting the way for the useful idiot. "Dammit, Pip, pay attention to where you're going."

"What about Spud?"

"Will you forget about Spud? He's a grown man. He can take care of himself."

Reed leaned into the slope, keeping the weight of the pack above his center of gravity. Behind him, Pip imitated his father's movement. Reed grinned with self-satisfaction. There might be hope for Pip yet.

The three of them moved slowly, silently, down the wall, the roar of the cascade growing louder. The deeper into the valley they went, the more agile and confident Pip seemed to grow; he didn't complain or whimper. Reed wanted to beat his chest and yell: *I told you my boy is tough!*

At the bottom, Reed made his way to a row of boulders that curved across the river. The first stone was an easy step, but the second lay eight feet out. The water had jammed a fallen pine up against the rocks, a makeshift bridge. After that, they could leapfrog across the remaining boulders to the other side.

The three gathered on the bank, and Reed pulled loose a few more feet of paracord, increasing the slack between him and Pip. "Now watch what I do, Pip," he said. "One foot in front of the other."

"Can't you just carry him across?" Spud said.

"How's he ever gonna learn a damned thing if we do it for him?" Reed pointed a finger at Spud. "You need to shut up and let me raise my boy."

"You're putting his life in danger."

Reed looked away and closed his eyes. He took a slow breath to tamp down his rage. It would be a good lesson for Pip. The strongest will always prevail; the weak are expendable.

"He's tied to a rope," Reed said as calmly as he could.

Reed stepped onto the first boulder and then onto the pine trunk, the wood slippery beneath his feet. He held his arms out to the side like a tightrope walker and leaned forward slightly to keep the weight of the pack over his legs. "One foot in front of the other."

When he got to the second stone, he turned and beckoned Pip, holding the paracord in his hands, ready to pull his son out of the river if it came to that.

Pip curled his hands and arms into his chest, his eyes fixed on the rushing water in front of him.

"Don't look at the water," Reed called out. "Keep your eyes on the tree trunk."

"I can't," Pip said.

"Yes, you can."

"I'll fall."

"One step at a time."

"I'm scared."

"Damn it, Pip. I'm getting tired of you disobeying me. Take a step."

"I'll take him," Spud said.

"No! He's gonna do it on his own. He's not a baby."

"He's a little kid, Reed. For God's sakes."

Spud lifted Pip and held him tightly to his chest, Pip's face tucked into Spud's shoulder, his arms wrapped around Spud's neck. Spud whispered into Pip's ear and Pip turned his head so that the light from his lamp lit up the pale surface of the log.

"Goddammit, Peter!"

It was the first time he had said Peter's name in Pip's presence. They had been using the nickname Spud because Reed wanted him to believe that at the end of the journey they would part ways. Using the nickname was to ease Peter's mind; the boy would never be able to identify him. Reed mentally kicked himself for the slip.

Spud stepped sideways along the fallen tree, shuffling a few inches at a time. Pip didn't move a muscle as the two made their way across the log.

Spud's defiance burned hard in Reed's chest. He moved to the next rock to make way for Spud and Pip, and by the time they joined him on the opposite bank, Reed had almost convinced himself that the time for Spud's departure had come. That kind of defiance called for swift and decisive correction.

But they had a long way to go, and Reed still needed his pack mule.

Reed bit back his rage and untied the paracord from Pip's belt. He didn't say a word for fear that he might lose his shit. He had to keep his head together. He had come too far to let impulse overrule his plan. He tucked the cord away and headed upstream toward the cascade, walking on the rocks that lined the river and beckoning for the other two.

They would leave no footprints to follow.

CHAPTER 56

When Max could hear the rush of water from the Devil's Cascade, he slipped off his pack, and Lyle followed suit. They had both tied their headlamps to the end of their guns, so they turned them off and removed them, Max stuffing his into his pocket. The bloated half moon barely lit the path around them, but up ahead, where the trees parted against the pewter sky, Max could see that they were approaching the knob of a hill.

"I'm going first," Max whispered. "You stay back a ways. If Reed shoots me — take him out."

"I should go first," Lyle said. He was about to say more, but Max didn't stick around to debate the issue. Lyle had a wife and a grandson. Max had no one.

Max stepped lightly as he neared the opening to the camp. He listened for the crunch of leaves underfoot, but heard only silence. He walked out onto the stone cap of the hill, the far edge lined with pine logs to mark the perimeter of the campsite. A small breeze carried the smell of mud and river water up from the ravine. But there was no sign that Reed, or Peter, or Pip had been there.

They separated, circled the camp, and met back together at the precipice.

"If it were me," Lyle said, "I'd cross here. We've been heading north by northwest since the trailhead. But from here the trail turns east and circles back around. Cross here and head that way . . ." He pointed to the northwest. "And we'll come to another river that marks the Canadian border. There're only two places that I know of where you can cross that river. The easiest would be a place called Loon Falls, but if they're willing to get wet, they could wade through at the rapids a mile or so west of that."

"The question is, did they pass through here or leave the trail earlier?" Max had spotted a child's boot print along with two men's where they cross a beaver dam, but the trail over the last mile or two was rocky enough that he hadn't seen any prints.

Max turned on his dimmed headlamp and began looking for footprints along the edge of the ravine, circling back to the tree line, while Lyle went back down the path to gather up their packs. Something flickered in Max's periphery. He aimed his light at the tiny sparkle and saw a wrapper. He picked it up—an energy bar, and it was dry.

Lyle walked back into the campsite with a pack in each hand, and Max called him over. He squatted beside Max. "No rain on it," Max said. "Someone was here today."

"It was them. This is where they crossed. I knew it." Lyle strapped on his backpack and headlamp. "I'm going down."

Max too heaved his backpack onto his back and followed Lyle. They moved slowly down the side of the ravine, Lyle in the lead, both men holding on to patches of grass to keep from slipping.

"I can't believe they took a child down this," Max said.

"Reed has to know the noose is tightening," Lyle said. "He'll have no problem risking Pip's life, if that's what it takes. He's a selfish bastard."

When they got to the bottom, Max stood on the first stone of a natural crossing point, a slippery pine log spanning the rushing river. If the fall didn't crack his skull, the freezing water would likely drown him. And if that didn't do him in, there was hypothermia. "Reed took a six-year-old across this?" Max said. "He's insane."

"We gotta get to Pip tonight," Lyle urged.

And with that, Max stepped onto the log. It shifted slightly beneath him, but he held his balance and made it across. Lyle followed.

On the other side of the river, the land leveled out to the right, while to the left it climbed back up to the Devils' Cascade. Straight ahead lay a hill that rose up as high as any they had crossed on their trek. "We'll need to find their trail," Lyle said, dropping his pack. "If we don't, we may pass 'em and not even know it."

Max followed suit. They aimed their lights at the ground and walked in small circles, looking for a track. After half an hour, they had found none.

"We should wait for daylight," Max said.

"We can't wait. They can't be far."

"Yeah, but which way? Up the hill? Down the river? If we choose wrong, we may never find them."

"I can't stand the thought of Pip, out here in the cold. I'm his Poppy. I have to find him."

"I don't like it any more than you do, but we have to keep our heads."

Lyle put his hands on his knees, his body bent down in defeat. Still, he didn't turn back.

"They have to stop for the night at some point. We'll hit it at first light, find their trail, and double time it until we catch up. We have the upper hand. We aren't traveling with a small child."

Max could see that Lyle was struggling to give up for the night, so he added, "We'll find Pip. I promise."

Lyle nodded reluctantly.

As Max pulled his gear from his pack, a curious thought came to him. They had been in the woods for five hours or better. That was more than enough time for Bolger to confirm what they had found at the shack, more than enough time for him to follow up on the Tahoe, more than enough time even to call the State Patrol to launch a plane with night-searching technology. Max looked up at the sky. Where was the plane?

CHAPTER 57

By the time they set up camp, Spud was so cold he thought his bones would break.

It had been a hard slog once they crossed the Devil's Cascade. With no trail to follow, the forest clawed at them as they ducked and twisted through the scrub. Spud walked behind Pip, sweeping branches aside so that the boy wouldn't get scraped up. Sometimes the brittle pine shoots would snap off in Spud's hands and Reed would bark at him for making noise, but Spud no longer cared. The man was a psychopath. He had wanted Pip to walk across a log in the middle of a raging river. Had Pip fallen in, that rope would have done nothing more than pull a dead body out of the water.

And it hadn't escaped Spud's notice that Reed had called him Peter—not Spud. It had been Reed's idea to call him by a nickname. Peter chose the name Spud because that's what his father had called him. He didn't like hearing that name on the lips of someone like Reed, but when Pip said it, it warmed Peter's heart.

Spud wondered why Reed made that slip. Had it been a mistake? Maybe, but it seemed to Spud that a better explanation was that Reed no longer saw a need to keep Spud's name secret. Spud could think of only one reason why—Reed no longer planned for him to leave the Boundary Waters. Cogs turned in Spud's head as he walked. If he had been looking for a final justification for what he needed to do, Reed had just handed it to him.

They had marched uphill for what seemed an eternity, the sound of the Devil's Cascade becoming a distant murmur behind them, the trees thinning as they gained elevation. Spud had lifted Pip into his arms and carried him to the top, his legs burning with every step. His feet were wet—frozen—from walking through the muddy rivulets and sloughs. The pain was almost unbearable. Yet he willed himself to keep moving.

They crested the ridge and headed down the other side. Reed promised they'd set up camp at the bottom, where a creek would supply them with water. The promise of that relief kept Spud moving.

The downhill side was a bit easier. It might have been because he was distracted by thoughts of warmth and comfort, or it might have been because his legs had grown too heavy, but Spud tripped on a rock and went tumbling forward. He tossed Pip to the side to keep from falling on the child and went face-first into a slough of black mud, his knee cracking on a rock, the weight of his pack flattening him in the muck. Freezing water soaked his clothing and covered his face. Pain from his knee shot up the left side of his body. The toe that he had stubbed against the stone screamed to life.

"Goddammit!!" He spit mud from his mouth as he cursed. He tried to roll to his side, but the weight of the pack pinned him to the ground. His hands sank into the mud beneath him as he pushed to get up.

"Daddy, wait," Pip called out. "Spud fell."

Reed paused but did not return to help as Spud struggled to turn his body sideways. Alone, he managed to unclip the pack and work it off his back. Then he pulled himself up to his knees, the front of his blue jeans completely soaked, his face blackened with mud. He wanted to scream.

But he didn't. Instead, he dragged himself out of the morass and knelt down next to Pip. "Are you okay? I didn't hurt you, did I?"

"I'm okay," he said.

Spud forced a chuckle. "I gotta watch my step...do like you're doing."

He lifted his backpack from the mud and as he heaved it back onto his shoulders, he took note of all of the places on his body that hurt. It might have been simpler to tick off the few places that didn't. Then he picked Pip up and carried him across the mire and continued his march to the bottom of the hill.

Once there, they found a small clearing. No sooner had Spud shed his pack than Reed ordered him to fill the filtering bag with creek water. Spud could barely stand, but did as he was ordered, because they would need water. At the edge of the creek he began to shiver—powerful, uncontrollable shaking that knotted his shoulders and back and clenched his jaw so tight, he thought his teeth might break.

He carried the water back to camp, hooked the bag on a limb, and fell to his knees beside his backpack. He fumbled at the cords with gnarled fingers. When he'd opened it enough, he yanked stuff out until he felt his sleeping bag wedged in the bottom. He tried to pull it out, but his fingers refused to obey him. So close to warmth, yet so far away.

He stood, gripped the bottom of the pack with what strength he had left, and shook it violently until the sleeping bag fell out. His fingers failed him yet again, so he unzipped the sleeping bag with his teeth, threw off his coat and wet clothing, and crawled inside, curling into a fetal position as his body shook with cold.

Reed, in his warm coat, wool sweater, and expensive boots, went to work setting up his small tent, the clack of bungeed poles gnawing at Spud's concentration. Spud had convinced himself that he could kill Reed to save Pip's life, but now he believed that he could do it just to get Reed's coat. He needed a fire to dry his clothing and thaw his body.

"When I warm up..." Spud could barely get the words out past his chattering teeth. "I'll get... some firewood."

"No fire."

"What do... you mean? We gotta... dry our clothes."

"My clothes are fine. So are Pip's."

"Mine aren't. My shoes... are soaked—everything's... soaked. I need... a fire."

Reed spoke like a mother who was tired of her child's tantrum. "We can't have a fire, because if a plane flies overhead, we'd be spotted. I have Mylar blankets that'll keep us hidden from the infrared."

"I need...dry clothes...in the morning."

"Hang 'em in a tree. They'll be dry in the morning."

"The hell...they will."

"I—said—no—fire!" Reed punched each word.

Spud felt as though he had just been handed a death sentence. "I'm wearing...street clothes."

"And why is that?" Reed stopped masking his anger and hissed his words. "You disobeyed me and went to St. Paul after I told you not to. You brought a fucking tracker back to the cabin with you. You don't have clothes because..." Reed took a breath and seemed to settle down. "I brought food and sleeping bags. We have a water filter, a cookstove, and food. I didn't have time to get you better clothes."

Reed's explanation was nothing more than noise, the clanging of tin cans presented as music.

Reed set up a small burner about the size of a badminton shuttle-cock, the flame fed by a small propane tank. Beside Reed lay packages of dehydrated food, meals that would bloom once he added the boiling water. Reed controlled the food, the water, the gun.

Spud tucked the toes of his right foot behind his left knee to try to warm them up. They had been traveling north by northwest. Reed had talked about a river, and a place called Loon Falls, where they could cross into Canada. If Spud kept going in that direction, he would surely find the river. Then it was just a matter of walking along the bank until he found a place where he and Pip could cross.

He didn't need Reed any longer, did he?

CHAPTER 58

Max set up his bivvy and sleeping bag, unable to escape the question: Where was the search plane?

He had once been involved in a manhunt for a suspect in a triple murder. The man had disappeared into the Superior National Forest, and Max called the State Patrol Search and Rescue unit, who eventually found the man. They had launched both a plane and a helicopter out of Duluth, and within a couple hours had footage of the man hiding beneath a tree, the outline of his body fluoresced in the thermal imaging camera.

Lyle boiled water over a small burner, and Max ate a meal of teriyaki rice that tasted like heaven itself. He hadn't realized just how hungry he was. As he ate, he tried to make sense of it. How could Bolger not have called out a search plane? Even if he had doubts about the pillow at the shack, the Tahoe at the trailhead was proof that Reed was on the run. Was he really out to protect his old friend? It didn't make sense.

Max took another bite of his rice and cast his gaze skyward. "I don't get it," he said.

"What?"

"Where's the search plane?"

Lyle didn't say anything.

"They should be out by now."

Lyle kept his face to his meal. "Who knows? I told Bolger we found Reed's Tahoe, but I don't think he believed me."

"What do you mean, you told Bolger ...?"

"He started flapping his gums about not having evidence. You know the drill."

Max stopped looking at the sky. "You said you talked to Joanna ... not Bolger."

Lyle stopped eating for a second, lightly shook his head, and said, "I guess I did say that, didn't I."

"Let me see your phone."

Lyle took another bite of food before slowly saying, "You won't find 'em."

"Won't find what?"

"Those two calls I said I made to Bolger."

"What the hell, Lyle?"

Lyle looked up at Max, his features carrying no contrition or apology. "This ain't Bolger's business; I'm not gonna let him get in the way."

"In the way of what?"

"What do you think we're doing out here?" Lyle said.

"Saving your grandson's life."

"That's not where it ends, Max. He killed my little girl. You know it. I know it. There's no way she'd let Pip out of her sight like this—not if she had a breath in her body. Reed's not leaving these woods alive."

"I didn't sign up for an execution."

"If you don't have the stomach for it ..." Lyle pointed across the river. "You can head back anytime."

Have the stomach for it. Those words filled Max's head with a hundred uninvited memories, visions of Mikhail begging for his life. The irony! Killing was the easy part, Max knew firsthand. It was the aftermath that hollowed a man out. "You can't do this, Lyle."

Lyle dropped his eyes to the ground, looking far beyond the stones at his feet. "I wake up in the middle of the night, so broken I can't breathe. I get so mad ... I want to bust up anything in my reach. It took all my strength not to walk into that bar where Reed worked and beat him to death. He killed my little girl—I felt it in my heart. And now I know."

Lyle choked back something dark and heavy. "She was beautiful and sweet... and now I'll never hear her voice again. I'll never get to kiss her on her birthday or hear her laugh at my bad jokes. I was supposed to protect her. I'm her father... and I'll never..." His big hands trembled and his voice cracked. "You have no idea... the pain..."

Lyle reached into his backpack and pulled out the whiskey bottle. It was almost empty now. He twisted the lid off and took a big drink. Then he looked up at Max, his eyes narrowing to a squint. "When someone kills *your* daughter, *then* you can have a say. Until then, stay the hell out of my business."

Had Max looked that crazed when he set off to hunt Mikhail? Niki had described him as having tunnel vision in those last days. Is that how the search for Pip had become a mission to kill the men who took him? Judge, jury, and executioner. Max knew that path well, and he couldn't let Lyle charge down it without knowing what lay ahead.

"Six years ago, I lost my wife." Max spoke without thinking, opening a box he thought he never would. "She was a social worker at a hospital. One day, she overheard something she wasn't supposed to, and a man named Mikhail Vetrov killed her for it—ran her over in a parking garage. For a long time I thought she was the victim of an accident—a hit and run. Then one day I learned the truth. I found out about Mikhail. So I hunted him down, onto a frozen lake. When I caught him, I tied him up and made him watch as I cut a hole in the ice just big enough to feed him through."

Max's voice sounded threadbare, but the words expanded in his throat, thriving on the air, warming him like some healing elixir. "When he finally confessed, I dragged him to that hole and fed him to the lake."

"Jesus," Lyle whispered.

"Every time I look in the mirror, I see a murderer looking back at me. You wanted to know why I gave up my badge? Well, now you do. I went to the woods to take what I had coming. I went there to find a way to look at myself again. I used to think that I was a good man, but I crossed a line on that frozen lake, and now I can never go back."

"Why are you telling me this?"

"I'm tired of running from it. I'm done. But you still have a choice."

"Do as I say, but not as I do?" Lyle said. "As I see it, you're the last person in the world to be preaching to me."

Max had just confessed to killing a man. How could his warning fall on such deaf ears? "Lyle, I'm all alone in this world, but you have a wife ... a grandson. Killing Reed won't bring you the peace you think it will. How are you going to look Meredith in the eye? Pip?"

"I'll look 'em in the eye just fine knowing that the man who killed that boy's mother is dead. I came into these woods to kill Reed Harris and bring my grandson home, and that's what I'm gonna do. If you try and stop me"—Lyle looked hard into Max's eyes—"well, friend, that would be a big mistake."

"You gonna shoot me, Lyle? Is that what you're gonna do?" As if the threat ahead of him weren't enough, now he had a threat walking beside him.

"I'm putting Reed and that other guy down like the cur dogs they are. I'm just letting you know that nothing, not you, not them, not God Almighty, is gonna stop me."

CHAPTER 59

That night, after a supper of rehydrated eggs, with his wet clothing hanging in the branches of a nearby tree, Spud crawled back into his sleeping bag. Reed had brought a tent for him and Pip to share, but not for Spud, who stared up at the stars and pondered how he would kill Reed Harris.

Reed had made a point of carrying his handgun into the tent when he and Pip went to bed, so sneaking in to cut Reed's throat was out of the question. Reed was probably waiting for Spud to act; that's why he kept the gun ready. Besides, Spud couldn't bring himself to kill Reed with Pip lying so close.

Spud had been foolish to butt heads with Reed when they crossed the river. He had nothing to gain other than to put Reed on notice that the tide had changed. But the tide hadn't changed, had it? Reed still had the gun, and with the gun came power and control. If Reed left his gun alone even for a minute, that would be all Spud would need. If not, he would have to use his knife—and wait until dark so that Pip wouldn't see the blood.

Tomorrow night they would be in Canada. He would bide his time until then, do it along the trail while the gun remained zipped in the backpack. Reed sometimes rested on a fallen tree or rock to wait for Spud and Pip to catch up. That would be the best time to strike. Spud would have the knife out and ready. If Reed stayed still long enough for Spud to get close, it would only take one quick slash across the throat.

How had he fallen so far? An unexpected grief washed over Spud. A year ago he was a broke landscaper who gambled too much and hated his mother, but he wasn't a murderer. Now he had his mother's death on his hands—and Sandy's. So many times in his life he had thought about the spirit of his father, hovering over him, watching him. Spud stared up at the stars. How disappointed his father must be.

Spud had never given much thought to having a soul, although he wanted to believe that his father could still be near him. But now, he hoped that there was no such thing, because if there was, his own would be black, and forsaken, and damned.

Ten feet away, inside of Reed's tent, he could hear Reed scolding. "Stop squirming and go to sleep. We have a lot of walking to do tomorrow."

If Spud could find a path to redemption, would his father forgive him? Maybe that was the reason for Spud's journey. All of the planning and the pain—it all led to Pip. Yes, he could kill Reed. He was sure of it.

That was the thought that calmed Spud's mind as the night breeze lulled him to sleep.

What happened next started out as a dream. He stood in a marsh, the body of Sandy Voight at his feet. She looked up at him through clear water, her eyes seeking him out as if wanting to ask him, "Why?" She reached up from the depth, her hand tugging at his shoulder. He tried to pull away, but the tug became more demanding.

Spud awoke to see a shadow standing over him. At first he thought Reed had come to kill him, but then a tiny voice whispered, "Spud, can I sleep with you?" It was Pip with his sleeping bag in his hand.

Spud smiled in the darkness, his heart lifted skyward by the boy's small show of affection. Spud gave the child his sleeping pad, an extra layer of insulation to keep Pip's sleeping bag off the cold ground. Then he helped Pip get settled in next to him.

CHAPTER 60

Max awoke in the full-throated darkness of the night to the sound of rustling material. He had gone to sleep not sure what the morning would bring. He had confessed to murder, an act that had filled him with an overwhelming sense of relief. Someone else knew. It was out there for Lyle to do with it what he wished, and Max didn't give a damn what that might be.

But the relief of the confession had quickly vanished, eclipsed by Lyle's threat.

Max had gone to sleep with the hope that it had been the whiskey talking, although Lyle didn't seem impaired enough to blame it on alcohol. Max's hopes fell by the wayside when he unzipped the mouth of the bivvy to see Lyle rolling up his sleeping bag. Next to him, the flame of the tiny stove sparkled beneath a pot of water. Lyle was almost ready to hit the trail and Max was still wiping the sleep from his eyes.

"Why didn't you wake me?" Max said as he slid out of the bivvy.

"I want to look for tracks as soon as the sun comes up."

It didn't skip past Max that Lyle hadn't actually answered his question. He began disassembling the bivvy and rolling up his sleeping bag and pad. The morning air was cold. The moisture that had remained on the trees and leaves had frozen overnight, and the world around him had turned stiff and crisp. Max worked quickly to stow his gear inside

261

the backpack, pausing to get some of Lyle's boiling water for his break-fast before Lyle had a chance to toss it aside.

"Were you planning on going without me?" Max asked as he took the first bite of his rehydrated eggs.

"I don't need your help," Lyle said. He scraped at the sides of his food pouch with an all-purpose utensil, finishing the last of his breakfast. His pack leaned against a tree stuffed and ready to go except for the tiny stove. Lyle's deer rifle leaned against the tree as well. "You should go home; you'll only be in my way."

"I'm going with you," Max said.

"Why?" The question came out sharp and angry.

Why? Max thought to himself. This wasn't his burden to carry. Whether the men they hunted lived or died meant nothing to Max, but stopping Lyle from killing them did. Shoot them in a fair fight—in self-defense—fine, but he couldn't let Lyle execute them. Plus, he had promised Meredith he'd bring her family home. "That's my business," he said finally.

"And doing what I'm gonna do . . ." Lyle picked up his stove and folded it down to tuck into his pack. "That's mine."

Max finished packing his gear as the first rays of dawn reached down into the valley, giving the world a hazy glow. Lyle left without another word, working his way downstream, and because they were north of the Laurentian Divide, that meant he walked north. Max thought about following him. It made sense that Reed would head north, where the land was more agreeable, the hills more manageable. But Lyle had that covered. If there were prints, he would find them.

So Max worked his way upstream toward the Devil's Cascade, all the while keeping an eye on Lyle. If Lyle disappeared, Max would know that he had found tracks.

As the sun broke the horizon, it lit the woods with a luster that bordered on magical, the trees glistening with frost, the ice on the leaves and twigs sparkling like glitter in a snow globe. Every few steps, Max would turn and look for Lyle, his weathered figure hunched over as he searched for tracks. The longer Max searched, finding nothing, the more it made sense that Reed would have taken the easier path to the north.

Max was on the verge of giving up when he saw it—a small boot print on the bank. It was only the toe, but it belonged to a child. It was the same boot print he had seen the day before on the beaver dam.

He had found Pip. Something heavy lifted from his shoulders.

Max stepped into the woods and slid between a gap in the trees, the most logical place to walk. He was twenty feet in before he saw the second print, this time from the larger of the two men—Peter.

Max gave thought to following the trail alone, leaving Lyle behind the way Lyle had planned to leave him, but this wasn't about Lyle, and it wasn't about Max. This was about Pip. Max returned to the river and stood on a rock far enough off the bank that Lyle would see him if he bothered to look.

Max put his pinky fingers to his teeth and blew, but his whistle was swallowed by the crushing roar of the cascade. He waved his arms, the shotgun lifted high above his head. Lyle was about to follow the bend that would take him out of sight when he stood and stretched his back. Max thought he had looked his way, but he wasn't sure. Lyle stood motionless for a few moments before he began his jog upstream.

When Lyle got to him, Max showed him the tracks. "They took the harder trek," Max said. "Tried to hide their trail. They're worried that we're behind them."

"They should be worried," Lyle said.

Max and Lyle headed into the woods, zigzagging through gaps in the trees, looking for more prints. The trail led up the side of a hill that wasn't as steep as the ravine wall they descended the night before, but was a challenge nonetheless. At the top, Lyle looked through the scope of his rifle, using it in place of binoculars.

He spoke as if to himself. "If we knew where they planned to cross into Canada, we could hustle around and cut 'em off. But if we choose wrong…" He slung his rifle onto his back. "For now we follow their trail."

At the bottom of the hill they came to a small creek, the slow-moving water trickling beneath a thin cover of ice. The ground near the creek had been disturbed—trampled grass, matted pine needles—and food packages had been stuffed under a rock, a half-assed attempt to hide their trash.

"They camped here last night," Max said, getting excited. "If they left at daybreak, they're only…" Max looked up the hill in front of them, almost expecting to see Reed and Peter right there.

"We're close," Lyle said with a grin. He pulled the deer rifle from his shoulder and jumped across the creek, heading up the hill with the vigor of a man half his age, slowing only when he needed to look at the ground for footprints.

That climb seemed endless, the hillside laced with fallen trees, and rocks, and roots. There were sloughs and creeks that slowed them down, but those impediments would have also slowed Reed Harris. They had to be gaining.

At the top of the ridge, Lyle scoped the horizon in search of his grandson. He did the same thing at the top of the next hill. At the crest of their third hill, Lyle pointed at two peaks in the distance. "If he's going for the falls, he should be on that hill to the right. If he's crossing at the rapids, he'll be the one on the left. We'll know one way or the other once we cross the valley."

Max was about to start down the hill when the crack of a distant gunshot froze him in his tracks.

CHAPTER 61

By Reed's best guess, he should have been able to see the blue of a lake in the distance, yet he saw only trees. Loon Lake, a twenty-five-hundred-acre body of water, fed the river that they would cross to get into Canada. He took off his backpack and tried to get his bearings as he waited for Spud and Pip. Reed pulled the gun and binoculars from his pack and walked to a stone slab at the top of the ridge to get a better view, looking first to the northern horizon. It took a moment, but he spied a touch of blue peeking through the trees in a valley ahead of them. Loon Lake. The tightness in his chest lifted.

Spud carried Pip to the top of the ridge and set the boy down, taking off his pack and using it as a seat for them both. Two peas in a fucking pod.

Reed hadn't woken up when Pip left the tent the night before to sneak off to Spud's side. That Pip would choose Spud over him made Reed want to crush Spud's skull. He would do it with a stone, right in front of the boy. That would teach his son to be hard, prepare him for the tough world that awaited them. He had put up with the boy's softness to the point that Reed felt he might break.

Reed looked to the sky, the sun farther to the west than he would have liked. There were no search planes — a good sign. No planes meant that no one was looking for them yet. But how could that be? Something about that didn't add up.

He lifted the binoculars again and looked to the hills behind him.

Someone had put a phone in the box with Pip's toy car. Who? A cop? No. A cop would have gotten a warrant for a real tracker, and they would have wired it to the battery of Spud's car. So it wasn't a cop, which meant that someone else had broken into Spud's house to pull off that stunt.

Lyle? It had to be.

But Lyle knew about Reed's escape up the Sioux Hustler Trail the last time Reed had been a fugitive. If Lyle was behind the phone in the car trick... why hadn't he sent out a search plane?

As he scanned the southern horizon, a flicker of light on the ridge caught his eye.

Reed stepped behind a tree to hide as he tried to find it again. He waited... and there it was, a glint of light, brief but unmistakable, sunlight ricocheting off glass. He held the binoculars against the tree trunk to steady them. With his middle finger he rolled the focus wheel to get a fix on the hill. At first he saw nothing, but then it moved—a man, standing on the ridge. Reed got down on his belly, elbows on the ground. Not just one man, but two.

What the hell? They were shadows, tiny and distant, but definitely men, one facing north, solid and unmoving in his stance, aiming a rifle at the very hill where Reed lay hidden. The second man stood further back, his shape obscured by trees. Reed saw no one else.

It had to be Lyle. But if it was Lyle—and he'd found the cabin and probably the Tahoe as well—where were the search planes? Surely Lyle would have called the State Patrol. Reed put the binoculars down to ponder, and only one answer made sense. Lyle didn't want the State Patrol involved. Lyle wanted to find them himself.

Reed leaned against the tree to think. A few paces away, Spud and Pip sat out of sight of their pursuers, oblivious. Lyle was likely following the trail of broken scrub and footprints that Spud the ox was leaving behind. Spud had screwed them once again. Reed needed to slow Lyle down, maybe send him on a false trail—or both.

An idea came to him, but it seemed too easy. He ran it through one more time and, although it had flaws, it had a real chance of success. If nothing else, it would buy him time. Reed stood and pulled his gun from the waistband of his hiking pants.

As he walked toward Spud, Reed went through what needed to happen. He had told Spud about Loon Falls, hadn't he? Yes. Had he ever mentioned the rapids? No. Maybe Reed would mention Loon Falls one more time, work it into the useful idiot's memory.

He paused briefly to take off his coat, draping it over the gun before finishing his walk back to Spud.

Spud looked up at Reed and said, "I told you that no one's following us."

Reed smiled, put the muzzle of the hidden gun against Spud's knee, and pulled the trigger.

CHAPTER 62

Spud felt an explosion as the bones in his leg shattered and a thunderclap of pain shot through his body. He fell off the backpack, howling, his hands cupped around what was left of his knee. He could hear Pip screaming. He rolled to escape the pain, but every move awakened more agony.

The ringing in his ears gave way to the chaos of his own grunts, mixed with Pip's high-pitched squeal — "No!" — and "Spud!" screamed as loud as the child's lungs would allow.

Spud tried to look at Pip, but he couldn't see through the tears. Then he felt Pip's hands on him. The boy had dropped to his side. Spud wanted to put an arm around him, but he felt Pip's tiny fingers being torn away as Reed pulled his son back.

"I'm your father," Reed yelled. "You stay here and listen to me."

Pip continued to scream until a slap silenced him. Then he went rigid, his eyes cast up at his father in fear.

"I'm gonna teach you how to be a man," Reed said. "That's what all this is for."

Pip's jaw quivered and tears flooded his eyes, but he didn't make a sound.

Spud lay on his side, his busted knee resting on the ground. He wanted to reach out to Pip, but he couldn't. He had failed. He ran a gentle finger across where his kneecap should have been and felt the hole, the nerves coming alive with even that little bit of touch.

"Spud's a liability. You know what that word means?"

Pip's chest shook as he fought to hold in the cry.

"It means that he causes more problems than he's worth."

"He's . . . hurt," Pip said, pushing the words out between hard sobs.

"Listen to me!" Reed shouted. "There're two men chasing us. They're hunting us, and it's Spud's fault."

Spud wanted to call out to Pip, but his throat had seized shut.

"We need to get away from here," Reed said. "Go someplace where it'll be just you and me, a family. You want that, don't you? But we can't take Spud with us. He's the reason those men are chasing us. And if they catch us, we can't be a family. You'll be all alone. So the question is . . . what do we do with Spud?"

Reed walked to Spud and took a knee at his side. "A man has to be smart about stuff like this," Reed said more gently. "I want you to be smart, like me. I want you to think with your head. So tell me . . . should we kill Spud?"

"No!" Pip yelled.

Spud closed his eyes. Reed was putting this burden on the shoulders of a child. He swallowed hard and tried to speak. "This isn't your doing, Pip." The grunted words barely made it past his lips. "Remember that. Whatever happens, it's not you."

Reed jabbed a knuckle into Spud's shattered knee. Spud choked on the pain.

Reed said, "Because of you, I've got men on my tail, so you can shut the hell up." He returned his attention to Pip. "You're right, Pip. We shouldn't kill him. Do you know why?"

Pip didn't answer.

"If we kill Spud, those men who are chasing us will keep chasing us. But if we wound him . . . well, maybe they'll stop and help him. One of the men might even stay behind. Either way, we stand a better chance of getting to Loon Falls if Spud here stays alive. The question remains, how much alive should we leave him?"

Reed brought the gun up to his chest where Spud could see it. "Now, if you were to tell me how to get at that cryptocurrency..."

Spud thought about the knife in his pocket. Reed was close enough, but there was no way to get it out without Reed stopping him. Reed was offering a deal that Spud knew would never be honored. Whatever Reed had in mind for him was going to happen regardless of the money.

"Tell me how to get it and I'll let you go with a bum knee. That's not so bad."

Spud tried to control his breathing enough to speak. "Password... Fuck you Reed... all caps."

Reed stood up. "I didn't think so. The problem is... with just a busted knee, they might figure they can come back for you later. It's not like you're going anywhere. But if you're in danger of bleeding out..."

Reed aimed the muzzle at Spud's stomach. "This is gonna hurt, but with any luck, you won't die." He pulled the trigger.

The bullet entered Spud's abdomen, slightly right of center, a tiny squirt of blood splashing out of the newly formed hole in his coat. Like the first shot, it sent a shock wave through Spud's body, and although the second bullet burned hotter than the first, the pain didn't seem as all-consuming. Maybe he was losing his ability to feel.

Again Pip wailed, his scream piercing the air.

"Goddammit, shut up!" Reed barked. Pip stopped screaming.

Reed leaned close enough so that only Spud could hear what he said next. "One of those bastards following us is Lyle Voight, the father of the woman you killed. He's a former sheriff and you can bet he'll have a gun. If you tell him what we did, he'll kill you. I guarantee you that. The only way you'll stay alive is if you keep your mouth shut."

Reed went to Spud's backpack, pulled out Pip's sleeping bag, and strapped it to the outside of his own pack. Then he grabbed his son by the arm and disappeared into the woods.

CHAPTER 63

The sound—a crack—had come from somewhere north. It was muffled and weak, barely making it to them, but Max knew right away that it was a gun. He and Lyle stood still and searched the horizon as if the shot might have left a shadow to guide them.

"I think it came from that hill," Max said, pointing to the ridge on the right.

"I think so too," Lyle said.

The two men started down the hill and a second shot rang out, clear and crisp. It was still very far away, but definitely coming from the hill on the right. They took off on a dead run. Max slid around trees and crashed through scrub on the way down the slope, his backpack catching on limbs as he pushed through. On the climb up the next ridge, he slowed a bit and tried to step on rocks and lichen to maintain some semblance of stealth.

Traversing the ground between two ridges was a slog. A bird could have covered the distance in a matter of minutes, but it took Max forever to climb the hill, curling around trees, climbing over the dead ones, crawling on his hands and knees when the pines grew too thick. He had lost track of Lyle, and as he neared the top of the ridge he paused to listen for him and heard instead the faint groan of a man. Max unbuckled his pack and slid it to the ground, his shoulders unfolding as the burden fell. He slid the forestock of the shotgun back an inch to confirm the shell in the chamber, then released the safety.

He tried to be quiet as he crested the hill, but the brush was too thick, so he charged the position and found a man lying on his back. He couldn't see the man's face because a backpack blocked his view, but from the size of the man, it was Peter Molinar. A few feet away lay Lyle's backpack, but no Lyle—and for the moment, no Reed.

Max leveled the shotgun and turned in a circle, searching the trees. Then he stepped close enough to see Peter's face twisted in pain, and bloodied bits of what remained of his right knee visible through the hole in his pants. A patch of crimson bloomed on his right abdomen where Peter's hands gripped his coat, his fingers red and wet. Peter saw Max and whispered, "Help me." Then Peter's eyes shrank to a squint, as if he was confused. "You're . . . that cop?"

"Hello, Peter."

Something moved to Max's right. He spun and aimed the shotgun at the sound, but let the barrel drift to the ground as Lyle walked out of the woods, his rifle hanging low at his side. "They're gone," he said bitterly.

Max leaned his shotgun against a tree out of Peter's reach, but kept his eyes on Lyle, who stopped about ten feet away from the wounded man. "Where are they?" Lyle's voice was low and ominous. He slowly raised the muzzle of the rifle until it pointed at Peter's face, but Peter's eyes were closed.

Max stood on the other side of Peter, not sure what to do. He couldn't stop Lyle from pulling the trigger. Max needed to get control of the situation before it spiraled. He stepped around Peter in the hopes of getting between the two men, but Lyle closed the gap and stood beside Peter, the gun still aimed down at his face.

"Where's Reed?" Lyle said. "Where's Pip?"

Peter opened his eyes and looked at his bloodstained hands. It was as if Max, and Lyle, and the gun didn't exist. "He shot me."

Lyle kicked Peter's bloody knee, which caused Peter to howl like a wounded beast, his cry filling the trees. "I asked you a question."

"Stop!" Max grabbed Lyle by the arm, but in a blur of motion, the older man spun toward Max and raised the rifle as if to smash Max in the face. Startled, Max shoved his palms into Lyle's chest, sending him sprawling to the ground. Before Lyle could react, Max stood over him, ready to kick the gun away. He pointed a finger at Lyle and yelled, "Goddammit, Lyle, keep your shit together!"

Lyle, on his back, raised himself onto his elbows. "What the hell do you think you're doing?"

"You won't get anything that way."

"Son, don't you ever—"

"Beat him to death and we won't know where Reed's headed." Max softened his tone. "We won't know what happened to Sandy. Let me try."

"We ain't got time!"

"One minute. That's all I'm asking."

The flare of Lyle's nostrils eased a bit and he gave an almost imperceptible nod.

Peter was crying, his teeth clenched, spittle webbing his parted lips. Max knelt on the ground and spoke in a calm voice. "That woman you killed...that was this man's daughter. And the boy you kidnapped... his grandson. So you see, you're in a bit of a predicament—but I guess you already knew that."

Max could tell that Peter was trying to control the crying, but it wasn't working. "Don't leave me out here," Peter pleaded.

Max kept his voice calm, gentle, in the hope that he might settle Peter down enough to get some answers. "That depends on you."

"You gotta help me."

"That's the thing, Peter...we don't. But if you help us—"

"I don't want to die."

"No one wants to die. Sandy didn't want to die. Your mother didn't want to die, but here we are. So where's Reed headed?"

Something calm seemed to pass through Peter as he lay in the dirt, and for a second, Max thought that he might really be dying. But then Peter said, "You gotta save Pip."

Max was taken aback by that. Peter had killed Sandy and kidnapped Pip, but now, facing his death, he thought of the child instead of himself. "That's what we're trying to do."

"He's taking him to Canada."

"We know that. Where are they crossing?"

"A place called Loon Falls."

"Why did Reed shoot you?" Max asked.

"He wants...to slow you down."

"So he knows we're tracking him."

Lyle had found his feet again and was standing behind Max. "I knew it."

"Reed left him behind," Max said slowly. "He wanted us to find him. He knew we'd ask where they were going." He turned back to Peter. "Did Reed mention Loon Falls after he shot you?"

"Huh?" Peter blinked and winced but didn't answer.

"Did he say the words 'Loon Falls' *after* he shot you?"

"I think I'm dying."

Max asked the question the third time. "Did he say it after he shot you?"

"I think so."

Lyle said, "He left this piece of shit behind to send us the wrong way."

Peter started to cry again. "Please don't leave me. Please. I'm sorry for what..." He looked past Max, to Lyle. "I'm so...sorry. Please don't leave me here."

"Where is she?" Lyle asked. "What'd you do with her body?"

"I don't know. That was Reed. I—"

"You're lying," Max said.

"No—I swear. All I did was take her to Reed."

"Reed was at the casino," Lyle said. "Stop lying."

"You're gonna leave me to die."

Max dug the GPS communicator from the pocket of his hiking pants and showed it to Peter. "You see this?"

Peter wailed through his gritted teeth as something inside of him caused his body to go rigid.

"Stay with me, Peter," Max said, putting a hand on the man's shoulder. "Do you see this?" Peter blinked away tears and looked at the GPS. Max tapped the side. "I push this button here and it sends out a signal for help. They'll be able to find you and fly you out of here. It's the only chance you have."

"Thank you."

"I'm not gonna push that button unless you tell us the truth, Peter. It's that simple."

Peter looked at Lyle again and back at Max. Peter's hands were red with blood, his leg twisted unnaturally. He breathed in spurts. They were running out of time. Max turned the device to the side so that Peter could see the red SOS button. "Just press and hold—but first, the truth."

"He told me . . . he said she was abusive to Pip. He lied to me."

"Where's her body?" Lyle said.

Peter tipped his head back and let loose a deep, guttural cry. "I'm sorry! Please!"

"Where's her body?"

"Hill River State Forest. Just off the road, there's a marsh."

Max heard Lyle move and turned to see the deer rifle again aimed at Peter's head. Lyle looked like a man who had just walked through hell. His hair held sticks and leaves and his cheeks were hollow. He held the gun to his shoulder, but the barrel sagged with weight. His eyes burned bright with rage.

Max stood and stepped in front of Lyle's aim.

"Get out of the way, Max."

"Put it down."

"He killed my girl."

"Think about Pip."

"Dumped her like trash."

"He's not worth it."

"You're in no position to give advice." Lyle didn't have to say more for Max to understand the card that Lyle had just laid on the table. Silence for silence.

Lyle tried to step around Max and again Max moved into his way. "Do what you want with me, Lyle; I'm done running, but you're not killing this man."

"The hell I'm not."

Peter writhed on the ground behind Max, crying in pain. Had he been a dog, Max would have put him out of his misery, but he wasn't a dog.

Lyle moved the barrel to point it at Peter's head, and Max finally charged him, grabbing the rifle as Lyle fired, sending the bullet into the dirt. He slammed the heel of his hand into Lyle's chest, sending him sprawling to the ground again. Lyle scrambled to his knees and aimed the gun wildly at Max. "I told you not to get in my way!"

"You gonna shoot me, Lyle?" Max held his arms open. "Is that what you've come to?"

Lyle looked hard at Max and then at Peter, who lay behind Max's feet. Then Lyle tilted his head back and screamed like a banshee, his wail echoing through the forest. In the silence that followed, Lyle rose to his feet, slung the rifle over his shoulder, picked up his backpack, and marched into the woods.

Max was confused until he turned around to find Peter Molinar staring up at the sky through lifeless eyes.

"Aw, hell," he whispered. He knelt down at Peter's side and closed Peter's eyelids. He felt no sorrow for the death of this man, in fact, had he the opportunity he would have thanked Peter for dying all on his own—for saving Lyle from the ordeal of having to kill him.

Then Max ran back down the hill to where he had dropped his backpack. By the time he returned to Peter's body, Lyle was long gone.

CHAPTER 64

Reed walked with new purpose. He would leave no track for Lyle to follow. He carried Pip whenever the ground turned soft, stepping on rocks and moss and sticks to avoid leaving a footprint. The boy didn't help a lick, hanging limp in Reed's arms every time Reed picked him up. Had he been this way with Peter? Reed got so fed up with the extra load that he almost regretted killing Spud—almost.

He stopped at the top of every hill to look back through his binoculars. There was no way Lyle could still be following him, but that didn't stop Reed from seeing phantoms moving on the slopes behind him.

He and Pip had headed west, away from the Loon Falls, away from Spud, and hopefully away from Lyle and whoever Lyle had brought with him. If Spud had done his job, Lyle would head north to Loon Falls while Reed and Pip slipped quietly into Canada at the rapids. He and Pip would be home free; all he needed was a little luck—for once in his goddamned life.

As the afternoon sun grew weak, the temperature dropped below freezing. A slight breeze made the air even colder, yet Pip wasn't crying or whining. He knew he would get no coddling from his father. Reed saw this as a hopeful sign. He believed that, deep down, Pip could be tenacious and hard, just like Reed had been after his father pushed him. Reed had learned to follow orders and tough it out, and in the two hours since they left Spud, Pip had been a good soldier.

Still, it seemed odd that Pip hadn't spoken in those two hours. He walked like a zombie, never once looking up at his father. Reed tried to get Pip to talk a few times, but every comment landed on deaf ears, the boy's sullen disrespect grating on Reed's last nerve. Reed paused to give Pip a rest and to offer him an energy bar, but Pip didn't want to eat. Reed ordered him to eat, so he finally did.

They returned to the march, cresting yet another hill thick with trees and scrub brush. In the distance Reed saw the river, dark and calm, and beyond it, Canada. Reed wanted to jump for joy, but he was far too tired. He still had to get across. He still had to worry about Lyle and the other man.

Reed had expected to hear the sound of a gunshot announcing the death of Peter Molinar, but it never came. That could mean any number of things, the best-case scenario being that his pursuers had stayed with Spud. But if he knew Lyle, that wasn't likely. Reed had to assume the worst case—that Lyle would be showing up at the rapids that evening. Reed needed to be ready.

At the river's edge he paused to listen and heard the distant churn of what had to be the rapids coming from around the bend. He followed the bank as the river narrowed, emerging from the trees at a place where the river squeezed from a span of fifty yards across to a mere fifteen feet. They called that section the rapids because as the river narrowed, the water pushed through at a higher rate, the rush over the rocks that lined the bank creating a churning din. It sounded like a set of rapids, but was really nothing more than a bottleneck.

Reed walked to the edge and took in the sweet smell of the water and the trees—of freedom. Pip stood back from the river as still as a rock.

"I'll take the pack across first," Reed said. "Test how deep it is—then I'll come back for you."

Again, the boy didn't so much as twitch.

Reed stripped down to his underwear, the cold November air biting every inch of his exposed skin—and this would be the warmest part of the next few minutes. He lifted the pack over his head and stepped into the river.

The water was freezing, colder than he thought he could stand, its icy grip moving up his leg with every step: ankle, calf, thigh, and he hadn't yet reached the middle. He struggled to maintain his footing on the slippery rocks as the current pushed at him. When the water hit his stomach, he could only breathe in short bursts. When it reached his chest, he stopped breathing altogether.

Would Pip ever understand what his father had endured so that they could be together? Would he appreciate Reed's sacrifices? He lifted the backpack high above his head, and with his next step he felt his body lift out of the water a few inches. He had reached Canada.

When he was close enough, he heaved the backpack to shore, his mind reaching for when he was a deputy and took a water rescue course. How long could a man survive in water that cold before hypothermia stopped his heart? For some reason, he remembered it being around half an hour, although that seemed generously long.

He turned back to the Minnesota shore and found that Pip was gone.

Reed's first thought was that the boy had fallen into the river, the sound of his cry swallowed by the churn of water. He looked downstream and saw nothing. Then a flash of movement caught his eye. The boy was running through the woods, heading back the way they had come.

Reed charged across the river, climbing out on the Minnesota side and running barefooted and mostly naked through the woods, chasing after his son. The cold air on his wet skin introduced him to a whole new torture.

Pip didn't get far before Reed caught up. He spun Pip around and slapped him across the face, knocking the stocking cap off his head. Reed didn't think that the slap fell sufficiently hard enough, so he swung again, catching Pip hard on the cheek and sending him to the ground.

"Where the hell do you think you're going?"

Pip screamed and held his left cheek.

"Answer me!" Reed took a step toward Pip and raised his hand.

Pip rolled to his side and buried his face in his arms.

"Where were you going?"

"You killed Spud!" Pip yelled between sobs.

Reed picked Pip up by the collar of his coat, grabbed his stocking cap off the ground, and marched him back to the rapids, the boy struggling to break free from Reed's grip. When they got back to the rapids, he threw Pip to the ground, grabbed his face, and forced the boy to look at him. Then in a voice loud and clear, he yelled, "Spud killed your mother. Don't you know that?"

Pip stopped struggling. He stopped crying. He sat on the ground as though he had gone numb. "That's right," Reed said. "That day he came to your house... he killed your mom. That's why I had to do what I did."

He waited for Pip to say something—to react in any way—but the boy just looked at Reed with a blank expression. "I found out what happened and I did what a man has to do. You understand?"

Pip stared up at his father but still said nothing.

The cold ground sent shards of pain spiking up through the bottoms of Reed's feet, but he tried to sound calm. "It's just you and me now. We're a team—father and son. We gotta get across that river—and we have to hurry. Stand up."

Pip didn't move. He didn't even seem to blink. It was as though he had gone catatonic.

Reed lifted him off the ground and stood him up. Then, with his clothes in his hands, he hefted Pip onto his shoulders and waded back across the river.

On the other side, Reed scanned the Minnesota shoreline as he dressed. He had to get his head back in the game. If Lyle was still following them, he wouldn't be far behind. Lyle had some skill as a hunter, but Reed felt up to the challenge. The real question was, who was that second man?

If Lyle didn't take the bait of Loon Falls, there would have to be a battle, and it would be two against one. He needed to figure out a way to even the odds. He needed to set up an ambush.

He took in the layout of the rapids and the land around it. His pursuers would have to cross here. They would be vulnerable in the water and have their backs to the river once they crossed, cutting off any retreat. Behind him, Reed had a hillside full of trees for cover.

He was in a perfect place to bring this whole mess to an end.

CHAPTER 65

Max had flipped through his options as he retrieved his backpack. He could hit the SOS button, wait for rescuers to show up, maybe get a manhunt started, but that would take several hours, and by then Lyle and Reed and Pip would have disappeared into Canada. He dismissed the idea. He couldn't leave Lyle alone in the Boundary Waters with Reed. The passion that filled Lyle's head could make him careless, get him killed. He couldn't let Lyle go after Reed alone.

But more than that, Max thought of Pip. Max had once had a child taken from him, a child he had failed to save. And now he saw Pip's face every time he closed his eyes. He would not fail again.

The Canadian border twisted from east to west, following a labyrinth of connecting rivers and lakes. To cross, Reed would need either a boat or a choke point where the river thinned to a gap narrow enough to walk across. Lyle had talked about two such choke points: Loon Falls and a set of rapids to the west. If Reed wasn't heading for the falls, he must be headed for the rapids. If nothing else, Max could find the river and follow it until he found the rapids — or became hopelessly lost.

Max used the setting sun to gauge a northwest heading. He cinched the straps of his backpack and headed downhill, leaving the dead body of Peter Molinar on that lonely hilltop.

Alone in the woods, he thought back to his failed experiment as a hermit. He couldn't kill a rabbit to save his life. But that had been the problem, hadn't it? He really didn't want to save his life. Hell, he was half dead already. He had watched hundreds of sunrises and sunsets, yet as hard as he tried, he could not remember a one of them. Nights were dark and days light, but there seemed to be no color in either, not until this last week. And had he lost his sense of smell? Of taste? Eating had been reduced to a means to an end—existence. He had been taking up space, and nothing more.

But now he felt more alive than he had in three years. The aroma of mud and pine buoyed him as he crossed yet another valley. The rhythm of his breath, in sync with his footfalls, became like music as he leapt over rocks and fallen trees. He charged up slopes and pushed through scrub, undeterred by the biting limbs. He felt a sense of passion unlike anything he'd felt in a long time—not since that day he had chased Mikhail Vetrov onto that frozen lake. Max was a beast freed from a cage. A hunter—not of rabbits but of men.

He finished his climb to the crest of yet another hill and was about to start down the other side when he saw it—the river just beyond a short valley. He had somehow stumbled his way to the Canadian border.

As he marched down, his thoughts turned back to the mission at hand. Had he navigated to a spot east of the rapids or west? If he turned the wrong way, he would end up walking away from Lyle, and like it or not, Lyle needed Max.

The sun was already touching the horizon; he would be out of light soon. The terrain leveled off as he neared the river, the rocks of the hill giving way to a wetland. He was glad that Henry had found him a good pair of boots, impervious to the slop underfoot.

He paused at the river's edge to listen, but he was breathing too hard to hear anything. He took a few deep breaths then held one, straining for the slightest sound of rushing water, but hearing nothing. He tried again, but still nothing. He looked at the river in both directions, but he found no clue as to which way to turn.

He was about to head to his right when he heard the pop of a gun, followed by two more shots coming from around the bend to his left.

Max took off at a dead run.

CHAPTER 66

As Reed settled into his hiding spot, he thought about a movie he'd seen some years back, a story about three hundred Spartans who'd held off thousands of invaders by making a stand where the trail narrowed. The movie had been based on true events, and Reed appreciated the lesson: Choose the battlefield and you have the advantage. Reed thought that he had chosen wisely.

He sat on a hill overlooking the rapids, about fifty paces up from the river, a fallen jack pine in front of him for cover. He would soon know if his plan to send Lyle to Loon Falls had worked. He had decided to give his former father-in-law one hour to show. If Lyle didn't turn up by then, Reed could assume Lyle had gone to Loon Falls and Reed would have a hell of a head start. If Reed's plan hadn't worked, though, Lyle would have no choice but to cross at the rapids, exposed as he waded across the chest-deep water. And like the Spartans, Reed would be waiting.

He had taken Pip up and over the ridge before coming back to set up his ambush, tucking the boy into his sleeping bag and giving him an energy bar for food. He'd said, "I'm gonna do some stuff in the woods tonight. I need you to stay here."

Pip had looked at his father with empty eyes, and Reed had wanted to shake the boy. He didn't need gratitude from his son, but this sulking was getting old. But Reed had taken a breath to let his frustration pass. Maybe the despondency worked in Reed's favor. A numb Pip was less likely to run off again. He'd added one last touch to keep his son put. "Stay in your sleeping bag. The bears won't hurt you if you stay in the bag."

Pip sucked on the energy bar, not acknowledging that his father was even talking.

From his vantage point behind the stump, Reed had a clear view of the rapids, although the window of the firing lane was far narrower than he would have liked. And he would have preferred to be closer to the river than he was, but the trees at the river's edge were too thin to offer cover. Reed would make it work; he had always been a decent shot with his nine-millimeter.

To his right, the sun touched the horizon. It would be dark soon and Reed's advantage would be cut in half. There had been a gibbous moon out the night before. That might be enough light to see Lyle, but he'd be shooting at a shadow. Would it be better to give up his cover and wait in the thin scruff closer to the river? No. Lyle had a scope on his hunting rifle. He doubted that it was night vision, but he couldn't take that chance. Lyle would be smart enough to glass the woods thoroughly before crossing. It was best to stay hidden behind his stump.

Reed pinched his eyes shut, and when he opened them again, his mind had calmed. He smiled. He and Pip had made it across the border with enough cash to get them set up. He knew of a fishing camp a day northeast of them where a man with pontoon planes would fly them out of the woods for cash. He and Pip could start over. He would raise Pip alone. Sandy was dead. He had won.

Reed lifted his binoculars and searched the Minnesota side of the river, staying low just in case Lyle was doing the same on the opposite bank. The trees were thin but abundant, a curtain that could hide a man until he chose to make his presence known. But no one could hide once they stepped into the river. If there were two men chasing him, he would wait for the first to cross and get to shore, and hope that the second man followed closely behind — kill the first man on the bank and the second in the water.

His stomach growled with hunger. He'd only brought one power bar with him and he'd eaten it already. It wouldn't be long. If Lyle had followed him, he would be at the rapids soon. Reed slid the glove off of his right hand and stuck his cold fingers up under his armpit for warmth, raising the binoculars to his eyes again with his left hand.

He saw nothing at first, and was about to lower them when something moved at the edge of his vision. He sank behind the stump and scanned the area. Then it moved again—twenty feet up the bank, in a patch of birch, a man. Reed's pulse hammered in his ears. It was Lyle Voight. He was studying the Canadian shore through the scope of a deer rifle.

Where was the second man? Had he stayed with Peter? Had the plan worked? Reed watched Lyle step closer to the river and again scan the woods. Lyle didn't appear to be talking to anyone. He was acting like a man alone.

Reed leaned against the stump as he drew the pistol from the back of his belt, pulling the slide back and loading a round into the chamber. Gun at the ready, he eased another look, a sprig of dead pine needles hiding him.

He could make out the edges of Lyle's shape moving between stands of white birch trees, inching down the bank. When he stepped out of the shadows Reed could see that Lyle carried his backpack in front of him like a shield. Reed looked for the second man but still saw nothing. He would wait until Lyle reached the Canadian shore before he opened fire.

Lyle had slipped out of his coat, hiking pants, and boots, but had left his shirt on as he waded into the icy water. Reed tracked his every step with the sight on the pistol. Patience. Wait until he climbs out.

Lyle took careful steps as he crossed the river, stumbling a bit as he finally crawled up the bank on the Canadian side. The backpack blocked Reed's view of Lyle's chest, and although there was probably nothing in there that would stop his bullet, he lowered his aim to Lyle's thighs. He would cut the man down and then finish him off.

Reed rose up to his knees and held his sight on Lyle as he reached the edge of the clearing. Just a few more feet.

Lyle made a final push, climbing out of the river and stepping into the clearing a little off-balance. Reed fired once — twice — three times.

One of the bullets struck true. Lyle buckled and tipped backwards. Reed couldn't tell if bullets two or three hit meat, or backpack, or nothing, and was about to fire a fourth round when Lyle fired back over the top of the pack. The bullet splintered the bark on the stump. Reed tripped backwards. The old man was firing blind but had damned near hit him.

When Reed peeked out again, Lyle was gone.

CHAPTER 67

Max ran as fast as he could, with the thirty-five pounds of camping gear still strapped to his back. As the river narrowed, he dropped the pack and used the trees for cover, working along the hill until he overlooked the rapids. He slipped behind a pine tree to catch his breath and assess.

The Canadian side was flat for a stretch about the size of a racquetball court, with only a bit of scrub. Beyond that, the land rose steeply up into a hill thick with trees. Lyle's backpack lay in the clearing. Max scanned the tree line looking for Lyle, but the forest was too thick.

Then something in the river moved. It was Lyle, clinging to the Canadian shore, his body half in the water and half out, on his back. Pressed against the rocky bank, he held his rifle tightly against his chest.

Max was close enough that Lyle should hear him if he called out, but so might Reed, who had to be somewhere on that opposite bank. The trees on Max's side of the river were too scrawny to provide cover from a bullet, but there were enough of them that he might be able to sneak down closer to Lyle.

Shotgun in hand, Max got down on all fours and crawled through the brush until he was within spitting distance of the rapids. "Lyle!" His voice didn't carry beyond the noise of the rapids, because Lyle didn't move. "Lyle!" A little louder and Lyle turned. "Are you hit?"

"My leg."

"If I give you cover, can you make it back here?"

"I . . . I think so."

Max doubted that Reed was close enough to be in range of the shotgun, but the noise might cause Reed to duck long enough for Lyle to retreat. If Max did nothing, hypothermia would set in and Lyle would die right there in the river.

"He's just left of that big poplar," Lyle said.

Max saw the tree. Tall and white, it stood out from the shadows like a dried bone. He sidled up to a dead birch, no bigger around than a coffee can, and propped the shotgun on his shoulder. "Let me know when you're ready."

"I'm ready."

Lyle stood, fired one shot at the side of the hill, and pushed away from the bank. Max shot at the base of the poplar tree, pumped a new shell into the chamber, and was about to fire again when three quick shots rang out from a patch of pine trees well to the left.

Lyle went under the water, his rifle barely held above the surface.

Max fired at Reed's new position and Reed fired twice at Max, one bullet hitting the dirt near Max's right foot, the other chipping the bark off a tree in front of him. In the river, Lyle came up for air and lunged toward the safety of the northern bank. Max fired once more to cover Lyle and then dropped to the ground to await Reed's return fire, which never came.

Max's heart pumped hard. It wasn't the first time he'd shot at someone who was shooting at him. He had been trained for such things, and the training came back to him like muscle memory, but the rush of adrenaline, and fear—and yes, excitement—always seemed to punch him in the chest.

"You okay?" Max yelled.

"He got me." Lyle winced from the pain. "In the back."

Shit. That changed everything.

Lyle clung to the far bank, his bare legs dangling in the water, his back pressed against the tree roots. He still had his rifle. Max had no hope of getting Lyle back to the Minnesota side of the river as long as Reed held his position in the woods. He had to figure out a way to draw Reed away from the river.

Max stripped off his coat, held the shotgun above his head, and dashed to the rapids, jumping far enough out to splash down past the midway point, the frigid water punching the air out of his chest. He held the shotgun above the surface as best he could and came up for air only a few feet from the Canadian side, close enough to the bank to be out of Reed's line of sight.

Lyle had an exit wound just below his clavicle. His teeth chattered uncontrollably and his breathing came in hard, labored spurts. He looked like hell. Max needed to get him out of that river, and fast.

"I'm going to draw him into the woods, away from the river. My backpack's about twenty yards upstream. Dry clothes."

Lyle twisted in pain, but he managed to eke out, "I'll . . . cover you."

"You get your ass across the river as soon as you can."

Lyle's backpack lay about twelve feet ahead of Max and next to the pack lay Lyle's coat and clothing. Max would grab what he could as he ran by. He had only one shell in his shotgun, and would have to save that for Reed, if he could find him. The sun gave no heat, but enough light for Max to see the terrain. Little else.

"On three?" Max said.

Lyle gripped Max's arm with icy fingers. "Find—Pip," he said, his words hitting hard and sharp, like the blade of a cleaver. "Save—him."

Max couldn't think that far ahead. He needed to get Lyle out of the freezing water. He was about to run through a clearing that Reed had set up as a kill zone. But Pip was somewhere on the other side. How many bullets could Max take and stay on his feet? He had to get to the woods and then keep going—no matter what.

"I'm going on three," Max said. "One, two, three."

On three, Lyle rose to the top of the bank and fired a shot at Reed's last position. Max sprang over the bank and ran with everything he had. Shots rang out from the hillside, but whether Reed was firing at him or Lyle, Max couldn't tell. All he knew was that he hadn't been hit. Lyle fired back from the river.

Max charged past Lyle's backpack, scooping up a fistful of clothing as he passed. He cut right, knowing that Reed's last position was toward the left side of the hill. When he got to the woods, he kept moving, breaking sticks and thrashing through the scrub, making as much noise as he could, hoping to draw Reed away.

In the penumbra of the fading sun, the branches and thorns seemed invisible, tearing at Max's face and arms and chest from all directions. He pushed his way up the slope, his feet churning like those of a running back charging the goal line. At some point, the sound of gunfire had ceased, replaced by the thumping of his pulse. Had Reed been hit? Or had he given up his nest to chase Max? Either way, Lyle would be able to get to safety.

As he neared the top of the ridge, Max stopped to listen but could only hear his own heavy breathing. A few feet ahead, two fallen pine trees lay crisscrossed in a natural barricade. He crawled between the trunks, aimed his shotgun in the direction that he thought Reed would come from, and looked at the clothing in his hand: a coat and a wool vest. His core would be protected at least.

When he took off his wet shirt, he saw blood oozing out of a wound in his side. Had he been hit? He touched it and could feel that it was a cut—not a bullet wound. He must have hit a sharp branch on his dash up the hill. He hadn't even felt it. His knee throbbed with pain and he remembered hitting it on a rock as he came up out of the river. All in all though, he had come through the skirmish relatively unscathed.

And he still had that one shotgun shell left—one last chance to stop Reed Harris.

CHAPTER 68

Reed had been working his way around Lyle's flank when the second man opened fire, the boom of the shotgun sending Reed diving to the ground. A spray of pine needles and leaf confetti marked the path of the shotgun pellets. The man was shooting at the wrong spot.

That's when Reed saw Lyle lunge into the rapids, scrambling to retreat back to Minnesota. Reed took aim and squeezed off three rounds, at least one of the bullets dropping Lyle into the water.

"Die, you prick," Reed yipped with his first big grin in days.

The shotgun fired again, peppering the trees to Reed's left. Reed fired two shots into the far woods and ducked behind a tree just as a third shot ripped through the tree above him.

He pulled a handful of bullets from his pocket and reloaded the Glock's magazine. The second man had a shotgun. With a range of maybe fifty yards, it was no match for a nine-millimeter. All Reed had to do was stay out of range. The bigger question was whether the second man would attempt to cross the river.

Reed lifted his binoculars out and glassed the far shore. In the waning light of day the long shadows moved like mirages, but no man with a shotgun. He looked downstream for Lyle's body. Was that bastard still clinging to life somewhere along the bank? Reed thought about working his way down to the river to see, but shook that thought off. If Lyle was in the water, the cold would take care of him soon enough. The greater threat was the second man.

Reed scanned the woods again, and this time he saw something that definitely wasn't a shadow. He held the glasses against a nearby tree to steady them and saw movement. Before he could figure out exactly what he was looking at, the shape bolted from the woods and the second man leapt into the river.

Reed dropped the binoculars and raised the Glock, but the man was already beneath the cover of the near bank. Reed was out of position. He no longer had a firing lane into the clearing. He started making his way back to his first nest, and was almost there when Lyle stood and fired blindly at Reed's last position. Reed fired back automatically, shooting before he had acquired his target, the bullet missing badly and giving away his new position.

The second man came up out of the river and charged into the clearing. Reed fired at the moving target but the man kept running. Lyle fired again from the river, sending a spray of dead bark into Reed's face. Reed dove for cover behind a large rock, firing a shot back at Lyle while in midair.

Behind the rock, he rose to his knees and looked to the clearing. The second man was gone.

Damn it!

Reed took two deep breaths to settle down. He had to think. If he stayed where he was, the second man would take the high ground behind him and set up crossfire. If Reed left his cover to flank Lyle, he'd be pinned down against the river. His fingers shook with adrenaline as he listened to the second man crash his way up the hill, no more than seventy yards away. Then the crashing sound stopped.

Reed tried to think strategically. Lyle had at least two bullets in him and was in a freezing river. He was no longer a threat. Even if Lyle was too stubborn to die, he didn't have enough life in him to keep up the fight.

As for the second man, he would try to get behind Reed, stay uphill, where he would have the advantage. Reed needed to get around the back side of the hill, grab his son, and leave the battlefield. He would let his pursuer come to him—one on one. As Reed saw it, he had won this skirmish, and now it was time to set up the field for the next one.

He moved low and fast, looping wide to the west to avoid running into the second man. He would skirt around the ridge and come from the back side to collect his boy. From there, they would head north, and if the second man followed, Reed would be ready.

CHAPTER 69

Although Max's hiking pants and boots were wet, he now wore Lyle's dry vest and coat. He listened hard for any sound that might portend the arrival of Reed Harris, but heard nothing beyond his own breath. The woods on the hillside seemed too dense for anyone to slip through without making a sound, yet Reed had seemed to move like a ghost, like a man who had been hunting since he was big enough to carry a gun. Max suddenly wished that he had paid more attention to his father on their own hunting trips. Maybe he would have learned how to glide through the woods as quietly as Reed did.

Max propped himself against the downed tree and looked through the shadows for movement. He had a reasonable view of the slope below him and to his flanks, but the more Max examined his little barricade, the less his position made sense. A thin tail of sunlight leaked blue across the hills to the west, the dying light casting shadows in angry slashes. The woods had fallen dark enough that the only fight left for Max and Reed would be at close range, and what were the odds that Reed would get that close?

Part of Max wanted to circle back to Lyle. If Max's ploy had worked, Reed should have pulled back from the river and started hunting for him. But the thought of Pip stopped him. Surely Reed wasn't dragging Pip through the woods during a gunfight. So where was the child?

Max had stopped short of the crest, conceding the high ground for no good reason. If he were Reed he would circle the ridge and come up the back side—come at Max from the top of the ridge. Whoever held the high ground would hold the advantage, so Max abandoned his nest.

He climbed slowly, staying low to keep below the branches when he could, the sound of sprigs scraping against his coat rising like a cacophony to his own ears. He took the most direct path to the top of the hill, the crest flattening out for a quarter mile from side to side, but only a stone's throw from front to back. Max moved to the back side of the ridge and again listened. Reed couldn't have had enough time to travel that far, but underestimating him at this point would be deadly. Max held his breath.

Then he heard something that sounded like the chirp of an animal, somewhere down the back side of the ridge. He waited and heard it again. This time it sounded less like an animal and more like...a child crying.

He raised the shotgun to his shoulder and stepped lightly down the slope, doing his best to break no twig and rustle no leaf. Twenty paces down, he heard it again, clear this time.

Pip!

Ahead of him, a blue backpack lay on the ground beneath an enormous white pine, and next to it an orange sleeping bag, lumped in the middle where a little boy lay curled up. Max wanted to scream for joy, but instead, he squatted down and scanned the woods around him. He had to stay focused. Reed was out there still.

Pip had pulled the sides of the bag up around his ears and was sobbing. When Max got within a few feet of the boy, he stepped on a twig and Pip went silent.

"Pip," Max whispered.

The boy didn't move.

"I'm a friend of your grandpa—I'm a friend of Poppy's."

The boy peeked out upon hearing the name, but didn't speak.

Max looked around, cautious, like a man about to pet a bear cub knowing that the mama might be nearby. He put his gun down before peeling the collar of the sleeping bag back. There was Pip, his face dirty, his dark hair tossed, and his cheeks wet from tears. Max wanted to lift Pip up and hold him, tell him everything was okay now, but he couldn't risk the boy screaming. He needed to be gentle and keep Pip calm. He needed Pip to trust that he was there to protect him. He needed to be fatherly.

"I'm here to take you home," Max whispered.

Pip stayed still.

"We met at the grocery store just before Halloween, remember?" It dawned on Max that he looked very different on that first meeting. "I had long hair and a beard, but it was me."

Pip looked confused.

"What's a pirate's favorite letter of the alphabet?"

Pip looked hard at Max and Max finally saw a spark of recognition. Then the boy said, "Arrrr."

Max gave Pip a warm smile and held out his hand. "Come with me."

Pip rolled onto his hands and knees and crawled out of the bag, wearing his coat, boots, and gloves. Max lifted him with one hand, carrying his gun in the other, and walked up the slope with his finger resting on the trigger guard. The sun was fully down now, leaving no straggling rays, but a waxing moon floated above the horizon, giving Max just enough light to make his way.

The boy traveled well, holding on to Max's neck and tucking himself in tightly to keep from catching on a branch. At the steepest part of the slope, Pip locked his feet around Max's torso, freeing one of Max's hands to grab shoots and branches as he pulled them up the hill. His knee still hurt, but he had the boy in his arms; he had Pip. He pictured the joy on Lyle's face, in Meredith's eyes, and felt so light that he could have danced a jig.

At the crest Max slowed to catch his breath. If he was right about

Reed circling around the ridge, he would be there soon. Max had to hurry and get Pip across the rapids before Reed caught up to them.

But then what? Hit the SOS button on the GPS communicator? It would take hours for the float plane to come.

And what about Reed? There was no way he would simply walk away, give up on the prize that he had killed Sandy, and Olivia, and Peter to get. Reed would become the hunter, moving through the woods with the agility and speed of a wolf, while Max would have to protect both Pip and a wounded Lyle.

And even if Max managed to get them all out of the Boundary Waters alive, that would not end things. Reed would bide his time and strike again. He would keep coming for Pip until he got him—or until someone put a stop to Reed.

Max could stop him. He had one shell left; that was all it would take. He had done it before. He put Pip down and looked toward the back side of the ridge. For all of the unknowns that swam through Max's head, one fact was clear: In that five thousand square miles of forest, there was one small patch of land where Reed was guaranteed to make an appearance—the clearing where he had left his son.

He set Pip down. "Pip, I need you to do something for me." Max kept his voice low as he looked around for a place to hide the boy. He spied a cluster of small pine trees and he carried Pip to them and set him down in the middle. "I need you to lie down here—just for a few minutes."

"No." Pip gripped Max's sleeves, panicked.

"Shhh. It'll be okay. I promise. I need to go back and get your sleeping bag. It's gonna be cold tonight. You'll need your sleeping bag, right?"

"Don't leave me."

"I need you to help me. Can you do that? Can you help me?"

Pip looked at Max like he was peering over the edge of a steep cliff.

"I'm gonna get you out of these woods, Pip. I'm gonna get you home, I promise, but I need you to do one little thing for me. It's very important. I need you to lie down here until I get back. Don't make a sound — like hide-and-seek. You know how to play hide-and-seek?"

Pip nodded.

"It's like that, except I'll know where to find you. Nobody else will, but I'll come back and find you. Can you do that for me?"

"I'm cold."

Max took off Lyle's coat and wrapped it around the boy. "You recognize this coat? It's your grandpa's. He gave it to me so that when I found you I could use it to keep you warm."

A smile crept onto Pip's face and he pulled the coat close.

"I won't be long, I promise. Just lie down."

Pip sat down on the pine needles but didn't lie down, a compromise Max could live with. "Now stay here and don't make a sound, okay?"

Pip nodded.

"Good boy."

Max walked to the back-side slope and paused one last time to listen. Hearing nothing, Max crept down the hill.

CHAPTER 70

Pip's sleeping bag lay at the base of a white pine on a part of the hill where the terrain leveled out to a manageable pitch. Max slid a dead bough into the sleeping bag, its curve giving the bag the form of a sleeping child. He looked around for a place to hide, a rock or thick tree trunk, but nothing nearby fit the bill. He had to stay near enough to make his one shot count, but if Reed spotted him . . . well, Reed's gun probably had bullets to spare.

Max looked around again but this time glanced up. The lowest branch on the pine was just beyond his reach. He leaned the shotgun against the trunk, jumped up, and grabbed it, hanging and bouncing to test the limb's strength. It would do.

He loosened the canvas belt of his pants, checked the safety on the shotgun, and slid the barrel down his back side, sliding it through the belt, the trigger guard catching to hold it in place. Then he jumped and grabbed that branch, pulling with his arms and pushing with his feet against the trunk until he was able to reach another branch. He lifted himself up into the tree, the bark digging into his bare palms, the cut in his side shooting pain throughout his abdomen. The butt of the gun jabbed into his back like a spike. He gritted his teeth and suppressed the urge to grunt. Lyle would have been proud of his stealth.

He wondered how Lyle was doing. Max had a first-aid kit in his backpack, but he hadn't looked at it closely. The bullet hole in Lyle's shoulder appeared to be a through-and-through. He hadn't seen the leg wound, but he was pretty sure Lyle needed more than what that little kit could offer. If he could just patch Lyle up enough to hold him until the float plane came... But first he had to take care of Reed.

Standing on the lowest tier of limbs, he held on to the tree with one hand as he worked the shotgun out of his belt, unlocking the safety again. The branches blocked his view somewhat, but they would also hide him from Reed. He crouched with the shotgun across his lap and leaned against the trunk to wait.

His legs ached from the cold, his wet hiking pants setting like icy concrete now that he had stopped running. He hadn't worn gloves because he needed his fingers to be thin enough to find the trigger, and now they too had stiffened. He cupped his right hand over his mouth and breathed wet warm air into it, flexing his fingers to work the starch out of his knuckles. He knew that it wouldn't be long before he would start to shiver. When that happened, his aim would be hindered. He needed Reed to hurry his ass up.

Max ran his thumb across the safety once again just to make sure that it was off. In that squatting position, his sore knee felt like it was being crushed in a vise, but he dared not move. The moon offered enough light for him to make out the trees at the edge of the clearing, but not enough to see beyond them. Max scanned the woods in every direction, but paid special attention to the woods to his left. That should be Reed's path. It would bring him into the clearing and hopefully to the sleeping bag, which lay almost directly beneath Max's perch.

One shot. That's all Max had, but at that close range, that would be all it would take.

A dead branch cracked in the darkness to Max's left. He raised the butt of the shotgun to his shoulder.

Three and a half years of waiting for his conscience only to discover that he was the kind of man who could live with what he had done. Killing Mikhail had returned balance to the world. Killing Reed Harris would do the same.

Another crack, closer now.

Max searched the darkness for movement. He listened carefully for sound. He knew where Reed would enter the clearing and he aimed the shotgun at that spot. This would be a justified killing. Reed had killed three people and put two bullets into Lyle Voight. Reed deserved to die. Max pressed his finger against the trigger and sighted down the barrel.

Slowly, a shadow below took the shape of a man, stopping at the edge of the clearing. The jaundiced moon lit his form enough for Max to see Reed Harris, carrying his gun.

Max relaxed his jaw and breathed through his mouth, silencing the whistle of air that coursed through his nostrils. Reed scanned the clearing before whispering, "Pip, we gotta go." He seemed out of breath.

Reed stepped carefully across the clearing, stopping directly below Max, the barrel of the shotgun no more than ten feet from the top of Reed's head. One small pull of the trigger and Reed would drop, his skull opened to the night air.

Max felt nothing for the man. Reed Harris was a carcass, still breathing only because Max allowed it. Max knew that he would feel nothing once he pulled the trigger. No regret. No guilt.

Reed bent down to shake his son awake.

Max could easily kill Reed... but, he also knew he had a choice. Something powerful bloomed in his chest and Max thumbed the safety, locking it on. Then he lowered the butt of the gun down, gripped the barrel, and jumped out of the tree.

He landed on Reed's shoulders, driving the butt of the gun into the back of Reed's head. Reed dropped to his knees. Max rolled hard on the ground beside him, stumbling only a bit before squaring up, swinging the shotgun like a three-wood, and smashing it hard into Reed's face, snapping his head back, the pistol falling from his hand.

Reed fell backwards and rolled down the hill, but jumped to his feet and immediately charged at Max, swinging blindly. Max dodged a right hook, the momentum carrying a dazed Reed past him. When Reed turned around, Max threw a haymaker into Reed's face, catching him between the eyes and dropping him like a bag of oats.

Reed didn't move, and for a second Max thought that he might have killed the man after all, but then a gurgled breath escaped Reed's throat. Adrenaline coursed through Max's veins. His heart thudded hard. He wanted to kick Reed in the face for what he had done to Lyle—he wanted to howl his triumph to the moon—but he put his hands on his knees, took some deep breaths, and tried to calm down.

Max still had his headlamp in his pocket. He strapped it to his head and turned it on. Reed's nose was bent to the side. His forehead was red and swollen, and blood trickled out of his mouth. His eyes didn't move behind his slitted eyelids.

Max carried the shotgun and Reed's Glock to where Reed's backpack lay. There he unclipped a bundle of paracord attached to the outside of the pack. He used the cord to tie Reed's elbows behind his back, then rolled him over and tied his wrists together in front of his stomach. With plenty of cord left over, he knotted Reed's legs and feet together. He checked Reed's pockets for blades and found a Leatherman, which Max pocketed.

Then he dragged a groggy Reed to a tree about as big around as his leg. He removed Reed's belt, leaned him against the tree, and wrapped the belt around both the tree and Reed's throat. This was the same way that he had tied Mikhail three and a half years ago. For a moment, the similarity filled Max with sadness, as though he had learned nothing in that time. But that notion fell away as Max thought about the child waiting for him at the top of the ridge.

Satisfied with his effort, Max picked up the guns and Pip's sleeping bag and headed up the hill to keep his promise.

CHAPTER 71

Pip hadn't moved, just as he had agreed. He sat cross-legged, hunched under the pine trees, with a look of concern frozen across his face. Max realized that Pip was blinded by the headlamp and didn't know who was walking toward him.

"It's me, Pip," Max said. "I got your sleeping bag."

Pip walked out of the trees and Max lifted him into his arms.

The trek down the ridge took some time. Max could see well enough with the headlamp turned on, but finding a route that didn't require them to duck or crawl was a challenge. He had to backtrack a few times, but his feet were light and his mood buoyant as he descended the hill and entered the clearing at the side of the river.

Lyle's backpack still lay where he had dropped it. Max had hoped to see Lyle waiting on the other side of the rapids, but the woods were empty. Max wadded Lyle's coat and Pip's sleeping bag into the straps of the pack, lifted Pip onto his shoulders, and carried the pack in one hand and the shotgun in the other as he crossed the river.

In the dark, the sound of water churning over the rocks sounded more ominous than it had in daylight, and walking at that slower pace, with a child on his shoulders, made the crossing more treacherous.

Max put Pip down at the river's edge and they walked thirty yards upstream to the place in the woods where he had dropped his pack. It lay just inside the tree line, and just as he had dropped it—Lyle was nowhere around. The dry clothing hadn't been pulled out. The first-aid kit remained untouched. Max's heart became as heavy as a stone.

"We're gonna camp here," Max said. He laid out Pip's sleeping bag and tucked the boy inside. "I'm gonna go find some firewood. You stay right here. Okay?"

Pip nodded his assent.

Max put Lyle's coat on over his wet clothing and dug the military flashlight from his pack. His toes were numb and the cold had turned the skin on his legs tender, the material rubbing like sandpaper with every step. He considered changing into dry clothes, but Lyle was out there somewhere. "I'll be right back," Max said. "I promise."

Max walked back to the rapids, looking for Lyle, in case he had pulled himself from the river but hadn't found Max's backpack. He thought about yelling Lyle's name, but Pip would hear it and expect his grandfather to be nearby—alive. With every step, the sense of dread that squeezed Max's chest grew tighter. He followed the river downstream, scanning the river and woods with the light.

When he was out of earshot of Pip, he started calling out Lyle's name, softly at first, but louder the farther away he got from the boy. He was about to turn around and go back when he saw it, something smooth and shiny floating in the shallows.

"No...no."

Max ran into water up to his knees, the object taking the form of a man's body as Max drew closer. He recognized the shirt.

"No!"

He grabbed the shirt and turned Lyle over. His friend's face was white in the light of the moon, a bullet hole clean through his throat. Max tried to pull Lyle toward shore, but he slipped from Max's frozen hands. He grabbed Lyle's shirt by the collar, but his fingers wouldn't tighten, so finally he hooked his arms under Lyle's armpits and pulled, heaving Lyle through the mud and grass, onto dry land.

He laid Lyle on the shore and hit him hard in the chest with his fist.

"Come on, Lyle." Max opened Lyle's mouth and tried to breathe air into his lungs, but they were full of water. He turned Lyle onto his stomach and pushed his weight down onto Lyle's back, flushing river water out of his chest. He turned Lyle onto his back again and gave another breath. "Breathe, you son of a bitch.

"Don't do this to me." Max's eyes filled with tears as he worked the CPR. "We got Pip. He's waiting for you." Max gave two more breaths. Lyle's lifeless eyes stared up at him. Max pushed on Lyle's chest again. "You can't do this now. It's not right."

Max pressed three more chest compressions but then stopped. There was a rigidity to Lyle's body that Max recognized. He knew his friend was dead—he had known it when he pulled him from the river. Lyle had taken that bullet to the throat so that Max could make it to the tree line. He had saved Max's life. He had saved Pip.

Wet and cold and beaten, Max put his arms around Lyle's shoulder and hugged Lyle's face to his chest. Max was covered in mud and river water, his hands and arms drained of strength. He looked to the sky through tear-filled eyes, half expecting Lyle's soul to be looking down on him. The moon and stars were the only witnesses to the death of a good man.

"You saved Pip's life," Max whispered finally. "You did it."

Then Max heard Meredith's voice. It sifted through the trees around him, a whisper, gossamer-soft and floating in the breeze. *Bring my family back to me.*

Max dropped his head in defeat.

CHAPTER 72

Max shivered violently as he trudged back to where Pip lay wrapped in his sleeping bag. From his pocket, he pulled the GPS communicator. A push of a button would bring a plane. Max contemplated hitting the SOS button, but wondered if a plane would be able to land at night. Did he even want the plane en route yet? Reed was still in Canada. Once things became official, there would be jurisdictional squabbles and extradition proceedings.

Max picked up enough wood to build a fire and returned to Pip, who was sitting up in his sleeping bag waiting. The sight almost brought tears to Max's eyes. He was such a quiet child, a trusting child, and Max had failed him. He stared up at Max without speaking, as if he expected something, as though he was waiting for Max to understand what had to be done. Max felt lost.

But Pip needed to be taken care of. He needed food, and a place to sleep, and safety.

Max stripped out of his wet clothes and put on dry ones. Then he wrapped his sleeping bag around his shoulders and worked on the fire, using the small cookstove from Lyle's pack to get the wet wood going. Once the fire took hold he poured the last of his water into a small pot and set it on the flame to boil. They would be eating beef stroganoff.

Pip didn't speak until the food was almost ready.

"Is my daddy going to get us?" he asked.

Max carried the packet of beef stroganoff to Pip and handed it to him. Then he looked Pip in the eye and said, "No, Pip. Your daddy's not gonna get us. He's never gonna bother you ever again. You have my word on that."

"He shot Spud."

"Spud?"

"My friend. Daddy shot him in the knee and in the stomach."

"Yeah," Max said, "I know." How could a father do such an evil act in front of his son?

Pip closed his eyes and exhaled, as if the poison of the past few days could drift out in that breath.

Max sat next to Pip as they ate.

When they'd finished, Max asked, "Did you get enough to eat?"

Pip nodded.

Max didn't want to get out from beneath his sleeping bag. His core had warmed up, but his feet and hands were still ice. When he stood, his joints and muscles popped and creaked like he was busting the rust on an old hinge. He unzipped his pack and pulled out the bivvy. He would let Pip sleep in it tonight. He set it up in a matter of seconds and showed Pip his new sleeping quarters. "It's all yours," Max said as he scooted the boy inside.

After he put Pip to bed, Max talked to the stars so that the boy would know that Max remained nearby. The sky that night was extraordinary, the stars as thick as sand on a beach, the canopy almost silver against the dark shadows of the trees. He wondered if the sky had been that beautiful the night before. It can be astonishing how the noise in one's own head can alter the way the world looks.

Max wanted Pip to know that he was still nearby, so he continued talking to Pip in a low, soothing voice, the kind of voice he would have used with his own child, prattling on about constellations and Greek myths until he was certain that Pip had fallen into a deep sleep.

Then Max unclipped a roll of cord from Lyle's backpack and slipped away from their camp, heading back to the rapids.

At the river, Max stripped naked again and rolled his clothing and paracord into a bundle to carry across the river. He felt numb with exhaustion, but he had a lot of work ahead. Again he stepped into the frozen water and again it stabbed at his skin like a thousand small knives. "Jesus...Christ!" He cussed quietly to himself as the shock of the cold took his breath away. "God...damn!"

He climbed into Canada and put his clothes back on, fingers and toes throbbing. The temperature had to be in the twenties. One more job to do, then he could sleep. He picked up the paracord and headed up the hill to find Reed.

Reed hadn't moved from the tree. Not that he had a choice, with a belt strapped around his neck, yet he looked a great deal weaker now. His head slumped on his shoulders like he was asleep but his eyes were open. His body lay at a strange angle, probably the result of a struggle to get free. And his shoulders sagged like a beast who had given up his fight.

"I can't breathe," Reed said, his voice wheezy and cracked. "Help me. I'm freezing."

Max paid no attention and went to work checking the knots.

"Who are you?"

Who am I? Max considered. *I'm the man who deals with monsters like you.*

"You're the one who put the phone in the toy car," Reed said. "You broke into Peter's house, didn't you?"

Max ignored Reed and started unraveling the cord he'd brought.

"That's burglary, you know."

Max wrapped a second layer of bondage around Reed's legs. He would bind the man tighter than a mummy for the ride back to Minnesota.

"And what you're doing now is kidnapping. You're willing to go to prison for this."

You have no fucking idea what I'm willing to do, Max thought. He unbuckled the belt and threw Reed to the ground, shoving his face down into the dirt, then sat on his back.

"Jesus Christ! My wrist! You're breaking my fucking wrist. Get off me."

Max tied a second section of cord to Reed's elbows, insurance that he wouldn't wiggle free on the long walk.

"You're not taking me back. You'll never get me across that river. I'll drown myself first, and I'll take you with me."

Max pulled Reed's Leatherman from his pocket and cut the cord. He stabbed the blade into the ground beside him and rolled Reed onto his back.

"You think you're saving Pip?" Reed said. "Is that what you think? You don't know the whole story. You don't know the truth."

Max doubled up the bindings around Reed's wrists.

"Your buddy Lyle molested him."

Something hot came alive in Max's gut.

"He's got you fooled. He's got everybody fooled."

Max couldn't ignore him anymore. "Shut up, you piece of shit!"

"You teamed up with a child molester."

"I said shut up!"

"He's the one who should go to prison. Why do you think I took Pip? I was saving him from that child-fucking—"

Max grabbed the Leatherman and held the blade to Reed's throat. "You're gonna shut your goddamned mouth. You understand me?"

"Do it!" Reed locked eyes with Max. "Here and now—get it over with."

A drop of blood trickled down where the blade pressed in to Reed's skin.

"Do it, you fucking coward!"

Max dropped the Leatherman and punched Reed hard in the face, again and again until Reed's head swiveled loose on his shoulders.

Max rubbed his knuckles and shook his hand to get some feeling back in his fingers. He would get Reed across that river — he would see Reed Harris in prison for what he had done.

Max went to Reed's backpack and dumped its contents to the ground in search of something to gag him with. He wouldn't listen to one more bark from that cur. He settled on a shirtsleeve, which he cut free using the Leatherman blade.

Reed was awake, but dazed, unable to comprehend what was happening. With the gag in place, Max faced the problem of getting Reed across the river. Reed would buck and squirm all the way back, and once in the river, that squirming would become a wrestling match.

An idea came to Max. He returned to the pile of Reed's gear and picked up a hatchet. He walked through the mechanics in his head and nodded. It would work.

CHAPTER 73

Max tucked a loop of cord around the bindings at Reed's ankles. He slung the loop over his shoulders, the rope crossing Max's chest. With the hatchet hooked to his belt, he began his climb up to the top of the ridge, pulling like a husky at the lead of a sled. Reed lay on his back, his legs lifted in the air as Max pulled him feet-first up the slope.

Reed thrashed and jerked as Max dragged his bundle a few inches at a time, using the trees and roots to pull himself forward, digging his feet to keep from sliding back. He thought about the Roman soldiers at Masada building a path up the side of a mountain stone by stone. He thought about Sultan Mehmed II pulling a fleet of ships over the hills at Galata during the siege of Constantinople. He thought about the Little Engine That Could, and the tortoise who outran the hare. Inch by inch, he pulled Reed up the hill.

At the crest, he rested and worked a knot out of his shoulder. Then he headed down the southern slope with gravity on his side. The headlamp cast its light out far enough to plan his path, and when the trees grew too thick, he used the hatchet to clear his way. Reed still did his best to tangle himself on rocks and scrub, but a couple yanks of the rope and Max was moving again.

Max had no idea how many hours had passed since he'd left Pip at their camp. It could easily be midnight, or three in the morning. Finally, Max reached the rapids.

Max left Reed near the water's edge, tethering him to a tree so that he couldn't roll himself into the river. Then Max ventured into the woods and found a pine no bigger around than a soup can, a good twenty feet up to its tip. Max took the hatchet to it, keeping his swings light so as to not awaken Pip on the other side of the river. He chipped away until the tree fell, then he cleared most of the limbs, leaving only a Y-crux about fifteen feet up.

Back at the river, he rolled Reed onto his stomach and tied him to the pole with paracord, securing him at the waist, shoulders, and knees, his back hoisted at the Y-crux. Reed squirmed, but the ride down the hill had taken much of the fight out of him. With Reed bound to the pole, Max dragged Reed, feet-first, to the bank, the pole sticking out a good eight feet below Reed's boots.

Satisfied that Reed was ready for his crossing, Max gathered his strength for one last trip. He told himself that people jump into frozen water for charity—polar bear plunges. This was no big deal. He stripped down to nothing, lifted his clothing above his head, and waded in. "Son of a bitch!" he hissed. Why would anyone do this voluntarily? He hurried across, tossed his dry clothing to shore, and went back for Reed.

Reed fought as Max yanked the pole toward the center of the fifteen-foot passage, a lone tug-o-war. When he reached the middle of the stream, he dropped the pole. Reed angled out of the river on the Canadian side, the water rising up to his chest, his head propped against the rocks along the bank.

Now came the hard part. Max got behind Reed and pushed him up like a centurion raising a crucifix. Reed fought like a feral cat, kicking and heaving. The man truly wanted to drown.

He was heavy as he rose out of the water, but Max only needed to get him upright because gravity would take it from there. With the last bit of strength he had, Max pushed forward, lifting Reed straight up. Reed screamed into his gag as Max gave one final push and Reed toppled forward, dropping face-first onto the opposite bank. Even with the rush of churning water in his ears, Max could hear the crack of Reed's head hitting the rocky embankment.

Max climbed out of the river and turned Reed over to find him still alive. With his head and shoulders out of the water, he couldn't drown himself if he tried, so Max took a moment to put on his dry clothes.

From there, Max dragged Reed into the tree line and, while it seemed impossible that Reed might wiggle his way into the river, being still tied to that pole, Max made sure that his captive would stay put by tethering him to a birch at the edge of the woods. Then Max walked upstream to where Pip lay in the bivvy, pulled Lyle's sleeping bag from his pack, and carried it back to where Reed lay bound and gagged. It was more than Reed deserved, but Max wrapped Lyle's bag around him.

Reed was beaten and exhausted, his face darkened with bruises, his nose broken and crooked, but in the dim light of the half moon, Max could still see his rage.

Max walked back to where Pip lay asleep in the bivvy, listening for his near-silent breath.

Max wrapped his sleeping bag around his shoulders and dug into his pocket for the GPS communicator, pulling it and Jenni's bracelet out together, the gold chain wrapped around his knuckles. He fingered through the charms of the bracelet, stopping on the one with no name. He closed his eyes so that he could see Jenni's face. He tried to conjure his child, the eyes he'd seen in his dream.

Max kissed the charm, held it to his cheek, and whispered, "I miss you." Then he pushed the SOS button, and leaned against a tree to wait.

CHAPTER 74

The sound of the plane woke Max from a shallow sleep. The sun had not yet broken the horizon, but there was enough light to see the break between land and sky. The plane came in low from the east, dropping to tree height as it followed the river past him.

Max slipped out of the warm sleeping bag and stood, feeling the pain from his knee and the cut in his side. He limped upstream to a clearing, and when the plane flew by for a second pass, Max waved his arms. It circled and came in for a landing, turning in the river so that it could push against the current as it angled to shore.

A door opened on the copilot's side and Henry stepped onto the pontoon. The SOS must have gone to his shop. Henry unhooked a short rope and tossed it to Max, who pulled the plane as far into the sandy shallows as he could.

"You okay?" Henry said as he walked to shore through ankle-deep water.

"Not by a long shot," Max said.

The pilot, a woman in her sixties with rust-colored hair, stepped onto the pontoon. "How many do you got?"

"How many?" Max didn't understand the question.

"People," she said. "I assume we're here to evac some people." She pulled a longer rope from the cockpit and tied it to the pontoon leg. Then she waded to shore in search of a place to anchor the plane.

"One," Max said.

He waved Henry over to explain, pointing down the shore to where Pip had emerged from the bivvy. "That boy there...that's Lyle's grandson. You'll be taking him out on the first trip."

"First trip?" Henry said.

"Lyle's dead. His body's in the woods past the rapids. The boy doesn't know it, and I think it'd be best for all concerned if we don't fly him out of here sitting next to his dead grandpa."

"Lyle's dead? How?"

"It's a long story, but...let's take a walk."

Max led Henry downstream. When they got to Pip, Max bent down. "How are you feeling today?"

Pip looked at Henry and then at the plane. "Is that for us?"

"It is," Max said. "This is Henry. He and his friend are going to fly us out of here. You ever been in a plane before?"

Pip shook his head.

"See that woman up there?" Henry said, pointing. "Her name is Rachael. She's our pilot. Why don't you go say hi to her?"

Pip looked at Max, who nodded and gave Pip a small nudge on the back.

Max continued downstream with Henry until they got to the rapids. Max pulled the top of the sleeping bag back. Reed was tied and gagged but alive. He looked like hell. Blood had dried on the side of his face. His nose was broken and his eyes were black, his left one swollen completely shut.

"This is Reed Harris...Lyle's former son-in-law. He killed Lyle's daughter and kidnapped the boy. We came up here to track him down. Last night Lyle was crossing the river when this man shot him. Lyle's body is downstream a bit on the other side of those trees. I'm sorry, Henry. I did all I could."

Henry braced his hand on a tree as he absorbed the news. "I can't believe Lyle's dead. I didn't think there was nothing that could kill a man like that."

A lump formed in Max's throat. "He gave his life to save his grandson."

Henry leaned down, looked into Reed's eyes, and spit in his face.

"Take me to Lyle," Henry said.

Max led Henry farther down to where Lyle's body lay frozen, his skin pale and hard. "Oh, sweet Jesus," Henry whispered.

"I'd like you to take the boy back to Ely alone," Max said. "I don't want him seeing his grandfather or his father like they are."

Henry knelt and touched the frozen skin of Lyle's cheek. "You go back with the boy," Henry said. "I'll stay here."

"I need Reed back alive," Max said.

"I won't touch him," Henry said. "It'll take some doing, but I'll leave the son of a bitch alone."

"I have a gun if you want it. It only has one shell, but if he tries anything, that'll stop him."

Max also had Reed's Glock, but he had to take that back to Ely so that ballistics could match it to the bullets in Peter and Lyle.

They walked to the plane, where Rachael was loading Pip into the backseat. Henry called Rachael to shore and Max watched as Henry told her the news, her head slumping low. Then she looked at Max, nodded, and walked back to the plane.

As they taxied out to the middle of the river for takeoff, Max caught a glimpse of Henry downstream again, kneeling next to Lyle's body, his head bowed as if in prayer.

CHAPTER 75

Max sat beside the pilot and Pip rode in the backseat, staring out at the sky around them. In that moment, Pip lived in a sliver of respite between the tumult of his kidnapping and the maelstrom of heartache ahead. Max wished he could capture just a drop of that contentment to save for later when Pip would need it the most.

Rachael used the radio to try to get in touch with the sheriff of St. Louis County, which would have jurisdiction over the murder of Peter Molinar. It comforted Max that Tate Bolger would have no say. Max would push to get the Bureau of Criminal Apprehension to keep tabs on the investigation into Sandy Voight's death. Intentionally or not, Bolger had botched things from the beginning.

It felt strange to think like a cop again, the world defined by rules and procedures. But he wasn't a cop. He had bent and broken the law to serve his purposes and he felt just fine about it. All that time he had spent at the cabin trying to turn back some karmic clock, but it had never been about going back. The man in the mirror wasn't a wound that needed to heal; he was the scar that remained.

About halfway into their hour-long flight back to Ely, Rachael managed to reach someone from the sheriff's department in St. Louis County. She handed a headset to Max, and he introduced himself to Chief Deputy Aldo Bennet.

Max gave Bennet a thumbnail sketch of what had happened, lowering his voice as he talked about the deaths of Sandy and Lyle Voight. He told Bennet about the body they would find at Hill River State Forest, and about Peter Molinar. Then he asked Deputy Bennet to bring Lyle's wife, Meredith, to the dock to take care of Pip once they landed.

"No offense," Bennet said, "but I don't know you from Adam, and you want me to tell this woman that her husband's dead?"

"I used to be a homicide detective in Minneapolis. Call Homicide there and ask for Niki Vang. She was my partner. She can vouch for me."

After his chat with Deputy Bennet, Max must have dozed off, because the next thing he knew the plane was banking for its landing on Shagawa Lake, the northern border of Ely. Behind him, Pip stared out his window with a look of amazement. All that Max could think about was how he had failed. He should have been the one to take that bullet. It should have been him lying dead on the bank of the river and Lyle sitting in that plane with his grandson.

There were two squad cars waiting for them at the dock, and next to one stood Meredith Voight, her gloved hands clasped together and pressed to her lips. Even from that distance, Max could see the grief on her face.

"Grandma!" Pip beamed. He waved from his seat in the plane.

Because they were coming to the dock on Max's side, he opened his door and stepped onto the pontoon as Henry had, unhooking the rope and tossing it to a man on the dock. Once they'd secured the plane, Max undid Pip's seat belt and set Pip on the dock. Pip ran as fast as he could into the arms of his crying grandmother.

"Grandma, I was in a plane!"

There were three men in uniform as well, two deputies and one city cop. One of the deputies stepped forward. "Detective Rupert?"

Max nodded and shook the man's hand.

"I'm Chief Deputy Bennet. It's good to meet you."

He must have talked to Niki, Max thought.

"If you don't mind, one of the boys will give you a ride to the office. We'll need a full statement."

"That's fine," Max said. He turned and pulled his backpack from the plane and handed it to Bennet. In a voice low enough that only he and Bennet could hear, Max said, "There's a Glock nine in here. Reed Harris used it to kill Peter Molinar and Lyle Voight. You'll want to get it to ballistics."

Bennet took the pack and looked inside, nodding. Then he handed the pack to another deputy. "Take Mr. Rupert and this backpack to the station and wait for me."

The deputy took the pack in one hand and Max's arm in the other. Max pulled free and said, "I need a minute."

He walked to the end of the dock, to where Meredith knelt, hugging Pip tightly to her chest. When she saw Max coming, she stood.

"I'm so sorry, Meredith."

Her bottom lip quivered as tears streaked down her cheeks. Max stepped in and wrapped his arms around her. He felt her knees give as she leaned into him, a woman barely holding it together. For that brief moment at least, she didn't have to stand on her own. She hugged him back, and sobbed softly into his shoulder.

"I tried," Max said at last. "I promise I did."

She took a breath, held it for a second, and whispered, "I know."

CHAPTER 76

Max had spent a lifetime sitting in police interrogation rooms, but this was the first time that he had been seated on the other side of the table. He felt a new appreciation for the calculations that muddied a simple round of questions. Max had to explain how he and Lyle had tracked Reed to his shack without dropping the hammer on Niki. He hadn't yet prepared a version of the story that kept her out of it.

For his part, Bennet was all business. No smiles or chitchat. When Max asked how they were going to process a crime scene so deep in the woods, Bennet ignored the question. Max understood Bennet's position—a man shows up with one dead body and instructions for where to find two more. Bennet had to consider that Max might be a murderer himself. It helped that Max was a former cop and had brought Pip out of the woods, but that could only take him so far.

Max started with the day that Lyle Voight showed up at his cabin. He told about Tate Bolger's refusal to look into the disappearance of Sandy Voight, which, in a way, led to everything else.

"It almost seemed like Bolger was looking the other way on purpose," Max said. "You need to bring the BCA in on this."

"You think Tate Bolger would cover up for a murderer?" Bennet asked. The question seemed more accusatory than curious.

"There's a definite conflict of interest. He and Reed have been tight since high school. They were patrol deputies together. Because of that, Bolger flatly refused to see this for what it was."

"I know Tate, and I can tell you that you're barking up the wrong tree."

"Just consider it," Max said. "That's all I ask."

Max continued, but didn't mention that Niki had pinged a phone number for him, nor did he mention breaking into Peter's house. He simply said that surveillance of Reed had led them to Peter Molinar. When Bennet asked what that meant, Max smiled and said, "We were watching Reed very closely." That didn't seem to satisfy Bennet, but he moved on.

When Max came to hauling Reed Harris out of Canada, Bennet gave a rare smile and said, "I suspect the good people of Canada will thank you for that one."

Max had just finished his first run-through when a deputy stuck his head in the door and motioned for Bennet to come out. When Bennet returned he said, "It appears . . . they've found a body in the Hill River Forest . . . just like you said. I'm going to the scene. Can you stick around here for a while?"

"Do you have a cot or something? I could use some sleep."

"I'll have one brought in."

Bennet left the door unlocked, which was a good sign, but had he locked it, he would have had to read Max his Miranda warning. The line between a voluntary interview and an in-custody interrogation is thin.

Soon a deputy brought a cot and a blanket. The room was small, and Max had to push the table to the side and stack the chairs on it to make room. Once he had the cot laid out, it took no time at all for Max to fall asleep.

Just before two o'clock, Max awoke to the door opening. It took a second for Max to remember where he was and why. He was hungry, and groggy, and curious. He rubbed the sleep from his face as a woman in a black suit entered. She introduced herself as Agent Edith Miller of the Bureau of Criminal Apprehension, Duluth office. Max sighed his relief.

Agent Miller carried a legal pad and a briefcase. On the legal pad were several lines that Max couldn't read, but he assumed it to be notes of the story he had told Bennet. Max folded up the cot and reset the table and chairs for his second interview.

He told the story exactly as he had, again remaining vague on how they had linked Reed Harris to Peter Molinar. When he told her that it was simply good detective work, she asked that he explain that to her. He tried another dodge, saying that a good magician doesn't give away his secrets. She shook her head and said, "I'd really like to hear how you did that."

Through the window, Max could see that the world outside of the sheriff's office had turned gray and cloudy, the sun slipping toward the western horizon. It had been a long day. Max sat back in his chair and considered Agent Miller's request. He was tired of dancing around. He would be called to testify at Reed's trial, so he couldn't lie or it might screw up the case. At the same time, he wasn't going to give up Niki. But the thing about voluntary police interviews is that the interviewee holds all the cards. He had resented that as a cop, but now . . . Max leaned forward. "Agent Miller, I'm gonna end this interview and walk out of here now—unless . . . I'm under arrest?"

"I still have some questions—"

Max stood. "They'll have to wait. I appreciate that you have a job to do, but I've had one hell of a night. I'm exhausted, and I feel like I've gone ten rounds with a heavy weight. We'll need to pick this up tomorrow when my head is clearer."

"I'd really like you to stay."

"I'm free to leave, am I not?"

"You are."

"Thank you."

Max walked out and asked a woman at a desk to contact Bennet for him. She made a phone call and handed the receiver to Max.

"Deputy Bennet, I was wondering if I could get a ride to the trailhead to get my car."

"Your car's not there," Bennet said. "We towed it in for processing. It's part of a crime scene."

"Ah, shit."

"Gotta be thorough."

Max would have done the same, and he mentally kicked himself for not realizing that his car would be searched. "Is there a taxi service here in Ely?"

Bennet chuckled at that.

"Any suggestions on how I might get home?" Max asked.

"I'll tell you what. We have a Range Rover forfeited from a drug dealer some time back. We use it for surveillance. You can borrow that."

Half an hour later, Max was on the road, a burger and fries spread out on the console. As he drove the two hours back to his cabin, he ran through everything again. Had he tried hard enough to pull Lyle back from his rage? Should he have stopped Lyle when he wanted to kill Peter? Would that have changed anything? Had he made the right decision to bring Reed back?

Maybe he was too tired to see it clearly, but he felt that he had done his best for Lyle. And although sparing Reed's life came with a bitter aftertaste, one less ghost would visit him at his cabin.

The one regret that weighed heavy on Max's mind was the way he had treated Niki.

As he drove, the sky grew dark with clouds, and then dark with night. By the time he pulled onto the trail that led back to his cabin, the world around him was black. The Range Rover bounced along until he neared his cabin and saw Lyle's pickup still parked there, a small blade of regret piercing his chest. Then he noticed a reflection that seemed out of place—another vehicle. A few feet closer and he recognized Niki's car parked next to his door.

He wished that he had had more time to prepare. But a man can't always choose when his world will turn upside down. He eased up to the side of the cabin and parked.

CHAPTER 77

M ax approached the glass door wearing mud-covered hiking pants and a patina of grime from his two nights in the Boundary Waters. He was tired, and sore, and smelled like sweat and river water. This was not how he wanted to look when he and Niki met once again.

Niki sat on his couch beneath a dim floor lamp, watching as he stepped onto the front porch. She wore a flannel shirt, and blue jeans, and no smile.

Max opened the door slowly. "I see you found my cabin," he said.

"I'm a detective."

He closed the door behind him. "Bennet called you?"

"He said that some guy was being flown out of the Boundary Waters with a crazy story. He wanted to know if you were a nut job. I told him you were, but you were also a passable homicide detective in your day."

"I appreciate the reference."

"He said there were dead bodies?"

"You already know about Sandy Voight and Olivia Molinar. Add to that Peter Molinar." Max let his eyes drift to the floor. "And Lyle Voight."

Niki allowed a brief moment of silence before saying, "I'm sorry. The child's okay though?"

"Physically, but his mother's dead. His grandfather died saving his life. His father's going to prison. Just a few weeks ago he was looking forward to Halloween with his family. Now . . ."

"They said you brought the father back alive."

Something about that still didn't sit right with Max, like it was an admission of weakness. "I had him in the sights of my shotgun—ten feet away."

"He killed your friend? Lyle?"

Max started to answer, but something stuck in his throat, so he simply nodded.

"No one would have faulted you if..." Niki looked as though she were studying his face for some unspoken understanding. When Max didn't respond, she said, "It would have been self-defense."

Max thought back to those few seconds, how easy it would have been to cut the man down.

Niki continued, "But you brought him back."

"A little worse for wear, but yeah, I brought him back."

"Now he's in the hands of St. Louis County?"

"And the BCA. That guy Bennet seems to be a good egg. Spent the day giving him my statement. I kept you out of it."

"What do you mean, you kept me out of it?"

"The ping that led us to Peter Molinar. They don't have to know about that."

"Why not?"

"I don't want you getting in trouble for doing me a favor. I shouldn't have asked you in the first place."

Niki shook her head slowly, exasperated or maybe angry.

"What?" Max asked.

"You're still treating me like I'm your little sister. You were always like that. I did that ping because I was being a good cop. If anyone wants to make an issue of it, let them. I can take the heat. I'm tougher than you think."

"I never thought—"

Niki stood, her anger pulling her to her feet. "You have this twisted belief that keeping me in the dark is noble."

"Keeping you in the dark?"

"Christ, Max. I'm a detective. I make a living figuring things out."

"Things?"

"You were hunting for the man who killed your wife. I was there. I helped you look. I covered for you, remember? Then you disappeared without a word. Don't you think I know what happened? I may not know the details, but I'm not stupid."

Max lost his breath. Of course she knew. It had always been wishful thinking on Max's part, the hope of seeing a better version of himself reflected in Niki's eyes.

"I should have told you," he said, finally.

Max walked to the refrigerator, using those few seconds to think. Niki deserved to know the whole truth. He would tell her the details and let the chips fall where they may. Lyle had left two beers behind. Max opened them and took one to Niki on the couch. Max took a seat in a chair opposite her.

"The man who killed my wife...his name was Mikhail Vetrov. Jenni had a recording. One of the girls that Vetrov trafficked had told Jenni about his business. But she'd told it in Russian, so Jenni had no idea. He killed her before she could get the tape translated. I followed him from Minneapolis up to the border...and caught him about twenty yards into Canada."

Max thought back to that night: the cold, the wind, the ease he felt in his chest as it all played out. "I dragged him onto a frozen lake—tied up—and I cut holes in the ice with an old spoon auger. I had to cut eight little holes in a circle to make one big enough to fit a man through. I listened all day as he denied killing Jenni, but as I dragged him toward that hole...he confessed."

Max expected to see an expression of horror on Niki's face but saw what looked like...empathy?

"I told myself that I had no choice. His confession would never be admissible in court. He would walk free."

"Mikhail never made it off that lake," Niki said.

Max held Niki's gaze. He wanted her to see the lack of remorse, see him for who he was now. "No," Max said. "Mikhail didn't make it off that lake."

He stood and said, "Now that you know…you deserve to have some time to take it in. I'm gonna go take a shower and if you're not here when I come out, I'll understand."

Max took a couple steps and stopped next to the couch. Slowly, gently, he laid a hand on Niki's shoulder. "And what I just told you…my confession…you can do with that what you want. I'm done running. No matter what you decide to do…it won't change how I feel about you."

He gave her a soft squeeze, and then walked into the bathroom and closed the door.

The hot shower felt like a dream, soothing his muscles and easing the tension in his chest. The cut in his side, which had been quiet since the EMT cleaned it at the sheriff's office, woke up as the soapy water seeped through the bandage, but even that couldn't diminish the sense of peace.

Max closed his eyes and held his face to the stream. He had confessed at last, revealing his true self to Niki—a murderer, the kind of man she hunted. And if she chose to hunt him, he would gladly surrender. She could take his confession to a grand jury or she could keep his secret; it didn't matter. He was willing to face what he'd done.

Max tipped his head against the shower wall to listen for Niki leaving, but all he could hear was the water beating against the fiberglass. When he finally toweled himself dry, he slipped into a pair of flannel pajama bottoms left on the floor days earlier and the bathrobe that he kept on the door hook.

Before leaving the bathroom, he wiped steam from the mirror and looked at himself. It was the first time in three and a half years that he held his own gaze. Maybe it was because he wasn't looking for the man he used to be—or the man he thought he'd been. He was looking at a man who was flawed, but honest about the darkness inside. He was looking at a man he could live with.

As he turned the knob he wondered what lay on the other side. Did he want to see an empty room? How could he expect anything less? Yet deep down, he hoped to see her there, waiting. He ached to hold her and tell her how all those years of working beside her—denying what he had felt—had been a mistake.

Max opened the door to darkness, except for what little light spilled in from the sixty-watt bulb out on the porch.

CHAPTER 78

The pale light threw shadows across the floor, shadows that crawled onto the empty couch. Niki was gone.

When Max was a child, his stepmom had told him that, sometimes, you can't fully appreciate a thing until you know what it's like to lose it. She said that "the absence of someone truly special will leave a hole in your heart that you can feel every time you take a breath." Max wanted to be happy that Niki was gone. She had made the right decision. Still, her absence made him want to fold in upon himself. In all those years of exile, he had never felt so alone.

Then Niki spoke. "It's snowing," she said.

She stood near the glass door, leaning against the wall, her face turned to watch the tiny snowflakes gathering on the other side of the glass.

"Niki. I thought . . . you left."

"I almost did." She sounded mournful as she stared out into the night.

"What changed your mind?"

Niki turned to face Max, her eyes soft and kind. "Why didn't you kill Reed Harris?"

"What?"

"You said you had him in your sights. All you had to do was pull the trigger, right?"

"Yeah."

"He killed Sandy. He killed Peter and Mrs. Molinar. He killed your friend. Why didn't you pull the trigger?"

"It wouldn't have been right."

"After all that he'd done?"

"But letting Reed Harris live doesn't erase what I did to Mikhail."

"You want the world to be black-and-white, Max, but it's not. Good and bad aren't absolutes."

"I don't feel sorry for killing him. I'll carry that night with me for the rest of my life, but if I had to do it all over, I'd still send Mikhail to his grave. Do you understand now...why I needed to come here? Why I pushed you away? As much as I want to be with you — and, God, I want to be with you — you shouldn't be with a man like me. You deserve so much more."

Niki turned again to look out through the glass. Now the snow was coming down in larger flakes, covering the porch outside. She watched it fall for a while, then said, "My mother has a scar, just below her shoulder. As a child I asked her about it, and she told me that she caught her arm on a piece of tin when she was a child in Vietnam. I never questioned it. But that wasn't the truth."

Niki put a finger to the glass to trace a droplet of melting snow. "When I was old enough, my aunt told me the truth, a story I've never told anyone." She paused again, leaning her forehead against the cold glass.

Max held his breath, afraid to move.

"Before my family escaped Vietnam, my father spent four years in a reeducation camp. When he got out, he was half dead. My mother knew that she had to get him out of the country. She'd been working on a plan to cross the mountains into Thailand. She had forged their papers and sold all of their possessions to buy an old truck. Near the border, they were stopped at a checkpoint manned by a lone soldier. He must have spotted something wrong, because he started to arrest my parents. My mom..."

Niki took in a slow breath, her gaze fixed on the falling snow. "My mom knew that my father wouldn't survive another term in the camp, so she begged for mercy. When the soldier refused...she pulled a knife from her sleeve and stabbed him to death. Her scar came from the blade of his bayonet as he tried to stop her."

Niki turned and faced Max, the light outside softening the curve of her cheek. "That soldier was just doing his job. Maybe he had a family waiting for him. The world isn't black-and-white, Max; sometimes it's gray. I don't judge my mother for what she did. I don't have that right. I wasn't there. And I'm not going to judge you."

"You can't ignore it, either, Niki."

"True, but I refuse to ignore every other day of your life too. If you were as vile as you want to believe, you would have killed Reed Harris and left him in the woods. You didn't. My mother did what she had to do, and I know you well enough to know that if there were any other way to bring Mikhail to justice, you would have taken it."

He gave her a quiet smile, one with roots that reached down to his heart. Something had lifted inside of him, and he felt light enough to float. She had found him, and she brought to him the absolution he'd been waiting for all that time. He felt mended. He felt...happy.

And now Niki stood a mere ten feet away, leaning against the door— tough, witty, beautiful, and wise beyond her years. She meant more to him than he had ever let himself believe, but to admit it—even now— felt like stepping off the edge of a cliff. He loved her. He wanted to go to her, to tell her, but when he opened his mouth, what came out instead was "So...now what?" God, he was an idiot!

Niki shifted her weight from her left foot to her right. She folded her fingers together and then unfolded them again. Finally, she said, "I drove two hundred miles to be here...with you. These last ten feet... that's up to you."

Ten feet. Four short steps. The walls had fallen away and his rules lay in ashes on the floor. Max moved to her as though she were gravity itself. He stopped so close that he was sure she could hear his heart beating. Then he lifted a finger to her chin, tilted her face up to his, and kissed her gently, tenderly, her lips soft, and warm against his. And when the kiss ended, he felt dizzy. "That was nice," he said. *Nice* was a hulking understatement.

"Yeah." Niki was slightly out of breath. "It was."

He held her gaze. "Thank you for not giving up on me."

"I didn't have a choice," she whispered.

He was about to kiss her again, but she raised a finger and said, "Before we get carried away, I think you should take me..." She looked up at him in a way that melted something inside of him. "To the kitchen." Her mouth curved into a smile. "I've been here all day, and I am starving."

Max closed his eyes and laughed. It felt so good to laugh again. Then he wrapped his arms around her and said, "Will bacon and eggs do?"

She rested her head against his chest. "That would be perfect."

ACKNOWLEDGMENTS

Once again I find myself indebted to a small army of people who have helped me create a novel of which I am very proud. First and foremost, I want to offer my undying appreciation to my wife, Joely, for being my sounding board, my first editor, and my most endearing and enabling companion. Thank you. Also I want to thank Amy Cloughley, for being an agent extraordinaire and always having my back. Helen O'Hare, my editor at Mulholland Books, was remarkable in helping me put this story together, and I owe her a great debt of gratitude, as I do my whole team at Little, Brown/Mulholland: Michael Noon, Allison Kerr Miller, Bowen Dunnan, Gabrielle Leporati, Josh Kendall, and Lucy Kim.

I also want to thank my proofreaders, Joely, Nancy Rosin, and Terry Kolander, for spotting what I had become blind to. And finally, in researching this story, I took a trek up through the Boundary Waters Canoe Area to understand the journey that my characters would take. Joining me on that adventure were my friends, Greg Joseph and Scott Cutcher. Thanks for being good sports and hitting the trail with me.

ABOUT THE AUTHOR

Allen Eskens is the *USA Today* bestselling author of *The Life We Bury*, which has been published in twenty-six languages. It is in that book that Eskens first introduced the character of Max Rupert to the world, albeit in a supporting role. Max has appeared as a protagonist or co-protagonist in three more novels before *Forsaken Country* (*The Guise of Another, The Heavens May Fall*, and *The Deep Dark Descending*). Eskens has also published *The Shadows We Hide, Nothing More Dangerous*, and *The Stolen Hours*, all to critical acclaim. His books have won the Barry Award, the Silver Falchion Award, the Rosebud Award (Left Coast Crime), and the Minnesota Book Award. He has been a finalist for the Edgar Award, the Thriller Award, and the Anthony Award. Eskens lives with his wife, Joely, in Greater Minnesota.

...AND HIS MOST RECENT NOVEL.

In September 2023 Mulholland Books will publish Allen Esken's new novel, *Saving Emma*. Following is an excerpt from the novel's opening pages.

CHAPTER 1

I hold no faith in distant memories. To me they are as trustworthy as the boards of an aging footbridge, the planks heavy with decay. Time can corrupt a memory, spoil its shape, its color, its truth, wear it down to the point that it's barely recognizable.

For example, for many years I treasured a memory of my father. He died when I was still quite young, but I could picture the back of his head, his strong hands, when he'd carried me on his broad shoulders. It took me years to admit that image was stolen from a photo of us I'd found in my mother's closet, that my memory was only a fantasy born of my need to feel his presence.

When I went to college, and later law school, I allowed logic to blow out the last remaining flicker of that candle, my ersatz memories traded in for reason. Truth wasn't truth unless I could hold it in my hand or usher it safely through a gauntlet of logical debate. And although I sometimes mourned the loss of that part of me that could believe just for the sake of believing, I eagerly put it aside.

And so, I feel somewhat duplicitous writing down this account of those ten strange days, which, even with all the reason and logic and training I can muster, I still can't explain. Where does one turn when logic fails? And I worry that years from now this memory, too, might bear little resemblance to the truth. Will I come to embrace what has happened, or will I deny it? All I know is that I cannot trust time to bring clarity, yet I feel too close to it all right now to make sense of it.

For that reason, I've decided to put pen to paper, to capture my most accurate version of the truth before it fades from my mind, and hope there comes a day where I can look back with some new perspective on the ordeal of those ten days, an ordeal that began when I met Ruth Matthews.

I was in my office at the law school, grading Criminal Procedure exams—my least favorite part about being a professor—when she showed up at my door. My first glimpse of Ruth was like taking notice of a moth—she appeared quietly, her clothing and demeanor faded, like dust on a wing. A slightly plump woman with hair the color of fireplace ash, she wore a gray sweater buttoned to the throat despite the warm June day, and a brown skirt that brushed the tops of her shoes as she walked.

The one thing that stood out was the metal crucifix that hung on a leather cord around her neck. Thick and heavy, it looked more like a yoke than an adornment. As big as my hand, it had been made of two steel bars crudely welded together. Ruth brushed her fingers across it as she stood timidly in my office doorway.

"Professor Sanden?" she asked in a voice so soft that it barely carried the short distance to my desk.

"Yes?"

"I'm Miss Matthews…I have an appointment."

I had forgotten about the appointment but stood and smiled as if I had been waiting. "Please, call me Boady." I waved her to the visitor's chair and tried to recall our brief phone call. She had a husband…no, a brother who had been convicted of murder and she was looking for help from the Innocence Project.

I had once been the director of the Innocence Project, but handed the baton off when it became a full-time job. Now I handled cases only as a volunteer attorney. Because I was just finishing my spring semester and I had no classes to teach that summer, I'd decided to take a look at her case.

Ruth came in and sat, clutching the heavy steel cross against her chest.

"That's a…striking necklace you have there."

"I made it myself," she said, beaming. "I sell jewelry to help support my brother's ministry. Would you like one?"

"I'm not a jewelry person," I said, brushing the stack of essays to the side. "So, this is about…your brother?"

"Elijah, yes. He was convicted of a murder, but he's innocent."

They all are, I thought. "When was the conviction?"

"Four years ago."

"Do you know if there was an appeal?"

"I think so, yes."

I swiveled to face my computer. "His last name?"

"Matthews…like mine."

I typed *State of Minnesota v. Elijah Matthews* into a database of appellate cases. If it was a jury trial for murder, it was likely appealed. I could get the basic facts of the case from the Court of Appeals decision. The case popped up.

The first paragraph gave the procedural posture, a description of the trial and how the case came to be at the Court of Appeals. I was only a couple sentences in when I read the name of the attorney who took Elijah's case to trial: Ben Pruitt. The name reached up from the page to wrap its cold dead fingers around my throat. Looking at the date, I realized that Elijah's case had probably been Ben's last before his world collapsed and he took a bullet to the chest.

I turned back to Ruth, ready to tell her that I couldn't take the case. Four years and it was still too soon. She held my gaze as she rubbed her thumb up the center of her crucifix. It was then that I noticed a single word etched into the metal: *FAITH*.

Had she had faith in Ben Pruitt when he took Elijah's case to trial? She would have been better off putting her faith in the toss of a coin.

I turned back to my computer and began reading again. Her

brother had been accused of killing a pastor at a megachurch, a man named Jalen Bale. I read further and saw that Elijah had prevailed in his insanity defense after claiming to be a prophet doing God's work.

I swiveled to face Ruth. "He was found not guilty by reason of insanity."

"And yet he's locked up," she said coldly.

"At the security hospital in St. Peter. It's not a prison."

"Why is he locked up if he was found not guilty?"

"Not guilty by reason of insanity," I said. "He had what's called a bifurcated trial. In the first phase, the jury determines if the State proved beyond a reasonable doubt that he committed the act—the murder. After that, there is a second phase to decide if he was so impaired by some mental deficit that he shouldn't be held accountable for the crime."

"But he didn't do it."

I put on my mask of empathy, which I'd often worn when I spent my days in the courtroom advocating for people like Ruth's brother. "According to this case, your brother believes he's a prophet—as in the Prophet Elijah…from the Bible."

"My brother is a prophet. He speaks for God."

I held a flat expression, resisting the urge to roll my eyes. "Do you understand what it means that your brother was found to be not guilty by reason of insanity?"

"My brother's not insane, Mr. Sanden. I assure you of that."

"The judge in his case would beg to differ."

"And I am bound by my faith to forgive that judge, for he knew not what he was doing."

This time I closed my eyes to hide my expression, took in a slow breath, and then looked at Ruth again. "Your brother was determined to be so affected by a mental illness that he didn't know what he was doing. He didn't know that killing that man was a crime. The psychiatric experts who testified at his trial don't take that kind of determination lightly."

"Of course they're going to find him insane," Ruth said. "If someone in the tenth century tried to explain gravity, they'd have been locked up too. People are like beetles crawling on the floor of a symphony hall, unable to comprehend the greatness of the music around them. You can't fault them for not realizing. They don't know any better."

I had ungraded exams on my desk, and here I was discussing bugs and symphonies with a woman who believed her brother to be a prophet. "Miss Matthews, do you know how the Innocence Project works?"

She looked at me with unwavering eyes and said, "Mr. Sanden, contrary to what you may think, I am not an idiot."

The moth had some steel in her spine. "I never said you were, but, Miss Matthews, we have a limited budget." I turned back to my computer to peruse the case again. "We normally need substantial new evidence of innocence, like DNA. We have to find something strong enough to reopen Elijah's case. I need more than just a belief that your brother is innocent."

"It's not a belief, Mr. Sanden, it's the truth."

"According to the facts..." I pointed at my computer screen, which she couldn't see. "The victim was killed with a rock that had your brother's DNA on it."

"His DNA was on that rock because he had handled it. He'd brought it as a gift! He didn't use it as a weapon."

"As he lay dying, the victim wrote your brother's name in his blood. That's a bit on the nose."

"Every problem looks like a nail if all you have is a hammer."

"I don't even know what you mean by that," I said.

"They wanted to convict Elijah, so they interpreted all the evidence to reach that conclusion."

"I'm sorry," I said. "But I can't devote resources to a case unless I have something to show that the jury got it wrong. You don't happen to have anything like that, do you?"

Ruth Matthews gave a light nod and opened her purse. "I have this," she said, handing me two pieces of paper.

I unfolded them and saw one was a newspaper article about a magician scheduled to visit the Hennepin County Library. The article had a picture of a man in his forties standing before a herd of kids. The man had a clownish top hat and a cape, and he held a string of colorful handkerchiefs tied together—performing the end of a trick.

The second piece of paper was an email, which read:

> *My dear sister,*
> *I have done what has been asked of me. What happens now*
> *is God's will.*
> *Elijah*

I turned the paper over, expecting more but finding nothing. "What am I looking at?"

"The date of the email."

I compared the date on the email to the date of Pastor Bale's murder. They matched. "Okay," I said. "The email was purportedly sent the same day as the murder."

"Not just the same day but the same time."

"Emails can be programmed to be sent on a given date and time, so..."

"He sent the email from a computer at the downtown library. Elijah was at that library when Pastor Bale was killed."

"It's a Gmail account. It could have been sent from anywhere."

"It could have, but it wasn't. Look at the picture." She pointed at the newspaper article.

The magician appeared to be in a meeting room at the library. Seeing nothing else of interest, I shrugged.

"Not that one." Ruth leaned across my desk, plucked the article from my hand, and slapped it down. "Look!" She pointed at a smaller picture at the bottom of the page showing the magician next to a small "Events" sign at the reference desk.

I shook my head. "Okay...and?"

"The man sitting at that table in the background—that's Elijah."

I looked closer and saw a thin man with white hair, possibly balding but too far in the background to make out any specifics. The man sat hunched forward as though reading.

As I studied the photo, Ruth pulled another picture from her purse and slid it into my line of sight. It was a photo of a smallish man with white hair. "This is my brother, Elijah," she said. "And that's him in the library."

I studied the two pictures, but there was no way to say for certain that they were one and the same. "This really doesn't prove anything," I said at last.

"It proves that Elijah couldn't have killed Pastor Bale. He had an alibi."

"The jury found him guilty, so I have to assume they didn't believe his alibi."

"The jury didn't hear about the alibi."

I eased back into my chair and crossed one leg over the other, a move that gave me a moment to process that curveball. Could Ben really have missed something as important as an alibi? I didn't want to believe it, but then again, I didn't want to believe much of what I learned about Ben that year.

"Ben didn't—I mean, your brother's attorney didn't present the alibi to the jury?"

"No."

Ben, did you really fuck this up that badly? "Did the attorney ask your brother if he had an alibi?"

"I don't know. I wasn't there."

"But…you had this email. You could have said something?"

"If Elijah wanted my assistance, he would have asked for it. I don't interfere with his ministry without his guidance."

"Interfere? If this alibi is valid, you could have put a stop to everything."

"What happened to my brother was God's will."

"No. It was the judge's will. It was a court order that committed your brother, not God."

Ruth shook her head as if I didn't understand anything. "Mr. Sanden, my brother went to that hospital because God sent him there."

"If God sent him there…then why come to me?"

"Because God has spoken to Elijah. The time is coming for him to continue his mission elsewhere."

"If that's the case…" I heard the sentence form in my head before I said it, but I felt powerless to stop myself. "Why not just have God knock the walls down like he did in Jericho? You don't need me for this."

Ruth didn't seem insulted, although she had the right. Instead, she gave a subtle shake of her head, a gesture that came across as pity. "It's like trying to explain a symphony to a beetle."

Then she stood, placed her fingertips against the heavy cross around her neck, and closed her eyes. Her lips moved softly as she murmured something. When she opened her eyes again, she smiled at me and said, "I know you'll help Elijah. I can feel the Spirit moving in you already."

On that score, she could not have been more wrong.

Then she made her way out of my office, pausing at the door to say, "Have a blessed day."

After she left, I went back to grading exams, but I couldn't concentrate. I felt angry, and I wasn't sure why. I leaned back in my chair and stared up at the plaster ceiling. The man thought he was a prophet. I pictured him wandering the streets, lost in delusion, shouting incoherent ramblings at people who rushed past not making eye contact. I couldn't help but think that Elijah Matthews should stay in the security hospital. Surely that was the safest place for a man who followed the commands of a voice in his head?

But I was also thinking about my own days in Catholic school, where the nuns would preach God's love on Monday and then slap us in class on Tuesday. Was I letting my own baggage interfere with my judgment? How many times had I preached to my students that passions and prejudices had no place in the law? Facts, and statutes, and legal precedence, those were the stones we used to build our fortresses.

For my own peace of mind, I would look into this case, do my due diligence before writing Elijah Matthews off.

I picked up the picture from the library. I needed to nail down Pastor Bale's time of death and verify whether or not this man was Elijah Matthews. It shouldn't take long to punch a hole in Elijah's supposed alibi. Although I had no official quitting time, I felt restless and decided to work on the case at home. A few hours of research in my quiet study, I thought, and I could put Ruth and Elijah Matthews behind me.

If only it had been that easy.

CHAPTER 2

Our home on Summit Avenue wasn't a mansion, but it held its own. Not far down the street from the governor's residence and other esteemed houses that carried the names of men who constructed mills and railroads at the turn of the century, ours was a Victorian built in 1891 by a man who had made his fortune selling hats. It had a large stone porch, windowed turrets, and intricately carved gables. It was a house you might walk by and think, *A man must have his life together to live in a place like that.* The first time I'd seen it, I had certainly thought that. Glance our way as you passed by, maybe catch us in silhouette through a window, and you might assume us to be the epitome of an American family: father, mother, and daughter, every thread of this fine tapestry carefully woven. But these days I knew: One step closer and you'd see that we more accurately resembled a poorly stitched quilt.

You would see that my wife, Dee, and I are of different races, she Black and me white, which isn't as big of a deal now as it was back when we first got together. You would see the gray that peppered my brown beard and the silver that twined through my wife's black hair, and think that we looked too old to have that fourteen-year-old child. And then you would notice that Emma holds no resemblance to either of us at all. Her hair shines with a hint of red and her features are fine. But it all would make sense once you understood that Emma was not our flesh-and-blood daughter; she had been our ward for only the past four years.

When I pulled into our driveway, Dee and Emma were nestled on the front porch, sitting close together in our Adirondack chairs, heads tipped, eyes focused on something on Dee's lap. Emma was small for fourteen and looked even smaller curled up next to Dee. She had a smile on her face until she saw me pull in, at which point she retreated blankly back to whatever they were looking at. I tried to pretend that I didn't notice, but this was a reaction I had been seeing more of in Emma lately.

I parked beside the house, the warm summer evening nice enough that I left my car outside of the garage. Entering the house through the side door, I grabbed a glass of water from the tap and three oatmeal cookies from the cookie jar, a peace offering for a conflict I didn't understand, and headed out to the porch.

"Hey, ladies," I said in my cheeriest voice. "Who wants a cookie?"

Dee greeted me with her big smile and an outstretched hand for the cookie, but Emma didn't even look up. Over their shoulders I could see that Dee held Emma's sketchbook in her lap, open to a picture of our dog, Rufus, a black Lab, beautifully drawn. I looked at the sketch and then at Rufus, who lay on his rug on the other end of the porch. The sketch was spot-on.

"Remarkable," I said, setting Emma's cookie on the side table. "I love how you captured the light shining on his coat."

Emma stiffened in her chair but said nothing. It was as if the mere sound of my voice clawed at her skin. Dee noticed it too, but she covered her disappointment with quick support. "Hasn't she drawn it perfectly?" She slid a hand onto Emma's stiff shoulders, and with Dee's gentle compliment Emma relax a touch.

There had been a time, even just earlier this year, when Emma would spend her evenings in my study with me, sitting in one of my Queen Anne chairs with her legs crossed and her homework on her lap. I had offered to bring in a desk for her, but she always said she preferred the chair. But in the past few weeks, something had shifted.

Last week, as she'd finished up her last year of middle school, she studied for her exams up in her room.

And that wasn't the only change. She'd started searching for reasons not to eat with us at the dinner table, and when I forced her to take her seat, she acted like she was a hostage, her head slumped down, hair covering her face. At first, I'd brushed it off; Emma was a teenager, after all. They were supposed to be sullen. But I was beginning to worry this was more than normal teenage angst.

So I'd been trying to hold out an olive branch. A week ago, I had offered to take her to Como Park again so she could sketch—she'd had fun there last November, drawing a bonsai tree in the arboretum. But when I asked, she said no thanks and locked herself in her room. Two days ago, I asked her what type of pie she wanted me to get at the grocery store, a question that used to put a smile on her face. But all she said was "It doesn't matter."

As I looked at her perfect rendering of Rufus, I tried again. "Maybe we should send you to art school in the fall. Or maybe private classes? You really are talented."

"No thanks," she said, standing and taking her sketchpad back from Dee, who let it go somewhat reluctantly. "I wouldn't want to be a burden."

Emma walked past me and into the house, Rufus jumping to his feet to follow her. I watched through the window as they climbed the stairs. "She's going to her room again," I said. "I don't get it—what'd I do wrong?"

Dee and I had had this conversation each of the last few nights, so she merely shook her head and took a tepid nibble from her cookie.

"Does she say anything to you…about me?"

"No," Dee said with a sigh. "I try and get her to open up, but…"

"She was smiling when I drove in. Then she saw me."

I knew Dee didn't want to hurt me, but even she couldn't deny that was true. Instead, she crouched to pick up a scrunched piece of thick white paper from under her chair. A page from the sketchpad. She unfolded it to reveal a drawing of the three of us, a re-creation of a photo we took last summer at a colleague's barbecue. We were seated at a picnic table eating corn on the cob, pausing only to smile for the shot. Emma's sketch was an excellent likeness. I looked at the drawing, then at Dee.

"She said she didn't like this one," Dee said. "Tore it from the book."

"Why?"

"She didn't say, and I didn't push it. You know how she dodges things."

I looked away. It had been a wet spring and the lawn was a vibrant green. Two squirrels chased each other from one tree to another and birds flitted about. Soon, evening would fall and the yard would become dotted with fireflies. It was picture perfect, but none of that tranquillity could erase the heaviness in my chest.

"When you were her age," I asked, "were you...I mean...is this normal teenage stuff?"

"No," Dee whispered. "And I can't help but think it goes back to that last visitation with Anna. It seems to me, that's when the attitude started."

Visitation. Just the thought of that word made me want to spit. It had been a little over a month since Emma spent a week with her Aunt Anna, and it was true: Ever since that visit, Emma hadn't been the same.

"You don't think that Anna told her about...Ben...and everything?" I asked.

I was stepping into territory that Dee and I had grown to avoid. Emma knew bits and pieces of the truth; she knew that her mother had been murdered and that her father, Ben Pruitt, once my best friend and law partner, had gone on trial for that murder. She knew that her father died before the trial resolved, shot by a police detective.

But what she didn't know—what we had so far kept from her—was that Ben had been shot while in my study, after happily laying out in detail how he had killed Emma's mother. Most of those details remained buried in police reports, filed away after Ben died, the shooting deemed justified by an investigator from the Attorney General's office. Dee and I had always planned on telling Emma the full story, but Emma had been through so much. And how do you drag a ten-year-old girl through such horrors? There are no self-help books out there for that.

Because I was Emma's godfather, and had been granted temporary custody while Ben was on trial for murder, I fought to keep Emma with us, a fight that pitted us against her Aunt Anna. It was a slog, but in the end, we won and Emma became our ward. Despite our victory, Dee and I found ourselves second-guessing every decision, none more than the decision to grant Aunt Anna visitation.

I had been the one to convince Dee to give Anna three visits a year, and now I regretted it. We had agreed to a weeklong visit around Christmas and a week over what had been Emma's mother's birthday—that was the visit that happened a month ago. The third visit lasted a single day and was scheduled around Emma's birthday so that Anna could take her shopping.

Emma had turned fourteen just three days ago, so the shopping spree with her Aunt Anna was scheduled for tomorrow.

"It's got to be Anna," Dee said. "She's poisoning Em against us."

Dee had warned me about just such a thing. Dee and I were well off, but Anna was downright rich. "It'll be a constant competition," Dee had said. "Anna will try to outdo us—bribe her. We take Em skiing at a local hill and Anna will fly her to Switzerland. I'm not going to buy her love, but you can damned sure bet that Anna will try to."

My strongest counterargument was that Emma would someday turn eighteen. "She'll have the right to make her own choices," I'd said. "We might as well ease into that cold water while we still had some control over the situation. As long as we're her guardians, we have the law on our side. We can set the rules. That won't always be the case."

Dee had acquiesced. Now Anna's poison seemed to be taking effect.

I walked to the front of the porch, hoping that the cool evening air might help me calm down, give me an idea of how to patch these holes in my family's quilt. The breeze brought no answers. I couldn't help thinking that if I could just get Emma to open up, I could fix everything, change her back to the loving, sweet child she had been just a few months ago. Maybe the time had come to tell her about her father? But if I was going to down that path, I would first have to come to terms with my role in Ben's death.

ALSO BY ALLEN ESKENS

The Stolen Hours

"A riveting, hold-your-breath, frightening mystery...thoroughly captivating."   —Karin Slaughter, author of *The Silent Wife*

"Eskens captures the legal drama skillfully. But it's how he nails his characters, with believable dialogue and shrewd interplay, that makes this work stand out. Oh, and there's a fabulous twist at the end. Wouldn't you know it?"   —Ginny Greene, *Minneapolis Star-Tribune*

"There's not a moment misplaced or a second lost. With the precision of a watchmaker, Eskens assembles the fine parts of a mystery set to the tempo of a thriller, leaving the reader breathless."
        —Craig Johnson, author of the Walt Longmire Mysteries

"Even readers who predict the tale's biggest twist before it arrives will still have the breath knocked out of them by the surprises that follow."
        —*Kirkus Reviews* (starred review)

ALSO BY ALLEN ESKENS

Nothing More Dangerous

"A stunning small-town mystery...Eskens clearly has an affinity for clever boys like Boady and Thomas; but he also has lovely visions of the mighty trees and secret swimming holes that make them long for summer—and mysteries to solve."

—Marilyn Stasio, *New York Times Book Review*

"*Nothing More Dangerous* works well as a mystery, a dissection of hatred and racial prejudice, and a coming-of-age novel...Eskens gracefully moves the novel through the little moments that help to shape people and see the world with a different attitude."

—Oline H. Cogdill, Associated Press

"Both heartwarming and hard-nosed, *Nothing More Dangerous* is a coming-of-age page-turner that probes the dark heart of small towns and the resilient strength that keeps families together."

—Thomas Mullen, author of *Darktown*

"Magnificent...*Nothing More Dangerous* is the next best thing to Harper Lee's *To Kill a Mockingbird*...Setting, plot, and characterization are masterfully woven together to create a tapestry of a small town as a tinderbox of prejudice, fear, friendship, and dark secrets."

—D. R. Meredith, *New York Journal of Books*

Mulholland Books • Available in paperback wherever books are sold

ALSO BY ALLEN ESKENS

The Shadows We Hide

"A riveting novel about one man's search for his father that becomes a perilous journey into a labyrinth of deceit and lies. Eskens vividly renders how small towns try to keep their secrets, and how sometimes they cannot."
— Ron Rash, author of *Serena*

"Murder, arson, betrayal, and reconciliation will keep pages turning and leave readers eager for more of Joe Talbert."
— Michele Leber, *Booklist*

"'Talbert proves himself a true hero."
— Marilyn Stasio, *New York Times Book Review*

"Allen Eskens has drawn an intricate and intriguing search map full of sharp turns and returns. Suspenseful, revealing, clear-eyed, and brightly told."
— Fred Chappell, author of *I Am One of You Forever*

"Riveting...Readers will enjoy trying to untangle all the clues."
— Mary Ann Grossman, *St. Paul Pioneer Press*

Mulholland Books • Available in paperback wherever books are sold